THE LORDS OF VALDEON

HEART OF THE WARRIOR - BOOK ONE

BY

C. R. RICHARDS

Dedication

For my group of loyal supporters. Thank you for your encouragement. Your gentle pressure has prodded me into finishing this story as it was meant to be told. The wait is finally over!

Prologue

BLOOD AND BONE. MIKEL D'Antoiné's fields were buried in the remains of the dead. He shifted his bare feet, trying to find firm footing upon the blood-soaked ground. Pain radiated from the many gaping wounds that made tracks along his bare torso. Dark, sweat-drenched strands fell across his swollen eyes. A hand made steady with grim resolve wiped them away.

Eight Valdeonian men stood with him in the remains of their smoldering village. Farmers all, they were the last of those able and willing to stand in defense of their people. Desperation kills fear. Anger breeds courage.

A lone shack protecting what was left of their women and children stood behind them. Screams of the helpless shook the thin walls. Mikel's wife and son were among the first to perish. Their bodies remained in a pile at the center of the battlefield with the other dead, befouled and dishonored by men from distant shores. Returning from his labors among the crops, he and the other men of the village had been too late to save them. Flesh eaters had already claimed most of their people before the farmers had pushed them back. Those innocents left trembling behind thin walls would not be taken with this new surge of violence. Mikel would see his life drain away first.

In the distance, the murderers from foreign shores waded through the dead. They were rough men, unkempt and savage. Mercenaries. Their armor was thick and their swords strong. Covered in the blood of the innocent, they kicked away the bodies of women and children. Cold hatred filled Mikel's heart as his eyes took in their leering faces. A hundred strong, they had no fear of the nine men who stood against them.

Thunder crashed in the depths of the sky as a great light burned through the din. Mikel shielded his eyes against its searing beam. He staggered helplessly as the ground threatened to break apart beneath his feet. Panic and cries to an unknown god rose behind him from the shack. The men standing with him made no protest. They were all ready to die, whether it be by the hand of an army or the land that kept them.

Then the great light faded, leaving a band of pale warriors standing at the edge of the battlefield. Dressed in brilliant white, their pale skin and hair glistened in the light of their power. Cold faces remained indifferent, betrayed only by the burning blue of their eyes. Each hard glare was fixed upon the murderous invaders. Cautious hope rose within Mikel's heart. The mercenaries knew these pale warriors, and they were afraid. Whimpered cries bubbled from flesh-stained lips. A few mutterings for mercy drifted across the muddy fields. Still, the pale warriors showed no emotion and no inclinations for mercy.

"Protect the Innocent. Punish the Guilty." A voice — neither male nor female — resonated from the very Erthe and sky.

Brandishing twin swords, the strange men and women moved as one. Perfect features remained emotionless as they penetrated the mercenary battle lines. Mikel stood frozen with the rest, watching as their unstoppable blades carved a deadly gap between the killers and the villagers.

His attention was not captured entirely. A large ball of brilliant energy floated beyond the swinging swords and pale heads. Was it the same power commanding the pale warriors? Or was this another unknown threat? Leaving the warriors to their battle, he followed.

Chaos. Avarice. They radiated from a cluster of trees well behind the bloodshed. Mikel spotted something moving beneath the branches. Bulbous head atop a shriveled body, the creature gnashed its long teeth in warning at the ball of energy. It hissed like a feral cat and turned to flee. A bolt of power struck the ground before the creature's feet, halting its escape. The hideous thing hissed again with bared teeth.

"Did you think I wouldn't know you've broken our treaty, Sarcion?"

It was the same voice he'd heard commanding the pale warriors. Curious, Mikel kneeled down behind undistinguishable charred rubble. The stink of death was greatest here, though he could see no blood. Taking great care to remain hidden, he listened and watched. These strange creatures were clearly enemies. They'd chosen his village as a battlefield, and he wanted to know why.

The energy ball began to pulse. Light formed arms, legs, and a small torso. No distinguishable features appeared on its glowing head. Though it was a short being — roughly the size of a small child — Mikel strained against the power hidden within its body. He examined the two beings locked in their own battle of wills. They seemed to be made from the same ilk, though one was beautiful and the other ugly.

"You intrude, Jalora. Andara is neutral territory, ripe and ready for the plucking!" The Sarcion's teeth snapped in warning. *"I have won this land. It is mine."*

Moving with the tremendous speed its ethereal body allowed, the Jalora grabbed its twin by the throat and squeezed. The creature's form was thoroughly revealed in the light of the Jalora's glow. Encrusted with scabbed sores and dried blood, its sickly green skin peeled under the light. Flaccid lids drooped over large dark orbs. Hatred swirled in their depths. Mikel hadn't considered the notion of good or evil. Tending crops and raising a family consumed his time. If evil did exist, surely the Sarcion was its host. Growling, the disgusting evil squirmed in the Jalora's grasp.

"We divided this world evenly, agreeing undeveloped lands such as these would remain untouched. They are inhabited by simple farmers, not warriors." The Jalora released its evil twin. *"I claim this land for my own. Andara is under my protection now. Leave and never return or there will be war between us, my sibling. Never forget how much I would welcome such a challenge."*

"Do your followers know of the blood lust in your burning heart?" The Sarcion asked, spitting venomous drool to the ground .

Moving its clawed fingers within the space between them, the Sarcion formed a malicious sneer upon its malformed face. Their competition for Andara wasn't over. Mikel had seen the same stubborn look in the eyes of a wild boar roaming outside the village. The beast wouldn't retreat from their dogs. It had greedily charged into their fields for an easy meal rather than going elsewhere. Mikel and his friends had killed the boar, but it hadn't been easy. Ridding Valdeon of the Sarcion wouldn't be easy either.

"Andara is rightly mine. I will have it. Your puppets may have destroyed my warriors, but there are always those hungry for power. We will meet again, Jalora. You will have the war you crave."

The Sarcion bounded into the trees, leaving putrid fumes in its wake. An explosion of green and black filled the forest with a thick haze. Stepping into its foggy belly, the hideous thing of evil disappeared. The Jalora waved its hand. Haze made way for sunlight and a steady breeze, but the damage had been done. Leaves wilted upon dying branches. Undergrowth withered and died within a moment's haggard breath. Mikel clutched at the ashes of his village. How would he stand against such a creature when it returned?

Mikel stood away from the rubble, keeping his eyes upon the Jalora's back. This being of light and energy could easily destroy him. Common sense told him to strike while the being was distracted. Instinct told him to stay his hand. These warriors and their god-like master cared nothing for the people of his village. He must act on their behalf. There was no one else. Trusting his instinct, Mikel stood at his full height and waited as the Jalora turned slowly toward him.

"What manner of being are you? Why have you come among us?"

"The world is bigger than the borders of your farm, Mikel D'Antoiné. Valdeon is one of many nations upon this continent. I intend to protect all of Andara from evil creatures such as these. Will you and your men follow me? Will you be servants of the light?"

Others had joined them along the tree line. Mikel's brother, Malcolm, and their faithful men formed a half circle at his back. The deep cut down his younger brother's left cheek would be a constant reminder to be wary of strangers. They held their weapons at the ready. Their eyes too had seen enough violence and death this day. Trust would not be easily given.

White light glistened about them, finally stopping to circle the Jalora. The pale warriors held their weapons at elegant angles, ready to strike Mikel down if he made a move toward their master. Not one drop of blood or muck stained their uniforms. One hundred men cut down in less time than it took to walk his fields. He felt no pity for them.

"These angels you have brought with you have great power. Will you give these powers to us as well?"

"You asked what I was, child. I was born when the old world ended. Its destruction came without warning, striking from the heavens. The cataclysmic attack tilted the world on its side. Human life disappeared from the planet's surface. Everything civilization had created was gone in a matter of moments. Concrete and steel gave way to forest. Technology faded with the civilization, which once worshiped its flickering idols." The Jalora paused for a moment as it relived the memories. *"I was created from the energy of emotions bonded to the land. Love. Hatred. Their intensity could not be erased. Not entirely. I am all that remains of the light from those long dead."*

"And the other being? The ugly creature? What of it?"

"There cannot be light without darkness. My twin embodies all things evil."

Extending its hand, the Jalora showed him a large, oval crystal resting within its palm. Tiny tentacles protruding from the crystal's surface wiggled in antici-pation as they stretched out toward Mikel. Swirling its finger around the oval, the Jalora formed a silver band. The tentacles stopped moving as the crystal darkened in sleep. Then the head of a great beast rose to the sur-face, floating on a sea of black stone.

"Behold. This Heart of the Warrior Ring will mark you as my servant. I give this Lion Ring to you, Mikel, as a symbol of our covenant. Known as 'The King of Beasts,' it will mark you as my voice on Andara." The Jalora tilted its bulbous head. *"I see fond memories of a child's trip to the zoo. Yes. I had liked*

these strange and wonderful animals. Perhaps I will bring them back to Andara?"

"You speak of things I don't understand. Tell me. If I wear this ring of yours, will you swear to protect my people?" Mikel asked, bringing the strange conversation back to firm reality.

"My wisdom will always be available to you and your descendents. I promise to protect Andara from evil as long as you and your heirs bear the Lion Ring. Know this. I decide who shall be worthy among your line to bear this symbol of our covenant. Guard it well, for if this ring falls into the hands of evil, more than Valdeon will suffer. Lose or dishonor the Lion Ring and my power will fade from the land along with my protection."

Mikel clenched his left fist as he stared down upon the lion's head within the stone. He was willing to sacrifice his life for those innocent souls shivering behind the thin walls of the shack. This being was asking for much more. It was asking for the future of his family line. His eyes drifted to the dying leaves the Sarcion had left behind. So be it. His heirs would serve like their sire before them.

"I will wear this ring of yours and serve you for the sake of my people."

"And those faithful to you? Will they also serve me?"

Malcolm stepped toward Mikel, resting a hand upon his shoulder. "I will stand with you, my brother. You will not bear this oath alone."

The others joined the two D'Antoiné brothers, their eyes staring unabashedly at the Jalora. Each of them nodded their acceptance. They were all brave men, pulled together by desperate need.

"Very well. I name you the Sacred Guard. Great power will be yours. Fulfill your eternal duty to protect our covenant."

Warm energy ran along Mikel's skin as the Jalora brought the Lion Ring closer. The middle finger of his left hand grew hot, aching to touch the ring's silver band. Need, urgent and insistent, grew within his heart. The pull of the ring was strong. Would he lose himself and all he had been if he put this band upon his finger? Mikel's heart grew grim. No. He had nothing left to lose. Duty to his people was the only spark of meaning he had left.

"Never let this ring fall into the hands of evil, my Lion. It is the key to summoning my power. If evil should take this ring, your borrowed magic could be turned against the very people it was meant to serve."

"You have my promise. This ring will not leave the Lion's hand while breath still flows from our bodies."

Mikel kneeled down and stretched out his left hand. The Jalora thrust the ring onto his middle finger. Hungry feelers bit into his flesh. He swallowed a scream as tiny teeth burrowed and chewed. Searching for a stronghold, the feelers at last struck bone. Tiny tentacles latched tightly into the marrow. Other tentacles opened, sucking Mikel's blood into its stony belly. Its mortal host threw back his head, unleashing a mighty roar.

"Mikel! Your eyes burn with fire. Amber flecks form within the brown."

Malcolm clutched at Mikel's hand as he fell to the ground. Heat burned within his body as the Jalora's power filled him. Pain overwhelmed his senses threatening to send him into unconsciousness. Words came to him as from a great distance. Still, his brother held firm to his hand.

"You are the Lion's Right-Hand, second only to him." The Jalora's voice echoed in the mist. *"Mark those amber eyes well, Malcolm D'Antoiné. They are unique to the Lion. This is the mark I give the rightful heir of the king. Guard your Lion well. The lives of a great many depend upon him."*

Chapter One

OBSESSION WAS A DEMON, driving men with the whip of blind ambition. Julian D'Antoiné felt the sting of its whip as his ship fought against the perpetual downpour. A great hound's muzzle — encased forever in bronze — snapped at the frigid air from under the bowsprit. Its distorted reflection upon the water was a herald, an ill omen of death.

The forgotten land ahead, as if in retaliation for the impending violence, threw all its ill will against them. Brutal wind sent daggers of rain pounding into the solar sails of the air schooner. Rough currents pushed against the ship's descending hull, but the vessel held its steady course toward shore. Julian ignored the wet striking his face. All his focus and will remained fixed upon the prey trapped somewhere within the thick coastal bog. The object of obsession was, at long last, cornered in the most desolate part of Andara.

He smoothed at the ring gripping his finger. It shivered with anticipation. Mentor and friend, the Sarcion had shown him many things. His greatest ally had once belonged to a nation of great people whose magic had been called "technology." Much of what it told him brought only confusion, but its promise of power he understood well. Bitter rivalry between the Sarcion and its eternal enemy, the Jalora, fueled an infinite match. Julian and his fellow mortals were but pawns in their endless game. He accepted the diminutive role and was being richly rewarded for his part.

"My lord prince." Captain Nunez's scarred face leaned in close, his voice fighting against the winds. "We've received the signal from shore. They've found it."

A single lantern light flashed from the thick trees crowding the rocky shore. Its message came in steady pulses. The hand holding the lantern was insistent, urgent and hungry. Julian's grip upon these new soldiers was a tentative hold at best. Obedience in exchange for the promise of freshly slaughtered human flesh. The creature would obey his commands until the driving hunger overpowered its will. The scent of blood drove them into frenzy, but their need mustn't be satiated yet. His own need was greater.

"Get me to shore, Captain," Julian commanded, boarding the hovering dinghy. "We don't have much time."

Leaning hard upon the throttle, Julian sent the craft bolting forward. Crystal engines blossomed brilliant white. Vessel and rope ripped out of the hands of his human crew. Flying recklessly toward shore, the craft bounced precariously above the waves. Not far now. He sailed faster as his own demons gave chase. Julian reversed the engines when the hull drew near rock. They whined in angry fits of metal. He leapt out of the dinghy and onto the rocky beach. Discarded, the small boat drifted slowly toward the tree line.

A long shadow fell across the ground before a small break in the trees. He scrambled over wet rock and driftwood to the spot. Dignity be damned. The shadow brushed at his hand for a moment, and then fell away. Julian mastered his revulsion at the intimacy of the touch. No affection dwelled in the shadow's frozen caress, only a hunger to devour. He forced his eyes downward and scraped moss from the weather-worn stone with the toe of his boot. They'd found the ancient road leading to Sea Point Outpost. His father would be there, hiding like the animal he'd become.

He pushed through the overgrowth as the shadow retreated into the bog. Following its dark blemish upon moss and stone, he forced his way into the inhospitable barrier. The stench of things long dead assaulted his nostrils, making his eyes water. Muggy heat hung about the dead branches. Julian rubbed a strong-smelling balm under his nose. Fresh air was a stranger in North Marsh.

Tearing, scratching, and gnawing at his body, the land fought back until it revealed the secret it had hidden so well. He glared up at the ruined fortress, its skeletal remains stretching helplessly toward the ocean it once guarded. The Jalora Legion had abandoned this stronghold long ago, along with the continent of Andara's northwest coastline. Now it was nothing more than a rotting corpse slowly fading away into the bogs.

Much like a painful birthing, he pushed through the tangle of limbs and growth to stand upon the dried path. Someone had cleaned off the stone and cut away nature's fingers, leaving an island of rubble. He sneered, absently stroking the talisman upon his finger. It was unlike his clever quarry to be cornered with no means of escape.

"I've found you, Leo!" Julian's shout echoed among the stones. "I can feel the Jalora's life force pulsing within your Lion Ring. You have nowhere left to hide from my power as long as it is upon your finger."

Dark eyes flecked with fiery amber pierced through Julian from a small gap within the stone wall. Nearly eight hundred years had passed since the Jalora had first put the Lion Ring upon Mikel D'Antoiné's finger. Countless Lions had kept Mikel's oath to protect the people of Andara by bearing the ring. Leo was as blindly dedicated to upholding his ancestor's promise as any of those who had come before him.

"The Jalora will never allow you to bear its sacred talisman," Leo called out through the stone. "Take that thing of evil off your own finger, my son. It will see all that is good in Andara destroyed."

"You remain the Jalora's puppet to the end." Julian spat upon the ground. "By its word you have abandoned the people of Valdeon, neglecting your duties as their king. Now civil war threatens our homeland. A strong leader must take your place."

"Tell this man to come face us then, bastard prince!" Another voice called to his left. "For it shan't be you."

"Brave words. You may well call me a bastard from the safety of those walls. Come face me directly and we'll see how loudly you can bark!"

Movement from the trees forced Julian to master his temper. His hold upon his unstable allies weakened as he lost concentration. The defenders of this ruined fortress had seen his terrifying army easily take their last stronghold, an abandoned abbey in the middle of a Ghent meadow. They were purposely goading him. Were they so anxious to die?

A single arrow flew from the wall, striking the ground beside his boot. Laughter, coarse and proud, filled the bogs. This last act of defiance was no surprise. From the moment a ranger put the 'Heart of the Warrior' ring upon his finger, the Jalora took control of his mind. It was a parasite living off the ranger's life force, sharing his blood within the crystal mounted upon bands of silver. As a child, Julian had been fascinated by the carnivorous appetite of the crystal. He remembered watching in awe as the host's blood filled its stony stomach. Sickened with disgust, his gaze fell to the ring upon his own finger. The Sarcion demanded no such sacrifice. It was a partner to its host. He smoothed his finger tip along the surface of the black stone. Of course, it did have its own needs.

"Hell awaits all of you!" Julian raised his hand and sliced it down again.

Nine dark figures, shrouded in midnight robes, poured from the rotting trees and tall grass of the marsh. They moved like wraiths toward him. Their passing made no sound, and their feet left no prints. Sniffing the air as one, the creatures caught their quarry's scent. Their blood-stained teeth began to chatter. A nerve-shattering caterwaul emanated from deep inside their billowing forms. They were the Sarcion's advanced guard and special assassin squad. Those unlucky souls who had heard their terrible song called them the Dirge.

They stopped beside Julian, tense with anticipation and hungry for his command to take the fortress. He watched them, feeding on their savage hatred. They had been men once. The Sarcion had changed them into instruments of death, bound forever to its will.

The man who joins the Lion Ring and the Sarcion Ring will rule not just Valdeon, but all of Andara! The Sarcion whispered within Julian's mind, sending the euphoria pulsing into his body. It was a drug akin to the deepest gratification. The words — as they always had — gave him the courage to push on. For two years, he had patiently orchestrated his rise to power. He had eliminated any competition for the throne of Valdeon. Then the long hunt for Leo had begun. The final element for his victory was at hand.

"I will restore the glory of Valdeon!" Julian breathed in deeply the sensation of his invincibility. "My armies will force all of Andara to cower at my feet!"

Pushing his hunger down, he steadied his emotions. A cool head would see victory this day, not reckless desire. He turned to the Dirge, forcing his gaze to remain fixed on the lifeless orbs hidden deep inside their hooded shrouds.

"Take the fortress. Leave my father alive. I want to see him in his defeat."

The Dirge swept toward the walls, effortlessly dodging the volley of arrows showering down upon them. Agile like predator cats, their movements were quick and sure. Nightmarish forms disappeared and reappeared too quickly to anticipate. They were untouchable. Death's song intruded upon the silence of the marsh. Screams of anguish rose up as the Dirge melted into the gaps of the wall. It was feeding time.

"They move like phantoms," Julian whispered to the Sarcion.

Yes, aren't they beautiful? The Sarcion vibrated with pleasure upon Julian's finger. Its bloodlust never seemed to be sated.

The lifeless bodies of the defenders flew over the walls, landing with a sickening crunch upon the crumbled stone. Julian kicked the nearest corpse over. Three slash marks crossed the man's left forearm. He was one of Leo's "Lion Friends." There would be no pleadings for mercy in this battle. In their fanaticism to protect the old ranger, they recklessly threw down their lives for his honor. Julian stood away from the zealot. He didn't recognize the man. Leo had many such nameless worshippers.

Death's music had stopped. It was silent again upon the marsh. Julian followed the slippery stone toward a large, barricaded opening. The wet wood was easily pushed aside now that no one was left to hold the bracings. Bloodied bodies were scattered everywhere. Some were Valdeonians loyal to their old king. The greater majority were men of other nations, those Leo hadn't disappointed. Julian hurried around them, turning his face away as the Dirge munched greedily upon the corpses. They hissed in warning as he passed.

One of the Dirge was waiting for him at the top of a crumbling wall. He struggled up the mossy stone to join its floating visage. As it turned the hooded cowl toward him, gray-blue skin pulled taut over sharp bones in a hideous mockery of a grin. Black orbs took Julian in with calculating hunger. Then the Dirge turned away and pointed a thin finger to the ancient courtyard below. Leo knelt upon the stone floor directly beneath them. Gone was his carefully maintained uniform. The old king had allowed his gray hair to grow long, tying it back in the fashion of a commoner. The Crown of Sorrows, symbol of Valdeon's ruler, hovered upon his brow. Its magic had diminished to a weak glow.

He had once feared the ranger kneeling before him. Now, the mighty Lion — one of the highest-ranking officers in their legion consisting of kings and other nobility — had been reduced to little more than a peasant. It was no easy thing to stand against the power of a ranger — especially the legendary Leo. Julian's contempt for his father gave him the strength to push aside the last of his fear.

The old ranger's eyes swept down to the oval ring on his left hand. He seemed to be contemplating the lion's head etched in white within the stone. The Lion Ring flashed soft purple in the afternoon sun. Was it speaking to its human host? Julian's ring stirred in response. For one wild moment, he imagined his father would surrender. Then a dagger flashed in Leo's hand. His amber-flecked eyes ran across Julian's face. With a final cry of defiance, Leo brought the dagger down upon his left hand.

The mighty roar of a lion shook the marsh, throwing them back. Julian fell to the ground, covering his ears. Beside him, the Dirge convulsed in agony. A band of energy within Julian's mind — his bond with the Lion Ring — snapped, leaving him disoriented. Screaming, he pressed at the hot blood escaping from his nostrils. His stinging eyes stared at the Sarcion Ring pulsing upon his trembling finger. The mental link to the Lion Ring had been lost.

Get up! You must find Leo before he disappears into the marsh. The Lion Ring's life force has been drained. I can no longer track it now that the Jalora's power has left the stone!

He tumbled down the ruined walls toward the courtyard. The Dirge waited for him at the base of the wall, spotless though they had spilled a great deal of blood that day. Their fury at the Jalora's unexpected attack was evident in the gnashing teeth and vicious sword thrusts into still corpses.

Blood pooled on the ancient stone at their center. The heavy raindrops already mingled with the thickness of Leo's sacrifice. Soon any evidence of his escape would be washed away. The Dirge seemed to sense his intent. They sniffed at the muggy air. One of them brought its face close to the stone and snorted great gulps of air into its nostrils. Howling like a demonic bloodhound, it lurched forward. Julian hurriedly followed. Several drops of blood marked a trail leading toward the back of the ruins. He cursed when the Dirge pushed aside a loose stone. It was an opening to a hidden trail. Footprints led toward clumps of matted grass surrounding a large tributary. Bent reeds and muddied water revealed a boat had been hidden, waiting for Leo's escape. His old quarry had tricked them again.

Pounding impotently at the mud, he tried to reach out with the Sarcion once more. It was no use. He'd failed. Leo had disappeared and taken his ring with him. Something floated in the water beside the grass. He prodded it over with the tip of his sword. It was a human finger. A nasty-looking oval shape was burned into the skin. Leo had left a piece of himself behind after all.

"We should have anticipated this." He spat at the abandoned flesh. "Leo would cut off his own finger in order to hide the Lion Ring."

Ranger honor. He'd endured it his entire life, along with his father's disappointment. Neither Julian nor his brothers had been chosen to bear the Lion Ring. What was not given willingly would be taken by force.

"I must have the Lion Ring. You well know what is at stake." He held the black ring out before him. "Legends warn none but the bearer of the Lion Ring may touch the throne."

Indeed. The Jackal Emperor will be disappointed at this latest failure. Your contract with him must be fulfilled. The consequences if you fail will be…unpleasant.

Their shared thoughts moved back to his elusive quarry. Leo had lost the powers of a ranger now that the Lion Ring was no longer attached to his body. Even so, they must find him soon. Others would be looking for the ring too. He stared out across the inhospitable marsh.

"There is no one else, Father! I am the last! Your only choice is to give me the ring!" He waited, but there was no reply. Not even the sound of oars moving through the water.

Brilliant white light exploded from the marsh to surround the ruins. Pulsing with unbridled energy, it rose upward in a towering wave above the trees. Then the walls of the abandoned fortress shook violently, sinking slowly to the marsh floor.

Run, Julian! the Sarcion cried inside his mind. *If the Jalora's power touches you, death will follow!*

He scrambled to his feet and raced back toward the stone path. The Dirge followed. Some were overtaken in the wave of light. Their agonized screams hurried his pace. He dove into the tangles of branches. Hacking desperately with his blade, he propelled his body out of the thicket. He landed hard upon the rocky shore and kept rolling until the light finally faded.

Human hands lifted him to his feet. Several of the crew stood beside longboats, watching the five remaining Dirge warily. Julian shook off the hands and crept carefully back to the stone path. He peered into the dead trees and muddied waters. The ruins were gone. Only the stillness of the marsh remained.

The Jalora was supposed to be a great champion of good. Today it had shown its ruthless side.

Chapter Two

OVER THE WAVES AND PAST the horizon, four emerald towers rose above the foaming sea. Formed with solid rock, the Grey Cliff Isles defied time and the elements for centuries before man was able to conquer their surface. They offered a simple life for those hearty souls willing to endure harsh conditions and hard work. The smallest isle, Marianna, could be traveled around by pony in half a day. Difficult to reach from the mainland, it was the farthest point west in the realm of Andara. For Seth McCloud, the little isle may as well have been on the other side of the world.

His amber-flecked brown eyes stared up toward the vast heavens as the hull of an airship floated slowly out to sea. He'd watched airships come and go from the town of Haven Bay's port for most of his sixteen years. One day he'd be onboard a vessel headed for freedom. Nothing could kill his dreams of adventure on Andara, not time or the lack of funds.

A well-placed elbow poked at his ribs. Carrot-colored curls atop a short islander frame bounced along beside him. Bright blue eyes shimmered with impatience. His best friend, Riley Logan, was not one to be ignored.

"I said Stan swears the ribbon and bows will be walking through the market anytime now. We need to pick up our pace. Great gulls, Seth. You've seen airships a thousand times."

"Ribbons and bows" was Riley's pet name for the girls of Haven Bay. He and the other boys from the outlying farms made it a point to be in the market at week's end. It was their only chance to catch a glimpse of softness other than the fuzzy tails of their woolie herds.

They walked down the little alley separating McTavish's Mercantile and Old Ned's Tailor Shop. Haven Bay Town Square opened up before them. Salty air filled Seth's nostrils as they walked. The soles of his boots pounded upon the stone of the square, scattering a gaggle of seabirds in his wake. Far below, watery fists slammed against the rocks of the cliffs. Everyday sounds of children laughing and men arguing about the cost of feed announced they were entering the market. He leaned his head back, taking in the briny air.

Long rows of chalk-white shops stood like sentries. Windows filled with tantalizing goods beckoned to the ambling crowds of market time. Each gray door sported a shop's name in bold, white letters. Each letter was in perfect uniformity with its neighbor. He rolled his eyes. Was it too much to ask for a missing letter or two?

"Ho! Seth! Riley," Charlie McDermott called from the hitching post in front of Morgan's Stable and Feed.

He brought a large, rough hand to smooth at the tiny bits of fuzzy stubble upon his square jaw. It wasn't a handsome face, but Seth found it likeable. Jamie Newcastle and Stan McBride stood beside him. One stout and the other pole thin, they were an unimpressive pair in Charlie's massive shadow. The boys nodded their greetings as Seth and Riley joined them.

Seth leaned against the empty buckboard wagon. His eyes drifted up to the thin gray patch of autumn sky peeking over the eaves. Palms sweaty and stomach squirming, he tried to summon an attitude of calm in front of his friends. After months of excuses and hesitation, today was the day he'd walk up to Alice McKenzie and start a conversation. Perhaps they'd talk about harvest? Riley's family threw a big party every autumn. Imagine if he walked onto the dance floor with the prettiest girl in Haven Bay upon his arm?

"Have you seen them yet?" Riley asked, fingers combing through his untamed curls.

"Tea shoppe's serving those nasty little powdery cakes today. Alice fancies those." Stan gave Seth a sideways grin. "I expect she'll be along soon with the others."

Jamie pointed at Seth's front. "Have you been rolling around in jam, McCloud?"

Cherry filling dotted the front of his best black waistcoat. Seth wiped at the sticky mess, his fingers managing to spread the preserves rather than hide them.

"That's a stain for sure. I was helping my mother pack her baskets this morning."

Jamie grunted and shook his head. "No offense to your mum, but I don't know why she bothers with such things. Your family isn't well off either, and that uncle of yours has a tight fist. Where does she get her money to waste on those who won't work?"

"We can't let the little ones go without."

Seth kept a tight grip on his anger. Jamie was the elder's son. He'd never had to do a hard day's work in his short life. His belly had never been empty nor had he been too cold to sleep. People like him couldn't understand need until they experienced it for themselves.

"Careful, Jamie." Charlie leaned forward, a mean look upon his face. "If not for Mrs. McCloud, Dad and

I would have been in a hard place last spring when the feed went bad."

Riley stepped around Seth to stand before the elder's son. Bright blue eyes turned hard as an angry splotch of red formed on his neck. The infamous Logan temper was coming dangerously close to the surface.

"You and your fancy clothes. Seth and I will be rolling in riches when we make our fortune on the mainland."

"Ha! You two will never see the mainland. Do you expect to buy airship tickets with woolie dung? McCloud there can't afford proper clothes — stomping about in his uncle's worn-out trousers." The elder's son poked a chubby finger toward them. "He'll end up a poor book mouse in a little schoolroom someplace, while you'll be up to your knees in woolie dung the rest of your life."

Charlie stood up straight with his arms crossed. "I'd rather do an honest day's work than wind up like you, Newstuffle, working as a clerk in my father's mercantile. You'll be sitting on a stool until your backside's too wide to fit through the door."

Skirts swept by them, trailing the scent of flowers and apple. Seth took a deep whiff along with the rest of the boys as they let the group of pretty Marianna girls pass. Light-headed and a bit dazzled by the swirl of fabric and dancing ribbons, his palms began to sweat again.

"I have half a mind to ask Alice McKenzie for a walk down Farm Row come week's end," Charlie told them.

"You say you will every week's end and every week's end you don't." Riley tilted his head with a chuckle. "Aye, and I can guess your reason."

He pointed to the mercantile where two massive men pounded down the steps toward their wagon. Hands the size of shovels effortlessly gripped heavy sacks of feed. They were Alice's brothers, Danny and Mike. Hardened from life on the farm, the brothers enjoyed brawling for money on the docks. Even the Logan boys, Riley's six older brothers, gave them plenty of distance.

"I'd ask her. I have no fear of them."

Stan lifted his chin with a sniff. A strand of blond hair fell across his wind-burned cheeks. His scrawny frame stood straighter as he took in a great gulp of air. He made an unimpressive figure despite his usual boasts. The group of boys burst into laughter. Seth couldn't find the humor to join them. He well knew what it was like to pine for a girl who wouldn't spare him a glance.

"Why don't you go on and talk to Alice then, McCloud?" Stan grinned, catching Seth unaware. "Everyone knows you fancy her."

"McCloud? Talk to a girl? Don't be stupid."

Jamie's chubby fingers reached up to play with the large brown mole on his chin. Two hairs matching the muddy color of the mop atop his head jutted out wildly from the growth. His malicious grin widened as the barb struck home. Seth had just enough time to catch Riley's fist as it flew toward Jamie. Riley may have been short on stature, but any one of them could testify his temper made up for it. The elder's son blanched and fell quiet.

"Well, McCloud? They've stopped on the row. There won't be a better time." Stan pushed Seth toward the group of girls. "I should think Marianna's field ball team captain would need to have courage."

"Let's see you go first, McBride!" Riley turned on Stan, stepping toward him.

"It's all right. I'll go."

Squaring his shoulders, Seth moved toward the group of girls like a man making his final walk to the gallows. His hands were shaking, and an uncomfortable shower of sweat had broken out upon his forehead. Strange buzzing filled his ears. Tingles raced up his arms and neck. He fancied Alice, but the sensation of being near her was typically more pleasant. These new symptoms — the buzzing and tingles — certainly didn't feel like love's tender touch.

He ran his open hand along the back of a metal bench. Stopping to take a steadying breath, his fingers gripped the metal tightly. The bar collapsed under his touch with a sharp pop. He yanked his fingers away. The top piece on the bench's frame had been crushed and twisted. He stepped back, staring down at his hands. What had happened? He'd sat upon this bench many times. It had never shown signs of decay. Marianna's weather was harsh, but certainly metal could withstand more than a few seasons under its skies.

"Hurry on, McCloud!" his friends called behind him.

Alice McKenzie stood at the very center of the skirts and ribbons. Her golden hair showered in little ringlets upon the soft yellow bodice of her gown. Meadow-green eyes watched Seth as he moved toward their numbers.

"Hello, Alice," Seth blabbered, tucking his hands awkwardly inside his pockets.

"Well, Seth McCloud?" She brushed her curls aside and put her hands upon her hips, waiting.

Sunlight blanketed her hair setting it aglow with golden shimmers. By the green, green fields she was a beauty. He struggled to say something. Anything! The heat upon his skin rose to a feverish temperature. His palms had broken out into a sweat. He cleared his throat, suddenly aware of the gurgling sound as he tried to move his tongue.

Alice flipped her hair as she turned from him. The girls burst into giggles and twirled away, leaving Seth standing red-faced in the throngs of onlookers. He let out a choked breath and turned quickly toward the stables. His friends fell silent, letting Seth have a little of his dignity back.

"I don't understand it, Seth." Charlie shook his head. "You are the very devil on the back of a horse and on the ball field. But get you around a girl and you wilt like a hot-box flower."

"Not to worry." Riley slapped Seth on the back and gave him a reassuring grin. "You're better off. Old Alice McKenzie has her nose up in the air."

Seth gave him a half-hearted shove. His eyes followed Alice's bouncing blond curls down the row until she was out of sight. Well, he had found the courage at last to talk to her.

"Here comes old Fussbottom." Riley folded his arms, letting the contempt form on his face. "What is he doing out of his cave?"

Fergus McCloud, Seth's uncle, was the Haven Bay School headmaster. Coarse gray hair neatly bound in a short tail, black robes impeccably laundered, he was the personification of ruthless order. Seth's father had died before he was born. Fergus took his mother in while she was still pregnant, but he hadn't done so gracefully. Each day he found new ways to show them how much of a burden they were.

He stopped before them, hand clasping the handle of his walking stick. Shifting off of his crippled leg,

Fergus remained a rigid tower of unpleasantness. The hard glare he ran over each of their number made them shrink back like they were small boys again. Seth's childhood had been spent learning to withstand the iron glare. He lifted his chin and returned the headmaster's contempt with careful indifference.

"Loafing about, are we?" His disapproving gaze landed on Seth. "I hope this doesn't become a habit. The day when you must fend for your own livelihood comes sooner than you think."

"Yes, Uncle. You've reminded me many times."

"How very much like your father you are. He had an appetite for beauty too. It is unfortunate he allowed his interests to get the better of him. Marry young Alice if you will. Have a litter of pups while your education wastes away. Do not think of coming to me when you can't afford the roof over your heads. I will not support a loafing bum and his offspring."

Ever the masterful artist of humiliation, his uncle had delivered a strike in Seth's most vulnerable area. He struggled to keep calm. Showing any sort of hurt or emotion to the headmaster would provide Fergus another lever to manipulate. Seth gripped the side of the buckboard and remained silent for his mother's sake. She would be the one to suffer should he provoke the headmaster.

Fergus left them without another word. Heading toward the academic world he'd built for his own ego, he offered no greeting to his fellow Haven Bay residents in the square. The dark cloud lifted from the market to follow him.

Years of resentment exploded from Seth's chest. Raw power ran down his arm and into his fist. Pulsing with its energy, he swung at the buckboard with all the impotent rage in his heart. The wagon lifted off its wheels and slammed to the ground, swaying until it stayed upon its side. Bits of shattered wood spilled about his feet.

"Great gulls! How did that happen?" Riley stammered.

"A wind gust?" Stan asked.

"Don't be daft." Jamie circled the wagon with the others. "Clearly the wheels or the axles broke, and it tipped over."

Seth held his hand out, turning it over as he inspected the skin. It was devoid of bruising or marks. The intense feeling of fury had made him feel powerful, as if he could smash the wagon in one angry strike. Reveling in the sensation, Seth grasped at the feeling of invincible strength. For a brief, unsettling moment, he was ready to wound. His fingers gripped the air around an imaginary neck.

Any secret pleasure he held for the sensation of strength disappeared as Seth lifted his gaze. Anne McCloud stood in the row, clutching at her basket of packages. His mother's gentle face wore a trembling frown under the shade of her bonnet. Eyes accustomed to vibrant cheer now held deep sorrow as she looked upon her son.

She walked around the other boys, skirt sweeping unheeded in the dried horse droppings. Seth stayed put as she came to stand before him. His mother dropped the basket in his outstretched arms. The aroma of pastries and herbal medicines mixed into a nauseating blend.

"I'm afraid I'll need to pull you away, Seth. This basket is much too heavy."

"Yes, of course, Mother." He waved a hasty farewell to his friends and followed her.

Impatient autumn winds swept upward from the sea. Damp, wispy fingers tugged at Seth's untidy mass of dark waves. Arms full with bundles of baked goods and medicine, he whipped his head against the wind. The stubborn curls would not behave. Blowing urgently at the strands falling into his amber-flecked eyes, he followed his mother down the Main Row of Haven Bay.

"The McDonald home is just ahead. Come now, Seth. We must help those who are less fortunate than ourselves, mustn't we? Mrs. McDonald has taken ill, and her poor husband has no one to help him with the little ones. We do them a kindness."

"Yes, Mother, but don't you think we should consider looking after ourselves as well?"

"I know it hasn't been easy for you, dearest, but we must stay with your uncle for a little while longer."

"Why, Mother? He doesn't want us living with him any more than I want to stay under his roof. If you'd just let me get work."

"Do you know why I endure Fergus?" She squeezed his arm. "I would do anything to see you with a good education, Seth. Don't you see how much your schooling will aid you in your future? Please, dearest, be patient a little while longer. For me?"

Seth's grip twisted at the basket's handle. He nodded curtly and began to count the thatch roofs and gray-trimmed eaves as they passed to ease his impatience. White was the traditional color marking Haven Bay from any other town in all of the Grey Cliff Isles. Sometimes he had a devilish impulse to paint one of them a fiery red.

His mother opened the little iron rod gate of the next townhouse and held it in place. The sounds of chaos reached them as they walked the short distance to the door. She raised her fist to knock, but the home's inhabitants had seen them coming. Mr. McDonald stepped outside, dragging a toddler on his leg. The newest member of the McDonald household, a tiny baby boy, was crying in his arms.

"Heaven bless you, Mrs. McCloud! Please come in."

The relief was palpable on Mr. McDonald's face. His good wife had taken ill, leaving him to care for their two small children. Unshaven with clothes wrinkled and dirty, he looked utterly defeated.

She turned to Seth with a gentle smile. "I shall be here for a time. We'll have a nice long talk later, just you and I." She kissed his cheek and took the basket from him. "Go on, now."

The little girl, still hanging on her dad's leg, kept her eyes on Seth. Then she gave him a shy smile and waved goodbye as the door closed. He shut his eyes and released his remaining anger with a long sigh. His mother was right to take care of those in need, but he wished sometimes she would show as much kindness to herself. Anne McCloud was a soldier in the battle against poverty. Nothing deterred her commitment to those who sought her care.

In a way, he was relieved her sense of mission was so strong. It would make saying goodbye easier. He'd find his own destiny away from Haven Bay and Fergus McCloud. His thoughts turned back to the strange incident with the wagon. Perhaps life on Marianna was pushing him toward madness? It was plausible. Fury had almost turned him to murder. Seth shoved his hands into his pockets. He had to leave Marianna before he hurt someone. There was no choice now.

Chapter Three

Silent wind brushed at the trampled grasses of the
Ghent meadow. Its unrelenting pressure bent the
blades over telltale signs of battle. Xavier De Vincente,
bearer of the Wolf Ring, knelt beside a cluster of arrows
jutting from the mud. The dozen or more distinct boot
prints belonged to the airship crew he'd been following.
Traces in the mud indicated they had walked the short
distance from their landing site to attack the abbey. Yet
there was no blood. The abbey's archers had missed
their mark.

"It doesn't make sense, Wolf."

Rafael Cristiano — Jalora Legion uniform pressed
and perfect — stood at his shoulder, staring across the
empty distance at the horizon. The legendary airship
captain had the honor of bearing the Fox Ring. Despite
their hard journey from Valdeon, he remained the
elegant naval officer.

"There's no cover. Leo would have seen the ship's
mast long before they arrived. He wouldn't have been
taken unaware."

Fox had landed their airship five miles to the south
for that very reason. Wolf and his squad of rangers had
crossed the distance at a full run, using their skills of
camouflage to arrive undetected before the abandoned
abbey.

"Perhaps the men sailing in our mystery ship
weren't the first to arrive. Look. Their boots step

around the arrows or in some cases step upon them. These prints were made after the battle was over."

Wolf came to his feet, hooking his thumbs under his belt. What bangtail mischief was this? Something, an uneasiness, crept along his spine. He lifted his augmented vision to scan the horizon. The Jalora gave its rangers many superhuman gifts. Discernment was perhaps the one he relied upon most. He remained perfectly still, allowing the Jalora's power to reach over the grassy mounds. Others felt his searching and paused in their work.

"What is it, Wolf?"

"The Jalora is unsettled." Wolf shook his head. "I can't quite see…"

A low whistle came to them upon the wind. Berto Mendoza, his second-in-command, was signaling the all clear. Wolf took a strong hold upon his uneasiness. The other rangers were already troubled. No good would come from sharing his fear. Marching across the battlefield, he joined Berto at the edge of the ruined abbey. Unlike the Fox, Berto was a man who was used to rough living. Bearer of the Jaguar Ring, he was an army officer and one of the best trackers the legion had produced. Wolf trusted Berto's judgment. There was no enemy waiting for them in the abbey.

Eager faces watched him from beneath the safety of their camouflage cloaks. The two youngest rangers entrusted to his care were still enamored by the idea of adventure. They hadn't seen battle yet, and if Wolf had his way, they wouldn't for a long while.

"No signs of life, Wolf." Berto saluted with a nod. "Even so, I don't like the feel of this place."

"Agreed. Split up and search the ruins. I'm going to check the building for any clues Leo may have left behind."

Wolf turned to catch the flicker of ash fabric as it rushed by him. Yuli the Otter and Tulio the Rabbit blinked at him with anxious eyes. Between hay and grass, they weren't out of their teens yet. He'd had to use a stern hand to keep their mischievous wanderings checked.

"Stay together. No wandering about on your own. Understood?"

"Yes, Wolf." They gave him careful salutes and darted off to the west.

A single building standing tall against a cloudless blue sky was all that remained of the abbey. Bits of old stone, knocked loose by cannon fire from battle, littered the ground about its base. The abbey was another victim of the last great war. A Jalora Master born in the royal line of D'Antoiné had walked the earth then. Much of Andara had been torn asunder upon his death. A hundred years had passed since the dark day the Jalora Master fell. His descendent, Edmund D'Antoiné the Leo, was feeling nostalgic for old family stories it would seem.

Wolf ducked inside the building, careful not to hit his head on the doorjamb. He and his countrymen were gifted with a height surpassing their Andarian brothers. It was useful in battle, but challenging when visiting neighboring countries. Stretching his senses into the building's shadows, Wolf waited for any sign of supernatural danger laying in wait. Nothing. The abbey was empty.

He walked past several mess kits left behind by their owners. Rotting food abuzz with insect life confirmed his suspicions that the battle had taken place at least two weeks prior. The evidence about him suggested these seasoned men had been surprised in the middle of a meal. Since Leo's disappearance, Wolf had heard rumors of a new enemy from a distant land possessing the power to move about Andara undetected. The Jalora Legion was unable to confirm these reports. Now it would seem they had tentative proof.

Wolf let his frustration bubble to the surface again. Valdeon's Chancellor would not embrace suspicions Julian D'Antoiné had somehow managed to ally with the unknown enemy. The bastard prince had something to do with his father's strange behavior. He was certain of it. The tragic deaths of Leo's other sons had been thoroughly investigated. Julian agreed to be questioned about their deaths. In fact, Wolf had conducted the interrogation personally. Something, however, had blocked Wolf's probing into Julian's mind. Some power he couldn't overcome had protected their primary suspect. It didn't take a great mental leap to follow the logical flow of clues. Julian was after the throne of Valdeon and was eliminating the obstacles in his way. He'd been very careful to hide his tracks. Wolf couldn't accuse the slithering little worm until he had proof.

The fragrance of orange and spices drifted toward a stone stairwell. The distinctive smell was Leo's scent, given to him by the magic of the Altar the day he was anointed king. Wolf climbed the stairs, hunching within the suffocating space. The short climb took him to a second floor hall in which a single chamber had survived the ravages of time. Inside the cramped room was a small cot with a rickety crate next to it. A single candle still stood upon the makeshift table, its wax cascading down through the boards. It wasn't suitable accommodation for a king or a Jalora bishop, but both Leo and Wolf had slept in worse environments in their service to the legion.

He gripped the silver encrusted belt hanging about his waist until the metal dug into his fingers. Releasing the belt again as his frustration eased, Wolf turned his attention to the base of the abandoned abbey. Crafted during the time of their ancestors, it had slowly fallen into rubble. Leo had managed to turn the crumbling ruin into a fortress. He was a gifted warrior and strategist — too gifted to be found unless his hunter had help.

Resting a hand on the brittle stone railing at the edge of the small patio, he breathed in the scent of sweet grass below. Rays of fading light from the setting sun shimmered into the depths of the blue stone upon his finger. The image of a wolf's head shifted slightly to face the sun and then returned its eternal gaze back upon its ranger. He took a breath and let his hands drop to his side. It seemed all of Andara was waiting for Wolf to find Leo. He was, after all, a Lord of Valdeon and third-in-command of the Sacred Guard. Who but the elite ranger and long-time friend would their missing king turn to for aid?

Leo had come to him in secret during the darkest hour of the night a year earlier. He'd been injured. Wolf remembered the steady stream of blood dripping in the nursery of his hacienda in San Rudalfo. Angered their king would endanger his family by leading an enemy to their door, Wolf had not greeted him warmly. Leo's mysterious behavior, his long absences, and disregard for his duties had driven a rift between the two of them. Indeed, Julian's unchecked behavior had pushed their families to the brink of open bloodshed.

Wolf and Leo argued, but the king kept his secrets close. Turning to leave, Leo had called Wolf an "Oath Breaker" and disappeared into the orchards surrounding Wolf's home. The Lion had not asked for help after that night. He'd kept his distance from his comrades, hiding in lonely places like this abbey. Wolf lowered his eyes to the rocks below. Guilt and shame were constant reminders of his dishonor. He had spoken to no one of his argument with Leo. Not even his wife, Dulcina.

A flash of ash cloak alerted Wolf the Lords of Valdeon had not been idle while he looked for Leo's chamber. Impatient youth. Wolf's mind drifted to the rest of the Sacred Guard. In his early forties, he was the eldest among them and had become their leader in Leo's absence. The young Lords of Valdeon were impressive in their skills, but at times like these Wolf wished for the company of his old comrades again.

During the time of the first Jalora Master, Mikel D'Antoiné, nine Valdeonian men made an oath to the Jalora. They and their heirs would lay down their lives protecting the Altar of Providence. It had been his deepest honor to bear the Wolf Ring upon his finger. He'd gladly taken up the oath that so many of his forefathers had kept before him.

One among the Sacred Guard had forsaken his duty. Esteban, brother to the king and bearer of the Hawk Ring, broke the code and was banished from Valdeon. His whereabouts were still a mystery. Now Leo had abandoned his people too. Seven of the Sacred Guard remained, but could they save Valdeon from civil war without the Lion?

He turned back into the room to find Cardinal Dragon regarding him from the doorway. Short white hair clung tightly to his sweaty scalp. The neatly trimmed beard contained evidence of his last quick meal. Peppered with mud and filth, the ash tunic and trousers of his uniform reflected the hard travel he'd endured reaching the abbey. Eight hundred years had passed since Mikel and the Sacred Guard had served. Many Heart of the Warrior rings joined their numbers over the centuries to form a powerful force. Seeing the leader of the Jalora Legion disheveled gave Wolf a momentary shiver of foreboding.

"We've found Leo's missing followers. Their bodies had been dumped in an old gravel pit a few miles to the south. They were tortured and then beheaded." Dragon kept his expression perfectly blank. Those intelligent, knowing eyes regarded Wolf with expectation. "We've been able to find Leo thus far, because of the bond you share."

"What are you asking, Dragon?"

"I must know if Leo was taken by these villains. If the Lion Ring is lost, the legion must be prepared for the worst."

"Very well, I will try."

Wolf turned his attention back to the few belongings Leo had left behind. Sometimes the Jalora would grant him insight if he kept his mind peaceful and focused. He rested a hand upon the pillow and closed his eyes. Images and impressions of his missing king began to form. Residual memories of Leo, sharing a meal and conversation with his companions, danced across Wolf's mind. The images moved faster, finally stopping at a memory of Leo holding a letter. Wolf saw his tears of grief and felt Leo's intense need to flee. Then the images evaporated, leaving him no closer to Leo's whereabouts than he had been before.

"The Jalora has shown you something, Wolf." The commander of the Jalora Legion came to join him beside Leo's cot.

"Yes." Wolf nodded, failing to keep the disappointment from his voice. "Leo was here a few weeks ago. He is still fleeing from those who would take the Lion Ring."

"Why? Why hasn't he asked for aid from the legion?" Dragon rubbed at his dirtied beard. "If the Lion

Ring is lost to evil, our world will crumble. He puts all of Andara in jeopardy."

The Lion Ring was the key to the Jalora's power on Andara. If it was taken and overpowered by evil, then the Jalora's power would fade from the Altar of Providence. Every ranger in the legion would lose his extraordinary skills. They'd be helpless in the face of impending evil. The raw guilt twisted in his heart again.

"The Jalora will not abandon us. We must trust its wisdom. Leo received a letter which caused him to flee this fortress. I can only hope it is the answer to what he seeks."

"A letter," Dragon whispered absently.

The silence erupted in a thunderous roar, reverberating against Wolf's skull like cannon fire. He fell from the cot to his knees, slapping his hands over his ears. Deafening in its intensity and painful in its sorrow, Leo's death cry shattered Wolf's being. He cried out in pain and grief. His own cries were soon joined by others sharing his bond. The Lords of Valdeon were the Sacred Guard, bound in body and soul to protect the Altar of Providence. When one of them died, the others felt the pain as well.

Dragon helped him to the cot and took Wolf's face in his hands. "What has happened? Tell me."

"It's Leo." Wolf sucked in a miserable breath. "He has passed from the world. The Lion Ring is black with death."

"The ring? Where is it?" Dragon gripped his face harder.

He let his hands fall away when Xavier shook his head. Dragon stood away from him. He closed his eyes, but opened them soon after.

"The Jalora will not answer my pleadings." He leaned his back against the wall, turning pale and sick. "Lost, the Lion Ring is lost."

Rafael the Fox fell into the room. His handsome features mirrored Wolf's own grief and horror. "Sir?"

Wolf stood, projecting absolute confidence to his much younger guardsmen. "Have our ship ready to depart immediately. We must return to San Leonora, before news of Leo's death causes civil war. And Fox, we don't have four days to waste in the air. Drain the last crystal in the ship's engine if you must. Get us to San Leonora in all haste."

Fox saluted and darted out the door. The other rangers called after him as he ran. Wolf's grip tightened upon the cot. The Lords of Valdeon were still boys. They should not have to carry this burden Leo had placed upon their shoulders. It was up to Wolf to lend them his strength. He kept the confidence wrapped around his being like armor.

"I don't know why the Jalora remains silent, Dragon, but I still have faith it will not abandon us."

"The legion is at your disposal. Any assistance you need, we will make our top priority."

Wolf nodded his thanks. Forcing his trembling legs to obey, he moved toward the door. Above all else, he must be there to support the Chancellor of Valdeon and protect the Altar. They were weakened now, exposed to their enemies. Edmund's death could not be hidden once the court saw the Orb of Valdeon black and lifeless. Using the magic of the Ancients, the Crown of Sorrow had left Edmund's brow the moment the Lion Ring was severed from his life force. It's silver would be gripped tightly once more in the golden jaws of the lion's head within the throne. Such omens could not be mistaken. Watchful traitors were keen to strike.

They'd be disappointed in their treachery. The Lords of Valdeon were duty bound to stop them just as they had been since the first rings were forged.

The weight of his new responsibility settled into a permanent ache at his temple. In all of Valdeon's history, the bearer of the Wolf Ring but served. Now with Leo dead and his worthless brother the Hawk banished from San Leonora, leadership of the sacred guard fell to Wolf. The people of Valdeon looked to him to keep their society at peace and stem the tides of civil war. Somehow he would see his duty done. The Jalora would not abandon them. He had faith its wisdom would see them through tragedy.

He cast one last look at Leo's meager possessions. Why? What could be so important to Edmund D'Antoiné that he'd been willing to risk his life and his country to hide? Wolf turned his back on the mystery. Leo's reasons didn't matter anymore. Their king had passed from the world. He and his secret pain were beyond them now. The Lords of Valdeon had their duty to perform, and they would see it done.

Chapter Four

THE TINY ISLAND OF MARIANNA stabbed the ocean's surface as if a gigantic hand had thrust it into the waters. No beaches or cheerful harbors gave welcome to visiting ships from faraway places. Sailors delivered supplies to the inhabitants of Haven Bay at its three-berth airship port. They loaded their holds with woolie wool and left again as quickly as they could. No man wanted to be stranded in the middle of a desolate ocean with no escape. Seth sat upon his isle pony at the southernmost point of the island. He understood well the desire for escape. Once free, he'd never return.

The angry ocean struck impotently against the immovable cliff a thousand feet beneath him. Rabid foam swirled against the rock. Its frothy body was quickly sucked under by the dangerous undertows surrounding the island. The chaotic and endless battle perfectly reflected Seth's mood.

"Easy, Nan." He patted the isle pony's neck to reassure her.

The amber within his eyes burned as he stared into the horizon. Endless water met thin gray clouds over an orange sunset. No one knew what waited across the water. Many believed the continent of Andara and its island neighbors were the last inhabitants of Erthe. Seth wasn't sure. Sometimes, when he came to Land's End and closed his eyes, he could hear a voice upon the breeze. It called to him in soft words he couldn't quite understand. Perhaps it was his future calling? Anything would be better than the dull, endless days trapped on Marianna.

He brushed a stray bit of chestnut hair from his eyes. It had escaped the tie of his neatly arranged ponytail again. He let his hair fall onto his shoulders with an impatient tug. Nan shifted beneath him, sensing his stormy emotions. Leather reins circled tightly around his other hand as the animal tried to pull away. He lifted the material under his nose. The long tether had a musky smell.

Seth smoothed his sweating palms on his knee-length trousers. The toes of his boots dug into the stirrups. This was utter madness, but a little madness was what he needed.

"Yah!" he cried and spurred Nan forward.

Creamy white ribbons of fine horse mane streaked on the wind, taking on a silver shine as they caught the light of the setting sun. Seth laced his numb fingers through the white hair and spurred the animal on faster. He guided the pony closer to the cliff's edge. Mist from the water rose slowly up the base of the perilous cliff. Sometimes if the air was cold enough, the mist could reach up to the grassy fields, making clouds. Today the autumn air held a chill to it, coating the wet grass with a thin layer of frost. Nan's footing stayed true despite the slickness of the misty ground.

Hair whipping wildly about him, he breathed deeply. The exhilaration made him lightheaded. It was almost enough to chase away intrusive thoughts. Reluctantly, he steered Nan away from the edge and slowed her to a trot. They were drawing nearer to civilization. Paddy's Pub and Inn was up ahead. Beyond its door the Marianna Militia would be standing guard upon the Lookout. Racing along the cliffs was against the law. Seth had been warned before against what the constabulary called "reckless behavior."

Nan flicked her ears toward the inn. Seth pulled up on the reins, bringing her to a stop. He heard it too. The distant whinnies and jingles of harnesses signaled fellow travelers just ahead. A carriage was parked upon the row next to Paddy's. It was one of Mr. Morgan's rigs. Someone had spent a fair bit of money to take it out.

The inn's door swung open with a boom. Anne McCloud and their housekeeper, Emma, hurried down the steps. His mother's frame was dwarfed under a heavy shawl of green and red. He'd given it to her many years before as a birthday present. She lovingly took care of the hideous garment, wearing it often. In her haste to reach the carriage, she allowed mud to splatter upon the cloth.

Seth's uncle leaned against the carriage, supporting his crippled leg. He banged his walking stick upon the ground with a violent rhythm. As headmaster of the Haven Bay School, his uncle was used to bullying those weaker than himself. Anne and her son had endured years of his angry tirades.

The headmaster grabbed his mother's arm, pulling her roughly down the hill toward a small grove of trees. Emma hurried after them, her hands clasped together in a pleading gesture. The headmaster's temper and belligerent tone were legend around Marianna. Many claimed they would throw him off the cliffs if it weren't for his popular sister, Anne.

Fergus had struck Seth once when he was a small child. The men of Haven Bay had been bent on killing the brute. Seth had pleaded for his uncle's life that day. His defenders relented, but they did leave Fergus with a warning. His crippled leg was courtesy of their family friend and protector, Thomas Logan.

Spurring Nan forward, Seth jumped down off the pony as soon as they reached the hill. He guided her to an old tree beside the road. Loud voices broke through the thin branches, pulling away his attention. Worried his uncle would forget the circumstances in which he'd gotten his crippled leg, he tied Nan's reins to a branch and hurried into the trees.

Emma stood at the edge of the small grove, sobbing into her apron. Her body leaned weakly against a decaying tree trunk. Strands of gray hair wilted away from the bun atop her head. She cried harder when she noticed Seth. Reaching a hand toward him, Emma's eyes pleaded for him to stop.

He pushed through the branches thick with autumn colors, moving quickly into the small clearing. His uncle loomed over his mother like a black-robed specter of death. Fergus's coarse, gray hair — normally tidy — had come loose to float about him in whipping strands. Wild eyes shifted from his sister to the trees. The rough hands gripping Anne's arms shook violently.

His mother stood in the wet grass, holding a shaking hand to her bleeding mouth. Her long, dark hair had come out of the tight bun. It danced in the wind like a wild horse, freed from the rope of constraint. Anne McCloud wasn't crying or cowering. She glared back at her tormentor, strong and defiant.

"Let her go." The cold rage in Seth's voice broke the spell over the scene.

His uncle let his hands fall away with a short, grating laugh. "So, you show your anger to me at last? And what do you think you will do, boy? Are you man enough to challenge me?"

His dismissive sneer found its mark. He was a master at manipulating emotions and twisting them to cause pain. Members of the McCloud house knew well to guard their hearts.

"There is one who will put you in your place!" Emma shouted behind Seth.

Always his protector, she put a restraining hand upon Seth's shoulder. He didn't want her interference this time. Fergus had put violent hands upon his mother. Nothing would stop his rage. His uncle's tyranny would end here in this small grove. Then they would leave his house forever. He took a step forward, but Emma's iron grip held him in place.

"Enough," Fergus hissed spinning on his heels toward the small dirt path. He pushed past Seth without a word or a glance.

"My son and I will leave for the mainland," his mother cried.

"Use your head, woman. Who would have you? The boy must stay, but you are welcome to leave."

The headmaster paused for a moment among the dying foliage. He gripped the worn handle of his walking stick, squeezing it until his knuckles grew white. In his other hand, he clenched a crumpled sheet of his sister's stationary. Fergus stuffed the letter in his pocket. His rigid form pushed through the trees toward the road, leaving them in the damp grove.

Emma burst into fresh sobs as his shuffling steps crunched upon the fragile leaves. Releasing her death grip on Seth, she lifted her skirts and burst through the trees as fast as she could run. Seth guessed she was fetching Thomas Logan. This time he wouldn't plead for the headmaster's life.

He came to stand before his mother, hoping for an explanation behind his uncle's words. Her green eyes remained distant. She didn't seem to see him. Tears escaped unnoticed as she relived some long-ago memory. He gripped his mother's chin to bring her back. Finally returning to the present, his mother clung to him.

"What's happened? Please tell me."

"He's right, Seth. Who will have me now?"

He pulled his mother's small frame tighter against his own. Fear was beginning to replace anger, but he managed to control his worry for her sake. It was nothing new for them to argue, but it was Seth's mother who always relented in order to appease Fergus. Most people did.

"You have me, Mother. I'm almost seventeen and old enough to start work. Let us leave his house."

"We're alone here now without aid or means. Fergus will not forgive who you are. I must protect you somehow."

"You're not making sense. Won't you tell me what happened? Why is Uncle so angry?"

"Fergus McCloud is not your uncle!" She pushed away from Seth.

He stared at his mother as the world closed in and only the two of them were left among the trees. The woman before him was no longer someone he recognized. She was a fierce, wild thing, trapped in a cage of lies.

"Oh, Edmund," his mother cried to the empty sky. "Where are you? Why did you abandon me to this life? Why did you abandon your son?"

Edmund? He'd been given the same name as his dead father in accordance with islander tradition. No. There had been no such person. His mother's agonized face was testament to the lie.

She closed her eyes tightly and threw her head back, shaking with angry sobs. Seth stood frozen, regarding the woman he thought he knew struggle to regain control. Her face relaxed at last, and when she turned back toward him, her eyes were hard with determination.

"How much money have you and Riley saved for your adventure to the mainland? Don't look so surprised. You could never keep things from me. Come, now, how much?"

"About two hundred credits."

Riley Logan had been his best friend since their mothers had put them on the same baby blanket. They'd grown up together, kept each other's secrets, and explored every inch of Haven Bay as an inseparable team. He didn't know how he would break the news to Riley they wouldn't be traveling to the mainland together after all. Things had changed. His mother had changed.

"That won't be enough. We'll have to borrow the rest. I want you to get the money from Riley and hurry home to help me pack. Our time is short. We leave for the mainland tonight."

"Leaving?" Seth shook his head. "I don't understand, Mother. Tell me what's happened!"

"Everything will be all right once we reach our friends. They'll know what to do. Hurry, Seth! Race to the Logan Farm. No dawdling."

Seth stared after her as she ran through the trees toward the carriage, his body frozen in place by the chaos of her words. Then he turned away, heading for the safety and solitude of the trees. The golden leaves were growing thin as winter grew nearer. He came to the tree where he'd tied Nan. Moving around the trunk, he expected to see her munching on the last of the wild grass. Instead, he found broken branches and over-turned earth. The little isle pony was gone, and she had taken the branch with her.

"Nan?" Mr. Morgan would box his ears if she'd wandered off into the far fields. Seth leapt toward the nearest overhanging branch. His fingers gripped the rough bark. Pulling his body up, he wrapped his arms about the trunk and looked out over the surrounding fields. Hoof prints and drag marks pointed Seth in the direction Nan had gone. She was headed back home to the stables. Perfect. Mr. Morgan was already upset Seth had been late getting Nan back yesterday. If the pony returned without him, well, there would be no hearing the end of it. His trip to the Logan Farm would have to wait. He had to find Nan.

Sunset crept across the fields, sending its shadows over the hills. Gone was the comfort of the familiar as imaginary phantoms haunted the darkness. Seth stayed within the sun's fading rays, ignoring the images from his troubled thoughts.

Edmund.

Crying a child's tears many nights under the head-master's roof, he'd prayed for his real father to rescue him. Life with his uncle forced Seth to face the truth. The man who had sired him was long since dead. If he was to escape his uncle, then it must be under his own power. Today the truth he had reluctantly accepted was proven to be a lie. Was the real truth about Edmund any better?

Know your father. Know yourself.

It was a saying that guided the Grey Cliff Islanders. They held firm to its simple wisdom to define futures and keep their way of life. Seth tugged his cloak tighter about him. His seventeenth birthday was a few months away. Soon he'd take his first steps into manhood. He wasn't prepared to enter his future as a bastard.

A cream-white tail whipped against the backdrop of dying meadow grass. Seth ran to catch the broken limb trailing behind Nan. She turned her head at the tug from her fallen reins. Blades of grass hung from her mouth as she casually chomped.

"Great gulls. Must you always stuff your stomach?"

His fingers, chilled by the cold mists, couldn't manage the knot. He growled down at the branch. A great pop filled the empty field as it broke apart in his hands. Splinters of wood showered down upon his boots. Nan tried to bolt at his unexpected show of temper, but he held her reins tightly. Jumping into her saddle, he hurried them back toward town.

The road took his pony a little closer to the southern cliffs. Distant waves crashed against rock. Seabirds circled over his head as they sailed upon the wind. Strange. Darkness was a danger to the birds. The winds dashed them against the cliffs well enough during the daylight hours.

Putting them out of his mind, he concentrated on his own worries. Seth took a deep breath and held it before lifting his hands from the reins. Tilting them under the fading sun, he found no bloody scratches or bruised skin.

"The branch must have rotted through, Nan. How else could you have broken away so easily?"

It was a reasonable explanation. And when the headmaster had insulted his father in front of his friends, a tremendous gust of wind had helped him flip over a wagon. Many such strange things had happened over the past year. All of them had been coincidental. Seth frowned down at his unscathed hands. Lies would not still his troubled heart. Something was happening to his body. The changes were growing stronger each day. Soon he would be unable to hide it from his family.

Sighing, he looked out across the empty fields in the dying light. Herds of woolies normally roamed here, feeding upon the tasty meadow grass. The sheep farmers had taken their herds closer to the barns for the fast approaching winter season. Seth shivered at the silence the absence of their soft bleating left. It was lonely on this stretch of road.

The reassuring flames of the Lookout danced in the swirling winds. Their movements flickered shadows upon the stone structure. Small figures of the Haven Bay Militia walked lazily up the steps toward the stone platform. Facing out into the open waters, they stood watch for Amity Island raiders. It was an unfortunate islander who met raiders alone at night. The villains were vicious men from a nearby island who made their living robbing their neighbors. Isolated with limited protection, little Marianna was their favorite target.

"Easy, Nan. We'll be home soon."

Seth patted the pony's neck to calm her. Cutting across the fields might get them to the stable master's barn before his impatience grew to anger. Taking the lantern from its tie upon his saddle, Seth ignited the comforting flame. He spurred Nan off the Main Row and into the fields, heading toward town. The orange of sunset had left Marianna behind. Stars speckled the sky around a bright half-moon. He rested the lantern's base upon his thigh as the darkness engulfed them. It was peaceful in these empty fields. No lies or secrets chased him here, only the hidden mysteries of the darkness.

Something stirred in the grass ahead. He reined Nan in and lifted the lantern. Sweeping the light back and forth, he almost missed a silent figure waiting feet away from him. Seth kept the pony's head steady, soothing her with his voice until Nan stopped trying to bolt. Raising the lantern a little higher, he shifted the light until it struck the stranger. A face, completely covered with a tight black mask, stared back at him. The image of a white dagger ran down the very center of his featureless countenance.

Seth gulped in a shallow breath and held it. Tales of islander boys snatched by smugglers were often told in the common room at Paddy's Inn. Enslaved and forced to work aboard smuggler ships, they were never heard from again. He made ready to spur the pony into a gallop.

"Identify yourself. I warn you. I'm expected at home. Any delay and the constabulary will come looking for me."

"We both know you tell a half-truth."

His harsh accent marked the stranger as a Tslavian from the mainland. A deep hood encased the stranger's head in rich midnight. His cloak swept from his shoulders to his black boots. Dark leather gloves held the fabric firmly closed, hiding secrets in the shadow of the garment. Quick hands grabbed Nan's reins, ruining Seth's chance for an easy escape.

"What is it you want?" Seth yanked at the reins, but the stranger's grip stayed firm.

"How strange you must seem to these bumpkins."

He shook his hooded head, moving a little closer. The smell of rotting flower petals and sweat emanated from the dark man's body. Seth slowly forced his feet from the stirrups. A hard kick might loosen his grip upon the reins. Then he'd show this stranger the meaning of haste as he hurried to warn the militia.

"You may adorn yourself with sheep dung and farmer's boots, but nothing can hide the amber fire of your eyes. How they burn with your anger! In another setting that fiery look may have frozen my heart still, but here upon this speck in the ocean, I can only laugh."

"You've confused me with someone else. My deepest pity goes to the young man you seek."

"Have pity for yourself first. He is here. Hurry!"

Two Amity Island Raiders rose slowly out of the grass behind their leader. Their shaved heads were painted black with red markings swirled in angry circles. Dark brown tunics covered their bodies, from the shoulder to below their knees. Mud-colored cloaks served to hide them in the night. The Amity Raiders stood fast in the tall meadow grass, clearly not frightened of the dagger-faced man.

A girl struggled between them. Her honey blonde hair whipped wildly against her captors. Seth recognized her. It was Alice! Her home was one of the neighboring farms to the north. How had the raiders reached so far inland without the militia spotting them?

"Fools! I've paid you enough for the boy. You'll draw attention to us."

"We require additional payment." The shorter raider grinned at the girl as Seth's mind raced to translate the ancient Islic language. "She'll fetch a good price in the Azure Isles. Besides, I've been watching this boy. He fancies her. I don't doubt these simple-minded dung farmers will believe the two of them ran off together."

"Very well. Take her if you must, but make certain you dispose of the boy's body before you leave. I don't want any awkward questions."

The masked man dropped Nan's reins and turned away as if Seth were no longer of any consequence. His hired men stepped back as he passed. The dislike upon their faces needed no translation.

"You have the wrong person!" Seth called after him.

"I have exactly the right person. I know who you are, Seth McCloud. It is regrettable you never shall know the truth about yourself."

His laughter faded in the endless dark of the fields. Its grating tones drenched their group in harsh silence. Outnumbered and unarmed. Seth's options were few. One of the raiders spat into the emptiness where the man had disappeared. He turned back to Seth, giving him a rotting smile.

Chapter Five

"GET DOWN OFF THE pony, boy. Don't make me chase you." The shorter raider waved a hand toward Alice. "You can see we have valuable cargo to stow aboard ship."

Struggling against the ropes binding her feet and hands, Alice screamed through the gag in her mouth. Her captor, a towering man with an ugly expression, wrapped his tree-trunk arm around Alice's waist and squeezed. Crying out sharply, her eyes pressed shut and her body became still. Seth thought for a moment the brute had crushed her. Then Alice's defeated green eyes found his face. Tears escaped through the lashes as they pleaded for help.

These despicable villains had managed to travel inland past the militia without being noticed. They could just as easily disappear again. Alice would be taken and sold. He couldn't leave her to such a fate.

"You'll not be taking Alice anywhere. Let her go."

"I'd worry for yourself first, boy." The short raider regarded Seth with the keen eyes of a greedy merchant. "You must be someone important. The Dagger paid us thrice our price for the gutting. He doesn't typically bother himself with common sheep farmers."

Shaking his head, he shrugged and pulled his sword. Its blade was chipped and unpolished, probably a trophy from a recent burglary. The weapon looked sharp enough and its wielder well practiced in killing.

"I think I have the right to know why he wants me dead."

"They always ask why. You bore me now, boy." The short raider turned to his big companion. "Kill him quickly. We need to make the slave traders by morning to unload this tart."

He threw Alice to the ground, kicking her out of his path. Tree-trunk legs stomped toward Seth as the big man thrust powerful hands before him. Scarred and rough, those hands appeared to have killed many times.

"He may be big, Nan, but you're bigger!"

Seth spurred the Isle Pony to a run. Snorting and pounding her hooves, Nan toppled the big man. Rocking his body from side to side, the raider tried to get up. Seth wouldn't have a chance if the villain were able to stand. His enemy was much too strong to fight outright and a surprise move would only work once. The raider had to be put down permanently. Cold acceptance stilled his fear. He brought Nan around again. Spurring her forward, he charged his pony. Nan's agitated hooves stomped over limp flesh. He prodded her away when the brute fell silent and still upon the grass.

Seth's cloak pulled tight about his neck. The clasp held firm as he was yanked roughly from Nan's retreating back. Escaping his grip, the lantern sailed across the night sky to finally break upon the ground. Oil drenched a clump of dried underbrush. Raging flames swept across the grass. The fire grew closer as the quick seconds passed. It wouldn't take long for the entire field to be consumed in flames.

A form materialized out of the smoke to pounce upon him while his attention had been drawn to the fire. The short raider held his naked blade above Seth's body, ready to strike. Seth kicked his leg up and connected with the man's exposed side. The raider rolled away and onto his feet. He pounce forward again, whisking his blade at Seth's face. More swift strikes targeted his chest. Hot fire blazed along his upper torso as the blade slashed tender skin.

"I'll cut that grin off your face, boy!"

"Come ahead, Raider!"

Something primeval and ferocious had broken out of the cage in Seth's heart. It radiated from his body like a savage animal. He felt powerful and wild. This new animal within him anticipated the raider's next move. It welcomed it with savage glee. He spun away as the raider's sword came for him. Missing his heart, the slice drew a bloody line along his right arm. Uncontrollable fury overpowered the last of Seth's fear.

"Marianna!"

Seth dove at the man and knocked him off balance. The raider's sword dropped into the grass. Seth kicked it into the hungry flames. His opponent growled a fierce battle cry and pounded his fist into Seth's stomach. His grip wrapped tightly upon Seth's arm. Then Erthe and sky exchanged places. Seth found himself flat on his back in the grass with the raider straddling his body. The stench of dung and sweat hung over them. He gagged at the smell. The raider had covered his tunic in Woolie droppings to avoid the militia dogs. Disgusting, but clever.

"You're no farmer." The raider twisted Seth's face toward the light. "D'Antoiné. No wonder the Dagger wants you dead."

He pushed away and hurried to his feet. Suspicious eyes remained fixed upon Seth as he back-stepped toward the unconscious raider. Shoving at his fallen friend with a rough boot, he cursed when the other man didn't move.

"Your eyes do not lie. I'll remember your name, boy. The Dagger isn't the only one who'll pay to know where you are." He abandoned his friend and hurried away toward the coast.

Euphoria raced through Seth's blood like fire even after the raider disappeared into the darkness. He came to his feet, brushing absently at the bits of grass and filth. Something about Seth's eyes had terrified the man. He knew well enough his eyes were unusual. Flecks of brilliant amber shone against the brown. This group of mad men had confused Seth with someone else, someone who shared similar looks. No. It didn't explain how the Dagger knew his name. Perhaps Seth looked like his absent father? Edmund seemed to have passionate enemies willing to go to great lengths to kill. But why go after a son this Edmund had never bothered to find?

Muffled cries behind him brought Seth's mind back to the field. The flames had grown into a fiery mouth, devouring dried grass and any other tinder it could find. Alice was in its path. A sudden gust of wind stoked the flames. Thick smoke filled the space between them. He couldn't see her anymore.

Running into the wall of smoke, Seth began to call for the girl. "Alice! Help me find you."

Urgent thrashing guided him through the blinding smoke until he tripped over her bound legs. Seth's fingers tugged at the rope, but the knots held firm. They had to get out of the smoke before both of them were overcome. He lifted her over his shoulder. Staggering forward, he prayed he was headed out of the smoke and not into the flames.

Fresh air struck them. His watering eyes made out the still form of the big raider. He kept well away from the man and lowered Alice to the ground. Disheveled hair fell over the rips in her dress. One of the sleeves had fallen in rolls at her bound wrists, its fabric smoldering as a stray spark from the grassfire found her arm. Seth ripped the burning sleeve from Alice's arm and threw it toward the fire. He dropped down beside her and began to untie the bonds with trembling fingers. The ferocity Seth felt moments ago left him as he looked into her eyes. Shock swirled about in their depths. She stayed still, staring at him.

He pulled at the cloth in her mouth and waved a hand slowly before her face. "Are you hurt?"

The raider had clearly frightened Alice out of her senses. He turned from the disturbing intensity of her eyes. Trying desperately to focus on the tight rope at her ankles, he fumbled with the knot. It was a challenge keeping his fingers from accidently touching the ruined petticoat. Its tattered lace hung loose from under her dress. He did his best to avert his eyes until the knot finally worked free. Marianna's strict rules were clear about such things. A man did not see a woman's petticoat until his wedding night. Doing so would give the girl's father good reason to stick a musket in the impetuous young man's back.

He stood and pulled Alice up with him. Her body swayed a bit as the blood rushed to her limbs. Seth awkwardly gripped Alice's shoulders to steady her. She burst into sobs and threw her arms around his neck. Great gulls. The girls of Haven Bay hadn't paid Seth much attention with Riley's older brothers strutting about the markets. He wasn't quite sure what to do with Alice. Her body was soft and warm. He should be enjoying this chance — possibly his last — to hold her in his arms. Her strong embrace, however, was irritating the cut upon his chest. He managed to keep from howling when Alice pressed tighter against him.

"You're safe now."

"Fire! Go fetch the militia!" A man's voice boomed into the night.

Boots and angry shouts approached them to his right. A group of Marianna men had come to investigate. Faces, masked with alarm and anger, shown in the torchlight as they raced toward the burning grass. Alice's father appeared to be leading the search. He raised a hand to stop the men. His eyes rested upon his daughter in Seth's arms. They took in her dress in shreds and the wild state of her hair. His large musket came up. The barrel pointed at Seth's forehead.

"I can explain!"

Seth pushed Alice gently away. Honestly, what ill-favored moon had caused everyone to go mad?

"Seth McCloud? Is that you?" Mr. McKenzie slowly lowered the weapon. "What are you about, boy? I nearly put a hole in that foolish head of yours!"

"What are you waiting for? Bind him. The young hooligan has set the entire hill on fire."

The torches parted as the wide frame of Elder Newcastle pushed to the front. Sweat beaded on his balding head despite the cool evening. His large burgundy waistcoat expanded under the torchlight as he took great, heaving breaths.

"Wait a moment, Elder." Constable McTavish elbowed his way through the men to stand beside him. "Look there by young McCloud's feet."

The men followed his finger to the raider sprawled on the ground beside them. Mutters of astonishment circled around the mob. Several of them pounced upon the unconscious man, holding him down though it was unnecessary. Slowly their eyes turned to Seth.

"Did you best that raider, McCloud?" Constable McTavish asked, leaning over the raider. His bushy brown eyebrows arched to mimic the frowning mustache.

"Yes sir. Another man was with him. He ran off toward the Lookout."

"What an absurd lie," Elder Newcastle snorted. "How could the weakling nephew of the headmaster best a raider when the militia cannot?"

Seth let out an irritated breath. Of course the man would question anything he said. A feud between Fergus McCloud and Elder Newcastle had been raging for as long as Seth could remember. Oftentimes he found himself in the middle.

"I saw him!" Alice cried. "Seth saved me. He was wonderful."

She threw her arms around Seth's neck and kissed him on the lips. Hot flashes moved up and down his spine. He'd never been kissed before and hadn't imagined his first would be with the prettiest girl in Haven Bay.

"Alice!" Her father snapped. She released her death grip on Seth with a small grin and ran to her father.

"Thank you, Lad." Mr. McKenzie regarded Seth with a frown for a few moments and then began to pull his daughter across the field toward their farm.

"You there," Constable McTavish called to one of the farmers staring at Seth. "Take some men with you to the Lookout. Tell Sergeant Gunn to keep half his men at their posts. The other half are to go out into the fields and beat the grass until the other raider is found. We'll need every other free hand to fight this fire."

The constable led his volunteers toward the flames. Elder Newcastle followed, casting one last dark look at Seth. Letting out a pent-up growl of frustration, Seth leaned his hands upon his thighs. His cuts and bruises were beginning to ache. Fighting a grass fire with the others would be a feat his body might not endure.

A fist as large as a shovel struck Seth's face. He plummeted to the ground, landing on his backside. Danny McKenzie stood over him with his massive fists raised.

"Thank you for saving my sister, but that's all you'll do, McCloud." Danny stomped over to join Mike.

"My brother's right, McCloud. Alice can do better for herself than to marry a poor school mouse. Come on, Danny. We're going to take this brute for a midnight walk by the cliffs."

The twins nudged aside the group of men holding down their prisoner. Danny and Mike pulled the dazed raider to his feet, holding him in place when he swayed. Mike nodded at his twin when Danny smacked their prisoner across the face. Seth brushed off his trousers, glaring angrily at the departing men. He wiped at the fresh blood dripping from his lip. Well, a punch was what a person got for risking his life to save their sister.

"Keep her on the farm next time," Seth grumbled under his breath. He pulled at the front of his ruined shirt. No amount of washing would see it clean.

"Get the dirt off the wagon! We need to smother those flames and block the fire's path!" Constable McTavish shouted orders to the silhouettes around the flames.

Seth watched mutely from his seat upon the ground. Marianna had finite land mass. A grass fire could easily destroy every bit of life upon its surface. The Islanders were well practiced in fighting fires caused by the angry lightening storms pushing in from the sea. This particular fire had seemed larger than it was, and they quickly smothered it.

"I don't envy the greeting you'll get at home, young McCloud." The constable joined him at the edge of the smoldering grass. "I'll have more questions for you." He helped Seth to his feet. "Why don't I stop by to see you in the morning? I can have a word with your uncle about what happened here tonight. Off you go, then, and stay on the row. We don't want you mistaken for a raider and shot by one of your own."

"Ho, Constable!" The elder beckoned from the wagon. His large bulk took up most of the seat, leaving the driver to hold the reins at an odd angle.

Constable McTavish's mustache squirmed upon his frowning lip. He nodded to Seth and headed to join the other men in the back of the wagon. The comforting lights from their lanterns suddenly faded as the wagon dipped down into a dale. He was alone again in the darkness.

Spinning about, he looked for Nan. The pony was nowhere to be found. Alarm bells rang in the distance. Their ear-piercing clamor had most likely driven the already frightened pony back to her stall.

Rubbing his arms to keep warm, he headed across the lonely fields. Damp grass and other soft remains squished about his wet boots. He tried not to imagine what else he may be stepping in along the abandoned woolie fields. Lifting his eyes up to the heavens, he breathed in the familiar stillness of a Marianna autumn night.

Crystal engines roared over Seth's head, knocking him to the ground. It was a small airship flying dangerously low. He brushed the wet grass off his filthy shirt, watching the bright glow of the crystal chamber flicker toward Haven Bay Airship Port. It was a good day's airship ride from the coast of Andara to the nearest tower of the Grey Cliff Isles. Take another half day and that would see you to Marianna. An experienced crew would wait for daylight to avoid being dragged into the massive cliffs of the tiny island. The captain who flew that ship must either be mad or in a great hurry. Seth shook his head. Who would ever be in a hurry to visit Marianna? It was the most remote stretch of land upon which a man could stand.

Marianna had stood unpopulated for many centuries. Seafaring vessels could not find a safe haven from the turbulent ocean surrounding the little island. The cliffs were impossible to scale. It was the mastery of air travel that finally conquered the little island's difficult shores.

Many people, tired of the booming population of Cliff Bench on Larkspur, had volunteered to colonize the little island. Haven Bay had hired Seth's uncle to organize a school just before he'd been born. Fergus had agreed. He'd left Horner Isle with his pregnant sister to colonize the one-town island with the rest of the hearty souls out for a new start.

Tiny lights flickered in the windows of Haven Bay as Seth mounted the last grassy knoll. The residents of Haven Bay were all at their suppers by now if they weren't hiding from the raiders in their homes. He clutched at his rumbling belly. A hot meal and some of Emma's nettle ointment for his cuts would see him right again.

He hobbled down the footpath, passing the Haven Bay School on his way toward town square. It was the only building in Haven Bay made from real stone. Stories still circulated around town about the headmaster and his treasured schoolhouse. Somehow Fergus was able to convince a crew of wayward sailors into chiseling pieces of the cliff side away. He used most of it for the tall building. The rest went to make the Lookout and the base of the airship port.

The school's solid frame towered over Seth as he hurried around the corner to the Main Row. Its empty windows watched as he passed, judging his worth. Resentment filled his heart. He hated each and every cold stone. The headmaster's office window was dark. His uncle had already returned home . He looked down at his bloodied shirt. Perhaps his uncle would postpone the usual angry tirade once he noticed Seth bleeding? The thought cheered him a little.

His mother would have her own words to say to him. She'd been waiting for him all this time and was probably worried by the alarms. He hadn't wanted to believe her words spoken in anger. The Dagger and his raider friends had changed Seth's mind for him. Passing through the small garden of fading flowers, he jumped over the stone bench and pushed through the little iron rod gate leading to the residential neighborhood. The McCloud home was the last house on the row.

"Mother? Emma?" Seth called, closing the door behind him. No answer. That was strange. Mother had told him she was coming home to pack her things. Perhaps she had gone to the Logan Farm instead?

Seth pushed through the kitchen door to find Emma. She had heard everything and would know what the argument was about. Someone had to explain why his world had suddenly fallen into chaos.

Their well-ordered kitchen was empty. Copper pots rested unused upon their hooks. The kettle sat cool on a dead fire. Seth backed away from it. The world may have been topsy-turvy, but his stomach still expected supper. He pulled day-old bread and cheese from the cupboard. After eating a quick meal, he filled the basin. Soapy water washed away the stench of ash and blood.

Emma's medicines were kept on a high shelf in their pantry. She'd been anxious to keep them out of 'little hands' when Seth was a child. Now they stayed where they were out of habit. He grabbed the jar of nettle ointment and sniffed its contents. Crinkling his nose, he dipped his finger in with a grimace. The ointment stung when he rubbed it into his cuts. They weren't deep and the bleeding had stopped, but that didn't diminish their throbbing. Perhaps in the morning someone would actually notice he had been wounded in battle.

He let the satisfied grin come. The struggle had been frightening, but oddly exhilarating. Seth's daydreams were full of adventurous deeds. Tonight, he had been the hero he had always wanted to be. He couldn't wait to tell Riley.

Seth climbed the stairs to his bed chamber. Pulling off his tattered clothes, he winced as the fabric brushed against the knife cuts on his chest and arm. Fresh clothes had been laid out for him on top of a traveling trunk. His mother hadn't been idle that evening either. She'd emptied his wardrobe.

Floorboards squeaked down the hall in his mother's bedchamber. He replaced the board and put the table back. Easing out of his chamber, he tiptoed out into the hallway. A sudden movement cast shadows over the small band of light coming from under her door.

"Mother? Why didn't you answer me earlier?"

He tapped lightly on the door and pushed it open. Interrupted in her packing, his mother's things had been strewn about in piles of chaotic clutter. Her trunk was open, dresses and her cloak had been scattered upon the floor next to it. Anne McCloud lay on the bed wearing her best gown. Her dark hair streamed across the fabric. The glossy wood of her treasured Valdeonian guitar rested upon her chest. His mother's face was pale and her lips were an odd blue color. Something was clenched in her cold hand. Seth moved to her side with unsteady legs. His own hand reached for her dead fingers, prying away a tiny glass vile. Eyes locked upon her blue lips, he put the vile in his pocket and sat down in the rocking chair across from the bed.

The bedchamber door slammed shut. Seth turned in a slow daze at the noise. Standing beside his mother's wardrobe was the Dagger. His thick cloak opened exposing a naked sword. The blade twisted slowly in its master's hand.

"I underestimated you, boy. You escaped those bumbling idiots with just a few scratches. Let me guess, you rescued the girl as well. Of course you did. It's in your half-breed blood. You can't help but play the hero."

"Did you do this to my mother?" Seth managed to stand.

"Your mother married outside her race and then came you." He spat upon the floor between them. "I've watched this house for years. Anne grew more unhappy each day. You were such a burden for her."

"No. You're wrong. She loved me." Seth shook his head. "We're leaving together."

"What a fool you are, boy. Do you honestly think either of you would be welcome? Who do you think sent me here? Your family wants you dead." The blade's tip lifted until it was level with Seth's chest. "I have given your mother peace. Now I can finally be rid of you."

Seth yelped when his mother's dead hand brushed against his own. Anne McCloud had been a kind and loving woman. He had no doubts in his heart about her feelings toward her son. It was the only thing he didn't doubt now.

"I had hoped to make your mother's death look like suicide, but you've necessitated a change to my plans. How shall I finish the job, I wonder? The sword? No, we don't want that fool of a constable to suspect foul play." The Dagger's masked face tilted until the white blade was at an awkward slant. "What a tragedy for the crippled old headmaster! He comes home to find his household struck down by a mysterious illness. What a pity. Poor man."

Reaching his gloved hand inside the dark folds of his cloak, the Dagger pulled out a small vial matching the one hidden in Seth's pocket. A sickly green liquid splashed inside as he shook it gently. Such a small concoction, yet it had utterly ruined his life.

"The mastery of poisons is a proud tradition in my family. Century upon century we have developed the skill of assassination to an art form. I am their finest son." He lifted up the tiny vial, examining it fondly like a master craftsman. "This gem is very special. The Tslavian hillside beside my home is the only place this rare and deadly plant grows. It was once called 'Love's Bonnet' until my great, great grandmother discovered its deadlier purpose. She first used it to seek revenge upon her faithless lover. Ah yes, this special plant is now called, 'Devil's Cape.' One simply must pluck the young leaves off the plant before it flowers, mash them, and boil slowly until you have this concoction. Of course the real trick is not poisoning yourself by touching the juices."

The dark mask lowered to fix upon Seth once more. "Your mother was well versed in its use."

Seth's eyes were irresistibly drawn back to the woman he thought he knew. She had been a tireless supporter of the poor and a friend to every soul on Marianna. The thought of her creating such an awful substance was inconceivable.

"Now drink this like a good boy."

"Never! You'll have to use your sword, murderer."

"Aren't we full of ourselves. Do you imagine yourself to be a warrior now simply because you fought off raiders?"

He flew at Seth, throwing him to the floor. Air rushed out of his lungs in a painful burst. Struggling for breath, Seth was helpless to prevent the killer from pinning his arms. The Dagger pressed his knee down hard upon Seth's chest. He was forced to take a hand away from Seth's arms as he popped the top off the vial. Seth gagged. The poison smelled of dying flower petals and rotting fruit. He clamped his mouth shut and turned his head away.

"Now, be a good boy and open your mouth."

Desperate to break free of the killer's grip, Seth thrust his body upward, throwing the Dagger off balance. He slammed his free fist into his attacker's side and pushed at the man's body. They rolled along the cold floor until Seth found himself pinned again.

"One last show of spirit!" He jabbed Seth in the midsection with a lightning blow. His mouth involuntarily opened as he gulped for air. The Dagger's hand slammed Seth's head against the floor and poured the murderous liquid into his mouth. It tasted bitter, almost like berries that weren't quite ripe. His tongue and throat began to burn. He tried to spit the poison out, but the Dagger held firm. His killer pulled away at last.

Seth turned onto his stomach, vomiting the nasty liquid out of his body. The floorboards began to swirl and blur beneath him.

"Try as you might, D'Antoiné, death comes for you and your house."

Power thundered into the room with the force of a savage storm. Its large gray body slammed into Seth's killer, propelling him across the room. The Dagger's body disappeared from Seth's blurring vision behind the wall of gray. Angry flashes of red and gold hues crackled around the new stranger's body. When he finally spoke, the walls of the room shook under the power of his voice.

"Sandor, you fool! We had an agreement. I need this boy."

"Anne!" Emma's sobs lifted the haze about his heart. It was true. His mother was dead and he would soon join her.

"The boy, woman! See to the boy. Are we in time?"

Insistent fingers pushed at Seth's throat, then moved to his face. They gripped a clump of his curls, forcing Seth's head back and a cup to his lips. A nutty fragrance mixed with the scent of dried herbs made his stomach lurch. He tried to pull away.

"Drink it, Seth." Emma forced his mouth open again. He swallowed the bitter liquid. Then he fell back on the floor, coughing as the burning in his throat grew worse.

"Will he live?" the new stranger asked.

"We reached him before the poison stopped his breathing. There's still a chance he'll survive."

"How many will thank you, woman?" The Dagger's blurry body came to join them.

"This boy has grown dangerous, though his mother tried to hide it. Don't deny you feel the power radiating about his body. It has drawn out his temper. One can only imagine what he'll be capable of when he reaches his seventeenth year in a few months' time." The Dagger turned to the stranger. "I've grown weary of this island, ranger. You cannot expect me to continue to languish."

"Be grateful you still draw breath after betraying me! You will continue to watch over this boy until it is time. I found you once, Pavel Sandor, don't think I won't hunt you again. Now do what you do best. We need everyone to believe the raider trash is responsible for this mess."

Strong, rough hands lifted Seth's torso off the floor until he was sitting up. His head fell on his rescuer's chest. The proximity brought the patch on the man's uniform into focus. Embroidered into its shape was a golden sword stretching over a bright star. The words "Jalora Legion" had been sewn in crimson. He was a ranger, and someone Emma knew well enough to run to for help. More lies and secrets. What else had they hidden from him? What other dark secrets would he discover about the woman who bore him?

"Mother!" Seth screamed.

"She's dead, boy," the ranger told him. "You still live."

"Will you summon the Sacred Guard then?" Emma asked.

"No. I will come for him at the appointed time. You must resume your normal lives as best you can until my return."

The ranger lifted Seth over his shoulder as easily as if he were a small sack of flour. His body bounced weakly when they descended the stairs. Emma hurried after them, staying close to the ranger's back. His mother's killer didn't follow.

"You must keep him alive."

"Yes, it will be as you say," she told him.

Seth reached out his hand to her. "Emma, who am I?"

"Hush, boy." she rested her hand upon his head. "You're very ill. The masked man and the Ranger are only dreams."

Seth shook his head, gripping the ash cloak. They were not dreams. They were nightmares. The image of his mother's dead face swirled before him. She'd left him with no answers or explanation.

Chapter Six

RILEY LOGAN DUG HIS FEET into the ooze. His bright blue eyes glared at the insistent mouths surrounding him. He gripped the pitchfork tighter, trying to keep from slipping on the dung underneath his boots. It was a difficult job to remain standing in the middle of a herd of hungry woolies. The sheep bumped and charged at him as they fought to reach the hay at the end of his fork. Riley pushed through them with a growl.

His dad lectured the family at least once a week about the gratitude they should show the fuzzy creatures. The little island of Marianna had struggled during the first few years of colonization and would have failed if not for a happy accident of nature. A herd of larkspur short-hair sheep, known for their hardiness, mixed in a field with Heidelbreckt country long-hairs. Springtime overcame them, and Marianna was blessed with a new breed of sheep — the Marianna woolie. Softer or warmer wool could not be found in the Grey Cliff Isles or Andara.

"Get out of the way!"

The herd pushed at him even harder. Their superior numbers were more than a match for his temper. He dropped the bale in the middle of the yard and jumped out of their way. With his pitchfork raised in defeat, he scrambled out of the pen and fell on his backside in the grass.

"Careful, Little Whiskers." His brother Patrick snorted, lifting his lantern. "Wouldn't want Mother's baby hurt."

"Hurt? He'll wish he'd been trampled to death if Dad finds out he forgot to do the afternoon feed again."

George, another of the Logan boys, led his younger brothers to gather around the pen. They snickered as Riley hurried to his feet. Mr. Logan had fathered seven sons. Each of them had quick tempers and a smart mouth. Bright copper hair marked the boys as kin. While it was true they did fight amongst themselves, heaven help the fool who picked a fight with one brother. He'd have to face seven pairs of fists.

"I should hang a bucket of sheep dung around your neck to help you remember." Patrick hung his light on the post beside Riley's lantern. He grinned and leaned on the pen's rail.

"Come ahead, Patrick, and I'll show you the business end of this pitchfork!"

"I'll take it away from you and smack your bottom with the handle." Patrick pushed away from the pen and started toward Riley.

"Standing around like lazy bums, eh?"

Thomas Logan rounded the corner of the barn and marched toward the pen. The copper hair framing his weather-worn cheeks had begun to show signs of gray. Age hadn't slowed Mr. Logan. His iron will and tireless nature had made the Logan Farm Marianna's highest producer of woolie wool. He regarded his brood with naked anger. Riley kept quiet. He'd learned well not to argue with his dad when his temper was up.

"Do you think I pay to put food in those bottomless bellies of yours so you can lie about all day? I'll have you all cleaning the barn from top to bottom in a minute. Now, get to the house. Your mum has supper on the table."

"Aye, Dad!" The Logan boys sang out with better precision than a church choir.

Riley grabbed his lantern off the post. He followed his brothers, not wanting to tempt his dad's anger. He'd already had a good tongue lashing today for knocking the weather vane off the barn roof. Thoughts drifting to the coins he had hidden in his waistcoat, Riley mentally counted them until his foul mood subsided. He and Seth were very close to having enough money saved for their journey to the mainland. They'd make their fortunes in one of Andara's rich cities. Riley's days of mucking pens would be far behind him.

A horse and wagon raced at a reckless pace down the hill and through the stone pillars marking the entrance to their farm. Riley shook his head. His horse must be kicking up enough dust to cover their porch in dirt. And one guess who'd get stuck washing it down.

"What's he doing, the damn fool? His horse could break a leg charging about in the dark." George spat out the piece of straw hanging upon his lips. "Mum won't be fit to live with if the supper gets cold."

"Aye," Riley told them, waving at the dusty cloud floating under the lamps of the farmyard. "She'll make us take another wash by the time we've made it to the house."

His brothers groaned under their breaths. Mrs. Logan insisted on keeping them abnormally clean. Insisting they wash once a week. Imagine! The McKenzie brothers only had to wash once a month as was proper. It was Anne McCloud's doing. Seth's mother was like family. She was well loved around the Logan Farm, but some of the odd things she did were out of place on Marianna. She wouldn't let Seth use the Islic brogue — the customary language of the Grey Cliff Isle — or allow him to curse. Mrs. McCloud absolutely refused to allow Seth to leave the island no matter how much he pleaded. Riley felt sorry for his best friend sometimes.

"McTavish's Feed and Supply" stretched along the side of the buckboard in dark blue letters. Angus McTavish reined in his ponies and stopped in the farmyard close to the house. He was an older man, with no shortage of middle-aged plump about his belly. Struggling off the buckboard, Mr. McTavish leaned breathlessly upon its side. He waved wildly as they approached.

"Thomas, I have news!"

The farmhouse door creaked open and Riley's mum came out on the porch. Drying her hands on a long apron covered in flour, she ran quick fingers across her blonde hair. A few strands had escaped the tight bun she wore upon the top of her head. The omniscient eyes of a mother of seven took them in.

"What is it, Angus?" She dusted off a bench for their guest. "Come in, have some tea."

"No thank you, Laura. There's no time." Mr. McTavish shook his head. "I hardly know where to start, so much has happened."

Riley moved a little closer as the man took a seat on their front porch. He was itching with curiosity. This must be big news indeed. The militia had their share of skirmishes with Amity raiders in the summertime, but little happened to disrupt the boredom of a Haven Bay autumn night.

"Amity raiders came up to the McKenzie farm and carried off their girl, Alice."

"Raiders this close to winter? That doesn't make any sense."

Haven Bay guarded her coastline year around. They'd put in a relay system of alarms to warn their neighbors along the Farm Row. Each alarm was constantly manned during raider season. This time of year, however, the farmers turned their concerns to the oncoming winter months. The alarm bells outside Haven Bay remained silent and forgotten.

Patrick pounded up the stairs. The rest of the Logan boys followed. They circled about their guest, waiting for the story to continue. Mr. McTavish patted his forehead and cheeks with his linen. His eyes sparkled with the glee of a storyteller who'd been rewarded with a free meal. He was clearly pleased by the cries of shock.

"The McKenzie men with my son Rob, Elder Newcastle, and some of the other local farmers went looking for her. Guess what they found?"

"Tell us, man." Patrick grunted and got a good whack on the back of his head from their dad.

"They followed the smoke from a grass fire in the far fields to find Seth McCloud with Alice in his arms. Five Amity raiders were dead at his feet!"

Riley stared open mouthed at their visitor. Seth had fought and won a fight against five raiders? And stuck-up Alice McKenzie had let Seth touch her? What in the green, green fields had happened to his best friend? Seth McCloud wasn't a warrior or a lover. He'd barely been able to talk to Alice or any other girl during school. Then again, Mr. McTavish's son Rob was the constable. He'd seen it with his own eyes.

"Scrawny Seth McCloud?" George stammered. "Riley's friend, Seth McCloud, fought raiders?"

"And won." Mr. McTavish tapped his finger tip at George with each syllable.

"Is he alright? And what about Alice?" Riley's mum asked. "I must go to the farm. The poor girl is probably in hysterics."

Mr. McTavish stopped smiling. He stood to face Mrs. Logan. Riley didn't like the nervous look in his eyes. Something else was wrong. He pushed through his brothers and came to stand beside their mum. Her hand clutched at his arm.

"Seth is alright," Riley asked. "Isn't he?"

McTavish shifted his gaze uneasily away from Riley. "Constable wants you and your boys to help find the murdering raider who escaped, Thomas."

"Aye." Mr. Logan turned to his boys. "Michael, Stephen, Riley, stay here with your mum. Go into the house, lock the doors, and don't open them until we've come back."

"Alice will need looking after, Thomas. A girl needs a mother after such a horrible experience."

"No, Laura," Mr. Logan told her. The fear in his voice was unnerving. "I want you safe in the house. Don't worry. We'll bring her here if her dad agrees."

Riley gripped Angus McTavish's arm. "Seth? What about Seth?"

"He was bloodied some, but he seemed none the worse for wear. The men who found them said young McCloud, well, they said he seemed changed somehow. He wasn't acting like himself."

"And they just let him wander off on his own?" Riley pulled away from his mum's grip. "You don't know Seth like I do. He wouldn't show he'd been hurt."

Fighting off raiders. What had Seth been thinking missing the night bell again? He'd been warned so often, Sergeant Gunn had threatened to make him wash all the uniforms in the militia. This was more serious than a joy ride along the cliffs. Seth was in real trouble.

He needed help, and he'd get it whether he wanted it or not.

Riley raced off the porch and charged at full speed toward the corral beside their barn. Their only horse, Bluebell, drank lazily from the trough. She lifted her head when he threw open the gate, expecting her usual evening apple. He leapt on her bare back and thrust his heals in her girth. She snorted angrily and bounded up the lane toward the Farm Row.

"Riley Logan!" His dad yelled as he rode past. "You get your pasty arse back here before I beat it bloody!"

The Logan Farm was to the northeast of Haven Bay. Riley and his brothers could walk the distance into town in under thirty minutes if they cut across the fields. In his haste, Riley had left his lantern behind. There would be no shortcuts this time. He'd have to keep to the Farm Row using the moon's light to guide them. It was a well-traveled road connecting the farms in the far north to the town of Haven Bay at the southern end of the island. Over the years, wagons full of woolie wool and other supplies had worn the soil down to the hard stone beneath. Farm Row's slowly winding path through the farms eventually brought travelers to the Main Row and the east end of Haven Bay. Unfortunately for Riley, the McCloud home was in the southwest end of town.

Bluebell came to the top of Settler's Hill, allowing Riley a view of the night's chaos. He brought the pony to a halt. The strong odor of gunpowder and scorched grass traveled upon the constant breeze. Torchlights swarmed across the countryside like a luminescent fishing net. Every farmer and militiamen on Marianna must be in those fields tonight or soon would be.

"Ho, Riley Logan!" Someone called from the field to his right."What are you doing, charging at us in the dark? You could have gotten your damn fool head shot off."

Sergeant Gunn, leader of the militia, banged the cover of his lantern open. Light circled about him as he lifted the lantern higher. Streaks of dirt and sweat covered his face. He didn't look happy to have a visitor. Neither did the two men walking beside him. Each of them carried muskets, their barrels pointed at Riley.

"Don't shoot my dad or he'll have your head. He and the boys are coming in Mr. McTavish's wagon. I'm looking for Seth."

"Shoe and stocking. Always together. I'd wondered where you were, Riley." The Sergeant frowned and took a strong hold on Bluebell's mane. "Does your dad know you're out here by yourself? I didn't think so. Off you get. You and this horse are going to stay put with us until your dad gets here."

Riley slid off Bluebell. "Where is Seth?"

"You don't need to worry about him. He fought off those raiders in the first place." The Sergeant shook his head and pointed toward Haven Bay. "Constable said he headed through the fields toward home."

Riley sprinted into the darkness, ignoring the sergeant's angry shouts. Dodging torch-wielding volunteers, he crossed the small pasture land bordering Farm Row. A waist-high stone wall helped Riley get his bearing. The east end of town was close. Shadows from the church steeple stretched over the iron rod fence surrounding many a headstone. He shivered. They buried their dead in its lonely yard. Old or young. The boneyard didn't care who you once were in life. Death turned everyone back to dust.

The lights of town were a welcome comfort as he made his way through the empty alleyways of the market place. His work boots hit the ornate stones of town square. Businesses and homes along the square had their shutters tightly closed, hoping to guard against raider mischief. Though the alarm bells were no longer ringing, the residents of Haven Bay remained cautious. Riley didn't blame them. They'd been looted enough over the years.

The McCloud house stood at the northernmost point of the square. Its windows were dark as if the house had been abandoned. Riley stopped beside the line of benches along the little ornamental fence. Anne McCloud kept a warm home despite being kin to the isle's meanest resident. Tonight its friendly light and the fragrant smells of a busy kitchen were missing.

Their front door swung open. A huge man dressed in a heavy gray cloak filled the doorway. Seth's unconscious body was hanging over his shoulder. The stranger stopped. His hood lifted as if he were listening. Riley squatted down behind the benches lining the square. Something about the man warned him to stay hidden. The moments clicked by as he waited, motionless and watchful.

Emma broke the spell over the square when she shut the door behind their visitor. Words, low and quick, passed between them. Then they hurried down the Main Row with Seth's unconscious body. Riley stayed low and followed. Emma was having trouble keeping pace behind the stranger. In truth, if Riley hadn't been able to fix his eyes on Seth's stained white shirt, he wouldn't have been able to see the man at all.

They stopped before Doctor McFadden's home. The stranger lowered Seth to the garden bench beside the doctor's front door. He exchanged more hushed words with her and then turned in a flourish of gray. The stranger disappeared into the night, leaving Emma alone with Seth. She banged on the door, but there was no answer. Lights blazed on the lower floor in the doctor's surgery. He was either with a late-night patient or preparing for wounded volunteers.

Riley left his hiding place and joined her on the porch. "What has happened to Seth, Emma?"

Her cloak flew between them, blocking his vision. The fabric fell away as Emma's hand stopped inches from his throat. Hard eyes held him in place with their intensity. Her hand dropped as recognition came to her face. Riley fancied he saw a glint of steel under the lamplight before her hand disappeared under the folds of her cloak.

"Why aren't you at home, boy?" She turned from him and pounded upon the door again. "There have been terrible goings-on tonight. Go round to the surgery and tap on the window. See if you can get the doctor's attention."

He backed away from her. His early memories were filled with Emma baking sweet cakes for him and Seth. She'd been there to kiss hurt fingers and clean skinned knees. The idea of her holding a knife to his throat was completely mental. He'd been mistaken. Emma wouldn't hurt him or anyone else.

Riley stood on his toes and peered into the surgery window. Doctor McFadden wasn't inside. Two bright green eyes and a head of strawberry hair suddenly appeared on the other side of the pane. He jumped back, nearly falling on his backside again. The window lifted open and Beatrice McFadden, the doctor's daughter, stuck her head out.

"Why are you peeking in windows this time of night, Riley Logan?" She clutched at the neck of her shawl. Bits of ribbons from her dressing gown popped up over the fabric. Freckles sprinkled on her nose and cheeks made her look much younger than her fifteen years.

"Well, I'm not here to see you, so you can stop your hinting." Riley tugged angrily on his waistcoat. "I've come for your dad. Seth's ill."

"Dad's gone around front. You'd best go find him and stop loitering." She slammed the window and stormed away, braids bobbing as she walked.

Loitering. He wasn't loitering. Beatrice was a little pest. It was lucky for her dad he was the only doctor on the island. Rude greetings from that daughter of his would send the town folk running from his door.

Riley hurried around the corner. Emma stood hovering over Doctor McFadden's shoulder as he examined Seth. She murmured something low to the back of his balding head. He turned at her words, face pale and eyes wide with shock. The stunned look on his face dropped the bottom out of Riley's stomach.

"Let's get him inside." Doctor McFadden gripped Seth's limp form, struggling to lift him. Riley bolted forward and took his other arm.

"Great gulls, he's grown! It was a good thing Riley was there to help you, Emma."

"Sometimes we find the strength when those we love are in trouble."

The half-lie flowed easily out of her mouth. There was no sign of remorse or guilt. It was as if Emma was someone used to telling lies. Riley looked away before she could see him watching.

Doctor McFadden led them inside. "I don't know what you boys have been up to tonight, Riley Logan, but you are going to stay in this house until your dad comes for you."

They laid Seth down on the infirmary table, and Emma began to undress him. Seth moaned a few incoherent words. Thrashing about weakly, he resisted Emma's efforts. She began to drop Seth's clothes to the floor as she stripped the layers. A tiny glass bottle slid across the wood to stop at Riley's feet. He picked up the funny little bottle. It was an odd sort of thing for Seth to carry about with him, but he'd hold onto it for his friend all the same. Riley stepped back and put it in his trouser pocket along with his hands. He didn't know what else to do with them. Nothing he could think of would help Seth now.

The doctor pulled Riley to the hallway. "Can you use a gun?"

"Aye, Doctor, I'm a fair shot."

"I want you to stand guard."

He opened his gun case and handed Riley his musket. It was a heavy weapon with a good polish on the handle. Doctor McFadden had spent many hours on their farm hunting game birds. He nursed his musket like a fragile babe. Giving it to Riley now was telling of just how much trouble might come their way. The doctor shoved an ammunition bag into Riley's arms and stood back to have a look at him.

"Mrs. McCloud has been murdered in her bed. Emma says the door was wide open when she found her mistress. I'd guess some murdering raider villain caught her unawares." Hate crossed the doctor's face. "There's no sign of her brother."

Anne McCloud was dead? Riley shook his head, ignoring the sweaty curls as they stuck to his neck. What fiend would raise a hand to a gentle soul like Anne McCloud? It didn't seem possible unless her foul brother had finally snapped. By the look on Doctor

McFadden's face, he was weighing the possibility as well.

Riley passed in front of the surgery door and stopped. Seth was drenched in sweat. Wetness had pasted his thick hair flat against his head. Low moans full of grief and worry filled the surgery as Seth struggled against Emma's hands. Riley stared at his best friend's writhing body. Seth could die. He tried to think back on their last words to each other. Had Riley said his goodbyes? He couldn't remember. Great gulls! It was nonsense thinking such things. Seth would recover. He was strong and one of the most determined people Riley knew.

"Well, don't stand there gaping. Go stand guard like I told you." The doctor pushed Riley toward the front door and stepped into the surgery to look after Seth.

The crystal lamps of the square were still glowing brightly, though their light hadn't kept the raiders at bay. Riley took up position just outside the front door. He held the musket before him, scanning the dark streets. Raiders had murdered Seth's mum. What if they did come back to finish the job on Seth? Would Riley have the stomach to kill a man to protect his friend? He didn't know, but he wouldn't stand by with Seth helpless while someone tried to…

"Who goes there? Show yourself, I warn you. I'll put a hole in your fat head!" Riley lifted his musket and pointed it at the movement in the darkness.

"Stand down, Riley!" Constable McTavish and a handful of men from the militia ran out of the darkness. "It's true then? We've had a killing?"

"Aye, Constable, Anne McCloud has been murdered in her bed." Riley brushed at the wetness stinging his eyes. In his shock, he hadn't noticed the tears before. "Seth's inside out of his head with sickness. We don't know what happened."

Constable McTavish nodded and looked with a pale face toward the McCloud home. "You men stay here with Riley and watch the house. One of you go to the stables and ask Mr. Morgan for the loan of a wagon. If these raiders are after the boy, then we must move him to a safer place."

The constable walked at a sharp clip to Seth's house. A strange sort of dread fell upon Riley's heart as he kept his eyes upon the constable. He had the right idea moving Seth. This wasn't the first time Amity raiders tried to hurt his best friend. He'd escaped their vile hands at age four when the raiders had crept into the farmlands and tried to snatch him away during the Logan's Harvest Party. Dad and the other men of Marianna had seen justice done that night, but it had come too late for Charlie McDermott's tiny twin brother. Though Riley had been only a few months older than Seth, he still remembered the killing with nightmarish clarity.

Constable McTavish came slowly toward them again. His face was solemn. He gripped Riley's shoulder briefly and walked into the doctor's house. Reality had come with him. Anne McCloud had passed from the world. Haven Bay wouldn't be the same without her kind, gentle ways.

"Seth shouldn't be moved!" Doctor McFadden shouted, following the constable back out into the street.

"If you'd seen the terrible things they did to Anne McCloud, well, you'd know why it's necessary. Think of your daughter, Doctor. You'd best send her to the neighbor's home and pray these bastards don't return. Get him ready."

A wagon approached them carrying the militia men. Their driver stopped the nervous ponies before them. Constable McTavish took the doctor's arm and hurried him back inside. Their wagon bumped and swayed along the Main Row a short time later. Judging by the stars, it was well past midnight when they reached the Marianna Airship Port. Its lonely skeletal frame stood with empty docks reaching out over the sea. In the past, visiting sailors had been willing to help fight off the thieving vermin to protect their cargo. The men of Marianna had defended their lands with fewer numbers this time. Luck had certainly been with the raiders tonight. They'd had an easy time of it.

Riley turned on his perch beside the driver for a quick glance at Emma. She'd said something about terrible things happening. He was beginning to wonder if this raider attack had been a diversion. Maybe the real purpose behind the night's trouble was to get Seth and his mum alone.

The lights from Paddy's Inn and Pub burned brightly against the darkness. Its owner answered the pounding at his door with a loaded musket. His bulbous pink nose protruded through the gap. Sharp eyes examined the constable and his companions before he swung the door open.

"Paddy will show you where to take Seth." Constable McTavish ushered the men carrying their charge through the door. "Do you want a lift back to town, Riley?"

His legs were shaking when he jumped off the wagon. "You aren't staying? What if those raiders come back after Seth?"

"We've still got a killer roaming about Marianna." The constable rested a hand on Riley's shoulder.

"Paddy and Teb are armed. Seth will be safe enough now. Are you coming? "

"No, Constable. I'll be staying right here with Seth." Riley gripped the musket tighter. "Someone needs to watch over him."

He pushed into the common room. Paddy and his barkeep, Teb McKinney, had cleared all the tables and locked up the drink for the night. The pub had long since closed to customers. He headed through the empty tables toward the stairs leading up to the bed-chambers. A strange spark of energy lifted the hairs on his arms when he walked close to the bar. There sitting upon its surface was a single glass. The remains of a dark liquor coated the bottom.

"Miss Emma is with Seth in the last room on the right." Paddy whisked up the empty glass and put it behind the bar. "She'll be needing your help."

Riley nodded. He stretched the tense muscles in his shoulders as he climbed the stairs. This day had turned into a long one. He was beginning to imagine things. An empty glass was common enough in a pub. His nerves were getting the better of him with good reason. Seth close to death. Mrs. McCloud murdered and her killer still on the loose. Peaceful Marianna had become a killing ground.

Smelling the pungent odors of herbs, he found Seth's sickroom. Emma was already inside. She leaned over the bed to straighten Seth's covers. Aging hands lovingly dipped a cloth in the basin of cool water.

"His skin is still hot to the touch." She gently wiped his forehead. "He'll survive, won't he?"

Doctor McFadden ran a hand over his balding head and frowned. "Only the Creator can say."

"Of course he will, Emma." Riley lifted a hand to lightly touch her shoulder and then let it drop. "Seth is too stubborn to quit on life."

He sat down in the uncomfortable wooden chair by the window and rested the musket over his lap. It was going to be a long night. Fatigue nudged at his body, but Riley ignored it for Seth's sake. Paddy knocked on the open door. He had a kettle of tea with three cups. Riley took his eagerly and let the warming liquid pour down his throat. It was nice and strong. His eyes were bound to stay open now.

An unsettling stillness fell upon Marianna as Riley kept watch at the window. It was like the aftermath of a storm. His eye lids drifted downward, lulled by the constant rush of ocean toward rock. In the wee hours of a dark morning, Riley lost his battle with fatigue and fell into sleep.

Angry shouts pierced through the temporary peace. Riley started awake, sending his forgotten teacup shattering to the floor. It splashed upon his bare shins. The liquid had gone cold hours ago.

Emma wasn't in the room. She'd left her shawl hanging over the back of her chair at Seth's bedside. Nothing could pull Emma away unless more trouble had come for them. Then the shouts invading his sleep erupted again. He didn't like leaving Seth alone, but curiosity won over caution. Casting one last look at his best friend, he crept out of the room. It was black in the hallway. Riley's foot took another step and didn't find floor. He clutched at the wall, feeling his way with an outstretched boot.

"That's enough out of you, Headmaster!"

He couldn't mistake the voice. Elder Newcastle and Fergus McCloud were quarreling again. Imagine bickering at a time like this. Two grown men should be able to put their hatred aside for a few days. If he was pressed to pick, Riley wasn't sure which side he'd choose. Elder Newcastle owned the only wool mercantile on Marianna and half the buildings in town. He overcharged the business owners on rent and tried to cheat the woolie farmers on the price of their wool. Dad was there to make certain he behaved.

Mr. McCloud, on the other hand, built their school, the Lookout. and the airship port with his own money. It seemed to Riley the headmaster took pleasure in reminding everyone — especially Elder Newcastle — that nothing would come or go from Marianna without his say-so.

They were standing toe to toe when Riley reached the base of the stairs. Both men were in a rage, ready to come to blows. Emma sat with Doctor McFadden at a nearby table. Her head slowly rocked upon her open palms. The doctor gripped her shoulder, encouraging her to sip from a glass of liquor.

"Your nephew has put us all in danger." Elder Newcastle stuck his pudgy belly into the space between them. "It's a wonder the entire town wasn't murdered."

"Young McCloud is one of us. We watch over our own. Talk to the constable if you're so worried." Doctor McFadden lifted tired eyes to the elder. "Seth is still very ill. I daresay he should remain under this roof until he can travel. Satisfied?"

"I'm satisfied if the entire McCloud household remains here." The elder lifted his chin and threw a spiteful glare at Fergus.

"I won't be caged in this hovel while my work suffers." He slammed the tip of his walking stick upon the floor and headed toward the door.

"You cold-hearted creature! Anne just died and Seth is upstairs fighting for his life. Is your work all you can think about?" Riley's mum cried, coming into the light.

Dad was right beside her with a look of murder on his face. He kept a steady arm about her. His dad was a fair, law-abiding man, but there were a few times he'd taken justice into his own hands. Riley recognized the glint of poorly contained rage about his eyes. Dad was close to giving old Fergus Fussbottom a long overdue beating.

"Look at him, Mrs. Logan." Elder Newcastle pointed at the headmaster's snarling face. "There's your answer."

The elder turned his great bulk and headed out into the dark morning air. Fergus Fussbottom's cold glare stabbed at his departing back. He struck at the floor with his walking stick and then stormed toward the lower level of the inn.

"Just a moment, Headmaster!" Dad shouted, stepping forward to block his way. "Seth is still..."

"I endured your intrusions upon my family's private business for Anne's sake. She is dead now, so don't think your interfering is welcome any longer. If you are concerned about the boy, take him to your home to live in squalor with the rest of the pigs."

"Thomas, don't!" Riley's mum grabbed Dad to restrain him. "Perhaps it is best if Seth comes to our home."

Riley pressed against the wall among the shadows as the crippled form of Fergus McCloud limped by. He couldn't recall a man more deserving of an entire island's hatred. Seth was best rid of him.

"His dear mother would want the boy to finish his studies." Emma's voice sounded frail through her tears.

"What would she think if I didn't make certain Seth went to school?"

"Emma's right, Thomas." Mum clutched at his arm. "I wouldn't know how to help Seth with his lessons."

Dad nodded, throwing an uneasy look up at the ceiling toward Seth's room. "I suppose it's the least we can do for Anne. You'll promise to send for me if McCloud gives you any problems at all, won't you, Emma? My boys and I are a brisk walk away."

"I think we should try to send word to Seth's father. He must know."

Riley's ears pricked up. What was Mum talking about? Seth's real dad had died before he was born. He and Seth had made a crude headstone along the fence of the cemetery when they were boys. The small act seemed to have helped Seth cope with his life in the headmaster's house.

His parents joined the others at the table. The doctor poured more liquor into small glasses. They sat in silence for a long moment. Private thoughts kept them silent, pushing Riley's patience to the edge.

"What do you know about him?" Doctor McFadden finally asked.

"Anne didn't speak much about Seth's father," Dad told them. "She did tell us once he was in the Andarian Army. Their families didn't approve of the affair for some reason."

"Foolishness." Mum wiped at her eyes and took a rare sip of spirits. She didn't approve of drink. "Such things mean nothing once the babies start coming."

"Did Anne tell you the father's name?" the doctor asked. "I know it wasn't Seth. The night her son was born, I asked Anne if she would name the boy after his father. She said she'd been told to name him Seth."

"It doesn't matter now. The boy is alone in the world. He needs his father." Dad threw back his glass and downed the liquor in one gulp.

"Very well." Emma nodded. "Anne had a confidant south of the mainland who knew about Seth's father. I'll send word and hope she can help us."

"Eavesdropping, are we?" Paddy boomed behind Riley on the stairs. He held the scruff of Riley's neck in his hand as they propelled into the room.

"Here now, boy!" Dad gripped at Riley's ear. "What did you just hear? Enough, I'd wager. You listen to me, Riley. Not one word to anyone about Seth's father. That includes Seth."

"Why? He should know his father is alive."

"Not a word to anyone. Use your head. How do you think people like the elder would take the news about Seth's father being alive, and he and Anne never married? Well, just imagine how Seth would take it and right after his mother died? Give me a chance to find out what's what first. We don't even know what manner of man Seth's father is now, do we?"

"Aye, Dad," Riley muttered, seeing the sense in it now.

"I must check on Seth." His mother patted Emma on the hand. "Get some rest. I'm here now."

His dad kept a restraining hand on Riley as his mum followed Emma up the stairs. Grief kept them to a slow pace. They all were saddened by Anne McCloud's untimely death, but Mum had lost her best friend tonight. Things would never be the same again.

"You're to stay here with Seth. Understand? You tell Paddy or the doctor if Mr. McCloud bothers Seth, won't you?" Dad shook his head and followed his wife up the stairs. "I should have thrown the bastard off the cliff when I had the chance."

Chapter Seven

LEGENDS SPOKE IN QUIET TONES of the fall of the last great civilization inhabiting Andara. In their obsession to harness the magic of their so-called "technology," the ancients had split the lands asunder. The world had tilted upon its side, spinning awkwardly around an angry sun. Mankind vanished from their cities as nature rebelled. Then the Creator gave the abandoned world to the Jalora and its rival, the Sarcion, to rule as they wished. Mankind returned, but in the new order their worship was demanded, not offered.

The death of the old world and the rebirth of the new left many inhospitable locations on Andara. Julian had found one such place on the rocky shores of the Northern Buells. Days away from the nearest outpost or village, these shores were safe to speak of treason. He kept his eyes out to sea, ignoring the sensation of being watched. Mighty evergreens lined the shore and stretched hundreds of miles in thick patches of green and snow. Visitors from the south rarely dared to challenge the dangers hiding behind those thick evergreen boughs. Julian and his guests were safe enough as long as they stayed out of the trees.

A massive Jackal airship anchored offshore. None of the usual shouts and scrambling by the crew announced their coming. Stealth rather than fanfare seemed to be the Jackal way. Indeed, it had approached shore without warning to catch Julian relieving himself in the waves. A masterful design in flight, the heavy ship defied gravity. The featureless hull was blanketed in sheets of heavy armor. Great guns waited for battle behind seamless shutters. This was a ship that could take down an armada.

One ebony longboat lifted over the railing of the ship and sunk low to skim over the rough waves. These brutal barbarians from faraway shores held a strange fascination for Julian. They were very different than the spoiled soldiers of Valdeon or the bumbling fools who joined the United Realm Army. One would hope men gathered from all the nations of Andara could acquire better discipline. Instead , UR soldiers spent their service swilling drink and gambling their credits. Jackal warriors, in contrast, covered their body in hard chest armor, never taking it off again until death. Long braids, soaked in the blood of their enemies, fell in twisted strands down their backs. They were fearless and unwaveringly loyal to their commander. Soon he would have an entire army of these unstoppable warriors obeying his every word.

Julian, however, well knew how dangerous it was to disappoint this new ally. His failure to capture the Lion Ring would not be well received. He kept his chin raised and arms still at his side. He was the Prince of Valdeon and the only viable heir to the throne. Justifying his actions to these barbarians was beneath him.

The longboat hovered over the rocks to anchor itself upon the beach. No one moved. Were they expecting a Prince of Valdeon to wet his feet racing to hold the longboat? He folded his arms and planted his feet harder upon the muddy shore.

A familiar blob of bald skin appeared over the bow of the boat. Whisper's impish grin widened across chubby, golden cheeks. Long fingers gripped the side and pulled his pot belly over the rim. Hovering a few feet above the rocks, the Akutarian Emissary approached Julian with excited waves.

He had first met Whisper a few years before, when Leo had still held a stifling grip upon the throne. Julian had been wandering along the coast of Valdeon to escape his father's insufferable judgment when the little creature appeared to him in his tent. Whisper had brought him a very powerful gift. Julian stroked a fingertip over his ring fondly at the memory.

"Greetings, great Prince of Valdeon." Whisper gave him a lavish bow and kissed Julian's Sarcion Ring. "I bring you gifts of welcome and friendship from my emperor."

"I return his greetings and yours, Whisper. It still is a mystery to me how he knows when I wish to meet with his emissaries."

Whisper shrugged its fat shoulders and slapped long fingers over where Julian guessed was its heart. "Think of me as my emperor's thought brought to life, Prince Julian. He created me to travel quickly across great distances to communicate his wishes."

"Your emperor must be very powerful indeed. Will I meet him soon?"

"My master cannot leave Akutar at this time, Prince, but he has sent you a gift." Whisper turned to the longboat and nodded. "He has sent you Akutar's greatest warrior to aid in your liberation of Valdeon."

A man — or at least Julian hoped it was a man — rose slowly from the center of the boat. Covered in a deep plum hood and cloak, he towered above the barbarians groveling before him. Disembarking gracefully from the vessel, he moved across the stone and mud in effortless strides. Julian resisted the impulse to step backward away from the towering stranger as he approached them. Gloved hands threw back the folds of the hood. A sharp cry choked in Julian's throat as he faced the hideous, skull-shaped metal helmet covering the man's head. Bright blue eyes trapped behind steel mesh were the only bit of flesh visible.

"You are Julian D'Antoiné, Andarian?" his gravel voice asked.

"I am. And you are?"

"I am called Lord Gorman, General of our Emperor's Army."

He stretched out a Sarcion ring in the space between them. The depths of the black jewel swayed in chaotic waves as if to absorb the hazy light of a coastal sun. Great power lived within its stone. It hung about the man in a mantel of danger. Murderer was a brand Julian wore with no regrets. He accepted what he'd done as necessary. Being in Lord Gorman's presence made him feel like an innocent again. One killer knew another. This man had taken many lives. Death walked in his shadow. He was indeed dangerous, but it didn't excuse his use of the term "our emperor." Julian was not a subject of Akutar. It very well may be within a season he would be the new emperor of Andara. The giant before him was a servant sent from Julian's ally. It was best to remind him of the fact at the start.

"Welcome, Lord Gorman. Your emperor is most generous to send you and your men to aid me as I take my throne." Julian stepped back a pace when the steel mesh covering Gorman's eyes flash with anger

"That is not the only reason I have come, Andarian. My emperor is concerned with your lack of progress in obtaining the Lion Ring. He fears your continued failure jeopardizes our conquest of Andara. I have come to guarantee our success." Lord Gorman lowered his metal face toward Julian. "Be warned, Andarian, I have no love of your homeland. If not for my orders, I would separate your head from your shoulders and invade with brutal force. Your overly complex plan does not inspire much confidence."

"But you are under orders, so we'll be doing things my way." Julian stepped forward, coming inches away from the insufferable barbarian.

Whisper came between them in a gust of frigid air. "Come now, my lords, we are here for a common goal. His imperial majesty wants the Andarian Northlands and he is generously offering his aid to our great ally in securing the south. We must clear the way for Akutar's armada. Valdeon must be destabilized before they arrive."

"He's sent his forces? We agreed he would not move until I obtained the Lion Ring." Julian turned an angry glare upon the emissary. The Sarcion had assured him this Jackal Emperor would be a worthy ally, but it had failed to mention how hungry this foreign lord was for Andara's rich resources.

"His hand was forced." Lord Gorman grunted a humorless laugh, guttural and ugly under the mask. "We can no longer wait for your clumsy attempts to find the Lion Ring. Valdeon must be taken by force."

"That wasn't our agreement."

Julian gripped at the handle of his sword, wanting nothing more than to thrust its tip deep into Gorman's heart. Low growls began to circle them. Crimson jackals painted upon chest plates moved in threatening waves. Sword hilts pounded on metal armor as Gorman's men circled around them.

"You must listen to me." Julian slowly moved his hand away from his own weapon. "I know of another way to take the throne without Valdeonian bloodshed. Valdeon may be ruled by another if there is no lion upon the throne. The Regent Medallion gives its bearer the power of a king in the eyes of the people. When the court sees me wearing it, they must unconditionally support my ascension to the throne."

Julian had devoured every word he could find about the legendary Altar of Providence. Despite his searching, little remained from the accounts of the Regent Medallion. Worn only once by a forgotten leader, its power remained a mystery. A single entry mentioned the Crown of Sorrows had allowed this regent to place it upon his brow. It was unclear whether or not Valdeon's throne had allowed the man to touch its golden surface once he obtained the medallion's magic. Julian may never be able to sit upon its golden seat. These jackal barbarians didn't need to know the uncertainties. They were best used and then eradicated from Andara.

"Another fairy tale!"

"You must trust me. I know where the medallion is right now," Julian told him. "Those loyal to me are securing it as we speak. I have absolute confidence that I will be the Regent of Valdeon before the week is out."

Gorman's cold and unmoving metallic face managed to project his disbelief. Julian's confidence wasn't shaken. He knew exactly where this treasure rested. The Regent Medallion had gathered dust in the same cabinet for centuries. It wouldn't be missed right away. Most had forgotten its existence. He would enjoy making them remember, especially the troublesome Lords of Valdeon.

What of the medallion's magic? Have you considered its power, Prince of Valdeon? The Sarcion whispered in his mind.

It seemed more amused than concerned. Gorman snorted in agreement. The Akutarian lord had heard their exchange. A thread of mistrust began to worm its way through Julian's heart. He stifled his irritation at the teasing.

"You warn me against tales designed to frightened children? I have no fear of ghost stories. You will see. I'll take the throne with the Regent Medallion around my neck. Valdeon will be mine, and I won't have to spill more blood to see it done."

Gorman lifted his hand and motioned behind him. Two warriors brought a bag forward and dumped it upon the sand. Julian staggered back as a man's head rolled by his feet. The face was Andarian, possibly from one of the southern counties of Valdeon. The man's dead eyes were bulging wide in terror.

"This man was taking a message to the playthings of the Jalora." Gorman pulled out a parchment from inside his cloak and handed it to Julian.

He smoothed his thumb upon the seal of Edmund D'Antoiné. Loyal to the last, Leo had tried to send his legion a warning. It would never arrive. He nodded a reluctant thanks. They were very impressive, these barbarians from the north. They dared show their hatred for the Jalora. In fact, they seemed to bask in their blasphemy.

"I want someone on the inside with you, Prince of Valdeon."

Gorman turned as a cloaked figure came to stand beside him. Skinny grey fingers with dangerously long black nails threw back the cloak, exposing an inhuman face, sharp in feature and strangely pale. Cold black eyes blinked back at Julian as it grinned. The odd face blurred as it changed. Dark eyes and hair began to form until Leo's dead compatriot stood before them.

"This changeling will be your new companion."

"The rangers will know he…it is not human."

How dare the brute! Did he imagine Julian would allow himself to be monitored like a common foot soldier? Gorman was supposed to be an ally, not his task master. The man was forgetting his place.

"The Sarcion protects me." The changeling's accent was a perfect impression of a Valdeonian landowner. Educated, but not too formal.

"See you don't make too much of yourself, Changeling. The Lords of Valdeon will not be easily fooled."

"It will be as you say, Prince of Valdeon." The changeling bowed, an insolent grin upon its borrowed face. "I will stay in this body until I have need of a new one."

A shimmer of malicious delight flashed in the creature's eyes. Julian turned away. His knowledge of changelings was limited, but one couldn't be too cautious with such creatures. He didn't want Lord Gorman having delusions he could replace Julian rather than uphold his emperor's contract. Perhaps it was time to remind these barbarians just how invaluable Julian was to their plans.

"We have much planning to do," Julian told him. "The Lords of Valdeon are the Sacred Guard. They are powerful rangers whose duty it is to protect the Altar of Providence. They won't be easily defeated."

"They are still human." Gorman shifted the steel mesh covering his eyes toward Julian. "I've faced many challenging foes in my conquests."

"Don't underestimate them. They are servants of the Jalora. The overconfident fall easily under the sword of a ranger."

"You fear them, Prince of Valdeon?" The changeling's black eyes sparkled with amusement.

"Let us say, I respect their power. We must separate the Sacred Guard somehow. They are stronger together, but if we can divide them it is possible they could be defeated individually." He waved a hand at his own ship anchored well away from their meeting place. "Come, I have food and wine onboard my ship. Such things are best discussed over a meal."

Lord Gorman turned bored eyes to Julian. "We must endure such trivialities for the sake of your ego, I suppose."

He walked away, leaving Julian seething in the sand. The deal with the Akutar was balancing on Gorman's blade. He'd have to watch this new threat carefully. One wrong move and Valdeon would be taken from him. Julian swallowed his pride and painted on a statesman's false smile. He fell in step beside Whisper as they moved in the wake of Akutar's most infamous warrior.

Chapter Eight

Dark silence filled the Grand Atrium of the Palace of Kings. Starlight glistened within the glass panels of the three-story structure. Xavier the Wolf led the Lords of Valdeon along the dark wall of windows. Soon the pink of sunrise would paint the glass. Servants would begin their bustling as the palace woke to start the new day. For now, the only ones stirring within the massive building were the rangers and the being whose power beckoned them forward.

Wolf paused before the golden doorway to calm his mind. They were about to set foot upon sacred ground. The throne room of the Palace of Kings was built upon the very spot the Jalora had created its Lion Ring. Standing in stark contrast to the ancient white stone in which it was based, the Altar of Providence stood in the glory of power and hope. The Jalora and its god-like servants, the Luminawni or Ancients as they were sometimes called, formed the Altar's cathedral with perfect white stone from their lands. Then they had forged the three parts making up the Altar of Providence — the throne, the crown, and the orb.

The beauty and grandeur of the Palace of Kings paled in comparison to the throne room. White stone stretched beneath them circling toward a gigantic gold medallion. A crown sat upon the likeness of the orb which in turn rested upon a throne. Engraved deep within the medallion, the symbol of the Altar of

Providence marked the absolute center of the room. Spiraling into a great sphere, the throne room had been lined with beautiful white marble pillars. Each had the symbol of the Altar of Providence chiseled within it. Chairs with rich, blood-red fabric resting upon a tiered platform lined the main aisle on either side, drawing every eye to the most magnificent treasure in the world.

Housing the earthly energy of the land, Valdeon's throne, known as the "Lion's Seat," had been crafted from solid gold. Great paws made up the legs and arm rests. Its golden mane flowed to the diamond encrusted spiral ceiling. Massive lion jaws bared their teeth above the head of the king. Clasped tightly in the eternal jaw was the Crown of Sorrows. Worn upon the bearer of the Lion Ring's head, it was a brilliant band of magical energy. Now, as it rested within the gold, it looked like an unimpressive piece of lead. Many a lustful conqueror would attempt to take the crown from its resting place, but only the bearer of the Lion Ring could touch the Altar's surface. Any blasphemer foolish enough to try would meet with a painful end.

Wolf had seen the Altar's punishment firsthand. As a boy eager to see the famed Altar, he'd attended the king's court at his father's side. A clumsy servant had accidently fallen against the throne as he tried to hand Leo a scroll. Even the Lion could not stop the Altar's punishment. Sometimes in his nightmares, Wolf still heard the man's screams of agony.

His attention was drawn to the Orb of Valdeon next to the throne. The Altar's last piece tied the land and the ranger to the spiritual body of heaven. Its midnight color floated listlessly within the sphere. Once a bright purple pulsing in unison with Leo's energy, the Orb's power had faded when the Lion Ring was separated from its human host. As they approached, the black within the orb exploded with a surge of angry red.

Wolf kept his rangers at a steady, respectful pace. They were the Sacred Guard, defenders of the throne and keepers of the Altar of Providence. Despite best efforts and intentions, the Lords of Valdeon had failed in their duties. The Lion was dead, and his ring had been lost. Wolf's grief and guilt surged through him once more. They'd searched every location Leo had been rumored to hide and hadn't found the ranger or his ring. His heart wanted to keep searching, but by Valdeonian law they must acknowledge the king to be dead. A Regent must be selected to rule until the rightful heir could be found. If one could be found.

They kneeled at the back of the hall, waiting for the Altar to grant them permission to enter. The Altar's touch surrounded Wolf, probing his thoughts and heart. He remained motionless, letting the power course through him. Wolf was its servant, bound to follow its command or accept its punishment. The Jalora had remained silent about Wolf's encounter with Leo, but he suspected its wrath would come today considering what had happened as a result of their argument. He waited in complete submission for its judgment. The young rangers waiting behind him suddenly stood. They turned as one and marched out of the throne room, leaving Wolf alone with the Altar.

Destiny.

The word filled his mind. It was the Altar who spoke to him now. Not in words or images, but by infusing his mind directly with its will. He lifted his head. A young man with curly chestnut hair and amber-flecked eyes stood before him. The Lion Ring pulsed with brilliant light upon his finger. In an instant the image was gone, and he was alone in the throne room.

The Altar's power left him. Their brief meeting was over, and the punishment he had expected hadn't come.

Wolf rose slowly to his feet. A thousand questions ached to be asked, but no answer would be given this day. Keeping his eyes upon the Altar, he backed away slowly until his boot struck one of the golden throne-room doors. Wolf hurried into the Atrium. A mighty groan behind him shook the windows. The massive golden doors began to move. Hinges — unused for decades — forced the door closed by their own power. The chill of fate ran along his spine as the handles of the door dissolved into empty air. No one could reach the Altar of Providence now. The Jalora had sealed it away from all conquerors, but it had also closed itself to its guard. This boded ill for Valdeon and Andara.

"What does it mean, Wolf?"

Otter's young, impish face was a checkerboard of shadow and early morning sunbeams. He moved closer to his older cousin, Berto the Jaguar. Other young faces cast troubled gazes at the golden doors. He had no comfort to give them.

"It means we must prepare ourselves for war." Wolf turned from the golden doors. Perhaps they would open again for the young man in his vision? Or had he been a mere memory from the Altar's past?

"See to your duties. I go to speak with Chancellor Benito."

Crushing silence ripped the warmth from Chancellor Benito's eyes. His wrinkled face grew taut, washing away any complexion against the purple robes of state. The fabric rustled in hurried movements as he sought warmth from the cold fireplace standing empty in his chambers. Benito, stricken, clutched at the cold marble mantle with trembling fingers.

Wolf had brought ill news with him, news capable of ultimately throwing Valdeon into civil war. If the Lion Ring fell into the hands of evil, the Jalora's power would fade from the land. The legion's extraordinary power and their ability to keep the peace would diminish. They would be regular men, greatly outnumbered by those who wished to aid evil. Indeed, there were several such men with their covetous eyes fixed upon the throne of Valdeon. Backroom deals and alliances were being made as many listened to talk of treason.

He stood quietly, waiting as the old man stared into the empty fireplace. Summoning power to his eyes, he probed Benito's mind gently. Wolf trusted the chancellor, but he had to make sure. No one was above suspicion. Swirling hues of crimson, yellow, and black clung to the chancellor's body. Terror, feelings of betrayal, grief. The emotions were all there in his energy, but no sign of treachery.

"Are you certain it's missing?"

"The location of the Lion's Ring has been blocked from us," Wolf told him. "Cardinal Dragon can't explain why the Jalora remains silent."

Dragon was the highest-ranking ranger in the legion. It was rumored the Jalora sent him direction for its legion in visions. Wolf smoothed at the worn silver adorning his belt. The Jalora had hidden much from its faithful servants. It had kept Leo's location from them, hiding him in mists of darkness. Wolf 's frustration came to him again. He quickly let it go. It was not for him to question the Jalora's perfect wisdom. He had faith it knew best for the legion and Andara. Wolf rested his life and the lives of his family in such faith.

Benito leaned his forehead against the cold stone. He, with the help of the Lords of Valdeon, had held a feuding country from the brink of civil war for two years. The bright light of hope they had shared was the promise of Leo's return. Now the king was dead, his ring and the orb lifeless. Hope had deserted them. Wolf took the old man by the arm and helped him into a chair. He poured a glass of spice wine and put it to Benito's lips. He stood away, allowing the chancellor to gain composure. They had much to discuss. It was best to give Benito a chance to muster his nerve.

He took a strong military stance before the chancellor, projecting confidence and strength. As a ranger, Wolf could not lie. The Jalora would not allow it. He could, however, omit his own worry and confusion from their conversation. In the coming days, it would be crucial for all to see the Lords of Valdeon as their pillars of strength. The Lion Ring was the key to the safety of Andara. When news of its disappearance reached others, their world would be thrown into chaos. It was critical the legion and Valdeon be of one mind upon their course of action.

"What is to be done?" Chancellor Benito's voice was little more than a whisper.

"We must wait for the Jalora to reveal the ring's location. I would sleep better if I could be certain Julian does not have it."

Benito turned to regard him. Cheeks sunken with age and worry drooped in disapproval. His shriveled lips struggled to remain expressionless. "Can't you put aside your family pride at such a time?"

"Why can't you see the black heart behind Julian's sincere face? He is not the grief-stricken son you believe him to be. Where is our wayward prince? I don't see him here paying respect to his father's memory."

Anger brought the blood back to Benito's face. He pushed out of the chair with an irritated howl and stalked to the window of his office. It was an old argument between them, one neither would let go. Benito, in his love for Edmund, forgave the many indiscretions of his son. He refused to hear the truth, even from someone who was compelled to tell only truth.

"I have summoned our western prefects. They must know. Perhaps some of Edmund's old allies will help us look for the ring?"

Wolf said nothing. He had no great faith in the chancellor's plan. The prefects of the East and West had been in bitter feud while the king still sat upon the throne. Their hatred and rivalry would only grow worse now that the Lion Ring was lost.

"The Lords of Valdeon will help you all we can to maintain control, as will the Legionaries here in San Leonora. Dragon also sends his offer of aid if you need it."

The chancellor wagged his finger. "I don't require the intervention of the Jalora Legion quite yet, My Lord De Vincente. No matter how much they pressure."

"The Jalora Legion has no interest in taking control of Valdeon, Benito! The Lords of Valdeon have sworn upon our very souls to protect the Altar of Providence. Every ranger in the legion is honor bound to help us in this duty!"

Benito came to stand behind his massive cherry wood desk, keeping it between his body and Wolf. Spreading his hands along the desk's surface, he leaned in to regard Wolf with narrowed eyes. Benito was playing the politician again, maneuvering circumstances to his own favor.

"I am certain they will help you, My Lord the Wolf. You are well admired by the Jalora Legion. Many call you the perfect ranger and the favorite son of Valdeon. Even the Dragon has showered his favor upon you."

Wolf regarded Benito with growing rage. Did he imagine his time as chancellor was a coincidence? Benito had no idea what he'd endured on his behalf. The old man should know better than to question. Wolf squeezed at his silver belt and took a deep breath. He had promised his wife, Dulcina, not to lose his temper with the old man.

"You attempt to flatter me?" Wolf folded his arms and returned Benito's gaze. "Ask your question directly, Benito. I have no patience for such beef-headed foolishness."

"I would know where your loyalties lay, Wolf!" The chancellor slammed his fist upon the desk. "Will your loyalties rest with the legion or Valdeon when trouble begins?"

The Jalora flared in angry outrage within his ring. It would not be questioned or tolerate such blasphemy. Its anger would be satisfied. Nothing, not the regret of breaking Wolf's promise to his wife or his fondness for Benito, could prevent the Jalora from using its host body to exact punishment. Their symbiotic relationship allowed Wolf to summon forth the full power waiting within. The Jalora's vast presence filled the room, pushing the Chancellor of Valdeon back against the fireplace.

"I am a servant of the Jalora and will follow its perfect wisdom as long as I draw breath! It guides my hand, not Dragon and not you." Wolf spat upon the ground. "Do you recall the circumstances of your appointment as chancellor? Many from both the

D'Antoiné and De Vincente families plotted for this office you now hold. It was the Jalora who commanded I place you in those robes, and I obeyed its will even though my family opposed me. Do you question me now?"

"Forgive me, My Lord De Vincente. I meant no disrespect. Valdeon and I are both grateful to you." The chancellor dropped to his belly on the ground, terror permeating from under the robes. "Our king approved of your choice after he…he punished his uncle, my predecessor."

"Edmund killed him in a rage after he learned your predecessor helped to spirit away his Tslavian bride and annulled their marriage. Let us speak clearly with each other."

Leo's taste in women was always exotic and dangerous. When his fancy had turned to the young princess of their bitterest enemy, Leo had rashly married the girl twenty years his junior. Her disappearance had caused a rift between the two thrones none could ever heal. War between Valdeon and Tslavia had narrowly been avoided. A stern intervention from the Jalora had stopped certain bloodshed. The hate, however, would eternally remain.

"Very well, you have my renewed oath of allegiance to this office and my word I will hear your guidance."

The Jalora, satisfied with Benito's penance, released Wolf's body and returned to the depths of the ring. Benito had been fortunate. Men were killed for lesser insults by its power. Benito struggled to his feet as the energy dissipated. Pride would not allow him to look into Wolf's face.

"If you will excuse me. The western prefects should be arriving soon."

"Very well, My Lord Chancellor, go and greet them as you will."

Purple robes rustled behind Benito as he hurried away. Beef-headed nonsense. Wolf had expected better from a man full grown. Though the Jalora had released its power, his body still held the remnants of anger. He swung a fist at the door with residual power behind his punch. Flesh tore through wood. The unlucky door slammed against its jamb with a harsh boom. He stalked past the splintered wood and into the lavish halls of the palace once more.

Depravity, selfishness, and greed. Their presence heralded evil. Wolf pulled his sword and swept its tip to rest upon the jugular of the woman who had been eavesdropping on his conversation with Benito. He spat in disgust when he saw her. Julian's younger sister, birthed by their mother and sired by hell only knew. Leo had banished his adulteress queen while the hell child was still within her womb. Rumors spoke of her dying in childbirth, but were never confirmed. Whether by neglect or nature, Zoya had grown from a child of unfortunate circumstance to an unbalanced creature of evil.

"Your very presence offends the Palace of Kings, Zoya No-Name. I have commanded your banishment from San Leonora. Why have you disobeyed me?" In his current mood of frustration and anger, Wolf couldn't keep the power of the Jalora from swirling behind his words.

Zoya's blazing dark eyes lifted to his face with a hatred spelling murder. She rested a fingertip upon the edge of his blade and pushed the sword away. A coquettish grin spread across full lips. Hers was a dangerous beauty, deadly to any man foolish enough to play the games she loved so well. Wolf, seeing her through the clarity of discernment, kept his attention upon her twisted face.

"Julian has said I may stay, My Lord the Wolf. He, and not you, will rule Valdeon as king." Zoya lifted her chin with prideful defiance. "I will sit beside him at the Altar of Providence, while you grovel at our feet."

"Blasphemy!" Wolf lifted the sword to her throat again. "The Jalora's curse upon you, Zoya Bastard Child. May it give you the painful death you so richly deserve."

"Curse me all you want, Wolf. You can't touch me. Rangers may not hurt women or children." She curtsied, lifting her black-laced petticoat up to mid-thigh. "Too bad you have to be so saintly. I would love to play with you."

Her tongue licked across his exposed blade and then she stepped away with a sigh. "You'll just have to spend your energy with the sow you married. Mayhaps the pup who follows you would like to play? I could show him the pleasures of manhood."

Wolf heard the shock and fury coming rapidly from behind him. His second-in-command swept toward Zoya. She shook her petticoat and let the green satin of her dress spill around it as if she were shooing away a mouse.

"Stop." Wolf thrust out an arm to block Berto. "This thing of evil is trying to goad you."

Zoya laughed as the young ranger struggled with his anger. It was true Wolf and the other rangers could not strike women and children. They were bound by the Jalora Code and could not break it without punishment. The Jalora would reject them, taking the ring from their hand and stripping them of power. But they weren't the only stewards of justice in Valdeon.

"Crawl back into your putrid basement, harlot!" A lightning hand smacked across Zoya's face, sending her spinning away. Eyes full of hatred glared at her punisher. She put the back of her hand to her bleeding lip and stared down at the blood. Her laughter, when it came, was harsh and manic. Zoya fled down the corridor at full speed.

"Well, Xavier the Wolf!" their defender boomed. "I thought I heard the roar of a hurricane, but alas, it is only you!"

A man of middle years with straight, dark hair and sparkling eyes laughed at Zoya's departing back. Wolf well recognized the mischievous grin upon Fausto De Quintaro's face. They had served in the legion together for many years and through many adventures. Now they both were a little grayer and a little more careful in their antics.

"Fausto!" Wolf burst into laughter and embraced his best friend. "When did you arrive?"

"I landed yesterday to bring lumber from Varianne." Fausto pushed away to grin at the broken door. "What a happy coincidence, yes?"

Wolf gave him a reluctant grin, though he knew Fausto could no longer see the expression upon his face. The Jalora's power hid all weakness and emotion, giving its rangers the advantage on and off the battlefield. They were the tools of justice, and justice must be immovable.

Other rangers, however, were able to see the facial expressions of their comrades. The little smirk on the Jaguar's lips didn't escape attention. Wolf shot him a look. The smirk disappeared quickly as his second-in-command stood at attention.

"Dulcina and the children are with me," Wolf told his friend as the three of them began walking down the corridor. "Will you come to dine with us this evening?"

"Of course! And we will be joined by another old friend. Cesar arrives this morning."

They came to the main corridor acting as the central artery for the Palace of Kings. Fausto cast a longing glance at a group of Valdeonian rangers marching past them. His hand smoothed along the side of his left leg, ruined in battle. The injury had ended his career as a ranger.

"I am glad to have you here with us, Fausto." Wolf gripped his best friend's shoulder. "I need your help."

"You will always have my friendship and support, Wolf."

Fausto gave them a quick nod. He was a good friend, brave and true. Wolf let a bit of his tension ease. He and his comrades weren't alone. Loyal subjects of the Jalora still remained in Valdeon. Time must be spent gauging who he could trust and who the bastard prince had lured to his treacherous side.

Jaguar followed a step behind him as they made their way down the corridor. Wolf regarded the young ranger's square face and weatherworn skin a moment. His second was from the rugged San Marimosa plains, home of the fabled Marimosa stallions. Jaguar had served in their cavalry before being called to the legion. Time in their numbers had taught him discipline, but certainly not patience for the social traditions of court. Wolf and Jaguar were kindred spirits in that respect.

"You would ask me a question, Jaguar."

"I was wondering about what the chancellor said to you, Sir."

"You wonder why I didn't punish him for going against my word."

"Sir, you are a Lord of Valdeon and third-in-command of the Sacred Guard! Not even the chancellor has the right to…"

"Each of us has a duty. Benito was chosen by the Jalora. I have sworn to protect him while he holds office. Would you have me betray my duty?"

"No, Wolf."

"By the look on Benito's face as he scampered past me, I'd say Wolf gave him something to think about." Fausto chuckled, winking at Jaguar.

"Our conversation has given me something to think about as well." Wolf lowered his voice as two members of court gave them curt nods. "I no longer know who to trust in this nest of vipers. Benito has summoned the western landowners. I know I can trust Cesar and your father, Berto, but the rest must be tested. We need to know how far Julian's treachery has run."

"You have a plan, Sir?"

Wolf nodded. It would take a great deal of patient watching, but he was confident they could chase the rats out of the palace. Once they exposed Julian and his treacherous comrades, the Lords of Valdeon could focus on finding the Lion Ring. Leo was a rash fool at times, but he would have had a plan to safeguard it. Wolf rubbed at his tired eyes. He needed sleep. Then perhaps his refreshed mind would remember any clues Leo may have left for them.

Chapter Nine

MASTERFUL FINGERS MOVED ALONG THE five hollowed reeds bound together by dyed horsehair. The musician's breath puffed out beneath high, sharp cheekbones as chapped lips blew upon the tops of the reeds. Jorge Pacarro played his flute with the passion of a man who knew sorrow as a constant companion. He understood loss. He was the last son of the plains. There were no more full-bloods — only he, the last of the Pacarro tribe.

Jorge leaned against the railing, letting the notes fade upon the wind. He tucked the rust-colored warrior braids behind his ear. Copper, intertwined among the strands, clicked softly as the airship raced through the clouds. The braids added to his exotic appearance. They were a tradition handed down from an ancient tribe once inhabiting the grasslands of eastern Valdeon. Jorge tried to keep some of his heritage alive. Out of necessity, however, he had adopted the Andarian culture in order to serve as squire to his ranger.

It had been many years since he had first set foot within the Palace of Kings to greet its young monarch. Now time and age had taken hold. His ranger had retired and stepped aside for his son. The once vibrant and daring young king had passed away from the world. Jorge let out a long sigh and played the funeral song of his people once more for Leo. He would not be allowed the chance once they reached San Leonora. Such simple homage would not seem worthy in the eyes of their eastern cousins.

His ranger, Lord Cesar Santiago, and their king, Edmund D'Antoiné, had served in the same battalion. They fought side-by-side in many a glorious battle. No more battles or adventure for any of them. Jorge was ashamed to admit it, but he loved wandering on his own land, cutting weeds and listening to the birds sing. He had seen too much blood spilled in his service to the Legion. His life in retirement was a peaceful one spent with his wife and children.

"Valdeon will not be the same without him, Jorge."

Cesar's bald head came to his shoulder. Bright, dark eyes and a round face touched with grief looked up at him from inches away. It was not easy to sneak up on a Pacarro. His lord may be growing older, but he still kept the stealth of a ranger. Jorge's hand dropped from the handle of his hatchet. Old habits from an old life. He reached for the pouch he carried in his coat. Carefully placing the flute inside, he tucked the instrument away.

"Are the others still bickering about trade agreements and sanctions against the east?"

Most of his fellow prefects couldn't think past their own lands. They had no idea what the ramifications of Leo's death would mean. Valdeon's future rested with the new heir to the Lion Ring. Who would be named as heir would certainly be the topic of many hours of heated discussion. Leo had produced two sons by blood and claimed a third, the bastard prince, as his own. Two legitimate sons had mysteriously died, leaving only the bastard behind. Jorge suspected Julian had a murderer's blade hidden behind his back.

"I truly think the fools would declare war this very day." Cesar gripped the railing and stared out at the vast sky before them. "Alberto and I have warned them to guard their tongues while we are in San Leonora. The men of the west cannot draw first blood. It would ignite the flames of civil war smoldering in the heart of the treacherous."

The prefects were bound by honor to follow their lords. Cesar Santiago ruled the northwest in his son's name. Lord Alberto Mendoza, steward of the famed San Marimosa fortress, also governed for his son, the Jaguar. Their lands were in the southwest. Another steward reigned along the western coast, but his was a treacherous nature. He was Julian's puppet in the west.

"What is to become of Valdeon?" Jorge shook his head. "I see very little hope if Julian is allowed upon the throne."

"Nonsense, the Jalora would never put a wicked creature such as that upon its sacred throne." Cesar nodded as if to assure himself as much as Jorge. "Our friend the Wolf is a clever man. He will know how to lead us."

Jorge returned his smile. Wolf was a wise man and a powerful ranger. He'd seen Leo's strange behavior and warned them of the danger it meant to Valdeon long before their king had disappeared. Keeping their country stable for two years, he'd remained loyal to the throne. Many wanted to see Xavier De Vincente rise to power. He had supporters from every corner of Andara. No matter how ardently they argued with him to take on the role as Regent, he refused. He could think of no greater man of honor than the Wolf.

"Will you help me, Jorge?"

"My lord?" Jorge tore his thoughts away from Wolf and the throne. "I would do anything for you, of course."

"You were always a faithful friend. I want you to help me keep the peace and our brethren out of trouble. I fear Julian will use any little infraction to start a civil war."

"You have my word, Cesar. I will do what I can."

The great ship's crystal engines rumbled as its thrusters went into reverse. They were beginning their descent. San Leonora stretched out beneath the airship like a tapestry. It was the largest city in all of Valdeon and indeed rivaled Lea as the greatest city on the continent. The home of the Lion was the undisputed center of Andarian culture and learning.

"They have hung the mourning banners for Edmund."

Cesar shook his head sadly at the city beneath them. His ranger eyes could see what was simply a blur to Jorge. Then details in the streets became visible as the airship began to land. Flags of black lined every street in San Leonora. Their fabric sailed upon the soft breeze.

"Let us join the others, Jorge. Idle children are prone to mischief."

Jorge followed silently as they moved across the deck toward the group of men assembling near the gangplank. Angry mutters and grumblings were suddenly silenced as Lord Santiago approached. Their tempers wouldn't be tamed for long. Sweet Erthe Mother. How was he to keep them under control when Cesar could not?

Running across the stretch of land between Lake Leonora and the Leonora River, the Great Inland Wall rose up to meet them as they moved through the airship port. Thousands of stone lion heads lined its top, ever watchful against invaders. Jorge cast a discreet look among the stone animals. Human eyes were hidden behind the teeth. He had accompanied his ranger many times on patrol along its rim. No better view could be found in Valdeon.

The eyes upon him as he walked didn't belong to the soldiers on the wall. He was well known among their numbers. Instead the rude looks and murmurs drifted over the row from stands in the market. Savage. Barbarian. He had heard such slights many times. Deeds and heart didn't matter to San Leonorans if a man's blood was not pure Valdeonian.

Jorge stayed close to his lord more out of habit then concern as they moved down the docks to the waiting carriages. Soon they had passed through the gates of the Inland Wall and were moving up Kings Row toward the Palace of Kings. His attention was drawn out the carriage window by the grandeur of San Leonora. Each time he visited the city it held something new to capture his imagination.

Sparkling in the sunlight just above the other rooftops stretched the golden tiles of the famed Art Museum of San Leonora. Next to it stood the library. It was said within the fabled structures was contained the greatest collection of work to be penned or drawn in Andarian history. How he longed to walk those rooms, running his fingers along the bindings of leather. He ached to throw himself into the words of the greatest minds their continent had ever known.

Their carriage entered a roundabout. Mounted on his San Marimosa stallion several stories above the row, Mikel D'Antoiné greeted them as they entered the palace grounds. Mikel had been the first Lion and Jalora Master. His was a great legacy of honor and courage. Edmund had shared his ancestor's bravery, but his offspring sadly lacked the Lion's strength.

Chancellor Benito was waiting for them on the palace stairs. He stood in the purple robes of office, clutching at a pointed ceremonial hat with one hand. The horrendous contraption tilted precariously atop his head as he tried vainly to prevent it from taking flight in the breeze. The scene was reminiscent of a child's spinning top toy. Jorge didn't care for the chancellor. Their first and only meeting had been a cold one. The prefects traveled to San Leonora to attend his taking of office after Leo had…well, ended the last chancellor's rule. Jorge had sworn to follow the man's leadership, because he'd been Wolf's choice. He'd made his concessions very clear to Benito at the time.

Cesar Santiago exited the carriage first in accordance with his station. The former Lord of Valdeon led his prefects to the base of the stairs. Giving Benito a nod of acknowledgement, Cesar remained upright. He had only bowed to one man in his entire life. Edmund the Leo had earned his respect rather than demanding courtesies due to his title.

"Greetings, my lord chancellor. We have answered the call to…"

"So I see, my Lord Santiago."

Benito's crisp tone severed Cesar's formal greeting. Jorge noticed the man's eyes resting upon his braids. Many in the west were used to seeing other tribal people like the Duhnish. These eastern folk knew only their marbled corridors and their silken clothes. Courtesy for visitors had been lost in San Leonora, it would seem.

"We have no time for refreshments or rest, gentlemen. I have grave news which must be delivered first. This way."

Benito set a quick pace up the long staircase and into the Grand Atrium. Jorge followed with the rest, expecting to feel the deep sense of awe he'd become accustomed to when nearing the Altar of Providence. Today, the sensation was missing. It had been replaced with the heavy weight of tension and fear.

Cesar's advancing age didn't stop him from catching up to the chancellor and blocking his path. "Something has happened, hasn't it? Something worse than Leo's death."

"What could possibly be worse than the death of the king?" Alberto Mendoza grunted. The graying mustache formed a bushy arch over his frown.

Benito pointed across the atrium toward the golden doors of the throne room. They were closed. The Altar of Providence was a beacon of hope and justice for the people of Andara. Its doors were always open for those seeking counsel or on pilgrimage. Jorge had never seen it locked away from the people it protected.

"Come, the others are waiting."

Benito led them into the Great Hall. It was an opulent room with long tables carved in dark wood harvested from the forests of Varianne. Red velvet upholstery covered each chair and sofa around the room. Massive chandeliers of gold hung over the guests as they dined at state dinners or held diplomatic meetings. It was also the room in which a country mourned departed monarchs. Black ribbons waited in crates. Soon they would lay Leo's empty coffin in the family chapel. Jorge's grief surged unexpectedly when he saw the ribbons. He turned away quickly, following Cesar to their table.

Several men had already arrived. Dressed in their rich finery, they sat sipping wine and speaking in quiet tones. A few cast suspicious glares toward Jorge and the other prefects. Their eastern cousins had been busy building up resentment for this day. Leo's funeral would not be uneventful.

"Rise." A voice echoed against the walls of the Great Hall. "The Sacred Guard approaches."

Jorge stood with the rest of the crowd as the doors swung open. Rangers dressed in their finest ash gray uniforms marched in the throne room, boots striking the ground in perfect unison. A man set the pace at their head. His dark hair, flecked with silver, had been cut short. Sharp lines etched along his chin and nose drew the eye upward into steel orbs. His predator gaze swept the room slowly. The crowd cowered like prey as the ranger's eyes moved over them. Xavier De Vincente's ranger friends called him 'Wolf.' Jorge could not imagine a better name.

The younger rangers circled about him like pups. Wolf tilted his head to the side, listening with patience as they yelped at once. A single bark from their pack leader sent the pups circling the crowd. Jorge kept his attention locked upon their alpha. The pack would pounce upon their prey only by the Wolf's word. Their leader turned and moved to the ornate ceremonial bell hanging at the head of the hall. Two poles made from the masterfully sculpted wood supported the golden bell. Wolf pulled on the velvet ribbon attached to its clapper. Its song silenced the room. He rang the bell nine times in honor of the nine Lords of Valdeon. Then Wolf let his hand fall from the ribbon and turned his head to the back of the room. He gave a small nod and lifted his chin with pride.

"Heaven blesses Valdeon for the Sacred Guard has come!"

Chancellor Benito raised his hands and the crowd rose from their chairs as six men marched ceremoniously into the room. Wolf moved to their head. Most of the men were dressed in gray uniforms belonging to the Jalora Legion army divisions. Two of the men, Rafael the Fox and Yuli the Otter, wore slightly different uniforms reflecting their Naval Division. Great power radiated about them. The hair on Jorge's forearms stood on end as it moved over his body in a wave. The Lords of Valdeon had come to San Leonora.

"Look at my Lucio. He makes a fine man and a noble ranger, does he not?"

Jorge moved his gaze to the young man standing at attention in the very center of the line. He remembered the proud day Lucio Santiago stood before his people in the courtyard of San Lucida. It was a bittersweet moment when Cesar had put the Ferret Ring upon his son's finger.

"Yes, Cesar, he certainly does."

Chancellor Benito bowed low to the Sacred Guard as they took their seats. The other rangers of Valdeon moved to their positions against each wall. Jorge hid his smile as several of their eastern cousins shifted nervously in their seats. The rangers weren't there for ceremonial pomp. Any skullduggery was bound to be squashed by Wolf's pack.

"I have dire news which must be carefully weighed." The chancellor raised his voice to carry throughout the room. "As you know, the Orb sits lifeless beside the Altar. Edmund D'Antoiné's body has not been found. Lord De Vincente has reported this to the Jalora Council."

Cesar Santiago rose to his feet. He held up a long, flat piece of wood, which had been provided on the table for each of them. Chancellor Benito returned his request for the floor with a nod.

"Do they fear the Lion Ring lost, My Lord De Vincente?"

"The Dragon himself searches for the ring, Lord Santiago. The Jalora has blocked his searching. We do not know what this means."

The men sat in stunned silence. If the Lion Ring was lost, Andara and Valdeon were in the gravest of danger. Jorge regarded the silent Wolf more closely. He had never known a ranger to be this forthcoming on such a dangerous subject. Their practice was to tell only what they must and to seek advice from the Jalora rather than mere men.

"Prefect Diego, you have the floor."

Benito gestured to the long table. A prettily dressed prefect stood across from Jorge. He paused to tug the tight waistcoat over his belly. Clearly the man had spent most of his days attending meetings and banquets rather than engaging in physical activity.

"I think it's very clear, My Lord De Vincente. Leo disappeared without a second thought for his duties. The Jalora is angry. It's punishing us for his indiscretions."

"Be careful with your words, Diego!" Alberto Mendoza slammed a fist upon the table. "Edmund was a Jalora bishop after all. It's not for you to question his actions."

"You have not been given permission to speak, Lord Mendoza!" Benito banged his hands together for quiet.

Prefect Diego puffed up his red cheeks, ignoring the chancellor's attempt to calm the room. "I am simply stating the obvious. Do you pretend these same thoughts have not occurred to you, Alberto? No, of course they haven't. San Marimosa was ever Leo's favorite. Our king considered it above his own prefects."

"He knew no dagger would be poised to strike at his back in San Marimosa!"

The words came from one of the western prefects. Jorge couldn't see who had spoken with such heat, but the effects were immediate. East and West leapt to their feet, throwing insults across the room. Jorge remained seated, watching the silent Lords of Valdeon. What were they waiting for? If the screaming didn't stop soon, bloodshed would certainly follow.

Wolf's intense gaze rested upon him. Was the ranger gauging their allegiance, probing for their loyalties? It would be a logical course of action to expose potential traitors, but the action was contrary to their goal. Bickering and harsh words would not help them find the Lion Ring or keep the peace.

Jorge stood, waiting patiently to be noticed by the harassed chancellor. He stared with great intensity until the man was forced to return his gaze. A single growl from Wolf silenced the room. Everyone was still as they waited for Chancellor Benito to recognize the strange man from the West.

"My Lord Pacarro, you have something to say?" Chancellor Benito's strained politeness was proof they shared a mutual dislike.

"I do. Many of you know me as squire to my Lord Cesar Santiago, a former member of the Sacred Guard. I was just a youth when I first met our king upon the steps of the palace. He greeted me with courtesy. We spoke for many hours of his plans for the future of Valdeon. In every word, every syllable, Edmund's love for his country shined. He gave his youth and his heart defending the Altar of Providence. Years passed, yet his love for Valdeon never faded. Do you imagine what he did over the past few years was done lightly?" Jorge let his words fall upon their hearts as the silence in the room grew. "Would you dishonor his memory by raising past slights when our king's body has not been found? Let us not decide Valdeon's fate this day, but wait upon the will of the Jalora to make itself known."

A pair of hands began to clap from the far end of the Great Hall. It was Felix Cristiano, steward of San Angelica. The massive port city on the western coast was home to Rafael, bearer of the Fox Ring. Its steward was expected to rule in support of his ranger son, but the two of them despised each other. While Rafael served in the Sacred Guard, his father had taken control of the city and allied himself with Julian.

"Bravo. I'm sure your impassioned speech turned every heart toward peace. You would make a great statesman, Duke Pacarro." Felix walked past the Lords of Valdeon and turned his back to his son. Rafael the Fox sat rigid, watching his sire take center stage.

"Many tales of Jorge Pacarro's courage circulate about the barracks of Valdeon's army. His loyalty to the throne and his ranger are well known. He was even given a plot of land and a dukedom by the king for his services. No one would question his motives for standing before you now. I would go so far as to say he believes what he has just told you." Felix stopped to clasp his hands behind his back. "But does this same loyalty blind Duke Pacarro to the truth? The Lion Ring is lost. Think, my friends. Why was it lost? Why would the Jalora allow such a catastrophic thing to happen?"

The room erupted in panicked murmurs. It was a question Jorge had asked deep in his heart, but hadn't dared voice aloud. A self-satisfied smirk stretched across Felix's lips. It was as if he knew Jorge's thoughts. No matter. Julian's puppet was deliberately trying to incite panic. He had to be blocked by the one weapon that could take him out of this verbal battle for peace.

"You are no one to judge the Jalora's motives, usurper. I will leave such questions to be answered by the Sacred Guard. If you weren't so driven by greed and ambition, you would trust the word of the rightful lord of San Angelica." Jorge's fingers ached to grasp the handle of his hatchet. One throw and the serpent's tongue would be silenced forever.

Face glowering with rage, Felix took a threatening step toward Jorge. "Perhaps the services of the Sacred Guard are no longer needed, Squire?"

The tip of a blade pressed against Felix's throat. It twisted until the tiniest of scratches drew blood. Rafael the Fox stood before his father with the expressionless face of justice. His eyes, however, glowed with fury.

"Your tongue has wagged enough for one day. Leave me before I have reason to silence you permanently." Rafael stared after his father until Felix had disappeared down the corridor. The room waited in silence until Fox had joined the other rangers once more. Wolf gripped Rafael's shoulder as he passed, then he gave Jorge a slight nod. Jorge bowed to the Lords of Valdeon and sat back down next to Cesar.

"I must get you home quickly, Jorge. The rangers might make you the Chancellor of Valdeon after today."

Jorge smiled. "You would never catch me in his silly contraption he calls a hat, my lord."

He turned his attention to the eastern prefects. They looked frightened, as well they should be. Julian's only hold in the west had been completely discredited. After Felix's inflammatory statement about the Sacred Guard, no one would dare associate with him. One plot had been extinguished, but how many more were smoldering in the halls of the palace? The next few days would be interesting.

Chapter Ten

SETH HELD A GREAT SWORD before him. The tip of its blade was fixed upon his opponent's murderous heart. Hungry fire devoured the grassland about them. Neither noticed its deadly flames slithering closer like fiery serpents. Every thought, every ounce of energy was focused on the life or death struggle with the mortal enemy before them. Heart pounding, the strange new power surged against his will. Then in a moment of uncontrolled rage, Seth threw back his head in a roar. Power shook the ground between them. He began to fall.

He lifted off the pillow, gulping in breaths. The pungent aroma of herbs and sweat hung heavy in the air. Seth's nose couldn't ignore the stench any longer. Getting out of bed, he hurried to the window and opened it. The cold air of early morning felt good against his face. Rubbing his eyes, he looked out across the empty fields. How had he gotten to Paddy's Inn?

Adjusting the small lantern on the table, he raised the lights in the bedchamber. A simple chest of drawers stood against the wall. He lifted the plain white pitcher from its top and poured cool water into the basin. The sensation was heaven upon his face. Seth closed his eyes, forcing the fog of illness from his mind. Memories, full of horrific images, came at him in a rush. His memory of that night grew stronger now as anger pushed aside the grief. Some moments were missing, but one detail burned in his thoughts. Pavel Sandor, his mother's murderer, was still on Marianna.

Clean clothes and a pair of boots waited for him in a chair next to the chest of drawers. Steadying his weakened body against the wall, he pulled on the trousers. The effort it took to finish this simple task helped him to understand how close to death he'd actually come.

Sunlight hadn't quite reached the hall as he made his way to the common room. The inn was quiet this morning, as if he were the only guest. A chair squeaked in the corner. Fergus McCloud sat at one of the tables. His stern features concentrated on the books and parchments spread out before him. Body remaining still and upright, he used his left hand to ease the walking stick a bit closer.

"Emma and I may leave this shabby prison today. Doctor McFadden insists you stay here until your strength returns." The headmaster's hard eyes remained upon the parchment in his hands. "I expect you to recover soon, boy. You've been enough of a bother. I will not have a malingerer living in my house."

"What makes you think I'd stay under your roof for a moment longer than I must? My reasons for remaining friendly with you are gone."

"So, the truth is out at last." Fergus lifted his gaze and gave him a humorless grin. "What will the town think of your sainted mother when her secret comes to light? Who will be the saint then, eh boy? Their dearly departed Anne McCloud or the man who raised her bastard son?" He struggled to his feet and began gathering his belongings. "Your mother may have catered to your every whim, but I will not. You will do as I say, boy, or you will be out on the street. And another thing. I don't want you near those Logans again."

"I'll be out of your home as quickly as I can manage, Headmaster. We need not see each other again except in passing."

Fergus' crippled figure lumbered out of the door. He spared Seth one last nasty look. It held the same wild anger he'd seen the night the headmaster had fought with Seth's mother. She'd warned Seth they were alone and without means the night she died. He understood now what she meant.

Paddy pushed the kitchen doors open with his back. Dishes rattled as he carried in a breakfast tray. Riley came in behind him, a half-eaten sausage link in his fingers. The other hand held firmly to the pot of fresh tea. He grinned a welcome, but his good humor disappeared when the headmaster's door slammed shut. Riley hurried around the bar to stand beside Seth.

"What did old Fussbottom have to say?"

"He was simply being his usual charming self."

"I'll bet." Paddy slammed the tray down a little too hard. Sausages rolled off the plates to hide amongst the utensils.

"Dismiss me out of my own rooms and complain about my food, will he? Good riddance to the foul creature. Teb! More breakfast! Seth's awake and hungry. Have a seat, boys."

They took their plates and plucked up the stray sausages. Seth sniffed at the meat in his fingers. It smelled of pork and thyme. His stomach growled in demanding gurgles until he took a bite. Even grief couldn't sway his need for food.

"Okay, Seth?" Riley sat down beside him when Paddy had gone back to the kitchens.

He nodded. "How long have I been here?"

"Nearly a week."

He'd been in a sick bed for almost a week while a killer was free to roam about the island? Too much time had passed. The trail for Sandor had grown cold, but there was still a chance. The villain's fear of the ranger had been evident even in Seth's stupor. He'd been warned to watch over Seth. Sandor was still close.

Other memories suddenly pushed their way into his thoughts. A white face and blue lips. Cold, dead hands. Seth pushed away the image quickly.

"They've buried my mother then."

Grief had come into his life without warning. Its heavy presence invaded the room, muting his quiet words. Forks clinked on plates as they ate in silence. Riley slumped in the seat next to him. Rubbing nervously at the back of his neck, he was struggling to find the right words.

"I'm sorry, Seth." Riley put a tiny vile onto the counter beside his plate. "You dropped this while you were, um, not yourself."

He plucked it up and held the tiny bit of glass closer. Remnants of a rather foul liquid coated the bottom. This vile he remembered well. The taste of death would haunt his nightmares for a good long while.

Their host pushed back into the common room carrying more eggs, potatoes, and sausage. He nodded with pleasure as he looked upon Seth's empty plate. The dish didn't stay empty for long. Paddy piled on more potatoes and meat.

"I'm sorry for quarantining your pub. Did it cost you business for an entire week?"

Paddy gave him a wave. "No worries, Seth. I made out the better for it. Someone gave me a full week's lodging for the entire inn. A stranger came just before the constable and Riley here brought you in the wagon.

He paid me a little extra to keep silent, but I reckon I can talk about him to you."

"A stranger? Was he tall? Taller than me, I mean? And did he wear a great cloak?"

"You met him then?"

"Yes. We've met."

This ranger was taking a great deal of interest in him. Seth sorted through his remaining memories from the night of violence. He'd worn a badge on his chest with "Jalora Legion" spelled out in gold letters. Sandor had feared him, but Emma treated the ranger with deep respect.

"Did this ranger give you any idea why he's taken such an interest in me?"

Paddy closed his lips tightly and pushed away from the bar. Sweat had formed along his brow and bubbled up on his bulbous nose. Shaking hands began to fuss with the dirty dishes as he stacked them on the tray.

"Raiders didn't kill my mother. Someone else murdered her and tried to kill me too. The ranger came into my room and saved me from someone with a heavy Tslavic accent called Sandor."

Paddy's face turned white and he gripped Seth's arm in warning. "Pavel Sandor? Are you absolutely sure? No. It's not possible. That murderous snake can't be here on Marianna. Seth, promise me you'll not speak to anyone about what happened or mention his name again. Danger will follow if you do. You too, Riley."

Riley shrugged. "I don't know enough to tell anything."

"That's enough excitement for you today. I should have kept my mouth shut as it is."

"Wait. What about the ranger, Paddy? What is the Jalora Legion? Please tell me. I've so many questions."

The older man frowned and wiped at his sweaty head again. Eyes normally willing to hold Seth's gaze waivered and looked down at his hands. He shook his head slowly.

"Please, Paddy. You don't know what it's like to find out nothing you thought you knew about yourself is the truth."

"I suppose not. Very well, you have to right to know about the ranger at least. Before I settled here, I lived in Lea where their legion headquarters is." His quick glance to the door was full of fear. "I've seen them in action. When a ranger pulls his sword, nobody stands a chance against him. Fastest thing on two legs, they are. Let's hope he doesn't return to Haven Bay anytime soon."

"He seemed willing enough to help me, though he definitely wants something in return."

"They aren't sweet and cuddly, boy. A friend of mine got himself into trouble with the law once. He made the mistake of trying to fight his way to freedom. One of those rangers split him right in two. There. That's enough of that."

Paddy picked up the tray and pressed his back against the double doors. "Keep what I've told you to yourselves. Trust me. You don't want to interfere in ranger business."

"Why don't we just ask Emma about the ranger?" Riley asked when Paddy had left the room. "I saw them together. Emma seemed very friendly with him."

"The ranger has left Marianna. He's not our primary concern right now. I have to find my mother's killer. He's going to pay for what he's done."

Somewhere Pavel Sandor was watching and waiting. Their battle of wits was about to begin.

The days passed much too quickly as Seth recovered. Dread at returning to the McCloud home was regrettably replaced with acceptance. His first morning back in the somber dwelling found him standing before the mirror to regard the unthinkable. The Grey Cliff Isles had many different waistcoats men wore to mark them in their trade. Marianna had four types alone. He'd been cursed with the dullest among them. Fingering the unadorned black waistcoat of a scholar, he frowned at the image. Even the buttons were dull.

"This is no longer my fate," he whispered to the sickly looking young man in the mirror.

The future with its unknown paths was no longer a worry. His will was intent upon one thing, finding his mother's killer. The father who had abandoned his child, his mother's true identity, and the mysterious ranger would have to wait. He'd seek out their mysteries after his next meeting with Sandor. Provided he survived the exchange, of course.

A loud bang beneath him announced the start of the day. Good. The headmaster had left for school. Now was the time to search for clues from his mother's secret life. Steadying his nerve, he crept to her bedchamber door. He reached up on the door frame where she'd kept her key. His fingers came away empty.

"Your uncle has the key." Emma came to stand at his back. "He refuses to let me pack up her things. I think he's taking her death harder than he'll admit."

Her sympathies for the man rankled. He let the cold facade he used with the headmaster stretch across his face. Emma, too consumed with her own grief, didn't seem to notice his bubbling anger. She patted her eyes with a worn handkerchief. Dressed in bonnet and cloak, she appeared ready for a long walk on a cold morning. Sprigs of dried heather peeked out of the basket she wore on her arm.

"Where are you going this early, Emma?"

"I've a bouquet for your dear mother's grave." She pulled out the heather. It was tied with white ribbon as was islander custom for a mother who had lost her daughter.

"Will you come with me today?"

The raw wound his mother's death had carved out in his heart opened again as he looked upon the white ribbon. Its purity, simple and honest, seemed unfitting for his mother or the woman gifting it to her. Lies upon lies. He no longer trusted his memories of home and family.

"I'll be late for class."

Seth slammed the front door and hurried into the square. White row houses with their tiny yards towered over him. His chest tightened. He was suffocating here. Many of the women stepped out on their porches to eye him as he ran by. They flew to each other in a frenzy of whispers and shaking heads. Seth ignored them, setting his attention on the towering school down the row.

Several of the students, friends he'd known his entire life, turned away and began their whispering. He wasn't in the mood to endure their curious looks or the sympathetic postulations from his professors. Passing by the gate at a fast clip, he headed for the fields to the north.

The Marianna countryside was a friendlier place in the daylight. Wet grass clung unnoticed to his boots as he hiked through the fields. His mind considered the possibilities as he walked. Sandor had to be someone familiar with Marianna. The villain had chosen the ideal location to ambush his victim, catching him upon a lonely road with no moon for a guide. Sandor had also mentioned he'd been watching Seth and his mother for years. The killer had to be someone who came to the island regularly. A sailor from a merchant ship or one of the Grey Cliff Island Revenue Men who came to Haven Bay twice a year, perhaps? Seth made it a point to speak with visitors. He'd met only a handful of Tslavians. None of them had been overly friendly.

Mind whirring with possibilities, Seth's feet took him to the charred field where the ambush had taken place. The fire had seemed more destructive during his fight with the raiders. Retracing his footing as best he could, Seth came across the cut ropes once binding Alice. He took a few paces forward to the spot he'd last seen the Amity raider. Kneeling down for a better look, he searched the area. Scorched earth and trampled grass were all that remained.

Then a sudden flash of sunlight on metal caught his eye. A golden coin was pressed into the ground within someone's muddy boot imprint. Seth plucked it from the dirt and wiped off the image minted into the gold. Great wings blanketed a creature with giant teeth and a misshapen snout. It appeared to be some sort of a monster. He rubbed the palm-sized coin against his coat, but the image was still encased in dirt. This coin wasn't from the Grey Cliff Isles. The Amity raider must have dropped it as they fought.

"Aren't you supposed to be in school, young master McCloud?"

Constable McTavish stood at the edge of the burned section of grass watching him. His uniform was pressed and neat. Boots shined under the morning sun. The constable's clean appearance didn't hide the red of his eyes or the pale face telling of many a sleepless night. Seth tucked the coin in his pocket. Standing, he brushed off his trousers and joined him.

"There are better ways to spend my time, sir."

"Like looking for your mother's killer?" The constable shook his head. "I know how you feel, Seth. You want to know the who and the why. I understand. I felt the same after my wife was killed. Her death is why I joined the constabulary."

The worn and solemn face looked out over the fields toward Haven Bay. He wiped at his tired eyes and gave Seth a patient smile. "These are hard men. It's dangerous for you to go hunting about on your own. They may find you. Next time luck won't be on your side. Do you understand?"

Seth nodded. He understood and knew the constable was likely right. It was foolhardy to investigate Sandor on his own, but even the risk of danger couldn't deter him. Nothing would stop him from finding his mother's killer.

"I'd better get to class, Constable."

Classes were in session when he entered the school. The double wooden doors of the library stood like guardians at the end of the empty hall. Seth had spent so much time reading the books within, the staff had given him a key. He hurried through the doors and locked them again. A cup with the shallow remains of the librarian's tea rested upon the desk. He dipped the coin inside and swirled it about until the dirt washed away.

Seth lit the fireplace and began wandering the shelves. He gathered all the books he could find on Tslavia. There weren't many. Islanders didn't bother with the other nations in Andara unless it directly impacted their industry. Most of the books were at least twenty years old and focused on economics or agriculture. He'd found a few pages about Tslavia's eternal war with its greatest enemy, Valdeon. Writings about the bloody wars didn't tell much about the people, rather they focused on loss of riches.

He pushed the books away and sunk down on the tabletop. Nothing. He'd found a clue, but had no way to interpret its meaning. A loud smack shook him from his morose thoughts. One of the books had fallen from the table. He picked it up and fingered absently through the pages. Then he saw it. The book's author had included an image of a monster matching the one on the coin.

Under the illustration was the notation, "The Gargoyle, symbol of the Von Wolkhurst Family."

He found their family name under the index. Fingers swiftly turning the pages, he came to the spot. Several pages were missing. Seth ran a fingertip along the rough stumps of paper. Someone had hastily ripped them out. Grabbing the next book and the next, he searched intently for signs of the Gargoyle and its family. Any reference to the Von Wolkhursts or the beast's image had been ripped from every one of the books in the school's library. He gripped the golden piece tightly in his hand. Who were these Von Wolkhursts and how did an Amity raider obtain one of their coins? One person could shed light upon its purpose, but Pavel Sandor was as much a mystery as the Von Wolkhursts.

Chapter Eleven

Seth joined the rest of the students returning home along the Main Row. Many a cheery greeting from passersby came their way. The citizens of Haven Bay were anxious to enjoy their week's end. Town had resumed its normal, ordinary routine despite the killing a week prior. Annoyed by their short memory, he left the Main Row to cross the small plot of land separating it from Farm Row.

Stopping to lean on the stone wall along the road-side, he brought the golden coin into his hand. His finger traced along the gargoyle's body. The hideous face snarled up at him in mockery. Humiliation and fury returned as his memory added more detail to the night Sandor had so easily defeated him. He shook his head with gritted teeth. If Seth were to stand a chance against the villain, then he'd have to learn how to fight with sword and fist.

"Ho, Seth!"

The Logan boys, sporting their finest togs, walked in a line upon the Farm Row from eldest to youngest. They were ready for a free night off the farm. Though the Haven Bay Pub was bound to be a little wild tonight, few were willing to start trouble with the Logan boys. They worked together, drank together, and fought together. Seth was glad he was a friend of the family.

Riley brought up the rear of their company. Hands stuffed in the pockets of his trousers, he stared at the back of the brother directly before him. He was mark-edly shorter than his siblings. Seth and everyone who'd ever met Riley were careful to avoid the topic. His brothers weren't as concerned about stirring his temper. They never let Riley forget he was the baby of the family.

Seth returned their greeting with a wave. A welcome face was with them. Tom, their eldest, had returned home from his service in the UR Army a few days before. He looked so different from the last time Seth had laid eyes upon him. Tom's straight auburn hair was cut short against his head in the military fashion. A well-trimmed mustache hung beneath his nose. Perhaps it was the way Tom carried himself or the worldly look in his eyes, which marked the biggest change.

"You've been busy while I've been away, Seth. I heard you took on raiders." Tom took his hand and shook it warmly.

"Seth rescued the McKenzie girl too." Patrick winked at Seth with a little grin while the others smacked their lips and laughed.

They quieted down when Tom gave them a sour look. A sad smile, genuine and regretful, dimmed the happiness in his green eyes. The eldest of the Logan boys had seen his own tragedy while he was away from them. Seth wondered if any of them would get a glimpse into Tom Logan's secret pain.

"I was sorry to hear about your mother. She was a kind woman."

He nodded and stuffed the gold coin into his trouser pocket. Somehow it had become a talisman, focusing his anger and will. It was his new constant reminder to never trust blindly again.

"Thank you, Tom. It's good to have you home."

"There's a tail on the dog." George motioned behind them with a mischievous wink at Riley.

Seth glanced over his shoulder. Beatrice McFadden, the doctor's daughter, was clearly following them. Strawberry hair bounced upon her shoulders. Her ruffled green dress rustled fiercely against her legs as she sprinted to keep their pace.

"What's she doing?"

"The pest has been following me for a month now. She pops up every time I come to town." Riley rounded on the girl. "Go home, Beatrice!"

She gave Riley a haughty look, much older than her fifteen years. "What do you think I'm doing? My house is this way. I should think you'd remember since you like peeking through our windows after sunset."

Riley muttered curses under his breath and turned his back to the girl. Red rushed from under his collar to invade the curly head of hair. His brothers burst into poorly contained snickers. Aching to join them in the first laugh he'd had in several weeks, Seth kept a tight hold upon his amusement.

Tom smiled gently at Beatrice. "You've missed the footpath. It's just there."

He pointed to a small, worn path winding across the field toward town. Beatrice gave Tom a quick smile and burst down the path with her strawberry braids trailing behind. Seth regarded Tom as he waited for her to run toward home. Time away from Marianna had changed him. This wasn't the Tom Logan who used to chase him and Riley around the farm with a rake.

Tom cuffed Riley gently on the head. "Somebody has a crush on you, little Whiskers."

"It's his charm!" Patrick's eyes watered as the pent-up laughter exploded onto the row.

Riley stomped toward Haven Bay. Colorful language spouted from his grumbling mouth. Seth hurried to catch his fast-moving friend. The stream of constant expressions about Beatrice and his brothers continued to bubble from Riley's lips in a rush. Seth hid his smile when he noticed Riley sneak a quick look at Beatrice hurrying toward town.

"They love to tease you because you get so angry."

Seth tugged at the hem of his waistcoat to straighten the garment. He winced a little as the fabric of his shirt caught upon his cut. It was healing without comment from anyone. Perhaps it would leave at least a small scar.

"Does it still hurt? Let me see."

Seth puffed up and stood a little straighter. Fumbling with the buttons of his waistcoat, he was anxious for the chance to finally show someone his battle wounds. He was pleased when the dark red line on his chest brought a gasp from Riley.

"Great gulls! How did you fight him off?"

"The raider gave me this cut. He would've slit my throat, but I was able to get his knife away from him."

New memories came back to him. He'd forgotten the euphoria surging through his body during the fighting. His mind began to conjure up more details from the battle, like golden rings set within black tattoos. The smell of burning grass and the feel of the man's sweaty hands on his throat. Then a name came to him.

"He called me D'Antoiné."

Funny. He'd forgotten the raider's look of terror and his strange words. More memories tried to come into focus. Words they'd exchanged. Details of the battle. Seth put a hand to his head. They weren't quite ready to come to light yet. One new memory, however, stayed with him. The raider had promised to remember Seth's face.

"Hated you, did he? What do you think D'Antoiné means? Some Amity Island curse, I'll wager."

"It's a name."

Sandor had called him a D'Antoiné too. He'd said Seth's house would die with him. The intensity of the man's hatred betrayed him. The mark on Seth's head wasn't just about his payment. It was personal for Sandor.

"What are you two girls giggling about?" Patrick marched over and pushed Riley out of the way. "Come look at this cut, gents!"

They gathered around Seth, whistling at the scars. A few of them touched the sensitive skin. Seth winced a little, but didn't draw away. It was a rare occasion when he could impress the Logan boys.

"I've seen worse scraps during boot camp." Tom shook his head at the pink line upon Seth's skin. Then he rolled up his sleeve and showed them a dark, ragged scar. It began at his wrist, twisting in an awkward arch to his elbow. The ghastly mark made the wound on Seth's chest look like a paper cut. Tom Logan had seen real combat in the army and it had changed him.

"Have you ever heard of D'Antoiné, Tom?"

"D'Antoiné?" Tom gave him a frown. "Course I have. The question is how did you come to hear of them?"

"One of the raiders said it."

Tom shrugged and began walking toward Haven Bay once again. Even talk of a mystery wouldn't curb his appetite for a pint. His brothers followed behind him, a new respect for the eldest in their eyes. Tom shook his head with a grin as they impatiently waited for his answer.

"D'Antoiné is the surname of two brothers — Edmund and Esteban — from Valdeon who became rangers together. They were both high up in the ranks of their legion until one of them disappeared." Tom kicked at a stone with the toe of his boot. "Never found him. It's quite the mystery."

Edmund. Was it possible this ranger from Valdeon was his father? Sandor had claimed Seth's mother had married outside her race. Could she have been part of the Tslavian family whose symbol was embedded upon the gold coin? If Sandor was telling the truth, then Seth was a child of two hated enemies.

Riley whistled low. "Did you know him, Tom?"

"Regular army like me doesn't mix with rangers, Little Whiskers. If you'd ever been up close to one, you'd know why. Now, come on. I'm likely to die of thirst!"

"Why would a raider from Amity Island confuse you with a Valdeonian ranger?" Riley put a hand on Seth's arm, slowing their pace until they fell behind the group. "I know you could pass for Valdeonian. Now, don't be angry. I'm just saying your hair and eyes are darker than the average islander. Maybe your mother's people had a little Valdeonian in them? You certainly don't look anything like old Fussbottom."

Seth looked away. Maybe his dark features hadn't come from his mother. What if he looked more like her Edmund? Perhaps he truly was the bastard son of this Valdeonian.

"Let's go to Paddy's. I could do with a little peace."

Riley bumped his arm and started back toward the west. His brothers, intent upon their thirst for a pint, continued on toward the Haven Bay Pub. Seth joined his best friend without an argument. He was in no mood for laughing crowds either. His mind was unsettled with bits and pieces of clues to his parents' past. He needed perspective from the one person he could trust in this new world of lies and secrets. Pulling the golden coin out of his pocket, he handed it to Riley.

His friend held it up against the light and examined both sides before handing it back to Seth. "What is it besides a sum greater than our farm makes in a year?"

"I found it this morning when I was searching the fields where the raiders ambushed me. According to one of the books in the school library, that beast is a gargoyle. It represents a Tslavian family by the name of Von Wolkhurst."

"They must be pretty well off to have a gold coin made for them." Riley rubbed at the back of his neck and shook his head. "Why would these Von whoever they are want to have you killed?"

The time had come to put their friendship to the test. Many would turn away from him if he disclosed what he was going to share with Riley. Bastards were either claimed by their fathers or shunned and forced to leave the island. What would the elder do if he found Seth's father was alive and Anne McCloud had given birth to his child without the vows? Swallowing hard, ready for the hurt, he mustered his courage. He needed Riley's common-sense point of view. Heaven help him, but a part of Seth very much wanted to believe his mother's old lies.

"My father isn't dead," he began. "On the day she died, my mother told me his name was Edmund. I believe he is one of the rangers from Valdeon Tom mentioned."

Riley looked down at his boots and rubbed at the back of his neck again. His best friend had a gift for speaking plainly and honestly. The trait made him someone most people readily trusted. It also made him a horrible liar.

"You knew? And you didn't tell me?"

"It wasn't my fault! I overheard my parents and Emma talking to the doctor. Dad said your mother told him their families didn't approve of their relationship. Well, and then Paddy caught me listening and Dad threatened to give me a good wallop if I told you."

Seth kicked angrily at a rock upon the row. "I wonder what else they're not telling me, like why he left?"

"You'll find out soon enough. Emma wrote to a friend of your mother's to ask her to help find your dad."

Perhaps his father had already visited Haven Bay and knew of his son? The ranger who saved him the night of the attack was a mystery. Memories of his voice were just beyond Seth's recollection, but his words had held little sentiment.

"What about the Tslavian family on the coin? Who do you think they are?"

"It's possible they are enemies of my father. Or perhaps they are my mother's people?"

Two large airships floated in the sunset above their heads. Another was moored upon the docks stretching over the cliffside. Three ships, foreign from the look of their build, visiting their tiny island upon the same day had drawn a crowd. Seth and Riley joined the curious spectators against the railings of the empty corral. In springtime, the pen was used to keep livestock awaiting transportation to and from Marianna.

"Can you tell where they're from?" Riley blocked the sunlight with his hand, straining with the rest to see.

"Those are trade vessels from the UR. They don't belong to any one country." Teb hobbled over to join them.

Seth waved a greeting, careful to keep his gaze off Teb's empty left trouser leg. He'd lost it in a war when serving in the UR Army. Many said Teb didn't seem to notice its absence. He was as full of life as the day he'd left Haven Bay for the mainland.

"Dock master says there's a storm between Larkspur Isle and the mainland. Supposed to be a sail ripper. A few ships had to be routed to Marianna until it passes." Teb pointed at the hovering ship preparing to dock. "Don't know what the Portsmouth vessel is doing this far from home though."

Sailors from the docked trade ship filed out of the port. Their disappointed expressions were almost comical. They were entering Seth's mundane world, but at least these lucky few could escape soon. One of them, an older man with silver hair and a face pocked by weather, let out a curse.

"Fighting wind and sea would be better than wasting away from lack of drink on this rock."

The man was a Tslavian. Seth swept his intense gaze over every inch of the old man. Heart beating quickly, he waited for any betraying sign of a disguise. Old eyes caught him staring. Hatred filled them.

"What are you staring at, Valdeonian pig?" The Tslavic insult hurled brutally from his mouth.

"I am an islander, sir." Seth gripped the railing tightly, forcing the anger down. His mother's killer could be standing before him right now.

"Is there a problem?" Teb, unable to understand the Tslavic tongue, gave Seth a puzzled look as he waited for the translation.

"Our guests need a lift to Paddy's." Seth kept his voice steady and forced a smile.

Teb nodded agreeably and hurried to his wagon with the sailors following. Seth stood away from the railing, watching the wagon roll toward the west. The Tslavian sailor met his gaze with an ugly sneer; then he turned away toward the promise of food and drink.

Riley knew Seth too well to be easily fooled. "What is it? What did he say to you?"

"That old sea dog recognized me, Riley. Or at least recognized me as a Valdeonian. He could be Sandor in disguise."

"What do we do now?"

Seth began the long walk toward Paddy's. "We follow him. I want to know if he's been here before."

Chapter Twelve

LIGHT FROM PADDY'S INN CAST box shadows upon Main Row. Laughter escaped the busy common room to echo in the night air. Three ships had brought thrice the business for Paddy and Teb. They rushed about on the warm side of the window to serve food and drink to their eager guests. Seth stomped his feet to chase the chill of the night air out of his bones. He wished they'd decided to spy on their quarry from inside the pub.

"Look at him in there, the old boozer." Riley pulled his cloak tighter about his body. "He's picked that place beside the window to spite us."

His friend did have a point. The old sea dog had remained where he was for hours, not moving to join his fellow crewmen. Occasionally he'd look out the window, smile, and then return to his drink. The other sailors left the old man alone, not wasting so much as a wave upon him. The harsh lines of his face and the curve of his frown discouraged such pleasantries.

"He's leaving, and about time too." Riley slapped at Seth's arm. "Great gulls. Frost has formed on the trees while we've watched him swill his drink. I should be home in a warm bed rather than following some filthy old drunk."

The sailor swung open the door to the common room and leisurely descended the stairs. Stretching his arms wide in a yawn, he stood upon the bottom step and took a deep breath. Then he began wandering in the direction of the docks. Hiding places were scarce on the stretch of road between Paddy's and town. They let the sailor move a good distance ahead before stepping out of their hiding spot to follow. It wasn't a challenge to keep up. The sailor kept to a slow pace, pausing now and again to kick at a stray rock.

Then a gust of breeze struck Seth's face. It carried the faint smell of citrus and spices. In that moment he remembered his mother. Each winter upon the Festival of the New Year's Birth, she'd somehow obtain a small jar of candied orange slices for the celebration. Their scent was distinctive, like the aroma he smelled now. Pausing on the road, he sniffed again. The scent had faded.

Torchlight danced against the midnight horizon. The airship port loomed ahead, rising in the night like a fleshless bird perched upon the cliffs. Seth froze on the row as the sailor's silhouette paused in the gateway. Crouching down slightly, the Tslavian sailor seemed to be preparing for something. Then he spun around quickly to face the Main Row.

Seth pulled Riley down with him as he fell to his belly upon the row. The old sailor stood in his crouch, eyes sweeping across the empty fields. Holding his breath, Seth waited as the moments ran by. Then the sailor lifted his arms over his head and took a deep breath. He disappeared inside the docks, leaving them sprawled upon the ground.

"Great gulls!" Riley wiped at the mud splattered across his cloak.

"Hush." Seth covered Riley's mouth with his muddy hand. "Sorry."

Crawling quickly to the side of the row, they tumbled into the darkness. More torches were mounted on each side of the gateway. Their circles of light overlapped in the center, ready to catch anyone sneaking onto the docks. While no high fences bordered the port, light and a vigilant militia were enough to discourage mischief. The threat kept most trespassers out, except for the youth of Haven Bay. It was a badge of honor to sneak through the back of the port and under its platforms. Tonight, however, they didn't have the option. The sailor was getting away. Sneaking around back would take too long. Seth didn't want to lose his best lead.

"If we're quick enough, maybe he won't see us. If we run I mean."

Riley pointed toward the far corner of the airship port. "We'll have no place to run if the law sees us."

Constable McTavish strolled along the road, absorbed in the pipe he was puffing upon. A bludgeon hung down the side of his uniform, bumping against his leg. The constable adjusted the barrel of his musket upon his shoulder. He was taking no chances this night. A full port was good for Haven Bay businesses, but too many strangers could mean trouble for the law. He pivoted upon his heals and headed back toward the cliffs.

"Coming, Riley?"

"Might as well. I've gone mad already staying out this late. Let's go."

Racing silently across the empty row, they plunged into the torchlight. Completely exposed for a few moments, Seth held his breath. He pushed through the gateway and didn't stop running until they were safely in the shadows of the pilings along the dock. Two levels of platforms hung above their heads. The docks, seemingly deserted except for lone sentries upon the nearest ship's deck, stretched out across the waters. The entire structure was still. Someone who knew these docks could hide in a thousand places. Seth had spent many a day here, hiding from his uncle among the cargo and rigging.

A strike, hard and excruciating, struck Seth's shoulder. It sent sparks of pain shooting across his eyes. Riley hit the ground beside him. The Tslavian sailor stood over them. A crooked sneer forced its way upon his chapped lips as he bounced the pipe in his palm.

"You've been shadowing me all night, Valdeonian pig. What do you want?" He poked the end of the pipe toward Seth. "Come, D'Antoiné, what have my comings and goings to do with you?"

Seth regarded the sailor before him, examining his movements and gestures. He must be Sandor. How many Tslavians visited Marianna and were so familiar with his father's people?

"I want your name. Are you Pavel Sandor?"

All expression fell from the sailor's face in a wave of white. "How do you know that name?"

He gave no answer, staring blankly instead at the surprise and fear upon the old man's face. Disappointment conquered any fear in Seth's heart. He'd been ready for denials, certainly not genuine shock. This sailor's journey to Marianna had been by chance, not by design.

"You think I'm Sandor?" His cackle came back in fits as he lowered the pipe. "If Sandor wants you dead, boy, then I would finish your business and prepare for the everlasting. Maybe I'll take care of you for him? We'll call it an act of patriotism."

The old sailor cackled louder, spinning the metal pipe. His fast-moving strike belonged to a much younger man. The pipe came down hard, whistling inches above Seth's head. He flattened his body upon the ground and kicked at the man's legs.

"You little mule."

The sailor reached into his boot and pulled out a knife. Brandishing it before him, he made ready to throw it at Seth's heart. Then a sudden gust of wind brought a dark shadow between them. It lifted as quickly as it had appeared, leaving behind a faint aroma of citrus. The knife was no longer in the sailor's hand. Eyes wide, he seemed as stunned as Seth.

"What goes on here?"

Constable McTavish came toward them from the darkness, musket held firmly in his hands. Intense eyes stared at them from within a hard face. Another person outside of Seth's household remembered the recent kidnapping and violent murder it would seem. He eased slowly to his feet and put his hands in the air. Riley followed his careful movements. A friend could easily be mistaken for an enemy in the darkness.

"Thieves, Constable! They tried to jump me. I'm an old man, an easy mark to their eyes. What choice did I have, but to defend myself?" The sailor tossed the pipe aside.

"Why, it's Seth McCloud and Riley Logan. What in the green, green fields are you boys doing here this time of night?"

The sailor let out a pitiful groan and began to gesture wildly. "I'll have no justice now. I'm a poor old man just trying to make a living. These two boys try to rob me, and it is I who will be arrested because they are friends of the constable! Who will give a poor old man justice?"

"Here now. I've known these boys since they were in nappies. These two would never rob you. Clearly there's been some sort of misunderstanding. Be off to your ship where you belong."

"He hit us both with a pipe, Constable! You can't let him go." Riley stomped threateningly toward their attacker. "Stop your howling, you old faker! I'll beat the truth out of you!"

The constable threw the torch to the ground and grabbed them both by their ears. Muttering angry curses, he forced them to the gateway. Seth followed his ear all the way from the docks to the town square. He let out a grateful sigh when the constable finally released the tiny appendage.

"Threatening an old man. I never thought I'd live to see the day. You boys have some explaining to do."

"He tried to kill us! Please listen."

Seth's protests stopped abruptly as his angry glare turned from the gateway. Constable McTavish had his full attention now. His mustache angulated in a mix of shock and fury. Angry fists gripped a pair of irons. He snapped one end on Seth's wrist and its twin on Riley's without a moment's hesitation. They had known the constable all their lives. It hurt to see the disbelief in his eyes.

Red heads appeared under the lights of the square. The Logan boys had come looking for their youngest. They approached them with a wave. Tom put his fists upon his hips as he caught sight of Riley in irons. Angry murmurs circled amongst the Logan boys. One sharp snap from Tom silenced their grumblings.

"We've been looking for you for hours. What will Mum say if you don't show up at the breakfast table in the morning?"

"He's been up to mischief, Tom." Constable McTavish shook his head. "I want you to march straight back to the farm and fetch your Dad."

Tom gave Seth and Riley a long look. "No sense in waking the whole house. I'll see these two get home where they belong."

A glimmer of hope worked its way into Seth's heart as Tom moved forward to grab his arm. The constable put the barrel of his musket between them. Tom's body tensed for a moment as his fingers reached for the hilt of a sword no longer there.

"This is no drunken brawl. Riley and Seth are under arrest for assault."

"We can't let Riley go to jail, Tom." Stephen grabbed his brother's arm, but Tom shook it off.

"And how will you stop it? Violence leads to more violence. I've seen enough to last a lifetime." Tom let a long sigh escape into the night air. "We'll fetch Dad."

Time passed a bit too swiftly when retribution came from across the Farm Row. Seth and Riley stood in the Haven Bay Police Station looking into the faces of their angry kin. It wasn't a new experience to see Fergus McCloud's disapproval, but Seth couldn't bear the look of disappointment upon Mr. Logan's face.

"Don't have enough work on the farm to keep you out of trouble?" He shook his finger in Riley's pale face. "I'll give you more, you young hoodlum. You won't have the energy to eat by the time I'm done with you. You'll earn every cent of the twenty credits I just paid to get you out of jail."

Seth stepped forward, hoping to block the anger aimed at Riley. "Please, Mr. Logan, it was my fault."

"Quiet. You have your own worries." The headmaster pushed him back with the tip of his walking stick.

Mr. Logan pulled Riley home by the scruff of his neck. Nothing Seth could do or say would sway his anger. He'd made a mess of things this time. It wasn't

Riley's idea to sneak into the docks. He'd pulled his best friend into this intrigue. In fact, if not for the strange disappearance of the sailor's knife, they both might have met their end in the shadow of the docks.

Constable McTavish tapped the desk, getting Seth's attention. "Now, young McCloud. Tell us again why you broke into the port tonight and threatened an old man? We'll be lucky if the ship's captain doesn't make too much of this whole affair. You know how important trade is to Haven Bay."

"I was trying to find my mother's killer. She wasn't attacked by Amity raiders. A Tslavian assassin named Pavel Sandor murdered her. I first met him in the fields above the lookout on the night the raiders attacked. It was Sandor who ordered them to kill me. After you and the other men left, Constable, I walked across the fields toward town. Hurrying home, I found the house empty, or so I thought. I saw movement behind the door of my mother's room, so I went inside and…and found her dead. She'd been poisoned." Seth stopped to compose himself.

Fergus's face drained of color. "That's quite a thing to say."

"I saw your mother's body." Constable McTavish swallowed hard at the memory. "She'd been brutally beaten. They'd have no need for poison after they fractured her skull as they did."

A wave of sickness came over Seth. What devilry had Sandor done to his mother's dead body? He shook his head, not wanting to hear anymore of the constable's words.

"The ranger told Sandor to cover up what he'd done, so you'd believe the raiders killed her. He must have beaten her after…after she was already dead. He's a master assassin, or so he claims." He leaned back away from them to calm his anger. "Sandor was hiding behind the door waiting for me. I believe he'd been paid to kill me by my mother's people." Seth looked into their disbelieving faces. "He pinned me to the ground and poured poison in my mouth. Sandor caused my illness. Don't you see? He killed Mother."

"What a preposterous notion. Use your head, boy. If this phantom had poisoned you, why aren't you dead as well?"

"A ranger saved my life," Seth insisted. "He came into the room and stopped Sandor."

"And the poor man you attacked tonight?" The constable spread his fingers across the desk. He looked tired.

"I thought he may have been my mother's killer. He's Tslavian and seemed to take an odd interest in me. He says he knows who Pavel Sandor is and was willing to kill me as a favor to him."

"I know you've been through some hard times, young McCloud, but think about how this story sounds. It may have been the fever playing tricks with you. People see all sorts of things when they're ill." Constable McTavish turned to Fergus. "Under the circumstances, I think we can spare Seth a night in jail. I'll have a word with the ship's captain."

"You're much too lenient, McTavish. Come, boy. We're going home and I don't want to hear any more foolishness."

Seth followed Fergus toward home, feeling very much alone. No one except Riley believed him, and now his only confidant was being punished.

"You think I'm mad."

"I think you like attention." Fergus poked Seth's chest with the metal handle of his walking stick. "Your mother isn't around to fuss over your every move, so you must call attention to yourself by making up these fantastic stories."

He grabbed the stick and pulled it out of Fergus's hands. Seth gripped it until his knuckles turned white. Anger turned to fury. He growled low as his hands twisted the metal handle.

"I am not making up stories! It was real! It happened, and I'll prove it!" Seth pulled open his shirt, uncovering his scar from the raider's knife.

"Hush, boy. Nothing you can do or say will convince me."

"I'll find this Pavel Sandor and make him confess to Mother's murder. You and the rest will see that he's real!"

Seth threw the stick back at Fergus. The headmaster held the handle under a street lamp. The once smooth metal had been crushed and twisted into an unrecognizable lump. Seth stared at the damage he had done with his bare hands. His gaze lifted to rest upon the eyes of his volatile uncle. For the first time, resentment for Seth had been replaced by fear.

Finally, the headmaster spun away and limped as quickly as he could toward home. Seth stood staring dumbly at his departing back. Words of warning spoken by Sandor the night his mother died echoed in his mind. He'd cautioned Seth would become dangerous to those around him. Those words, spoken by a killer, were proven to be the only truth he could rely on.

Holding his hands up to the light, Seth examined them as if they were foreign objects belonging to someone else. Though they had easily crushed the thick metal handle, he found no mark upon them. What was happening to him? How could he do such things and not feel pain? Anger. It gave him incredible physical strength. Standing before Fergus and listening to another round of insults had knocked away the boundaries of his control. He'd been compelled to reach out and strike the older man. It had taken all the will he had possessed to pull away. The longing to harm the headmaster was overwhelming.

Turning his face away from the place he had called home, Seth ran from the square in desperate strides. Going back to the McCloud house tonight was out of the question. He'd been able to stop his anger this time, but the next insult or hateful look from the headmaster might push him too far. Seth cast a glance toward the shadows of the port's pillars. The entrance to his favorite hiding place waited beneath the platforms. It would take him to a quiet place along the cliffside, but the climb was dangerous after dark. Heading west, he ran for the one place that could offer him a welcome distraction.

Chapter Thirteen

IT WAS LATE, A few hours from closing time when he reached Paddy's Inn. Business inside the common room showed no signs of slowing. Loud laughter and a poorly played fiddle shook the windows. Taking a tight hold upon his temper, he pushed into the common room. A quiet place to think was what he needed, not a party. His choices were rather limited on such a chilly night. Seth moved to the bar and squeezed in among the crowd. He wasn't much of a drinker, but tonight was a good night to pick up the habit.

Teb greeted Seth in a rush and took his order without comment. Cries for his attention rippled along the crowd pushing toward the bar. He snapped up Seth's coin and exchanged it with a full tankard. Seth, anxious to get away from the rush, moved uncertainly through the rowdy crowd of sailors. He spotted an empty chair in the corner. It looked like a good place for a nice long think.

Someone bumped into him, spilling Seth's full tankard down his ruined shirt. A small boy, no more than nine or ten, dressed in shabby trousers and a dirtied shirt stared up at him. Straw blond hair poked out from under a red knit sailor's cap. Small hands clasped tightly upon the handle of several tankards much too large for him to carry.

"Sorry, mate!" He hurried on through the crowd and out of sight.

Seth sunk down in the corner chair and stared into the nearly empty tankard. He sniffed at the dregs of ale. Sour and sweet mixed with the overwhelming smell of too many bodies in one room. He pushed the ale away and leaned his head back against the wall. This was turning out to be the perfect end to an awful day.

"Clumsy little nit!"

The music and laughter fell silent. Men who'd been sharing tales amongst their shipmates abruptly left their places. They hurried to the interior walls, giving the center of the common room to the evening's violent show. Trouble was about to begin, but it didn't discourage their taste for drink.

Seth stood with the rest as an unshaven, rough-looking sailor slammed his fist upon the table. He lifted out of his chair. Ale stained the front of his trousers and dripped down upon his boots. The young boy who'd spilled on Seth moments ago now cowered before the big man. He had bad luck enough to spill on the wrong person this time.

"Careful now, Tubs, Captain just got himself that new cabin boy. He'll be powerful angry."

A lanky sailor with a patchy beard and rat eyes put a hand upon the big man's arm. Tubs twisted away with a growl and reached for the cabin boy. He gripped the terrified lad by the collar and threw him against the far wall. His small body landed with a hard thud and a crack.

"Get up, you useless piece of rubbish."

Tubs marched toward the still body. Abandoned tankards shook on their tables as he passed. He kicked hard at the boy's side with his boot. Seth, frozen in place by shock, looked around the room. Why wasn't anyone stopping the man? He would certainly kill the boy if no one took action. The other sailors turned back silently to their drinks and their own business.

The little cabin boy groaned as the sailor turned him over roughly. Sad, frightened eyes returned Seth's gaze. He had been beaten before by the brute no doubt. Seth gripped at the table. His breaths were coming in angry gasps. He bolted out of his chair and gripped the heavy tankard in his hand.

"Leave him alone!"

He threw it as hard as he could. It struck Tubs in the back of the neck, dazing him long enough for Seth to pull the boy up. They hobbled together toward Seth's chair. Clutching his arm against his chest, the cabin boy cried muffled tears as he looked upon his hurt limb. It was bent in an awkward angle.

"You'll pay for that, woolie farmer."

"Call me what you will. In my turn I name you a brute and a coward. Decent men don't mistreat children."

He raised his fists. Power came to them as his anger surged. It was hungry now, ready to devour and destroy. This time he wasn't going to stop it.

Tubs stood at his full height. His broad shoulders shook as he laughed. Every ugly feature. Every habitual tick came into sharp focus as Seth regarded him with predator eyes. Scars covered his hands and arms. This man had seen many years of hard labor and hard fighting. He wouldn't be easy to defeat.

Touching his senses, the brute's shipmates came to crowd closer to Seth. They were a rough lot, smelling of old fish and too much drink. This wasn't to be a fair fight. All eyes in the common room were turned upon the ready combatants. The other sailors pressed harder against the walls. They wouldn't help him if they wouldn't help one of their own.

"Are you going to fight me on your own, farmer?"

"He does not stand alone."

A rich baritone voice cut through the crowd to his right. A faint scent of citrus caught Seth's nose again. He turned with his attackers to the next table. Two men, hooded and cloaked, sat drinking fresh tankards of ale. He couldn't see their faces fully, but the accent and their great height were unmistakable. They were Valdeonians. One of the men ran his finger along the steel of his naked blade. His other hand, the left one, was scarred and raw. Its middle finger missing.

"If you have grown weary of playing with small boys and unarmed islanders, perhaps you would like to play with me, yes?" Firm lips turned into a slow grin.

"No, sir."

A slight tremble had crept into Tubs's voice. He and the rest of his mob eased their hands carefully away from their weapons. Curious, Seth turned back to the table. He stared at the man running his fingertip along the cool blade. Deadly confidence hovered about him. His hands were steady as he laughed at the room full of men.

Seth — in contrast — couldn't keep his own hands from shaking. The angry power had left him the moment he'd sniffed the citrus perfume. His knees shook, threatening to give way any moment. This was a golden opportunity to hurry from the middle of the confrontation and find Paddy's musket. Yet, he couldn't look away from the fingertip as it ran up and down the steel.

"I've no beef with you, sir. It's between me and the farmer."

"I choose to make it my beef as you say." The finger finally stopped upon the blade and tapped it. "My blade has grown restless aboard ship. It wants movement."

Raw fear was on the brute's face now. Seth had no idea who this Valdeonian might be, but Tubs and his friends seemed to know him. They were terrified.

"Stand down, the lot of you!" Paddy stormed up with his musket loaded and ready. "I'll have no trouble from you in my pub. Get back to your ship and good riddance."

His loaded musket broke the spell over the common room. Tubs and his mob backed away from the Valdeonian. Heading toward the door, each of them glared at Seth on their way out. The rest of the pub's patrons went back to their drink while Seth leaned on his chair to steady his shaking knees. If not for the two hooded men, he would have been a bloody mess. He swiveled around to thank them, but found empty chairs and two full tankards instead. The two Valdeonian men had vanished as silently as they'd appeared.

"Are you well, Seth? What do you think you're about staying out so late?" Paddy cradled the musket in his arms, still watching the door. "You'd better stay here for a time until those drunken fools get to their ship."

A haggard old sailor approached them, his knit cap held in his hands. He rested tentative fingers upon the cabin boy's head. Cracked lips offered the boy a smile full of helpless pity.

"I'll take the boy to the ship's doctor. Tubs is a killer, though no man would dare try to prove it. I thank you just the same."

"You can't take the boy back to your ship. What if they try to hurt him again?"

The older sailor shook his head at Seth and gripped the cabin boy's slumped shoulders. "Don't have a choice. The boy's indentured to the Captain."

"He's a slave you mean."

"Some aren't as lucky in our life situations as you are, son. He has to go back. Got his Mum and other little ones to think of."

They made their way slowly out of the common room back to their ship. Seth was helpless to stop them. For all the troubles he had in his own life, he'd met someone worse off. It was his mother's war cry against poverty. Seth understood what she'd meant a little better after tonight. He'd been such a fool charging like a madman into a fight he couldn't win. Seth was no warrior, not like the two Valdeonian men.

"Paddy?" Seth touched his shoulder. "Those two cloaked men. Have you seen them before?"

"They came looking for rooms a few minutes after you arrived. I'm surprised you didn't run into them on your way from town. Forget them. Listen, Seth, you better have a care until those ships leave. It might be a good idea if you spent the night in the back room. I can drive you home in the morning."

Seth heard snickering from the corner and turned to glare at the group of sailors sipping their tankards. They turned back to their drinks again.

Paddy pulled him roughly to the bar. "Are you so certain those sailors just happened by? I told you not to mention Pavel Sandor's name."

"I'm sorry I did."

"So is the old sea dog. The militia found him hanging by his jaw on one of the docks. Someone had relieved him of his heart. Sergeant Gunn and Constable McTavish are calling it a drunken brawl, but we know otherwise, don't we?"

Seth stared at Paddy as the words sunk in. He'd been so certain the Tslavian had been Sandor. The evidence, his nationality, and his familiarity with the D'Antoiné family had been simple coincidence. Their clumsy attempts to investigate had gotten an innocent man killed. Well, perhaps not quite so innocent. One thing was certain, Pavel Sandor was still on Marianna and very close.

"Have a care. I plan to take this with me when I'm out in the open." He patted the musket.

"I'm not afraid. Let him face me. Sandor is going to pay for what he did to my mother."

Paddy rolled his eyes and threw up his hands. "Sit down, boy. I have mutton stew in the pot. Eat slowly. Hopefully those drunken bums will be well aboard their ship by the time you finish."

Three bowls of stew and a few hours later, his pride was satisfied enough time had passed. In the darkest time of night — just before the sun's rays began to penetrate the black — he stepped onto the front steps of the inn. No sign of anyone waiting out in the darkness as far as he could see. Those sailors were probably sleeping off their drink by now.

He slipped quietly down the steps and onto the Main Row. Stopping under the comforting glow of Paddy's hanging lanterns, he looked again into the trees where he and Riley had hidden earlier. Still no sign of movement. Now he was just being foolish. It was getting close to the dawn. Emma would be waiting to scold him as it was. He'd better not show his face after she had started the breakfast.

Hands grabbed him from behind and dragged him toward the darkness. The stench of stale brew and old fish stuffed his nostrils. Rough hands covered his mouth and held down his arms against his body.

"This don't seem like such a good idea to me. You know who was onboard ship with us. He seemed interested in this boy."

Tubs's friend, the lanky man from the common room, held up a small ship's lantern before Seth's face. Yellow teeth chattered in the chilly air. A dirtied leather eye patch covered heaven only knew, while the other eye darted wildly about them.

"He's no concern of ours." Tubs! His rough voice was one Seth would well recognize for a long time.

"Are you, barmy? Missing all this time and he just happens to pick Marianna as a vacation spot?"

"Shut it." Tubs pressed chapped lips against Seth's ear. "Your people won't recognize you when I'm done, farmer."

A rock solid fist thrust into Seth's abdomen, knocking the air out of his lungs. Eyes watering, he collapsed toward the ground. Several arms held him in place. Another strike hit his face with an explosion of pain. Laughter buzzed in his ears like a swarm of angry wasps. He began to wonder if he'd breathed his last.

Someone grunted close to his face. Thud. The many pairs of hands holding him suddenly let go of their grip. Seth fell to the ground, trying to get his breath back. He was alone beside the back wall of Paddy's. The group of mischief makers stood in a circle several feet away from him.

"Mercy!"

The call started from one sailor and was quickly taken up by the rest. Then a shadow moved through his attackers, deadly and swift. His movements were graceful and perfectly executed. Each raised fists sent another man to his back in a flash of movement. Seth had never seen anyone move so fast! He shivered, realizing the sailors could have been killed as quickly.

One would not be joining his friends when they woke. Tubs's lifeless eyes stared up at the morning star.

A form approached him. It wasn't a shadow or some warring angel from the beyond. The cloaked man from the tavern reached a hand out to Seth. He took it and was pulled to his feet as if he were a sack of yarn. Strong arms helped Seth under a small circle of light from one of the pub's lanterns.

"Beware the anger of fools, my young friend."

Though the man spoke in the common tongue, his words were accented by the musical tones of his people. He held Seth's face up to the light and chuckled at the cuts. His laughter was warm, not unkind. The bandaged hand pulled the hood from his head, revealing a handsome face. His hair was a fading chestnut overtaken by gray. A wave of citrus and exotic spices floated about him. Remarkable though the man may be, his eyes captured Seth's attention. They were a deep brown with specks of amber in them. A strange sort of power held Seth in their gaze.

Those dark eyes moistened as they scanned every feature of Seth's face. Gentle fingers smoothed around the bruises, stopping to cup his chin. The Valdeonian took a sharp breath and swallowed hard.

"His eyes do not lie, my lord." The other Valdeonian came to stand beside them.

"Have a care, Dante. Do not forget why we've come," his rescuer rebuked in the musical language.

"You have fire, my young friend. What is your name?"

"I'm Seth McCloud, sir."

He answered in the common tongue. Perhaps it was wrong, but a new instinct for mistrust made Seth hold back. He didn't want to let them know he spoke their language quite yet. The other man, Dante, may yet slip to reveal who they were. He was intrigued by the man standing before him. Why would such a cunning and skilled warrior be visiting Marianna? According to Tubs and his friends, this man wasn't here by chance.

"Well, Seth McCloud. You are safe now. Those men will not harm you again."

The two Valdeonians climbed the stairs, leaving him to go on his way. They reached the tavern door before Seth had the sense of mind to call after them.

"Sir! Do I know you?"

The warrior's eyes grew sad once more. He looked down at Seth for a long time, before answering.

"No. But you may call me Leo."

The Valdeonian entered Paddy's, leaving Seth staring after him in the dark. The scent of citrus and spices remained in the early morning air. He took one last sniff and turned toward Haven Bay.

Chapter Fourteen

SAN LEONORA, CITY OF Kings and capital of Valdeon, glistened in the afternoon sun like a treasure trove waiting to be seized. Beneath their descending vessel, merchants haggled with their customers. Young horses kicked against the corrals separating them from freedom. This deafening boom was the music of commerce. It heralded the Prince of Valdeon home.

Julian turned away from the bustling streets and markets. Waiting breathlessly for just the right angle, he marveled as the sun sent its beams in a halo around The Palace of Kings. Towering above the city, it rose like mighty peaks of stone and glass. Tiles of brilliant gold blanketed the roof. Endless mosaic arches formed supports to lift its massive structure. It was his childhood home and, as such, remained very dear to him.

A rotunda, built centuries before by the Ancients, stood at the southeast corner of the palace. Formed with rare white stone from their distant country, the very nature of the stone had been infused with the Jalora's magic. Andara's greatest treasure and symbol of power — the Altar of Providence — was kept within, safe from invaders. It was said that even the most powerful cannon could not blast through the walls of the mighty Lion's Den. Julian's lips formed the tiniest of smiles. The Altar could not be taken by force. This treasure must be won by other means.

"It is a great city, perhaps a little too flamboyant for my tastes."

The changeling, ever at his side, took delight in provoking Julian's anger. He wouldn't succumb to the creature's game this time. His temper, already strained from another failure to recover the Lion Ring, was close to breaking free. This creature was waiting to report every misstep, every moment of weakness to Gorman. Soon Julian would arrange an unfortunate accident for his annoying new companion. Perhaps someone would expose its true nature to the Lords of Valdeon. They were the great champions of the Jalora, after all. In his eagerness to defend its honor, the changeling's life would be forfeited at the Wolf's blade. Lord Gorman couldn't blame Julian for such a loss. No one could stand against a ranger.

"You will find the Palace of Kings distasteful then, Changeling. Please allow me to show you its every corridor."

The Great Inland Wall cast shadows upon them as they walked down the ramp of the airship port. Thousands of stone lion heads were carved across the top of the wall, teeth bared in warning. Running across the stretch of land between Lake Leonora and the Leonora River, it had protected San Leonora for centuries against invaders. His new allies, however, could not be thwarted by mere walls. He scanned the massive base for signs of the Dirge. They'd already dissolved into its shadows.

Marcellus De Costa stood awaiting Julian. He was a thick young man, built for battle and hungry for killing. A scar stretched from his right eye to the indentation in his cheek where a stone had pulverized the bone. He'd been caught indulging in his favorite gruesome pastime. Dissection of human bodies wasn't a crime unless those humans had been alive during the procedure. The villagers and his own father had found Marcellus too homicidal for prison. Putting this killer to death had been their best option. Julian tended to agree, though he'd never let Marcellus see his revulsion. The Sarcion had coerced Julian into rescuing Marcellus from the stoning. It assured him the madman would be of great value one day.

"Welcome home, my lord prince." Marcellus bowed low, eyes twitching in constant reminder of the damage his face had endured.

"You are a welcome sight, my dear friend." Julian forced his hand to remain steady as Marcellus took it up and pressed his lips against the glove.

Fevered eyes shifted to the changeling. "You've brought someone back with you, my prince."

"This is Armando, my new valet."

The changeling flashed an angry glare at them. Evidently it had expected to be treated as an equal. Marcellus noticed the look. He straightened and returned the sentiment with a hate-filled look of his own. A brief fluttering of hope came to Julian as his two irritating burdens sized each other up. Perhaps he could be rid of both of them as he played the two against each other.

"Fetch my luggage, Armando." Julian waved a dismissive hand to the changeling. "The other servants can guide you to my chambers when you're done."

Not waiting to see the resentful glare, he turned toward the street where an ebony carriage awaited them. A lion of gold, emblem of the D'Antoiné royal house, silently roared from its door. His little sister, Zoya, gave a delighted cry when Julian entered. She threw her arms around his shoulder and pressed her lips to his cheek.

"I've longed for your return, Brother." Zoya's smile twisted into a mischievous grin. "It has been frightfully dull with the Lords of Valdeon marching about the palace, keeping the peace. Their devoted worshippers praise them night and day. It turns the stomach."

"I do hope, my darling sister, that you haven't been provoking the Wolf. He is rather single-minded where you are concerned."

She shrugged and gave him a secret smile. He knew her well enough to suspect she'd gone against his word. One day she'd choose the wrong man to play with, and then her games would end permanently.

"The Orb of Valdeon is black with death." Marcellus changed the subject as he always did when Julian's anger with Zoya began to brew. "I knew you would not fail, my prince. What a battle it must have been! The Leo is…was a challenge."

Zoya's eyes glowed with desire as she leaned forward. "Let me see the Lion Ring, Brother!"

"I don't have it."

His dark glare weighed the look upon their faces. Bitter disappointment. Shock. Frustration. He couldn't fault them, having experienced each emotion upon the boggy shores of North Marsh. Understanding was one thing. Tolerance was quite something else.

"Have a care before you question, Zoya. My father still lives, but he severed his own finger to manage it. The ring is sleeping. It is powerless as long as it does not rest on a human finger. Leo is nothing without it, and it is nothing without the right bearer."

Their carriage moved through the massive arch in the Inland wall, and soon they were making their way up King's Row. The historic street had once been adorned with mosaics. Now, dirt and old bricks were the pathetic remains of the city's glory days. Two-story buildings lined either side of King's Row, blocking his view of the palace. They rode on in silence for a few miles. Any words spoken could only make matters worse.

The buildings ended abruptly, and they entered a large courtyard at the center of the city. Leo's first queen had commissioned a large garden with pathways and a bandstand for the people of San Leonora to enjoy. Now the garden was a weed patch and the bandstand a crumbling relic. Even the massive fountain had fallen into disrepair.

Valdeon had been grand once. Its power could not be rivaled by any on Andara. Of course those days of glory were before the Great War with Tslavia — Valdeon's fiercest enemy. A century ago, Tslavian soldiers plundered San Leonora. The city was almost lost, until a Jalora Master had come among them to protect the people. This Red Heart created the United Realms, claiming such an alliance between the nations of Andara would keep the peace. In truth, the fool had given away Valdeon's power over the continent, setting their once-great nation upon the path of mediocrity. It would take a strong leader to see Valdeon's power back again.

"What of the Regent Medallion?"

Marcellus and Zoya exchanged uncomfortable looks. She gripped the hem of her dress, lifting it to her chest. The unfortunate habit gave Marcellus a good look at her naked thighs. Julian slapped her hands and pulled the dress back down to the floor.

"Please try to behave like a lady, Zoya." He ignored her pouting face and stared hard at Marcellus. "What has happened? Why am I not holding the medallion in my hand at this very moment?"

"Your trinket wasn't where you said it would be, Brother." Zoya brushed at the front of her gown. "I had to spend a few evenings with one of the curators. Horrid little man. He helped me find the medallion. I've seen it with my own eyes. We were making plans for a midnight visit, but the Lords of Valdeon arrived in San Leonora before we could take it."

"Have I not made it clear? I must have the medallion!"

Gorman would be delighted to hear of this latest failure. Julian had underestimated his barbarian allies. Their hunger for Andara was keener than he had first supposed. In fact, he was beginning to suspect Whisper might be behind Julian's failed effort somehow. The medallion was his last chance to take the throne peacefully. He wanted to avoid the slaughter of his people by the hands of these barbarians if possible. Let them quench their thirst for blood on the rest of Andara. Valdeon belonged to him.

"Our country stands alone and unguarded at the very center of her enemies."

"What do you mean, my prince?" Marcellus, eager to avoid Julian's anger, grasped hold of this new talk of enemies.

"My informants tell me that Southbay plans to strike our eastern border. They seek revenge against our people for attacking one of their towns." Julian gave Marcellus a well-practiced look of concern. "Naturally, Valdeon would make no such attack. They falsely accuse us."

"Naturally." Zoya sat back, her eyes laughed at him.

"I fear they've been goaded into this by a powerful enemy. My informants brought back the broken sword of a Tslavian soldier. Don't you see, Marcellus? Tslavia believes Leo is dead and would take advantage of this to storm Valdeon! They concocted the raid on the Southbay town, knowing it would turn our neighbor against us. The fools would naturally go running to Tslavia for help."

"What are we to do, my prince? Has Chancellor Benito been warned?"

"The chancellor will not listen to my warnings. His ear belongs to the Lords of Valdeon. They refuse to heed the evidence."

Rumor of violence surrounding a few dead pawns would certainly spark outrage among the Tslavic court. He turned his eyes back to the window, letting Marcellus absorb the information. Andara was a powder keg waiting to explode. Tensions had been mounting since the day Leo had disappeared. Valdeon wouldn't be the victim of events this time. It would be the victor!

A tall pillar of white marble jutted up in the middle of King's Row. Mounted at its top was a large statue of a man riding his beloved San Marimosa stallion. Sword raised in defiance, Mikel D'Antoiné, the first King of Valdeon, remained dedicated in watching over his city. Julian smiled as he looked upon the famous Stallion's Gate. One piece of history at least remained.

"I must save Valdeon. I must restore its glory and make it strong again, or all will be lost."

"How will you do this, my prince, without the Lion Ring?"

"My ancestor, Cathmor the Conqueror, faced the same challenge as I do."

"Cathmor? Wasn't he named traitor?"

"Named by the very same Lion he overthrew. It was obvious the boy would be an unfit ruler. Cathmor had the courage to dethrone the weakling Lion Cub and conquer the southern countries. His rule was a grand one."

Yes, until the Lords of Valdeon found the Lion and set him free. You need the Lion Ring. The Sarcion's voice held the irritating tone of a reproachful teacher.

"Cathmor ruled his kingdom for a glorious two years!"

Julian lifted his hands in an impatient gesture. He quickly dropped them again, careful to keep the telepathic conversation and his performance for Marcellus separated. His sister gave him a knowing grin. He had few secrets from her.

Your Cathmor was never able to sit upon the Lion's Seat, Julian. How will you rule without the Altar of Providence? Pursue the Regent's Medallion if you must, but even its power cannot overcome the will of the Jalora.

Julian leaned back into the soft seat of the carriage. No creature on Erthe or in the beyond was capable of making him lose control faster than the Sarcion. It knew him too well.

"I will have the Lion Ring. Edmund D'Antoiné has run out of options. You will see. I will sit upon the Lion's Seat with the Crown of Sorrows upon my brow."

Their carriage pulled to a stop before massive stairs climbing up to the palace. Brightly colored tiles formed mosaics within the white stone of each step. Their designs reflected stories about the kings of the past. His jaw tightened as a bit of trash rolled across the bottom step, pushed by a gust of wind. So much for the days of glory long gone. Now the forgotten memories were trampled under the boots of the oblivious.

Their carriage began to sway as someone jumped off the driver's seat. Swinging the door wide, Armando flashed an insolent grin up at him. Turning his back on the changeling, Julian took Zoya's hand to help her out of the carriage. He completely ignored the creature. Zoya, on the other hand, was captivated. She stared at the changeling with undisguised curiosity. An all too familiar sparkle filled her eyes. Zoya had found her next game. Julian tugged her roughly toward the steps.

"Where is Benito? Why is he not here to show his respect for the Prince of Valdeon?"

It was customary for the chancellor to greet returning members of the royal family at the base of the steps. His gaudy purple robes of office were strangely absent today. Julian couldn't abide the old fool, but customs must be observed. It wouldn't do for Gorman's lackey to see moments of such disrespect.

"He is with the Lords of Valdeon, my prince." Marcellus's expression spoke of his anger at the slight. "They are making preparations for Leo's funeral."

"It would appear your lap dog of a chancellor knows his true master." Black clouded the changeling's eyes as it laughed. "Shall we?"

Marcellus pushed at Armando's shoulder. "You speak to the Prince of Valdeon. Show some respect."

A lightning jab to the stomach dropped Marcellus on his knees. Zoya helped the foolish young man to his feet, but her fiery eyes were on the changeling. Julian grabbed her arm, moving her away. He marched up the stairs, ignoring the low laughter from the creature.

They entered the Grand Atrium with its blinding sunlight and endless windows. Buttresses of white stone ascended three stories above their heads. Glass panels captured both dusk and dawn. These same panels changed in color during the hot San Leonora summer days, keeping the atrium cool. It was a marvel of engineering few understood.

Julian's memories of this place weren't fond. He'd spent many hours as man and boy, greeting dignitaries and listening to Leo's worshippers speak in hushed religious tones. The atrium was, above all else, the grand entrance to the throne room beyond. Through its golden doors stood the Altar of Providence.

"You failed to mention the throne room doors had been sealed. Considering they've stood open for at least one hundred years, did you feel the news was unimportant to share with me? I told you I wanted the throne room watched."

Julian's fists lifted toward Marcellus. Shaking with rage, they squeezed tighter. The fool was fortunate the Sarcion still had use for him. Then he remembered his new keeper and let his fists drop.

"No matter. Sealed, they will discourage those scavengers foolish enough to covet my throne. Never fear. The doors will open for the rightful ruler of Valdeon."

"Most reassuring." The changeling's grin exposed sharp canine teeth before disappearing under his guise of devoted valet.

"Those loyal to you are waiting. Many are eager to aid you in such a difficult time." Marcellus spoke with a zealot's passion. Julian returned his hopeful smile. He could use more dedicated followers like his mad friend in the days to come.

"Yes, I'm sure they are." Zoya gave Julian her knowing little smile. His greatest supporter, Zoya enjoyed helping encourage mischief. Unfortunately, she was difficult to control at times.

"What have you been up to while I was away, my little bird?" Julian wrapped her arm in his as they walked. "I do hope you've stayed out of trouble."

"Oh, you don't have to worry, Brother. I've finished my game." She offered him her most playful pout. "He wasn't anyone you knew. Don't worry. No one will find him. He's down in the dungeons with my other broken toys."

Julian gave her a harsh frown, but it quickly melted when she nuzzled her head against his arm. Zoya rested in the faith he would never harm her, and so far she'd been right. Yet, if she did ruin his chances to wear the Crown of Sorrows, their shared blood would not save her.

Marcellus respectfully cleared his throat. He motioned them out of the Grand Atrium into a large artery of corridors running throughout the palace. This corridor took them to the business center. The chancellor's offices were to their left. Elaborate tapestries showing images of horses and lions lined the walls. Benito's large double doors were closed. Julian smoothed at the stone as his Sarcion Ring stirred. The Lords of Valdeon were within his rooms, making their plans and poisoning Benito's mind against him, no doubt.

"The Jalora's playthings, these Lords of Valdeon as you call them, are behind that door. I can feel their great power." The changeling's perpetual sneer of superiority was gone from its face for once.

"I warned your general they would not be easily defeated."

The changeling nodded absently and followed the rest as they turned down another corridor. Julian was certain Armando would validate his opinion after having experienced the power of the Sacred Guard. Perhaps Gorman wouldn't take their existence so lightly now.

Plain doors lined the wooden paneled walls. Most of the meeting rooms were empty, their chairs standing neatly in rows. Light coming from the last room on the left fell upon the marble floor of the corridor. Many shadows crossed its beams, making impatient patterns upon the stone. Rumbles of angry, indiscernible words tumbled out into the corridor.

Then the ring of swords leaving scabbards announced imminent bloodshed. Julian hurried to the doorway. East stood against West in the confines of the room. Julian waited for the final trigger to their battle. These western lords were outnumbered. Some of them, long time friends of the Wolf, were not among these few. Their absence was disappointing. Such troublesome and rebellious leaders were best dispensed with right away. Giving titles to these bumpkins from the west was ridiculous. One of his first acts would be to absorb their lands and rule them as territories.

"Stop this foolishness!"

Xavier the Wolf's voice thundered into the room, shaking the chandeliers. Julian and his party hurried away from the Lord of Valdeon to freeze against the far wall. The ranger's form appeared to grow three times its size; though it was an illusion, Julian's very soul filled with terror. Power pushed at his body, threatening to crush him in its fury.

"We prepare for the funeral of our fallen king, and his subjects use the opportunity to bicker and fight." Wolf paused to look each one of the feuding men in the eye. "East and West are not to meet together outside of my presence. Now, get out."

Wolf left them as quickly as he appeared, not waiting for the men to move. He was a man used to being obeyed. The western landowners shuffled out like whipped dogs. Inside the meeting room, the eastern landowners huddled together whispering frantically. Their voices stopped abruptly when Julian entered. Many of his supporters were in attendance. He'd spoken to them each secretly before leaving San Leonora and knew their leanings. Others, newer faces from the eastern provinces, he was unsure of. Care would have to be taken.

"Please, gentlemen, please take your seats. Let us not stand on formalities at such a time." Julian moved to the front of the group and helped Zoya to a chair. "We are countrymen. My father's death impacts us all, as does the loss of the Lion Ring. Long have I worried this day would come. I have warned our chancellor and the Lords of Valdeon to be ready, but they have ignored my pleas."

Rumblings of discontent from his supporters fed Julian's confidence, but still their small numbers weren't enough to see him upon the throne. Observing the crowd for the newcomers' reaction, Julian hesitated. They seemed too frightened to seek favor from him. Could it be they hoped he would be their savior? The thought brought him a momentary rush of pride. He squashed it again. The Sarcion enjoyed bouts of pride too much. It could easily take advantage of such things.

"What was your counsel to them, my lord prince?"

One of his more fervent supporters, a low-level estate owner named Orryo, nearly jumped from his chair. He gave an imperceptible nod to Julian. This man was ever hungry for power. In circumstances like this he was valuable, but his ambition made him far too bold at times. No matter. Julian was easily rid of nuisances. Marcellus was anxious to continue practicing his unsettling hobby on humans. A word would send Orryo to the forgotten bowels of the palace never to be seen again.

Julian stretched out his arms, palms up in the perfect impression of a martyr. "Think upon the facts, my friends. The Lion Ring has been lost, and the Jalora refuses to reveal its location. The Orb is dark with death while the throne room's golden doors have hidden away the Altar of Providence." He waited for their fear to fester. "I believe these dark days have come upon us for a reason. The Jalora has lost faith in Valdeon."

"But, the Sacred Guard…" One of the newcomers rose from his seat, voice and hands shaking.

Julian shook his head with a surprising sensation of actual family shame. "My family has brought this disgrace upon San Leonora. First my uncle, a bishop in the Jalora's legion, was banished from Valdeon in disgrace. Then my father, the king, abandons his people for some unknown shame. It is up to me to save Valdeon and restore honor to the D'Antoiné name."

"What does the Wolf say about all this, my lord prince?"

The newcomer had found his voice, but he wasn't singing the tune Julian wanted to hear. His other comrades nodded, their faces full of adulation for the lord of San Rudalfo. Wolf. He had the peoples' trust. It was the leader of the Sacred Guard who ruled Valdeon, not the doddering old fool of a chancellor. Wolf had just become his biggest obstacle to the throne. He had to be taken care of, and quickly.

Chapter Fifteen

VIOLENCE. ITS DESTRUCTIVE ENERGY radiated from the drunkard charging toward him. Wolf stood perfectly still, blocking the fool's entrance into the Grand Atrium. Basilio, his squire, held a wary hand upon the hilt of his sword. Disciplined to the point of obsession, Basilio waited for his lord's command. He would lay down his life without question for Wolf. Such a sacrifice would be unnecessary today. Neither ranger nor squire were willing to draw their weapons this close to the Altar of Providence without cause. The sloppy drunk blundering toward them didn't warrant a weapon. Instead, he'd get a nasty beating.

"Die De Vincente pig!"

Basilio marched two steps forward to stand between the fool and Wolf. Drawing his blade, Basilio had his own plans for violence. A squire had many duties to endure on behalf of his lord. Defending his ranger's honor against insult was a matter of professional pride. Basilio was known as the deadliest blade in the Squire's Corps. His vengeance would be swift.

Ribbons of ash exploded into the corridor. They surrounded the approaching attacker in rapid streams too quick for human eyes to see. Two rangers grabbed the drunkard's body, disarming him and throwing his body to the ground. They were from Valdeon's eastern plains. One, tall and lean, bore the Owl Ring. His companion was a thicker man with a rugged look about him. He wore the Griffin Ring.

"Another troublemaker." Owl pulled the drunkard to his feet. "Where does the bastard prince find them all?"

Griffin picked up the man's dagger. "No crest or other markings. Julian's hiding his tracks."

"Take him to the dungeon with the rest. Question the fool when he sobers up. I want to know who encouraged him to attack a member of the Sacred Guard."

"Yes, sir."

Basilio flicked his blade at the side of the drunkard's head before the rangers could take him away. The man screamed as his ear bounced off his shoulder and onto the ground. Owl gave a hiss of alarm, but kept any objections he had from his lips. No one dared question a squire to the Lords of Valdeon. In many ways, they were more powerful than any soldier in the Valdeon or UR Armies.

Wolf nodded to Basilio and then turned to enter the Grand Atrium. Valdeonian dignitary filled the glass structure. Their murmurs of insincerities were deafening. Missing were the tales of friendship Edmund the Leo had cultivated from every corner of Andara. In his haste to squash rumors, Benito had not allowed time for Edmund's allies to attend his funeral. Many among the legion and Andara would not take kindly to the offense.

Cesar, Fausto, and Jorge were deep in conversation beside the exterior wall. Probing them quickly, his suspicions about more bangtail mischief were confirmed. The rangers had spent their morning breaking up fights and stopping vandals around the palace grounds. It would seem they were not alone in the struggle to keep the peace.

Wolf crossed the distance to join them. "You've seen some trouble, my friends?"

"Problems from our eastern cousins. I'm having difficulty keeping tempers from flaring. Young Herbert was lured into an empty section of the palace. His father and brother found him unconscious. He's in hospital now with a missing hand. Naturally, they are out for blood." Cesar shook his head. "It pushes the bounds of decency anyone would dare such a thing during our nation's tragedy."

"Who can understand such evil? The other rangers and I are prepared for skullduggery."

The atrium's growling murmurs subsided to hushed whispers. Julian D'Antoiné, Prince of Valdeon, stood at the entrance. Dressed in his favored black, he wore a sash of red. Its cheery hue proved the disdain he held for his father better than any word or action.

Marcellus De Costa, Julian's rabid dog, trailed behind him. Mad eyes darted around the room until they found Wolf. He whispered urgent words into his master's ear. Julian's attention rested upon Wolf and his friends for a moment. Then he gave Wolf a curt nod and headed into the crowd.

Zoya No-Name detached from her brother's arm. Coming closer, she tossed Cesar a small bundle wrapped in linen. Her smile was wicked when she saw him open the cloth. Puckering her lips in an insolent kiss, she hurried back to Julian's side.

"Curse the savage harlot!" Cesar spun his aging body around to go after her.

Wolf well recognized the determined scowl upon his old friend's face. He'd charge in amongst Julian's allies without thought for his own safety. Cesar may have been advanced in years, but he still had the heart of a warrior. Jorge pushed away from the pillar and came to grip his lord's arm. Fausto moved between them and the eastern lords lingering at the edge of the crowd.

"Please don't, for Edmund's sake, my lord." Jorge held tightly to Cesar's arm until the older man reluctantly nodded.

Jorge handed the cloth to Wolf. "It's Herbert's finger. I've heard rumors of the games Julian's she-devil plays, but hadn't realized she could cast her spells so quickly."

Wolf nodded his thanks to Cesar's former squire. The Pacarro tribesman remained fiercely loyal to his former ranger, though he had been released from service long ago. Five men loyal to Julian blanched under Wolf's gaze and disappeared into the crowd. Jorge's intervention had ruined at least one of Zoya's games.

A light touch rested on Wolf's arm. Love. Devotion. Dignity. They radiated from Dulcina De Vincente in waves, wrapping around her husband to strengthen him. Her very presence brought the beauty back into his heart in an instant. He lifted her hand gently to his lips. Dressed in widow's black, she paid homage to Leo. Her long hair had been braided in an intricate pattern stretching to her waist. Twisting among the strands of hair were ribbons of burgundy — his favorite color. Another hint of cheer had worked its way out from under her collar. It was a string of tiny blue beads formed into a crude necklace. Their little ones had made the present and given it to Dulcina for her birthday. She always wore it, even in the Palace of Kings.

Several ladies stood behind her. They too were dressed in black, showing Leo respect due him as King of Valdeon and a Jalora bishop. The women were known as Ranger Wives, picked and drawn to their rangers by the Jalora itself. Strong, intelligent, and devoted, their loyalty to their husbands was unshakable. Every ranger blessed the day his wife was sent to him.

Wolf's eyes drifted back to his own lovely bride. The other Ranger Wives followed Dulcina not because she was wife to a Lord of Valdeon, but for her own merits. Heralded as one of the greatest soloists on Andara, Dulcina used her voice for supporting many social causes as well as making heavenly song. He had been a confirmed bachelor for many years until he felt the touch of her hand. His heart belonged to only her.

"Cesar seems troubled, my love." She gave their old friend a fond smile. "Fausto. Jorge, how good it is too see you."

"I am far too irritable today." Cesar snatched the gruesome linen package from Wolf and tossed it behind him.

Wolf kept her hand in his and gave it a little squeeze. "Julian's friends are stirring up trouble, my love. I fear they will be outspoken in their objections during Leo's funeral."

"Julian has them ready to riot, I'd guess." Fausto's typical grin was missing. Anger replaced it.

"I suspect his plans may be far more subtle." Jorge ran his eyes across the crowd. "It would help his cause if the West was the first to draw more blood."

Dulcina let a sly smile cross her face. "I believe you may be right, my clever Lord Pacarro. Have you noticed the Ranger Wives are the only ladies present? I have it on good authority Prince Julian has ordered the ladies of court to leave San Leonora for the country estate of one of his allies. The only woman he will have near him is his half-sister."

Wolf shivered slightly as the Jalora's power ran along his spine. Prickles of warning lifted the hair on his arms. He hoped the other Lords of Valdeon were paying attention. Julian couldn't be trusted and would dare anything to take the throne. Edmund, the fool, had grown too bold in his dalliances with women. He had not waited for the Jalora's wisdom in choosing a bride. The black-hearted viper roaming the palace halls was a result of his disobedience.

"Perhaps, my love, the legion should leave intelligence gathering to our wives? You honor our house." He leaned closer to his squire waiting patiently for orders. "Basilio, tell Owl and Griffin the Lords of Valdeon fear a threat to our families. Have the Ranger Wives guarded. None of them are to wander about alone. Understood?"

His squire bowed low and hurried away. Heaven help any who tried to stop Basilio. Though he would never show his foul mood to his lord, others often suffered the brunt of it.

"May I escort you into the Great Hall, My Lady De Vincente, since this husband of yours must parade about with the other rangers?" Cesar took Dulcina's arm. "I warn you, Wolf. I may have Dulcina's heart by the time you've finished with the pomp and circumstance."

Dulcina gave the old ranger a kiss on the cheek. "You are the very essence of flattery, Cesar."

She and the other ladies entered the Great Hall. Their three escorts stayed close beside Dulcina, not just for the pleasure of her sweet company, but to protect her as well. He was grateful to them. If anyone tried to harm her, even the Jalora could not stay his hand.

Fausto reappeared at the doorway. Anxiety. Rage. Disbelief. They radiated from his old comrade's typically jovial energy. Something was wrong. Wolf cleared his mind and let the Jalora come to him. Yes. He could feel them now. Their hungry ambition was taking an ugly turn. Wrapping his power about him, he swept into the Great Hall to join Fausto. Shouts and rough shoves filled the room. Violence was moving dangerously close to Dulcina and the other ladies.

Julian sat at the head of the hall with his viper sister at his side. The pleased smile he gave Wolf was a clear sign his treacherous plans were already underway. His confidence was disturbing. The bastard prince's manner didn't contain any of his regular pretense as the grieving son. He knew something hidden from Wolf. It was time to probe the bastard prince whether Benito agreed or not.

"Someone must rule Valdeon until the heir is named. Julian is the last Prince of the D'Antoiné house. We must declare him Regent."

One of the Eastern prefects waved his hand toward Julian. Wolf recognized him. His name was Orryo. An ambitious man from a small province to the south, apparently he'd decided to enrich his station. What better way to move up in the world than to clutch at the Prince's coattails?

A western prefect, red-faced and patience exhausted, pushed through his comrades to face Orryo. "Esteban is the king's brother. The duty falls to him."

"You speak of a ghost! The king's brother has not stepped foot on these lands for years. What makes you think he'll come back?"

"I'll not see Julian the bastard prince upon the throne!"

Orryo flew at the western prefect with an angry growl. Wolf pushed his way through the crowd to reach them. Pulling the men off each other, he held them at arm's length as they struggled to continue their fighting. His demands for peace were lost among other shouts as the room exploded in furious movement.

Power raced suddenly along his back. Its warning alerted him just as another man with a dagger approached from behind. Wolf summoned the power to his arms. Yanking both men inward, he slammed the prefects together. They fell into an unconscious pile at his feet. Then Wolf turned in a whirl of ash to face his would-be assassin. Reaching the villain, he knocked the dagger away and grabbed him by the throat. Wolf lifted him off the floor until his feet dangled between them. He brought forth a ranger's deadliest weapon. A solid reflective surface completely covered Wolf's face, causing his features to disappear behind the cold silver. The death mask's power reached out to the assassin's very soul. It brought back the final moments of the man's life. His fear and his pain were reflected back to him within the cold surface. Many criminals and enemies described looking into a death mask as the single most terrifying experience a person could endure. Mortality is finite. Death is inevitable. None can escape it, but most feared what they would find at its door.

"Mercy! I beg you, my lord. Please grant me mercy!" He gripped Wolf's wrists, but his pathetic sobs were lost in the sea of fistfights.

Clang! Clang! The Great Hall's ceremonial bell pealed above the sounds of battle. Used for state dinners and other irritating court customs, its music was not designed to sooth. Rather its purpose in life was to drown out noise. Any noise. It worked well. Wolf turned with the rest of the men to see Jorge Pacarro standing upon a chair wildly ringing the irritating bell. The stunned crowd fell silent.

"Stop this bickering!" Jorge gave a final tug on the bell and then released its cord. "The welfare of the people of Valdeon must be considered first, not which D'Antoiné would be better suited to further your own selfish interests. You call me a barbarian from the West, but it is not I who dishonors the memory of our king and these ancient halls."

Wolf dropped the groveling man to the floor and released the mask. Jorge was right. He was only adding to the violence and dishonor. Resentment from the crowd thundered against Wolf's senses. The Pacarro tribesman's words had slapped them across the face. Jorge would have many new enemies after today. He hurried to stand beside Jorge, blocking a few of the prince's more ardent supporters.

"Do you imagine any but the Jalora will decide who rules Valdeon, you great fools? Chancellor Benito will remain in power. And the Lords of Valdeon will enforce his reign. Julian's plotting and planning will not see any of you rise higher within the court." Wolf let his furious gaze connect with each of the prefects. "Now, go and prepare yourselves to mourn our king. Do not test my patience further."

Julian's gaze bore through him from the doorway. The slithering snake had made certain his entourage was well away before the fighting began. He may not have ordered the attack upon Wolf, but Julian most certainly had instigated it. The challenge for battle had been issued. This fight, however, would not be fought like men upon the field of honor. Julian was using his weapons of deception to gain the throne. It would require all Wolf's cunning to win the day. Their country's future was at stake.

Eyes downcast and seemingly repentant, the prefects began to shuffle out of the Great Hall. Dulcina weaved her way between the sulking lords and came to stand beside Wolf. He took her arm, leading her out of the hall. She pulled gently to slow his angry march. He relented, allowing her to keep them at a dignified pace out the door and through the atrium. No one dared follow as she moved him out the door and into the palace gardens. Ignoring the beautiful flowers and shrubs lining the path, he sunk down on a bench under the nearest cherry tree. Dulcina rested her hands upon his shoulders and began rubbing away the tension she found there.

"Damn the entire D'Antoiné family!" he hissed, resting his head in his hand. "Hawk and Leo have both abandoned their duties, leaving that bastard son to lust after Valdeon. They have left our country exposed and weakened."

Oath breaker. He couldn't forget his part in the turmoil. The night Leo had visited, wounded and asking for help, Wolf should have locked him in a room and called the others. Leo may have listened to reason if Cesar were there. He shook his head. No. Leo hadn't heeded anyone's advice for many a year.

"My love," Dulcina wrapped her arms around his neck. "Valdeon has you to keep her strong. Why else would the Jalora grant you such strength and wisdom as its third seat? You have faith in the Jalora, and I have faith in you."

He clutched at her hand. She was his strength and his very heart. "I hope for the sake of our family I don't disappoint the faith you have in me."

"You never have." She came to stand before him and gently rested his forehead to her breast. "Our sons worship their father, and my heart could never be turned from you, my Wolf."

She brought his hand to rest on her belly and smiled at him. "Our new little one will love you as much as the rest of us do."

The happiness flooding his heart washed away Wolf's anger. He smoothed gently over his baby growing inside her. "Our third little blessing will bring much joy."

"You are one baby closer to those ten children you promised me, my love." Dulcina kissed the top of his head. "Now, you see? Everything will right itself. The Jalora will help you find the Lion Ring and its heir. He will rule Valdeon with your wise council, and our family will continue to grow."

Wolf stood and pulled her into his arms. He prayed she was right. Whatever the case, he must stabilize Valdeon until the Jalora was ready to reveal their new king. The future happiness of their family depended upon it.

Chapter Sixteen

J ORGE RAN HIS FINGERS ALONG the empty shelves of the vacant library. Once the Palace of Kings' book collection had rivaled the largest libraries in Andara. Now it stood vacant. Leo must have donated the precious collection to the San Leonora Library. A blessing in disguise. It would give him an excuse to visit the famed establishment while he was in the city. He was aching to find a book on the art of growing hybrid grapevines. The Pacarro family winery was due for a new blend.

A loud creek from ancient hinges echoed down the hall. He doused the light. This was a very old section of the palace. It housed many treasures from Valdeon's history. No one came here anymore except by special permission from the D'Antoiné Family. Despite being a friend to the Lords of Valdeon, it would be awkward explaining his presence in such a treasure trove of history.

Jorge backed into the shadows, waiting with the stillness of long years of training. His people were sometimes called the "Unseen Terror." They could disappear into the landscape and then sneak up upon their enemies, coming within feet of their quarry. It was a matter of pride that they could wear beads in their warrior braids and still not be heard. Other than a ranger in the Jalora Legion, only a Pacarro could move without making the slightest sound.

Three men passed by the darkened door of the library. The tallest was a bald man with a long scar along the back of his head. His short friend scampered alongside of him, regarding the treasures with a greedy eye. Orryo, the outspoken troublemaker, was among them. It was unlikely they had any more permission to be here than Jorge. He remained absolutely still as they crept by. Waiting until they were a little further down the hall, Jorge began to follow. The men were heavily armed. Obviously they weren't here to admire the priceless paintings lining the walls.

"Where did Prince Julian say it was?"

"It's supposed to be in one of these cases. He warned us not to break the glass." Orryo lifted his crystal lantern higher, casting shadows along the walls.

"How are we supposed to get it out then?"

"With the key, you idiot." Orryo held up a large brass key to show his inquisitive friend.

The bastard prince had sent his lackeys on a quest. Jorge, curiosity piqued, moved silently behind them. Orryo motioned to his friends when they stopped before the door of a massive space. Once a secondary dining hall, Leo's father had converted the space into a private family museum. Several glass cases stood in rows about the hall. Each case housed precious historical artifacts and family treasures. Strange. Julian was a son of the D'Antoiné Family. Why would he send these sneak thieves to steal what he could simply take?

Jorge kept to the tapestry-covered walls while they wandered between the rows of artifacts. Orryo finally stopped beside a glass case a few feet in front of Jorge. He gestured excitedly to his friends. They hurried over, their bodies blocking Jorge's view. He wanted to move closer, but cover was sparse among the glass cases.

Orryo leaned to his right for a moment, giving Jorge a brief glimpse inside. The case didn't contain any jewels or golden artifacts upon its shelves. Orryo carefully eased the key into the lock. Then a great whoosh sound burst into the silence of the room as the glass popped open. Jorge caught another unobstructed look at the contents of the case before the men huddled around the open door. Old music boxes and crude metal containers seemed unremarkable to him. Perhaps he'd been wrong about the importance of their quest?

"You take it." Orryo pushed at his bulky companion. "I unlocked the case. Someone else can touch it."

"What's wrong with you fools?" Their shorter friend pushed into the opening. He reached inside the case.

Orryo stopped him. "Have a care. They say magic protects it. Find something to wrap it up in."

Jorge crept closer to the open case as they scattered. The bright glitter of solid gold burst through its blanket of dust. His short burst of breath revealed an oval medallion attached to a heavy chain. Engraved within the gold was a chair with a sphere suspended above it. The image was very similar in nature to the symbol of the Altar of Providence. Only the Crown of Sorrows was missing. He didn't recognize the object, but if Julian wanted it obtained by dishonest means, then it was best protected.

Fast-moving boots echoed close by. Julian would do better to hire quieter thieves in the future. He grabbed the necklace by its chain, careful not to touch the medallion itself. One could never be too careful with magic, as his grandmother used to say. He crouched down behind a particularly dusty case just as the three thieves returned.

Orryo held a piece of fabric most likely ripped from one of the tapestries. Letting out a curse, he pushed aside the remaining artifacts within the case. Suspicious eyes turned back upon his comrades.

"It's gone! Which one of you took it?"

"Someone's over there behind the case. Hey, you there! Stop!"

Jorge ran through the cases in the direction of the door. Orryo gave chase. His two friends had taken rows on either side. It was a race to see who would reach the museum's door first. Their match ended abruptly when the glass case to Jorge's side fell over to block his path. The bulky bald man jumped over the ruined case and its fallen treasures. He pulled his weapon and stood like a human barrier between Jorge and the door. His short friend joined him seconds later. They had him surrounded. Jorge stood his ground with the chain hanging from his hand.

"Give me the Regent Medallion, barbarian." Orryo gripped his sword, waving its tip at Jorge's outstretched hand. "It doesn't belong to you."

Jorge's fingers tightened upon the powerful symbol he held dangling from his hand. Of course Julian wanted this treasure. Any man who wore the Regent Medallion around his neck would rule Valdeon — if there were no lion upon the throne, of course. It all made sense now. What better way to rule Valdeon if the king was dead and you knew the Lion Ring would never accept you?

The magic within the golden oval chose who would rule in place of the lion. And it didn't necessarily have to be a D'Antoiné. Even a minor landowner and thug could rule their nation if he had the medallion around his neck. The Lords of Valdeon would be bound by honor and duty to uphold his rule. They would have no choice. Any who opposed the new Regent would be called a traitor. He understood now the dangers Valdeon really faced. Hungry ambition began to grow in the eyes of the men surrounding Jorge. Julian may have commissioned Orryo to snatch the Regent Medallion, but the draw of power was sucking in another victim. Julian had competition for the throne.

"This medallion doesn't belong to you, either. It's going to the one man who can keep it safe."

Orryo lifted his wild eyes, taking in the new threat to his ambition. The tip of his sword swung slowly from one rival to the next. Jorge had seen such a look many times. Orryo was ready to kill all of them to take the treasure.

"Do you hunger for the throne as well, barbarian? A Pacarro tribesman as Regent of Valdeon, can you imagine such a ridiculous notion?"

"I am no more worthy to wear this than you are, Orryo. Listen to me. Valdeon's future is at stake. I must take the medallion to Xavier the Wolf. He'll know how to keep it safe."

Jorge chanced a look at the talisman in his hand. It could either save or destroy Valdeon. Magic or no, he must keep it safely out of the hands of Julian and his men. He tucked the medallion inside his shirt. Flinching at the cold metal, he let it rest against his skin. Power began to hum at his side, and a strange warmth grew within his torso. Saying a small prayer to the Erthe Mother, he readied his body for the desperate escape he must make.

"You aren't leaving alive, Ranger Stooge." Orryo's face had taken on a deadly, mad glower. "The Lords of Valdeon are relics like the trinkets in this room. We have no more need of the Sacred Guard or their Lion.

The Jalora, if such a thing truly exists, has no place in Valdeon anymore either. It is the dawn of a new era."

"Blasphemous fool! You dare insult the Jalora in its stronghold? You and your cohorts will never take the Regent Medallion."

Jorge pulled his hatchet and threw it in one well-practiced move. It stuck with a sickening thud in the bald man's forehead. Orryo and his short friend raced toward him, weapons striking downward. Jorge rolled across the broken glass and yanked his hatchet from its gruesome target. He swung the weapon up to meet Orryo's blade. Its deadly edge stopped inches from his throat. Tobacco and smoked meat scented his attacker's breath. Jorge kicked out, making contact with the man's knee. Orryo buckled. He fell with a howl onto the broken case. Jorge took the advantage and struck at his head with the blunt end of the hatchet. The short man's boot kicked the hatchet out of Jorge's hand before it could make contact. He lifted his sword, ready to thrust it into Jorge's heart.

"Halt or we'll fire!"

Four palace guards had their muskets trained on them. Brilliant red and gold uniforms stood out against the darkness. They were an impressive sight, almost too ornate to be functional. Jorge had seen them train for their duties. Vetted by the Valdeonian rangers, they were deadly shots. He raised his hands and stayed still. His short attacker wasn't as judicious. He jumped over the broken case and tried to run. A single shot echoed in the ancient halls. Howls of pain confirmed they preferred to keep their prisoners alive.

Their lieutenant stepped forward, taking in the scene. Men fighting among the treasures of the D'Antoiné family. One of the perpetrators dead. Jorge could imagine the criminal charges he was building up against them.

"It was the barbarian!" Orryo struggled out of the case. "He was trying to steal treasure. We stopped him. He killed my friend in his escape attempt."

"Would you like the lieutenant to search me, Orryo?"

Jorge slowly got to his feet, very much aware of the muskets trained upon him. He was bluffing of course. Jorge would do what was necessary to escape with the medallion. He had to make sure it was put safely into Wolf's hands.

"We can go before the entire court together and talk about tonight."

Orryo shifted his eyes from Jorge to the lieutenant. "An unnecessary inconvenience for the assembly during such a tragic time. You were stopped before taking anything."

"Silence," the lieutenant barked. "You'll get your chance to explain why you are in the museum without permission. I'm sure Prince Julian and Chancellor Benito will be very interested in hearing your case."

Going before Julian would be a death sentence. One Jorge was certain Chancellor Benito would enjoy carrying out. They'd have him buried deep in a hole before Wolf caught wind of any foul play. The Regent Medallion would find its way around Julian's treacherous neck while any hope for Valdeon faded away. No. He would kill or be killed before allowing such a thing.

"I demand you take me to the Lords of Valdeon. They are the only justice I will acknowledge in the East." Jorge retrieved his hatchet and put it in his belt. "Come now, Lieutenant. It is a simple request. If Wolf will not see me, then I will accompany you to my cell without further resistance."

The lieutenant regarded Jorge with the suspicious eyes of a man who knows he is on the verge of making a career decision. He dropped his gaze to the dead man again. To his credit, indecision was visible only in the small twitch of his fingers upon the trigger.

"Bind them."

Chapter Seventeen

WOLF RAN HIS FINGER DOWN the long list of names in the arrest log book. The rangers had found over a hundred possible traitors who had instigated violence around the palace in the past few days. He rubbed at his tired eyes. It was drawing close to midnight. Worry and frustration refused to let his mind rest. Never in his memory had so many foolish souls blatantly disrespected the Altar of Providence. In their arrogance, they were challenging the Jalora in its own house. He feared what their transgressions would mean for Valdeon.

Basilio placed a glass of amber liquid before him. Bourbon, a De Vincente family specialty, had been aged in barrels in caverns under his estate for as long as anyone could remember. Wolf took a long drink, closing his eyes as the warmth ran along the back of his throat. It was a much-needed taste of home.

His thoughts wandered to his estate in San Rudalfo. It seemed a lifetime had passed since he sat with Dulcina on their patio watching the stars. Their sons were tucked safely in their beds, sleeping in peace on such nights. Somehow he would find a way to restore order and take his family back to their simpler life.

Shouts and pounding boots invaded his daydream. He closed the log and covered his doodles of possible conspiracies. Wolf nodded to his squire with a sigh when the respectful knock came. Basilio didn't look pleased when he opened the door. He stepped back to allow the invaders entry.

Jorge Pacarro stood in the center of four palace guards. His wrists had been restrained. Several weapons were trained upon him as if he would break free at any moment. Wolf was well aware of Jorge's battle capabilities. They'd served together for many years. He was a fierce warrior, but he was also a wise man. The Pacarro tribesman stood patiently before them now, chin lifted high.

Basilio did not share his patience. "What the devil are you about? Release him at once."

"We've come to see My Lord De Vincente." Jorge gave Wolf a pointed look. "I will submit myself to his judgment."

Wolf probed Jorge quickly. The Jalora had wrapped its favor about him. Indeed, it had saved his life tonight. Strange. Something was different about his energy. Wolf scanned his body again. A palm-sized circle of blue-green power pulsed in the aura cloud just beneath Jorge's right kidney.

"You will release Lord Pacarro into my custody, Lieutenant."

"Yes, my lord. What of the other assailants?" the palace guard asked. "I have a dead man in the private family museum. Someone must answer for his murder."

"Hold them." Wolf gave Jorge another appraising look. "I will question these men personally in the morning."

The guards bowed, satisfied now that a Lord of Valdeon was going to solve the mystery for them. They released Jorge and left the room. Basilio handed Jorge a glass of bourbon with a huff of disapproval. Wolf ignored his show of temper. He led the other squires to the Lords of Valdeon and had once been Jorge's commander. The two men had come close to blows many times.

"And just what have you been up to, Jorge?" Wolf leaned against the desk. Curiosity had shaken the fatigue from his mind. Something important had happened tonight, and his old friend had played a key role.

"I went to the D'Antoiné family library to find most of the books packed away. Julian's men were roaming around as well. Their movements seemed suspicious, so I followed them into the museum." Jorge took a long gulp, emptying his glass. "They were attempting to steal the Regent Medallion. We have proof at last the bastard prince has designs on the throne, Wolf."

Basilio took Jorge's empty glass and refilled it. "They didn't get it, did they?"

"No, I was able to grab the medallion before they could lay their filthy hands upon it. I have it right here. I thought it would be safe with you, Wolf."

Jorge opened his shirt and reached inside to the spot where Wolf had seen the strange blue-green circle of energy. His face grew worried as his hand searched around inside. Stripping off his shirt, Jorge began to poke at the cloth. His fingers came away empty.

"That's impossible! I put it inside my shirt. I can still feel it's warmth upon my skin."

Wolf held his fingertips over the pulsing blue-green circle on Jorge's skin. He reached out with the Jalora. The strange circle of power was not a circle at all. Rather it was a shaft of energy penetrating deep into Jorge's being. He let his hand drop away.

A single word drifted into his mind. *Safe.*

Jorge's expectant eyes were upon him. Wolf took up his own glass again and drained it. The brave man before him had taken a great risk to save his homeland and defend the Jalora's honor. Would he be prepared for the consequences of his action? Perhaps it was wiser to keep the medallion's location to himself for the time being.

"Valdeon owes you a great debt, Jorge Pacarro. You have saved the Regent Medallion from the hands of the bastard prince and his followers. The Jalora is satisfied the medallion is safe."

Jorge nodded. "I heard them speaking of the medallion's magic, but wasn't sure what to expect. I'm glad it's safe."

Wolf nodded slowly and turned to look out the window at the darkened gardens beyond. This was troubling news. It was not surprising that Julian knew of the Regent Medallion, but the details of its magic were a well-kept secret. And such blatant blasphemy in the Palace of Kings must not go unpunished. The ruling class of Valdeon had grown complacent and disrespectful in the good graces of the Jalora. If they continued down this path, the Jalora's punishment would be fierce.

"We must take action, but without proof there can be no justice."

"I fear Julian and his allies no longer respect the Jalora in their thirst for power." Jorge had pulled his shirt back on and was fastening the front. "You're right, Wolf. We must have undeniable proof. I will be your spy."

He was a Pacarro, the last of the full-blooded plainsmen. If anyone could move about unseen — other than a ranger of course — it was him. His courage and loyalty were beyond question. It was a logical course of action, but the Regent Medallion must be considered as well. It had chosen Jorge's body as its new hiding place. The fatigue returned to Wolf's body in a wave.

"Very well, Jorge. I call you to service. Search these men out and discover their plan. We have no way of knowing how deep this conspiracy runs. You must stay hidden from everyone. Even Cesar and the other rangers. I want you to report directly to me. Tell no one else. Understood?"

"Yes, Wolf. It will be as you say." Jorge ran his hand over his right rib cage. "There's something you're not telling me. Isn't there?"

"Go, Jorge and the Jalora's blessings go with you." Wolf nodded to Basilio. His squire doused the lights and opened the window latch. Jorge Pacarro gave him one last look and then disappeared through the window into the night.

Chapter Eighteen

THE AUTUMN SUN AT HIS back, Seth stood facing his targets. An empty lantern oil can, discarded bottles, and a broken wagon wheel lined the short garden wall at the back of the McCloud home. He thrust the sword-length branch toward them. Twirling in unsure movements, he attempted to reenact Leo's battle the night before. The Valdeonian warrior's strikes, however, had been far more elegant than Seth's clumsy dance.

Lowering the branch, he rubbed at his sweaty forehead. Leo. He was another mystery to occupy Seth's thoughts. Clearly he was someone important. Why would he take a keen enough interest in Seth to journey all the way to Marianna? Perhaps it had something to do with Emma's promise to send a letter to his mother's friend asking for help in finding Edmund. Maybe his father didn't want to see the son he'd abandoned and sent this Leo in his stead? Sixteen years had passed on the island without him in their lives. Another sixteen could pass without his interference as far as Seth was concerned.

Body tingling in strange waves of power, he raised the stick again and struck at the wheel. Brittle spokes splintered under the savage attack. Collapsing into the ground in a pile of ruined wood and iron, the wagon wheel succumbed to its death blow.

"Put the silly stick down and stop messing about."

Emma let the back door slam shut as she tied her bonnet. A large, empty shopping basket teetered on her arm. He held it as she adjusted the ribbon at her chin. She hadn't worn her best dress today as was her usual habit. He suspected she wouldn't spend time gossiping among the other women in town. Not when her own household was the subject of discussion.

"I'll be at market for a few hours. You had best make yourself look busy when your uncle returns from town hall."

She gripped the handle of the basket, gave him one last disapproving glare, and exited the back garden toward town. He closed the back gate after her. Counting to ten, he hurried to the other side of the yard for an unobstructed view of the street. Seth was grateful for his unusual height this morning. He carefully peered over the fence, waiting for Emma's bonnet to disappear into the square.

Emma and Fergus had left him precious little chance to search his mother's bedchambers. Each time he'd paused by her door, one of them was quick to send him on his way. They weren't, however, as vigilant in guarding the rest of the house. It hadn't taken a great deal of searching for Seth to find his uncle's hiding place and the key to his mother's door.

Creeping across the floorboards toward the headmaster's study, he hurried inside. Sharp angled furniture and muted hues, the study was cold like its owner. He took hesitant steps toward the desk. A dull gray tobacco tin stood in a perfectly symmetrical line with the headmaster's quill and ink set. Seth opened it, crinkling his nose at the harsh aroma of strong tobacco. His fingers shifted through the dried leaves until they found the large silver key. He grabbed it, spilling some of the leaf bits upon the desk.

Turning away from the mess, he headed purposefully toward the staircase. His mother's bedchamber door stood at the top. Climbing the stairs, he was acutely aware of the silver key drawing closer to the lock. Anxious fingers slipped it into the keyhole. The lock popped. His hands paused at the knob. He'd waited for an eternity to look for answers; now the uncertainty of what he might find threatened to snatch away his nerve. Heart thudding in his chest and ears, he turned the knob and pushed open the door.

A wall of stale air stood vigil at the entrance of the darkened room. Cobwebs hung along the ceiling and bedposts, meeting in an intricate pattern along the wall. A layer of dust settled upon the neglected furnishings. Devoid of life, it looked like a tomb. He pushed through the feeling of gloom and entered the solemn chamber. His eyes were drawn to the bed where the Valdeonian guitar lay untouched. Unbidden memories came in a rush. Choking on her memory, he turned away.

Weak sunlight broke through the lace curtains. He pulled them open. A cloud of dust puffed into heavy air. He held a hand up to shield his nose and mouth. Well, there was light enough to search now, though the morning sun seemed irreverent in the room. Hardening his will with grim determination, he began looking through her wardrobe and trunks. Anne McCloud was all about him now. He rifled through her things, ignoring his hurt and the guilt he held invading her privacy.

Nothing. Piles of clothing and her drawings of Seth as a child littered the ground where he'd thrown them. He sunk down among her things in utter defeat. Weeks of waiting for a rare chance to search her room had turned up absolutely nothing. He'd convinced himself she'd hidden something important in her chamber. A clue to her past or the whereabouts of her Edmund would make the waiting worthwhile.

Then he noticed the nightstand beside her bed was a few inches out of place. Sliding across the short distance, he edged the tip of his finger between two floorboards slightly askew under its legs. One of them was loose. He pushed the nightstand carefully to the side and pried the board up. Inside a small, hollowed-out space in the floor were Anne McCloud's secret treasures.

He reached in and pulled out a stack of letters. They were tied together with an ornate pink ribbon. He ran his fingertip along the thick grade of the envelope. Expensive parchment, much nicer than any even Elder Newcastle used. He carefully flipped the bundle over and spread them apart for a quick glance. Ranging from sixteen years prior to a month before her death, they were all addressed to his mother in care of a post box in Port City on Eastland Isle. The handwriting was identical on each envelope and sent from the same address — Cottage on the Cliff, Isle of Carlotta.

Eastland Isle was a major air and sea port stop, connecting several island nations with the mainland and each other. He could understand why his mother had set up a post box for her secret correspondence there. Search as they might, it would take a hundred years to find someone on one of the many islands if they didn't want to be found. His mother's connection to the Isle of Carlotta wasn't as straightforward. Not much was known about the tiny island, except it rested a few miles off Valdeon's southern coast. How in the green, green fields had Anne McCloud come to know someone there?

It was best to read them away from prying eyes. He stashed the letters in his coat and reached in again. This time he pulled out a drawing sketched inside a banner from the Horner Isle festival. His mother — a beautiful young girl of seventeen or eighteen at the time of the portrait — smiled from the page. Ringlets draped along the material of the pretty dress she wore. It was a much different style than any he had seen her wear.

A handsome man dressed in a uniform of some kind had his arm wrapped around her waist. He held Anne against his chest, blocking Seth's view of the military insignia there. Their joined hands rested in his mother's lap. They looked happy. What had happened to make them part? Seth let out a long sigh. He had happened.

He held no doubt this was Edmund, Seth's father. The resemblance was striking. They shared the same cheekbones and strong chin. Even diminished in pencil and time, his father's amber-flecked eyes commanded full attention.

Rolling up the drawing, he tucked it inside his coat with the letters. The man who'd raised him would be home soon. No argument would be good enough to explain to Fergus why he had trespassed into Mother's room.

Satisfied her hiding place was empty, he almost missed the tiny crystal necklace. It glittered like the sun off the ocean's wave. A heart crystal, the very rarest of all gems. Could this be a love token from her Edmund? Seth absently lifted the silver chain over his head and let the stone fall inside his shirt.

"What are you doing in here?"

Fergus stood in the doorway. His body leaned forward in a rigid stance as if he were a cornered animal ready to spring. The headmaster's fierce gaze avoided the bed and stayed focused upon Seth. Guilt. He wore it like a cloak. Was his cold heart feeling remorse? Anne's death may have been avoided if Fergus had stayed home the night of her murder. He hoped the headmaster hated himself for it.

"Well!"

The frantic pitch of the headmaster's voice grated upon the last thread of patience Seth maintained. The growling scourge of Marianna was frightened. A frown began to work its way onto Seth's lips. This man was a coward and a bully. Too many years had been wasted pandering to his temper. Those days of dependence upon the headmaster were over. He wouldn't fear his empty threats ever again.

"I wanted Mother's guitar."

"Take it and get out. I won't have you dawdle inside your room all day. Go help Emma with the shopping, while I earn the livelihood for this household."

Seth grabbed the smooth handle of the guitar. It was thick with dust. He pushed past Fergus and headed toward his room. Resting the instrument upon the bed, his movements were slow and deliberate. Fury pressed at his self-control again. The strange, new power prodded impatiently, wanting to escape and take its vengeance upon the growling voice in his ear.

Suffocating in his rage, Seth left his room and headed toward the stairs. Fergus blocked his path. Arms gesturing wildly, the headmaster's body swayed in strange patterns of color. Distorted words passed through his growling lips. Seth grabbed the handrail to keep from tumbling down the stairs. His head buzzed with power. He pushed past his uncle, desperate for fresh air.

A hand gripped his arm. Seth tore it off his sleeve and twisted. Then he pushed the body away as if it were a lifeless lump. Fergus sprawled across the threshold of Anne's chamber, cradling his right arm. Seth stared blankly at the man. He'd pushed his uncle without thought or effort. He wasn't a killer, yet he ached to do the deed. It would be easy to make the groveling man before him submit. And why not? Hadn't he made others suffer? It would be a form of justice.

"I'm leaving. Don't follow."

The power intertwined with his words. Pictures hanging on the walls shook upon their nails. Plaster cracked and buckled beneath them. Seth stumbled down the stairs. He was suffocating in the living memories of this house. Reaching the door, he yanked the handle. It gave way, sending metal clanging to the floor.

Staggering along the iron rod circling town square, he headed west toward the edge of town. People crowded the busy marketplace. He tried to weave between them, but the control he had on his body was slipping away. Great gulls! He was going to hurt someone else. This time it might be an innocent.

Strong hands gripped Seth's shoulders, pulling him away from the path of a fast-moving wagon. Citrus and spices encircled him. Though Seth couldn't see his rescuer, he knew it was Leo. Falling against the man's body, he shook in helpless fits of rage.

"Deep breaths, Seth. The anger will leave when you are calm again."

Leo's words penetrated the buzzing in Seth's mind. He took a deep breath, taking in the citrus. The animal rage began to calm as if some memory brought about by the scent had sated its desire. He continued to breathe in the fragrance. The buzzing left his ears. He was in control of himself again.

"What is happening to me?"

Leo released his shoulders and stepped away. He was dressed in long, tan trousers with high boots and a white, billowing shirt. The sword Seth had seen the night at the pub was not on his belt. Leo looked quite ordinary in the afternoon sun.

"The question you ask is not an easy one to answer, my young friend. We must help you control your temper. Physical activity is good for this, yes? Dante and I load our wagon with supplies we've purchased for our farm."

He slapped a hand on Seth's back and guided him toward the front of McTavish's store. Dante was already loading supplies onto their flatbed wagon. Two isle ponies whinnied from the front as they approached. Seth hurried to lend a hand. Leo had helped him for the second time. Loading supplies was the least he could do.

"Dante and I have let the McPherson Farm to the west of town. Do you know it, my young friend?"

Leo's eyes suddenly shifted to the front of Seth's waistcoat. The necklace had worked its way from under his shirt. Glistening like a hundred stars, the heart crystal caught the sunlight and every passing glance. Seth quickly tucked it back in.

"That's a pretty thing, Cub. Where did you get it?" Dante waved a finger at the spot where the necklace rested beneath his clothing.

"It belonged to my mother, sir."

Dante nodded. He gave Leo a quick glance and then continued to load the wagon. Leo's hands were shaking as they gripped the side of the buckboard. He'd recognized the necklace. It held some meaning for him.

Seth bit at his lip. He wanted to know what relationship Leo had with his parents. What was the significance of the necklace Seth wore? Did his father suffer from the same fits of power? His nerve faltered.

"How did you move so quickly? I mean at the pub? Did you learn how to move as you did in the army? It was almost beautiful."

"Soon I will show you a bit more, yes?" Leo gripped his shoulder with a warm smile.

The Valdeonian's eyes shifted quickly toward the square where Constable McTavish escorted a drunken sailor outside the borders of town. Turning his face away from the two men, he leaned into the wagon and shifted a barrel of flour a few inches.

"Dante and I must return to our farm. You will come to visit us soon, yes?"

He jumped onto the driver's seat beside Dante. They pulled away without waiting for a reply. Seth stared after the intriguing man. Leo was entitled to his secrets. Heaven knew Seth had his own.

Walking down the Main Row, he headed toward the airship port. The entrance to his private sanctuary was hidden under the frame of the docks. The letters he carried weighted down his pocket. Hope was renewed. These secret letters must contain the answers he sought. Curiosity hurried his steps off the row and into the shadows of the port. Beatrice McFadden darted out of the structure as he circled around one of the pillars. Her hand covered her mouth as she wept. Eyes blurred with tears, she almost knocked him over. He caught the girl's arm to steady her.

"What is it? Are you hurt?"

"Ask Riley Logan if you must know!"

Seth pocketed the linen she refused to take from him. Stepping aside to let her go, he watched Beatrice make her lonely way back toward town. Tom Logan had been right about her crush.

He looked toward the cliffside. Riley must be there. Welcome news indeed. He hadn't seen his best friend since the night they'd landed in trouble with the constable. Mr. Logan had kept his promise to keep Riley busy on the farm.

A hand touched his shoulder. Staggering forward, Seth stumbled toward the ground. Riley gripped the back of his coat and pulled him upright.

"Sorry. Is the pest gone?"

"If you mean Beatrice, yes, she's gone and in tears."

"Well, serves her right I'd say. Following me around, calling me names." Riley tossed a stray rock at one of the pillars. "I can't wait to leave this rat hole. And I tell you this, Seth, I won't ever come back."

A loose board hung in the middle of the fence blocking entrance to the cliffs. He pushed it aside and shimmied through. The Sea Steps had been assembled and fastened to the rocky surface a few years after the colony was first formed. Spanning the height of the thousand-foot cliff, the steps ended upon a wharf. A lonely boathouse stood at its far end. Empty windows faced toward open sea. Seth spent many an hour inside this forgotten hideaway.

Intended for seafaring visitors, the steps had been decommissioned shortly after they had been completed. Amity raiders had used them to reach the surface in the most brutal attack in Haven Bay's history. Many settlers had been murdered and their woolies slaughtered.

Seth started down the steps, not stopping until they came to a large section of missing planks. The thick wooden beams used to support them extended empty toward the horizon. Beneath them, the sea raged in hungry anticipation. He placed his boot tips on the side beam anchored into the cliffside. The chain railing bolted into the cliff wall pulled taught under his grip. It smelled of rust and bird droppings. Sliding along the rock, he climbed to the next section of steps. These were intact and still strong. He landed on the first step with a thump. Riley landed beside him.

"Why are you in such a foul mood?"

Riley shrugged and continued the downward journey to the wharf. Seth waited. Something was bothering his friend, but nothing this side of a miracle would drag it from him before he was ready to talk.

"Dad will be glad to have me gone." Riley's voice was picked up by the constant breeze and carried over the waves. "The woolies got out again. They saw the fresh bunches of hay we bought from the McDermott farm and stampeded right over me. Dad thinks I'm useless. I'm a shame to him. Now don't shake your head, Seth. I heard him say it. Well maybe not in those exact words, but that's what he meant."

Seth gave his best friend a sympathetic nod. He understood perhaps better than anyone how much a word spoken in anger could wound. Mr. Logan was a kind man. Seth had no doubt he would mend things with Riley.

"You weren't meant for woolie farming. We'll find our own lives on the mainland. Come on. I have something to show you."

Boots pounding on the boards of the wharf, they headed for the boathouse. Seth yanked open the water-warped door. The familiar odor of brine and dust washed about them. Light from the sea-facing windows cast friendly patches of sunshine upon a long table and benches. Crates of unopened paper supplies stood beside a desk in the corner, waiting for a clerk who would never come.

Seth slid down onto one of the benches and pulled out the portrait of his parents. He handed it to Riley. His friend's eyes took in the picture for a moment and then lifted to search Seth's face.

"Dad said your mum told him this Edmund fellow was in the army. He looks just like you."

"There's more." He pulled the unread letters from his coat pocket. "They've been written in Valic. That's the language they speak in Valdeon."

"Oh. Can you read it?"

"Mother taught me." He unfolded the first letter and began to read aloud.

My dearest Anne. We've searched for Edmund, but the regimental commander refuses to give us any information regarding his whereabouts. They've promised to pass along one of my letters, but I haven't received word as of yet.

Courage, my dear friend. Edmund will come to you. He will be thrilled to find you carry his child. Do nothing rash. Your friend always, C.

"I wonder who this 'C' is? Mother never mentioned knowing someone on Carlotta."

"Maybe the other letters say where your real father is? Are you going to look for him?"

Seth stared down at the feminine ink swirls stretching across the parchment. "I honestly don't know. I can't think past finding my mother's killer."

He searched through the other letters, but they were simply responses to his mother's correspondence. This mysterious 'C' made reference to sketches his mother had drawn of Seth as he grew up. It was odd having a complete stranger know the intimate details of his childhood.

The last letter was almost as interesting as the first.

Anne. Of course you and your lovely son are welcome to come and stay with me at my cottage. It will be good to have company. I've been lonely since August died. Write to me and tell me when to expect your arrival.

Seth and Riley exchanged looks. This was someone who had answers. Would she share them with Anne's son? He tied the letters back up in the pink ribbon and put them in one of the desk drawers along with the picture of his parents. Mother had hidden them for a reason. It was best they remain hidden for now. The gargoyle coin and the vile he kept inside his waistcoat. They were his talisman.

"Remember the night we were attacked by the Tslavian man? I went to Paddy's after Fergus and I fought. A Valdeonian warrior was there. I suspect he knew my parents."

"Do you think this man could be your father?"

"This man's name is Leo."

He pictured those intense, amber-flecked eyes as they examined Seth's every feature under the light of Paddy's lantern. Was Leo his kin, or did all Valdeonians share their extraordinary eyes?

"He's a skilled warrior and faster than anything I've ever seen. Leo saved my life the night we met." Seth lifted his eyes to Riley's curious face. "He was a shadow of death moving amongst the sailors who attacked me."

"Why do you think he's here?" Riley plopped down on the bench across from Seth.

"He was in the square earlier loading supplies. They let the McPherson Farm, but I don't think they've come all this way to raise hay. I think he's here to help me."

A loud splash slapped water onto the wharf. It didn't sound like the steady beat of the waves. Something had fallen into the water. Seth stood up and went to the nearest window. Wet painted the boards at the edge of the wharf, but nothing else looked amiss.

"Could have been a seabird." Riley came to join him at the window.

The boards a few feet outside their window splintered as something round and black dropped from the sky. It had been heavy enough to smash through the wharf and into the sea. Then the roof above their heads rained down as another object found its mark. Seth and Riley dove to the side. The object, slowed by ceiling materials, rolled along the floor until it stopped at Seth's boot. It was a cannonball.

"What in the green, green fields is going on?" Riley stared at the cannonball as if it were a three-headed dog.

"Trouble. I think Haven Bay may be under attack again."

Chapter Nineteen

SETH GULPED IN THE BRINY air as they ran up the Sea Steps. The climb was a long one, even for young legs. Staying close to the rock face, they came to the missing section of steps. Jamie Newcastle stood waiting for them, thumbs stuck in his waistcoat pockets. The constant breeze from the sea tugged at his thick patch of brown hair. He smiled and waved.

"Ho, Seth McCloud. I've got news."

"What's happening in town? We were almost hit with cannonballs." Seth's shouts reached across the distance toward Jamie, but his urgency seemed to have no affect on the elder's son.

"I know. I dropped them. Needed to get your attention, didn't I?" Jamie rocked on his heels as he waited for them to climb across the gap onto the platform.

"You dropped them?" Riley lifted his fists. "The last one almost killed us, you half-wit!"

"Well there's the thanks I get for bringing good news. You've got visitors, Seth. Your mother's solicitors have come to give you an inheritance." Jamie poked Seth in the chest. "And here all this time I thought your family was poor. They gave me twenty credits to find you."

"My mother wore the same winter scarf I gave her for well over five years. Trust me. She had no inheritance money to leave me."

A bullet struck by Seth's boot. He and Riley pressed against the rock face, pulling Jamie with them. The shot had come from the airship port dock hanging above them. Another rang out, striking near the first. If they tried to go through the fence into the row, they'd be easy targets. Their only alternative was down.

"I hope you got your twenty credits in advance, Newstuffle," Riley grumbled and spat over the side of the platform.

"I don't understand." Jamie stared up at the docks. "Expensive clothes and nice manners. They seemed on the up and up to me."

"Come on. We're in for another climb." Seth pulled on Jamie's arm.

"Down again? There will be no escape off the wharf. What if they decide to beat us to death with cannonballs?" Riley stepped in front of Seth to block his path. "We have to get help."

"We'll be dead if we take one step through the opening."

Seth hurried across the beam, clinging to the rock face. If they stayed close to the cliff side, the shooter would have less of a target. He eased a boot onto the first step past the gap and moved down, so Riley could join him.

"Hurry on, old grandmum!" Riley called over his shoulder to Jamie.

The elder's son had one foot on the beam. The other was mounted like a stump upon the platform. He wasn't moving. None of the other Marianna boys were keen to try the climb to the wharf. Seth and Riley were the only ones who had actually made it past the gap.

Another shot struck the wood upon the platform by Jamie's foot. He yelped and pushed his body forward out onto the beam. Apparently Jamie had decided the threat of a bullet was more frightening than the thousand-foot drop down a rock cliff. Beads of sweat rolled down his pudgy face, matting dull brown hair against pale skin. Sheer terror shown in his eyes.

"Easy, Jamie." Seth switched places with Riley and extended his hand to the frightened boy. "Take it slow. Don't look down."

"Great gulls. If he moves any slower, we won't make the wharf until sundown." Riley leaned over Seth's shoulder. "Hurry on! You're almost done."

Jamie gave Riley a sour frown and shuffled a bit faster until he was within arm's reach of Seth. Batting away their hands, he made ready to jump onto the first step. A sudden sensation of unease rippled along the back of Seth's neck as he watched the elder's son. His eyes were drawn to the step his own foot rested upon. Odd. It was vibrating upon the breeze.

"Jamie, wait! Don't!"

He pushed Seth's hands away and leapt onto the step with a triumphant smirk. Wood cracked and split. Jamie fell toward the ocean waves as the step — which had held Seth and Riley's weight for years — snapped into pieces. Then Jamie was gone, leaving a panicked silence behind him.

"Help!" A voice came from below them.

Staying close to the rock face, they looked cautiously into the gap. Jamie was dangling from the side of the cliff twenty feet below them. Bruised and bloodied knuckles held an ancient tree root in their panicked grip. The wind caught his coat, twisting the top of Jamie's body a bit further out into the gap. He stamped the toe of his boots upon a tiny ledge to restore his balance. Jamie was a stranger to exercise. He wouldn't be able to hold on for much longer.

"I'm coming for you! Hold on tight and don't look down."

"Seth!" Riley pulled at his arm. "You can't climb down the rock face. You'll be killed!"

"I saw a rope at the top of the stairs beside the opening. It should be long enough to reach him. Go, Riley. Hurry!"

Riley slid across the beam in cautious movements. Troubled blue eyes cast a last look down at Jamie. Then he sprinted up the stairs. Seth's stomach tightened as the stomping of his work boots on wood faded. Jamie's frightened eyes found Seth. In the brief moment of contact, a horrible truth passed between them. Riley wouldn't make it back with the rope in time.

Seth took his boots and stockings off. He moved to the gap and stretched out across the rock to get a good grip. His bare feet and hands moved down the cliff face. He made the descent slowly. One slip could kill them both. Muscles feeling the strain, his body began to tremble.

"Hurry! I can't hold on much longer."

He was getting closer and chanced a look down. Jamie's anxious face stared up at him from ten feet away. It may as well have been a hundred. Nature was against him. Its elements challenged every inch of his climb. Briny wind slapped at his face and tugged at his hair. Moisture from the violent sea coated the rock beneath his fingers. Moss and other permanent ooze hadn't formed at this elevation yet. Jamie had been lucky there.

Seth eased down to the next set of footholds. Beneath him was a large mass of smooth rock spanning the width of the gap. It stood like a chasm between them. Great gulls. How was he supposed to get around it?

"Why aren't you moving?"

"Easy, Jamie. I don't have any more footholds. Hang on. I'll find a way to reach you. I promise."

Dull eyes fill with desperate hope pooled with tears. Jamie nodded. Seth forced an encouraging smile. Arms aching with effort, he leaned into the cliff and shifted his body weight onto his feet. Rugged terrain covered the cliff side to his right. Several hand and foot holds lined the way, but following the holds would lead them away from the opening. He turned his face to the left. The steps hung in a downward slope. Perhaps they could climb sideways until they reached the beams?

One look at Jamie's sweaty face dashed his hopes. He'd seen the look in the eyes of the woolies headed for shearing. Terrified, his natural inclination to run from danger had been thwarted. He, like the woolies, clung to the nearest mass. Fear was swiftly draining away the control over his body. He'd be frozen where he was if Seth didn't get him moving.

Something smacked against his back. He was so startled he nearly let go. It was a rope. Thank you, Riley Logan! He owed his best friend a night at Paddy's for this. Seth grabbed the lifeline and gave it a tug. It held firm. He wrapped the rope around his waist and walked his feet slowly toward Jamie. Balancing upon the small ledge, he untied the rope and wrapped it around Jamie's waist.

"Start climbing. Riley will help as best he can to pull you up."

The elder's son held firm to the tree roots even as the rope pulled taut. Seth, unable to let go completely of his hand holds, began swatting at Jamie's fingers. The second hard smack to his cheek woke the boy up. He let go of the root and was immediately tugged upward at a surprising speed. His feet soon disappeared over the edge.

Seth waited anxiously for his turn with the rope. His arms were beginning to ache with the effort. The tips of his toes began to shake. Keeping his mind off his tired body, Seth peered up at the bottom of the steps. It was a rare view. Then he saw something he'd not expected. Most of the wood on the broken end of the support beam was smooth. It had been partially cut hours before. Someone had hacked at the beam while he and Riley were reading his mother's letters. They'd known when some unsuspecting soul put his weight on it, the beam would give way. A shiver raced along Seth's spine. Luckily, both boys made it their practice to stay close to the rock wall as they climbed up and down the stairs.

The plan had been thorough. A fall from the Sea Steps would be readily viewed as an accident by the town. Only one person on Marianna had enough hate in his soul to devise such a plan. Seth rested his head against the chilly stone. He'd been searching for clues to Sandor's whereabouts. All the while, the assassin had been waiting for another opportunity to strike. Like a fool, he'd walked right into the trap. It wasn't a game of wits anymore. Rather, it was a matter of survival.

The rope slapped at his back again. Seth tied off and began the climb. A man's arms reached down as he neared the top. Constable McTavish helped him onto the platform beside a shivering Jamie. Sergeant Gunn kept a comforting hand upon the frightened boy's shoulder. His keen eyes searched the docks above their heads from which the shots had been fired.

"Constable McTavish!" Seth gripped at the man's arm. "Pavel Sandor set the trap. He meant the fall for me, not Jamie."

The constable kept a tight hold on Seth and Jamie as they pushed through the opening in the fence. It was much wider now after the militia had stripped off several boards. Drawn by the gunfire and commotion, a large crowd had gathered under the airship port. Riley stood in its center, held firmly in place by one of the militia. His head was lowered and he shuffled his boots in the dirt as the militiamen gave him an earful. They were in for it this time. Trespassing on the Sea Steps was against the law. It was one of Marianna's most serious offenses. Now the elder's son had almost died. This would be the talk of Haven Bay for years to come.

Sensations of foreboding returned along his neck and arms. Seth looked up at the docks. The tip of a musket barrel poked through two crates above their heads. Great gulls! The madman was going to shoot into a crowd of innocent people to get to Seth. What if he missed and hit one of the curious children hanging on their mother's arm?

"Listen to me. You have to let me go right now, Constable."

Seth planted his bare feet into the dirt. Tugging and twisting, he desperately yanked away from his captor. The constable, trying to hold onto Jamie as well, lost his balance. The hold on Seth loosened. Tugging his sleeve out of the constable's grip, he started to run.

Wagons, overflowing with multi-colored wool, filled the Main Row headed from Elder Newcastle's warehouse to the airship port. Seth darted between them. Coming too close to one of the skittish ponies, he rolled out of the path of its stomping hooves. The ponies tugged at their reins, startling the driver. Wool bounced precariously as the wagon veered off the row. It pitched wildly, finally tipping on its side. Bolts of wool flew into the dirt.

The driver, who had mercifully landed in the grass, hobbled out from behind the wreckage. "Young hooligan! You've ruined the wool. Families depend on the money made from their woolies. Have you no concern for your neighbors?"

Seth knew exactly how hard the woolie farmers worked to get their wool to market. He'd spent many an hour at the Logan farm on shearing day. Forgiveness would not come after what he'd just done. Angry faces approached the scene. Behind them, a lone man ran between the pillars of the airship port with a musket over his shoulder. They were safe from his weapon for a time.

Constable McTavish raced toward them, puffing and red-faced. He let out a horrified curse as he stared at the mess. Pulling out his irons, he grabbed Seth's arms and slapped them on his wrists. The weight of the metal couldn't be compared to the weight of the angry stares from the crowd.

"Look what you've done. What would your good mother say, Seth McCloud? There's no help for it. I have to take you in." Constable McTavish pulled him toward town. Seth hopped over pebbles and mud, trying to avoid sharp objects. The constable regarded his bare feet without much sympathy.

"You won't need boots where you're going."

Chapter Twenty

Wool and Wagon Littering the row. Farmers and merchants calling for Seth's head. This day couldn't possibly get worse. Riley scrunched down behind the corner of town hall. Afternoon shadows made criss-cross patterns across the dark blue door of the police station. The angry crowd of gawkers had finally moved on, leaving strained silence around the buildings. Seth had really made a mess of things this time. Every soul on Marianna had reason to want him punished. Even the two militia men holding Riley by the entrance of the Sea Steps had thrown back their catch. They were anxious to help corral the wild boy running around the row.

He'd stayed hidden, following the crowd as the constable paraded his prisoner through town square. People who'd known Seth his entire life were shouting for his removal from the island. Other eyes, strangers from what he could tell, were watching Seth's march to the police station too. He doubted their keen interest had anything to do with ruined wool.

The Haven Bay he'd known since childhood had become foreign. It was too exposed and dangerous now. He had to get Seth out of jail and into hiding somewhere. Maybe they could go to the northern farms for a while until things calmed down? He pulled out his purse and counted the coins they'd saved for their trip to the mainland. Two hundred credits, all he had in the world. He put them into the dirtied purse and stuffed it back into his waistcoat.

Two hands slapped down on Riley's shoulders. Convinced it was the militia or worse, he wiggled under their grip in a vain attempt to escape. Then he got a good look at the work boots and turned to see Tom grinning at him.

"You gave me a start."

"Aye, I'll bet. I can guess your plans, Little Whiskers." Tom crouched down beside him with a crooked smile.

"Seth and I have to leave Marianna. We don't have a choice."

"You do have choices, and the first you should make is talking this through with Dad. I used to be like you, Riley. The mainland was this exciting, faraway place I longed to explore. I couldn't wait to leave Marianna." Tom shook his head with a sad smile. "My adventure was exciting at first, but soon I came to realize the mainland is no place for Islander folk. You've no idea of the many terrifying things in the world. We're safe and protected here in the Isles."

Tom's eyes stared passed him at the stone of the hall. "I was in a war. I never told the family, because I wanted to protect you all from it. The horrors man commits against man…"

His face was stone. Warm eyes had become ice. The once familiar voice turned gruff before trailing off into silence. What had happened to Tom Logan? He'd changed into someone the family didn't recognize. In truth, Riley liked him much better this way.

Tom came back to himself at last. His lips forced a smile. "Go buy yourself a good time in Haven Bay, Little Whiskers. Come home late and get up early to work. If you set your mind to it, you can learn to handle the herd."

"And what about Seth? I won't abandon him."

"Listen to me, Little Whiskers." Tom gripped Riley by the arm and pulled him to his feet. "Seth has changed since his mother died. Now, stay still and listen. He has changed, and everyone sees it but you."

Riley folded his arms and gave Tom his sternest frown, but he couldn't escape his brother's firm grip. What was wrong with everyone? Seth McCloud was still the honest, kind person he'd always been. True, he was going through a rough patch, but Seth would come out of it.

"Paddy tells me Seth faced down a room full of sailors the other night in his common room. And he said Seth looked wild, half mad. He's headed for real trouble. I don't want to see you hurt with him."

Seth had fought off strangers on his own? He hadn't mentioned it on the wharf. Secrets. Seth's life seemed full of them. Riley had noticed the change in his friend. Tom was wrong there. Sometimes when he'd catch Seth brooding, a strange sort of barely contained rage hung about him. It seemed to grow stronger as the days passed. What had happened to the shy, polite-to-a-fault boy he'd grown up with?

"I can't leave him in jail."

"No, I suppose you can't."

Riley gave his older brother a grateful nod. A welcome bond formed between them, eldest to youngest. It was a bond he shared with Seth — more than mere friendship. The words wouldn't come to describe it. Riley supposed he would trust Tom Logan with any secret he had after today. Tom had come back a wiser man, but he was dead wrong about Seth. They all were.

Riley wouldn't abandon his best friend, no matter what anyone believed.

"I've got to get back to help George load the dry goods."

Tom gave Riley's shoulder a final squeeze and walked back toward the market. He was grateful his eldest brother hadn't tried to stop him from rescuing Seth. It hurt a little he didn't stay to help. Their dad had been right all those weeks ago. Seth was alone in the world, but he still had one friend left. Riley wouldn't let him down.

A loud bang brought his attention back to the police station entrance. Shuttering on its hinges, the door vibrated in blue streams. Fergus McCloud marched out of the jail, hands behind his back and robes billowing around him like an angry storm cloud. Constable McTavish, face flushed with anger, marched after him. He grabbed the headmaster's arm and spun him about. Low, angry words were thrown in a rush. Riley was too far away to hear the exchange, but he could guess at what was being said. The headmaster yanked his arm from Constable McTavish's grip and limped away in furious strides. The constable stared after old Fussbottom with obvious hatred. He headed back toward the station. Stopping at the front door jamb, Constable McTavish gripped its edge so tightly Riley thought the wood might crack.

"Where's Seth, Constable?" Riley asked, crossing the distance between them.

"The stubborn fool is leaving young McCloud behind bars." He gave Riley's face a good long stare. "You can go on home. The elder has his troublemaker behind bars to 'pay his debt to society' as he puts it."

"And after he saved Jamie. I don't suppose you'd let him out? Maybe release him into Dad's care?"

Constable McTavish shook his head. "No, Elder Newcastle would never allow it. Won't even listen to his son's account of what happened. Wish I'd let young McCloud go this morning. Our chase through the wagons was partly my fault. The boy has enough trouble in his life."

Riley nodded. Elder Newcastle had taken a dislike to anyone bearing the name of McCloud. He took every opportunity he could to put a bur in the family's boot. Seth's accident had cost the Newcastles a sizeable amount of profit today. It appeared the elder was intent upon getting his revenge this time.

"How much money will it take to get Seth out?"

The constable rubbed at his bushy mustache as it dropped downward. "The elder wants one thousand credits, but I supposed I could manage with five hundred."

It was a fortune! Riley walked dejectedly out across the town square. They had two hundred saved up between them. It had taken years to gather what only yesterday had seemed a good amount. Poor Seth. Riley couldn't leave him in jail alone. He stuffed his hands in his pockets and sank down on a bench to think. Who would loan him the money? Not many people in Haven Bay had three hundred credits hidden around the house.

"Paddy!" Riley snapped his fingers.

Racing down Main Row, he didn't stop until he came to the pillars of the airship port. They'd cleaned up the wool and wagons while he'd lurked outside the police station. No one was about. Piles of fresh fencing lined the old barrier next to the entrance of the Sea Steps. They'd be closing it up soon. He gave a quick scan around to make sure the coast was clear, and then stepped onto the platform.

Seth's boots were still propped against the cliffside. Unfortunately, they were on the wrong side of the gap. An unaccustomed anxiety sent his nerves twitching. He'd gone across the gap a thousand times. Of course the last crossing had been under musket fire. Gritting his teeth against the fear, he stepped upon the beam.

Riley stayed close to the rock face and leaned over from the safety of the side beam to grab the boots. Seth's stockings had been swept away by the wind hours before. He buckled the boots together and propped them on his shoulder. The trip back to the platform seemed much longer now that the winds had picked up to strike the cliffs. Most likely there would be no more climbs down the Sea Steps for him.

Keeping low beneath the pillars, he stayed to the side of Main Row until he was well away from town. He kept to an inconspicuous pace and headed west. Paddy's pub wasn't far. He could borrow the money and be back at the police station to pay Seth's bail by suppertime. A few months of working in the evenings would repay their debt. It may even be exciting being paid to spend time around travelers from different lands.

Music and chatter from the pub buzzed on the breeze. Riley flew up the wooden stairs and through the doors to the common room. It was crowded with men hooting in time to Old Ned's fiddle. Elbowing his way through revelers, he pushed his way toward the bar. Teb stood behind the long wooden island in a sea of noise. Practiced hands poured drinks for the patrons. Paddy had left him on his own.

Riley waved his arms to catch Teb's attention. It took several minutes for Teb to work his way to Riley's end of the bar. He'd had his hands full, taking orders and laughing at bad jokes. Each tankard robbed Riley of another hold upon his temper. Seth was locked in a tiny cell with no means of escape. What if one of those killers had gotten himself arrested on purpose or pretended to be a visitor? He had to get his friend out of Haven Bay tonight.

"Well, didn't expect to see you this evening, Riley." The young man gave him a nod as he leaned against the bar.

"Where's Paddy? I need to speak with him."

"You'll have to wait a while. He left this morning for Larkspur to pick up some supplies. Won't be back for a week."

Hopes dashed, he moved back outside in the late afternoon sun. Mum would be ready to serve supper by now. He'd definitely get a good tongue lashing for being this late. Sinking down on the bottom step, he put his chin in his hand. What would he do now? Perhaps he could go to Emma? She might have their household money. No, they couldn't pay it back before old Fussbottom noticed the money missing.

Two sailors walked past him, speaking in their strange tongue. Seth probably knew the language. He seemed to collect languages as a hobby. His best friend was as clever as they came. If their situation had been reversed, no doubt he would have Riley's bail by now.

His thoughts drifted to the Valdeonian warrior who'd saved Seth next to these steps. He'd been quick enough to lend aid before; perhaps Leo would be willing to part with the extra credits now? He took a deep breath and pushed away from the steps. It wasn't in his nature to beg — especially from a complete stranger, but for Seth's sake he'd try.

Chapter Twenty-One

It was a fair walk to the McPherson Farm from Paddy's. Riley crossed the Main Row, hopping over the short stone fence into the fields. His boots stomped over the soggy ground as he headed north. The McPherson Farm was the last property on Farm Row, before it headed away from Haven Bay and journeyed toward the northern farms. His legs were aching by the time he shuffled over the stone fence and landed on Farm Row.

Crumbled stone pillars marked the entrance. Riley shook his head, hoping this Leo wasn't a complete fool. Some deceitful thief had let the McPherson Farm to the two foreigners. Abandoned by its original owners years ago, the land had become overgrown with weeds and wild. A farmhouse and barn stood at the south end of the fields. Unkempt and vandalized by weather, neither was fit to house a stray dog.

Passing between the crumbling stone markers, he marched up the narrow lane, climbing the steep hill toward their farmhouse. Its surface had been grated smooth by horse and hitch. Weeds and overgrowth had blocked half the road for as long as Riley could remember. Now the shrubs were nicely trimmed away from the lane, and not one weed popped its head out of the dirt. This Leo had certainly cleaned up the place.

He stopped at the top of the hill. Rubbing the back of his neck with a sweaty palm, he gazed down upon the farmyard. Smoke puffed from the chimney. In the distance, an axe chopped firewood. He moved closer to the farmhouse, keeping to the cluster of trees along the hillside. The chopping stopped abruptly. Riley wondered if the man was going to his supper. A full stomach would make him more agreeable to a loan.

Stepping around a large tree in hopes of getting a better look, he tumbled into a man kneeling beside the trunk. The man rolled to his feet and turned on Riley with sword drawn. Another intruder jumped out of the thicket to Riley's right. Dark brown cloaks hid their bodies in the autumn dusk. Golden rings swung from piercings in body parts not meant for such things. Hideous black tattoos swirled in painted bands across their faces. Each design aimed at terrifying their victims. Amity raiders! How had they come to be this far inland without the militia seeing them?

"Where is D'Antoiné? No lies now, dung farmer. We've been watching you."

Cracked lips parted against blackened teeth as the man struggled to form unfamiliar words. Amity raiders stuck to the old Islic amongst themselves, but they knew enough words in the common tongue to rob their victims.

"I don't know what you're talking about. I don't know any D'Antoiné."

Riley had learned enough old Islic from Seth to hold his own, but responding in their own tongue didn't win him any trust. Their leader pulled his short sword and held its point at Riley's throat. Cold steel pressed into his exposed skin. No weapons and no aid within a field's width. He was done for unless he could fight his way out of the trees. Riley tightened his hands into shaking fists.

A flash of silver whisked past his face. Both raiders fell to their knees, a clean red line across each of their throats. Then their heads fell to the side, rolling into the grass. A tall Valdeonian stood over the bodies. Gray mixed with the dark of his shoulder-length hair. Strong features were checkered in shadow as the sunlight struck him between the branches. Intense brown eyes flecked with amber stared down at the two dead men. Great gulls! It could be Seth standing before him if age hadn't shown upon the man.

The warrior slipped his blade back into its sheath without a sound. Riley's knees buckled as those fiery eyes turned upon him. His stomach churned with an angry growl and he vomited into the dry grass. Riley sat back on the cold ground and closed his eyes, still seeing the blood leak from the two dead men.

"Are you well? Ah, here is Dante with the wine skin. Drink! You look as if you would crumble."

Dante was a balding older man with white grizzled hair and bright, dark eyes. He knelt beside Riley, lifting a bag made of smooth leather to his lips. Riley sipped the wine. It was strong and had a spicy bite to it. Dante lifted the bag a bit higher, forcing him to gulp rather than sip.

He pulled Riley to his weak legs with an amused chuckle. "I'm not sure we should be showing such hospitality to a trespasser, Leo."

"I came to see you, Mr. Leo. But I found these two instead."

The warrior's eyes focused on his victims again. He knelt down beside one of the dead raiders. Riley turned quickly away as he threw open the man's cloak to search the body. Dante put the skin back to Riley's lips. He drank gratefully.

"What did they want? I didn't understand them. Their accent is strange, yes?"

Leo came to his feet and stood away from the bodies. There wasn't a drop of blood upon his clothing or boots. The warrior didn't look upset in the least by killing two men. He could have been on a stroll through the countryside for all the emotion he was displaying.

"They wanted me to tell them where D'Antoiné was. How would I know unless they still think Seth is this D'Antoiné person?"

"Still? They have called Seth a D'Antoiné before?"

"He fought off the raiders last time they attacked the island. One of them called him by the name." Riley looked down at his hands. "Seth, well, he's the reason I've come to see you."

"Oh? And you are a friend of his, yes?" Leo asked, folding his arms and waiting calmly for Riley to continue.

"Aye, sir. I'm Riley Logan, Seth's best friend." He took a deep breath and burst into his explanation. "Seth is in trouble. He would never have sent me himself. He's just that proud. You see, we had some goings-on today in town, but it wasn't Seth's fault. Constable McTavish locked him up in jail. I can't leave him in there on his own."

Leo moved with a grace Riley had never seen in all his life. A spicy sort of smell came with him as he walked. It reminded Riley of those wonderful meals Anne McCloud had made for special occasions. Gripping his shoulder, the Valdeonian looked deeply into Riley's eyes. A soft wisp of a touch brushed against his mind. Then it was gone, taking his anxious thoughts and horror at the violence away.

"Let's walk to the constable together, my young friend. And you will start from the beginning. Tell me about the death of Seth's mother."

"I'll just take care of the bodies by myself, shall I?" Dante kicked at one of the dead raiders.

His cursing followed them as Leo guided Riley onto the lane toward town. The Valdeonian warrior didn't seem flustered by the other man's anger. He walked beside Riley as if he didn't have a care in the world. Listening intently to Riley's account of Seth's hardships, he limited his interruptions to ask questions about the night Seth had found his mother's body. Leo showed a keen interest in the stranger Seth said to have saved him from the killer Pavel Sandor. He was also pointedly interested in the death of the Tslavian sailor. Riley wished he'd known more, but Seth hadn't shared a great deal of details.

"Seth's had a hard time of it since his mother left us, sir. He's not mad or troubled like they say. The Creator knows he has the right to be, the way old Fussbottom treats him."

"Fussbottom?"

"Aye," Riley grinned. "That's what we call the headmaster, Seth's uncle."

A frown crossed Leo's face for a moment and then was gone. The amber flecks sparkled like Seth's did when he was angry. Sharp features upon the older man's face were a familiar match to a much younger bearer. He couldn't be a random stranger. Leo must be a relative to Seth and his father.

"Are you kin to Seth, sir?"

Leo smiled and began to laugh. "You might say so."

"Riley Logan!"

Mrs. Logan marched up the dirt path toward them, her yellow skirt gripped in her fists. Streaks of gray hair — she claimed her boys had given her — spilled out of her lopsided hair bun. Sharp green eyes flashed in a fury toward them. Pale cheeks glowed red from exertion. He'd not seen Mum this riled since, well, never.

"What do you think you're about, boy?"

Her voice crossed the distance between them with ear-piercing clarity. A few crows plucking at the empty landscape about them had sense enough to take flight. Riley shuffled on the road, feeling like a small boy. He knew she didn't want to hear any answer he could give her and waited for the angry tirade to finish.

"Woolies loose from their pen, while you gallivant with Seth all afternoon! And what happened to your clothes?" Her inflamed eyes looked past his shoulder toward Leo. "Who is this? One of the drunken bums from Paddy's, I'd wager?

"No, Mum! This is Leo, one of Seth's kin." Riley turned an apologetic face to Leo. To his relief, the Valdeonian was chuckling.

"It is a pleasure, my lady. I am kin to Seth as you say."

Mrs. Logan allowed Leo to take her hand. A blush swept up his mum's face as the Valdeonian kissed her worn skin. Leo had a charm and sophistication Riley knew he could never muster. It had the desired effect. His mum's countenance softened, and she gave him a begrudging smile.

"Are you now?" She looked Leo over. "I'm glad to know you. Anne was a dear friend to me, and Seth may as well be one of my bunch."

"You're most kind, Mrs. Logan. I'm sure Seth is as grateful as I for your friendship."

Riley's mouth gaped open as his mother gave Leo a deeper blush. He hadn't seen her this red since the washroom door fell open and the family saw her bare bottom.

"Won't you come to supper, Leo? Any kin to Seth and Anne are welcome in our home."

Leo kissed her hand again. "My thanks to you, Mrs. Logan. Another time, perhaps? Unfortunately, I must go to Seth. He has run into some trouble."

"Oh?" Mrs. Logan gave Riley a sideways glance. "Is it anything serious? Do you think you can help him?"

"I will try. Good night. Riley, I hope to see you again soon."

They stood quietly in the fading twilight, watching the handsome warrior walk toward Haven Bay. If anyone could help Seth, it was Leo. Confidence. Leo had it by the bucketful. Riley supposed anyone who could kill two men so quickly had the right to be confident.

A hard slap struck the back of his head. Leo's magic spell had left with him. Mum glowered at Riley with hands upon her hips. Her fury had returned.

"Back to the farm with you, boy! You'll have a full day's work catching up on your chores. Your dad will have a few words to say to you when we get home." She pushed him forward toward their farm.

Riley shoved his hands into the pockets of his breeches. Thomas Logan didn't have to say another word to his youngest son. He'd made himself clear. Riley wouldn't be a burden for his family much longer. He'd go with Seth and make his own fortune in the world. Casting a quick glance at his mum's stern face, he was certain he wouldn't be missed by the Logan family.

Chapter Twenty-Two

DEEP BREATHS. LEO HAD told him to take deep breaths to chase his anger away. Seth rested his head on the cell's hard pillow with his arm over his eyes. It wasn't working. Each jingle of keys and slamming cell door heightened his unease. Power prickled along his neck and spine. He turned on his side to face the wall. All this time he'd been hunting for his mother's killer, Sandor had been setting up a trap for him. The man was a renowned assassin. It had been foolish not to take precautions.

A hand shook him gently. Mulling his own thoughts, he ignored the touch. Then the hand grew more insistent, rolling him onto his back. Seth grumbled a curt, unintelligible warning and rubbed at his blurry eyes. Amber fire burned through Seth's mental fog. The intensity of those eyes brought him fully awake at last. Leo? Seth bolted upright on the little cot. Great gulls. Leo was the last person he'd wanted to find out about his criminal exploits.

"Come, we go." He put Seth's boots on the cot. "Your friend Riley went back for them when he came to ask for my help."

Seth nodded, silently brushing the dirt from his bare feet. Tiny scratches and a large bruise on his big toe ached as he pulled on his boots. Such discomforts and more were well deserved. He'd dragged Riley into more danger than a good friend should. Ruining such an important shipment for his neighbors was an inexcusable travesty. It had been a blessing Riley wasn't part of the accident. Better to have the shame follow him through the streets of Haven Bay rather than Riley and his family.

Leo pulled him up by the arm. Seth followed him out the cell door and past a disapproving guard. They stopped at the front desk where Constable McTavish sat staring at a pile of gold coins. Quick fingers plucked them up and deposited the coins in a lockbox. The constable tucked the box under the counter and reached for a small parchment.

"Here is your receipt for young McCloud's bail, sir." The constable raised an eyebrow of warning to Seth. "It's a good thing Mr. Leo has agreed to hire you to work off your debt, young man. I've agreed to release you into his custody. So, you'd better behave."

Seth cast a quick glance at the parchment before it went into Leo's coat. One thousand credits! Leo must be very wealthy, but even so, why would he spend such a large amount of money on someone he hardly knew?

The last tendrils of daylight peeked over the rooftops as they exited the police station. Absent were the curious onlookers who'd chanted for Seth's head. The town was still. He no longer felt a part of it or the people who'd once welcomed his mother into their homes.

Leo's firm hands guided him east toward the little chapel. The Valdeonian was taking great pains to help Seth. Perhaps he owed Seth's father, Edmund, a favor? Were they comrades in the army? Relatives, perhaps? Friend or relative, Seth couldn't take the man's money.

"Sir, I swear I will work off every penny you paid on my release."

Those amber-flecked eyes looked sharply upon Seth with an expression impossible to interpret. They held such firmness, Seth began to shrink away. Leo gripped him tighter.

"I knew your mother." Sorrow filled his eyes, spilling onto his face in a pained frown. "Will you take me to her grave, Seth?"

Leo had come because of his mother, not for Edmund's sake? He turned away from the man to look out across the fields. The pain and grief were still too close. Emma was constantly after him to talk about his mother, but Seth couldn't bring himself to admit that she was really gone — to admit that she had left him.

"I have never been, sir. She was buried when I was ill."

The sharp stab of grief struck his heart with a sudden thrust. He didn't want to see his mother laid under the cold ground. She'd spent too many seasons in the frigid wet cold of Marianna. He couldn't bear to think of her alone in the dark frost of death. Who was this stranger to ask so much of him? Unless he wasn't a stranger to their family. The sprouts of suspicion began to grow, bringing his stinging anger back toward the surface.

"It's time you spoke with her, yes? You must tell her why you are so angry."

Leo steered him toward the rolling fields beside the chapel. Seth suspected he knew exactly where they were headed. They walked side by side along the graveled path to the cemetery gate. A gentle mist from the sea rested upon Seth's cheeks and hair. He smoothed the wetness away and thrust his anxious hands in his pockets.

They made a silent pair as they passed through the iron rod gate. His mother's grave rested beyond a row of tiny headstones. They marked the little unnamed graves of the babes too weak to last in the harsh Marianna climate. Seth climbed the grassy hill and stopped before her white headstone. Several bundles of little winter flowers lay at the base. Their stark red and purple hues were obscene against the white. Emma. He knelt down to adjust a wayward bunch.

"I recognize these from Mother's box garden behind our house." He shook his head. "Emma must have picked them. Mother would be unhappy at the waste. Foolish! Leaving them out here in the cold."

Seth's chest and throat tightened. Hot tears escaped through the crumbling wall of his control. Sobs of helpless grief and frustration shook his body. Fist aimed at the ground, he struck again and again at the cold turf. The buzzing sensation at his temples and neck released its power into the ground, leaving a deep indentation by her headstone.

"Why are you so angry with her?" Leo's hand rested gently upon Seth's head. "We do not pick the time when the Creator calls us home."

"She lied to me! Mother left me alone with no clue as to who I really am."

"Anne loved you, Seth. This was not a lie, yes?"

He lifted his face to regard the Valdeonian. Wet glistened upon his cheek in the weak fingers of sunlight. He'd cared for her too. Seth let his fist drop. He wasn't the only one hurting. Exhausted, he sunk down into the chilly grass. It was an odd feeling to release the grief and anger he'd held inside for so long. He'd leaned upon them for courage in his efforts to find Sandor. Would he have enough courage left to finish their deadly game?

"Come, son." Leo helped Seth to his feet. "A hot meal should be waiting for us by now."

They walked side by side out of the cemetery gate and back toward the town square. Great gulls. The weariness penetrated his body down to the bone. Every muscle ached from his misadventures. Focusing on putting one foot before the other, he let his resentment for the man walking next to him subside.

"McCloud!" Elder Newcastle bellowed from the town hall steps. "What do you think you're about, boy? Who the devil let you out of jail?"

"Great gulls. I'm in no mood for him just now. We can take the Farm Row to avoid him."

"Never cower before fools such as these." Leo walked with firm conviction toward the elder. "Remember who you are! This fool is not fit to share the same road with the man who stood single-handedly against raiders, saving an innocent girl from capture. The shadow of his cowardice must never fall upon the only man with courage enough to defend a helpless child from villainous brutes. This buffoon dares speak your name in such a tone after you climbed down the fabled cliffs of Marianna to save his worthless son's life? No, Seth. Do not cower before such a one as this."

He stared open-mouthed at Leo. What in the green, green fields was he going on about? Seth was no hero. He was just…Seth. The Valdeonian warrior's words were true, he had to admit, but on each of those occasions it was his strange new power that had propelled him into action. Without its strength, his own bumbling efforts would have failed.

"If you have business with Seth, you must take it up with me. He is under my employ now. I won't have his time wasted speaking to you."

Elder Newcastle puffed up like a stuffed pig at harvest time. "Now see here! I am the elder…"

"Yes. You are the man who charges me three times its value to let the McPherson Farm." Leo marched passed the elder without another glance. "I know exactly who you are. Come, Seth. We go."

Seth gave a slight nod to Elder Newcastle as he hurried past to join Leo. A fierce grin stretched upon the Valdeonian's face. Leo burst into laughter. It was rich, deep, and very contagious. Seth begrudgingly joined him.

"Leo, who are you and how do you know my mother?"

He smiled and put a hand on Seth's shoulder. "I knew your mother before you were born. My troop was stationed on Horner Island while Anne was on holiday. I was in love with her, you see. We all were." Leo smiled at the memory. "She was an incredible woman. I swore to always be her friend if ever she had need of one."

"Did you also know her Edmund, my real father?"

"My friends call me Leo. It is a name I was given in my service to Andara." Leo gave him a small smile. "I am Edmund, Seth. I am your father."

The amber-flecked eyes matching his own waited for Seth to respond. He turned away and stared straight ahead. His life was changing quickly, too quickly. He needed time to sort things out. Questions he had for the man walking next to him were anxious to come out, but still he hesitated. Conflicting emotions pressed against his heart. Imagine coming from a warrior like Leo. No more lectures or dull classrooms. Leo could teach him how to fight, and he could show him about the world away from Marianna. Then he remembered his mother's sorrow the last time he'd seen her alive. Could Seth admire and trust a man who had abandoned his pregnant lover so easily?

Darkness covered the island, but Leo walked the row with the confidence of a native islander. He turned onto the small lane leading to the McPherson Farm. Leo took the steep hill at a steady pace, not slowing despite their long walk. Seth raced up the hill after him, clutching at his side. His father was not winded at all.

"Come, I smell Dante's stew."

The warmth of a comfortable home greeted them when Leo opened the farmhouse door. Floorboards missing for years had been replaced and covered with clean throw rugs. Fresh paint brightened the living area and kitchen. The home's large fireplace had been scrubbed clean of old ash.

His nose caught the scent of food. A bubbling pot hung over a cheery fire. The delicious smell of stewing meat and vegetables mixed with the aroma of fresh bread. Seth's stomach growled and his mouth began to water.

"Well, home at last!" A grizzled head popped out from one of the rooms down the short hallway. "You look like a shipwreck, Cub."

"Seth's had a busy day, Dante. Let's see how you look after scaling the cliffs of Marianna."

Dante snorted and marched toward Seth. The Valdeonian frowned and shook his head. He nearly ripped the waistcoat and shredded shirt off Seth. A rough, old finger traced along the scar on Seth's bare chest.

"And what battle was this from?"

"It's from a raider's knife, sir." Seth puffed up with pride when the two Valdeonians whistled in appreciation at the pink line.

"You will tell us of this adventure, yes?"

"What the boy needs is a full stomach, a hot bath, and a good night's sleep." Dante motioned impatiently toward the door. "Both of you go wash up. My stew is ready for eating."

Leo winked at Seth as they made for the side of the farmhouse. A barrel filled with water from the well stood upon the covered porch. Leo scooped out some of the water in a small bucket. He handed it to Seth and waved at a bar of soap upon a table next to the wall. Sniffing at the small block of soap, he began to lather. The bubbles smelled like wildflowers and spring grass. They'd not gotten this soap from the islands.

Seth rinsed off with the bucket and noticed Leo watching him. A strange sort of melancholy smile was upon his face. He turned away to grab a towel off the table and tossed it to Seth.

Dante had their plates full of stew and bread when they returned. The meat was seasoned with wonderful spices Seth had never tasted before. His tongue tingled as he savored the first few bites. Then he shoveled spoonfuls of stew in faster and faster. He gave them an embarrassed grin when he realized his plate was empty before either man had taken his first bite.

"You like my stew, yes?" Dante asked, taking his plate and filling it up again.

"I've never tasted the like, sir." Seth kept his eyes on his plate as the talk quieted around the table. "Why have you come to Haven Bay now, Leo? Why not before?"

He kept his tone measured, taking a tight hold on his anger. Growling and demanding why the man before him had ignored his son would be warranted. Despite his impatience, he couldn't bring himself to show his pain to a total stranger. He wasn't sure what to make of Leo. The evidence supporting his claim of being Seth's father was there in the portrait he'd found and the striking resemblance they shared.

"A month ago, a letter from a friend of your mother reached me. She told me of Anne's death and asked me to find you. I'm here to look after you, Seth."

"My mother told me she feared for me the night she was murdered. She didn't explain why."

In truth he could give a good guess why she had been frightened for him. Pavel Sandor. The killer was ruthless and determined to end them both. These attempts on Seth's life wouldn't end until he or Sandor were dead.

"Anne's fear started before you were born, Cub." Dante swirled his fork before him. "She disappeared one day and went into hiding. Now we know why. She'd found out she was pregnant with you."

"Dante!" Leo pounded a fist upon the table.

"Well, it's true. Your father didn't know you existed until he got our friend's letter." Dante took Leo's spilled plate away and came back with another. "We were on a ship bound for this island almost the same moment he found out you were here."

Seth stared at the man who'd sired him. The same pain and confusion striking at Seth's heart was etched upon his face. Life had been a bumpy ride on a rickety wagon. He'd grown up believing his father had died. Then he'd been led to believe, by his grief-stricken mother, that Edmund had abandoned them. Now these men were asking him to believe she'd kidnapped her own son away from his father. He didn't know what to believe anymore.

"Anne was such an exciting woman, so intelligent and kind. You remind me of her, Seth." Leo swallowed hard. "We were wed at the little church on Horner Island. Our witnesses were the people we thought we could trust. Before I had a chance to tell my family, my regiment was called to the Outpost Territories."

"What happened?"

"Our families didn't approve of us. One of my uncles used his connections to extend my tour and somehow stopped my letters from reaching your mother." His fist gripped at an unlucky eating utensil until the blood drained from his knuckles. "While I was away, the priest who married us was persuaded to annul our marriage. A dear friend of your mother wrote me about their plan, but your uncle took Anne away before I could find them. No amount of searching or threats helped my cause. In the end, I clung to my duty and an unhappy life."

Words wouldn't come as Seth regarded the father who'd been cast out of his life. The pain and grief Leo had shown at Anne's grave were real. He hadn't known his father long, but clearly he was a man of honor. Why would his mother hide from such a man? He shifted in his seat to ease tense muscles. Mother had her own secrets, and Fergus McCloud knew them. Contempt for his uncle grew to seething hatred. How could he steal away another man's wife?

"I don't understand. Why would Mother take me away from you? And why would she lie to me about who I am?"

"I think she was trying to protect you, Seth. Our families didn't approve of my marriage to Anne. They may have threatened to hurt you."

"It would explain Pavel Sandor's claims." Seth took another bite of bread and chewed as the two men stared at him. "Sandor and his raider friends ambushed me on the road. He told me he'd been paid by my family to kill me. Then he poisoned mother and tried to poison me as well."

"How did you escape such an assassin?"

"A Valdeonian ranger saved me. I didn't see his face, just the legion badge. He said he would be back for me at the appointed time. I'm not certain what he means to do with me."

"Traitor!"

Leo pushed away from his chair, sending the unlucky furniture smacking against the wall. Amber fire burned within his eyes. His father turned from the table with a feral growl. He fell against the windowsill and stared out across the farm.

Dante cleared his throat and shook his head. "Finish your bread, Cub, and there is a piece of pie for you. I go to fill your bath."

He disappeared down the hallway, leaving an uncomfortable silence hanging over the house. Leo's breath slowly calmed as he struggled to control his temper. Used to such angry fits of bad humor, Seth sat quietly. He kept a tight hold upon his own emotions. Nothing good would come of his powers striking at Leo.

"Forgive my anger, Seth. Your visit from the Valdeonian ranger concerns me. My side of the family knew about you and kept your existence from me. It will be more difficult to find a safe place for us to hide once we leave Marianna."

"I'm not leaving, not yet. My mother's killer is somewhere on this island. Sandor cut those boards on the Sea Steps in order to murder me. I'm certain of it."

"You don't understand, my son. I must get you to safety. This is important, yes?"

Seth rose from the table as quickly as his sore muscles would allow. He took a step toward the farmhouse door, but Leo moved to block his path. Two firm hands rested upon Seth's shoulders. His father's face softened, and a tired smile came to his lips.

"Very well. I want justice for Anne too, but you must promise to be careful. Sandor is the deadliest assassin Andara has seen in centuries. He won't be easy to find. I will help you look on one condition. You must allow me to train you in the sword. I can teach you many things, Seth. But you must want to learn, to carry on with your life."

"I do want to learn, Leo. You have my promise."

"The sword will wait. Come along, Cub. I have to chisel the dirt off you."

Dante led him down the hall to the back of the farmhouse. He swung open the porch door and stood aside to let Seth pass. The smell of mint and strong spirits made him stagger back. Dante pulled him forward onto the small back porch. A large metal tub stood at its center. Dante had filled it with steaming water. Slick liquid — bathing oil — floated on the surface.

"Take off the boots and get out of those filthy clothes."

The Valdeonian folded his arms, blocking the door. He wasn't welcoming an argument. Seth hurried out of his boots and stripped to the skin. He stuffed the vile and the gargoyle coin into his boot when Dante's back was turned. Then he hurried to stand by the tub, shivering in the breeze.

"In you go, Cub."

"You want me to get in the water, sir?"

"Well, I don't want you to drink it! Haven't you ever seen a bathing tub before?" He gasped when Seth shook his head. "What a barbaric country this is. How do you wash yourselves?"

He sank down into the water with a sigh. Heat penetrated his sore muscles. Stretching his arms and legs, the tightness in his body began to loosen.

"Did the tub come from Valdeon, sir?"

"Yes and stop calling me 'sir.' I'm not your grand-papa."

Dante poured a bucket of water on Seth's hair and began to scrub at it with a soap smelling of spices. He was beginning to resemble a rabbit in a roasting pan. It would be worth it if he could get a little more information out of Dante.

"The soap and the spices, they came from Valdeon as well, sir? I mean Dante."

"Yes, as did Leo and I. Your father will tell you all about his life in Valdeon when he's ready."

He rinsed the soap off and pulled Seth up from the water. The Valdeonian held out a long piece of fabric to wrap around his shivering body.

"And how do you dry yourselves, shake off in the breeze?" Dante snorted as he watched Seth finger the soft cloth. "Here, put this on."

He took the offered nightshirt from Dante. It was a rich fabric with ornate stitching upon the breast pocket. He couldn't imagine why a person would need a pocket while they slept. Pulling on the shirt, he found that it fit him very well. Hurriedly stuffing the vile and the coin into the pocket of his nightshirt, he followed Dante. They moved back into the kitchen to find Leo sitting by the fire, sipping at a small glass of amber liquid. The amber flecks in his eyes glowed in the light of the flames.

"Your nightshirt fits the Cub, Leo." Dante pulled at the fabric. "He has a bit of room to expand, but I'll soon fatten him up."

Leo nodded with a smile and poured two more glasses of the liquid. Seth took a seat beside him. He accepted the glass from Leo and sniffed it. Strong spices with the hint of fruit wafted from the glass.

"Let us toast to new friendships."

Leo lifted the glass toward them. Seth raised his too when Dante did. The amber liquid was spicy and rolled down his throat in warm streams of sweetness. The streams began to burn, and he coughed, clutching at his throat.

"This is special liquor made from the barks of cherry trees around my home in San Leonora. It is called spice wine."

"I like it."

He took another mouthful and turned to stare into the fire. The flames rose and fell in undulating bands of warmth. Seth pushed aside all the memories of the day to focus on Leo's words as they'd walked down the Main Row. His warrior father had called Seth a hero. No lie darkened his eyes when he'd said those words and none as he spoke of Seth's mother. It was time to tell Leo the rest.

Reaching into his pocket, he pulled out the tiny vial and the gold coin. He handed them to Leo, who stared at them silently. Slowly, careful to include each detail he could remember, Seth recounted the events on the day of his mother's death and everything he'd learned up to Leo bailing him out of jail.

"It is a promissory marker issued by the Tslavian Royal Family as promise of payment for large sums of money. They aren't given lightly." Leo handed the coin back to Seth. "Whoever lost that coin can't collect his money without it. He'll be back."

"Let us hope it belonged to one of the men you struck down today, Leo." Dante sniffed at the empty vile. "Devil's Cape. This is Sandor's calling card."

"I don't think the villain is concerned with money. He despises me. My death is personal to Sandor. Hatred compels him to continue his attempts to kill me." Seth touched the crystal beneath his shirt. "Why couldn't he let us go? The last letter from Mother's friend welcomed both of us to her home. We were leaving Marianna together with no intention of hurting or bothering anyone."

"Letter?" Leo lifted his eyes from the vial to regard Seth.

"I found letters and some other things in Mother's hiding place after she died." Seth pulled the necklace from under his nightshirt.

"May I see these things you found?" Leo's fingertips gently caressed the heart crystal at Seth's neck.

"I'll fetch them as soon as I can sneak down the Sea Steps again to the wharf. A portrait of you and mother was among the letters. I'm sure you'd like to have it."

"My thanks to you." His father leaned back in the chair, keeping his eyes focused on Seth. "Now you must go to your rest. I have kept you up too long."

A gentle touch pressed heavily upon his mind, pushing him toward sleep. His eyes closed as the heat of the drink seeped into his body. Warmth surrounded him, and he leaned his head against the side of the comfortable chair.

"He is very much like her."

"The Cub has his father in him too. He has courage."

"Yes, it is my hope he has more of his mother in him than his father."

"Well, courage or no, Leo, the boy looks half starved. What do they feed their young on this barbaric dot upon the water? He needs fattening up."

The fragrance of exotic spice and citrus wrapped gently about him. Seth breathed it in deeply, easing the last of his fears. His head rolled forward and he started awake. It took a few moments for him to realize he was back in the cozy farmhouse. Leo was close to him, kneeling at his chair. Seth opened his hand, letting him take the full glass of liquor. Seth stifled a great yawn. He must have fallen asleep in the warmth of the cozy kitchen. The night was full on now. He struggled to make his legs move as he staggered away from the chair. Leo seemed to understand and took his arm.

"Come, Seth. Your bed is ready. You need a good night's sleep, yes?"

The insistent power continued to lull him toward sleep. He nodded dully, trying to reason out where they were headed. Leo brought him to a small room with a comfortable-looking bed and a small writing desk.

"Into bed with you, my son."

Seth did what he was told and sunk down into the soft blankets. He closed his eyes with a contented sigh. Safe. The word echoed in his exhausted mind. He recognized the voice. It was the same soft whisper that came to him upon the breeze as he stood at Lands End.

"Sleep well, little one. You will live with your father. I am with you now and will keep you safe. This I swear."

Chapter Twenty-Three

OLD LIPS GRIPPED THE GLASS as thick, amber liquid passed between them. Julian sat across from Chancellor Benito, waiting as the old man finished his drink. The expensive liquor was a delicacy from Heidelbreckt. He'd taken great care to pick up a bottle on his last visit. The drink was one of Benito's favorites.

"You spoil me, my prince."

"It is the least I can do for the man who keeps our country at peace in such turbulent times. You carry a great burden, my lord chancellor." Julian brought the contrite mask of sympathy to his features.

Benito stretched his arms overhead and yawned. The tired smile came slowly to his face, but Julian wasn't fooled. Beneath the old visage burned the ambition of a young man. He would not easily give up the power he had been given.

"True. In my younger days, I could stay on my feet for much longer."

"The pressures of office, no doubt. It is your wisdom which guides us now, Benito. Younger men don't have your experience." Julian poured them another glass. "It is your guidance and wisdom I seek now. As the last surviving son of our dead king, I feel there is much more I could be doing to help. I ask you to use me, my lord, in any way you can."

He mustered the appropriate amount of patriotic emotion in the undertones of his voice. Benito, agreeably moved, patted his hand. A condescending smile touched the old lips. Julian returned it. Flattery was a tool he'd crafted to control the arrogant.

"I daresay we could use your help in calming the people. Were they to see their prince urging them to remain peaceful, they would follow your word."

Julian lifted his glass with a slight bow. The chancellor was offering to put him in a leadership role as the face of Valdeonian peace. What better endorsement could there be for his new role as regent? The old fool was practically handing him the throne.

Ash gray uniforms marched across the courtyard of the palace outside the chancellor's office. Julian moved to the window. His dark eyes followed the stomping boots with growing irritation. He'd make many changes when he was crowned king. The first would be the permanent removal of the Jalora Legion from Valdeon.

"Peace will not come as long as they occupy the palace, my lord chancellor." He waved a hand at the twenty-two lesser rangers as they marched about the grounds. "The Dragon has positioned his army at the very gates of the Palace of Kings! He has ignored your desires to keep the Jalora Legion out of the affairs of Valdeon."

"Come now." The old man shook his head with a tolerant smile. "The cardinal has allowed them to pay their respects to our fallen king. That is all. Wolf assures me they are necessary in helping him keep the peace."

Julian leaned a hand upon the window, bracing himself against his growing frustration. The Wolf's hold on Benito was stronger than he'd imagined. It was futile to keep to this course. He'd have to find another way to deal with Wolf.

"I hope you're right. One of those rangers could sweep through a troop of soldiers. I've seen them do it, and so have you."

Julian turned to go, leaving the old man to look out the window. Boots stomping in perfect unison thundered upon the ground outside. San Leonora's feeble dependence upon a fading legion with outdated religious beliefs was crippling the entire country.

"I would ask you to remember who leads them, my lord chancellor." Julian stopped at the door. "Would you discount my concerns so easily knowing the very man the renegades from the West would set upon the throne also commands this troop of killers?"

Julian left Benito and headed down the rear corridors to avoid the atrium. His chambers were located on the main level in the northernmost section of the palace. Away from the rush and noise of court, its location afforded him solitude.

"Out of my way!" He unleashed his spite upon an old woman scrubbing the tiled floor. She scurried out of his way, bowing as he passed.

He took a steadying breath, forcing down the anger. His plans had been delayed by the loss of the Lion Ring, yes, but he could still see hope. Two challenges stood in his way, Leo and Xavier De Vincente. His father was out of reach for the time being. It was best to focus on his nearest problem, the Wolf. He had Chancellor Benito's ear despite Julian's efforts to discredit him. Many of the other Valdeonian Lords also trusted the ranger. It sickened Julian to see how they hung upon Wolf's every word like weakling pups.

The Wolf has great power, Julian, the Sarcion whispered. *He is the only man who could steal the throne from you. The Wolf could take it without lifting a sword. Better to have done with him. Kill the Wolf! Kill the young Lords of Valdeon!*

Julian's insides twisted with rage. He had to take action. Something had to be done about Xavier De Vincente and the other members of the Sacred Guard. The young Lords of Valdeon would be easily vanquished if Wolf was out of the picture.

An elaborate arch made from the same stone as the throne room stood like a sentry over the entrance to an ancient wing of the palace. For centuries it housed the Lion and his family. During the rare times a Jalora Master walked among them, the Sacred Guard was housed in the wing as well. Even now, the Jalora's magic groped with angry fingers toward his ring. Julian hurried passed the entrance and continued on toward the chapel. He'd never been comfortable under the magic's judgmental touch and had moved his bedchambers out of the wing.

The double doors of the chapel stood at the entrance of another ancient wing at the very northern section of the palace. Julian headed to the left several steps, pretending to move to his bedchambers a few doors down. Satisfied no one was following him, he hurried through the doors of the chapel. Several small candles flickered at the altar. Someone was vigilant about mourning his father.

He walked by the altar without any of the usual rituals and stopped before an iron rod gate. The chains normally securing entry to the catacombs had been unlocked. He quietly opened the gate and took a torch from its holder. The same thoughtful soul had left another torch burning just out of sight from the chapel. Julian touched his torch to the flame. The light exploded in the darkness, revealing a set of winding stone steps leading downward.

The tombs of his dead ancestors lined the stairwell as he descended into the catacombs. His footsteps echoed in the eerie silence. This was the one place in all of Andara he could find peace. Walking amongst his ancestors fed his commitment to see the glory of Valdeon restored.

"Greetings, mighty prince." Whisper's bulbous head floated a hand's breadth away. Its hideous little face grinned in momentary glee. Julian staggered away on the steps, striking his shoulder hard against one of the tombs before righting himself.

"How is it you've come inside the Palace of Kings without being detected?"

Whisper may be maintaining its apologetic tone, but there was more to the little creature than he had first supposed. Great power would be needed to bypass the Sacred Guard. Their connection to the Altar should alert them to any breaches by creatures like Whisper.

"My emperor has gifted me with many powers, great prince." It spread tiny arms wide and cast its eyes downward. "I use them to serve."

"And you serve Lord Gorman today, I suppose."

"Indeed, mighty prince, I do. He has sent me to warn you. The Jalora's pets have not been idle. Lord Gorman intercepted a messenger sent by the one you call 'Wolf.' He was carrying a plea for aid to the Jalora Legion."

Wolf again! Curse the man. He dared call in the legion without the permission of the chancellor. What better proof of Wolf's lust for the throne could there be?

"Our general has dispatched the Wolf's lackey for you. No messages will be sent or received from parties outside Valdeon. Lord Gorman believes this knowledge will help you to focus on the important tasks only you can accomplish here in San Leonora."

"Lord Gorman is too kind. He needn't worry about me. I have everything well in hand."

"Wonderful news, Prince Julian! You have the Regent's Medallion then?"

He looked away, gritting his teeth. Insisting he take the changeling babysitter with him to San Leonora was one thing, but calling him to task like a subordinate was outrageous. Lord Gorman had made his desires for the use of military force against Valdeon clear. The man's impatience for bloodshed couldn't be quieted for much longer. Julian had to find the Regent's Medallion soon, or his control on the situation would slip away and he'd find himself bowing before Gorman. The thought sickened him.

"No? That is regrettable." Whisper shook his head sadly. "My Lord Gorman loses confidence in your efforts, mighty prince. He prepares his men for battle. Lord Gorman has won many thrones for our emperor over the decades. His passion is war. He cares nothing for the treasures and history of the lands he conquers. Even less care goes to the people of those lands. Many will die, Prince of Valdeon, if your plan fails."

His hopes of restored glory and power faded for a moment. Leo had taken his Lion Ring into hiding were Julian could not follow. The Regent's Medallion was missing along with the barbarian who had taken it. Things were not going to plan, but there was still hope. The Pacarro tribesman couldn't hide forever. He was still with them, spying for the Wolf.

"Tell Lord Gorman he has my assurances I will have the Regent's Medallion in my hands very soon. No one will dispute my right to rule. Valdeon is as good as mine. Then we can discuss the taking of Andara."

"You may tell him in person, Prince Julian. He will arrive in San Leonora when the sun sets on the third day." Whisper's voice faded into the stone of the catacombs. "I bid you farewell."

Gorman's coming would mean open warfare. It would be a catalyst for pulling the men of Valdeon together under the Wolf. In times of war, the Sacred Guard ruled Valdeon. No one would question them then. Julian's chances to take the throne would be soundly beaten.

"Ill news, Andarian?" The changeling stepped out of the shadows, a contemptuous grin upon its face.

Always lurking about, watching every move he made. Julian stormed past it without a word. Its sharp laughter thundered off the bones of his ancestors. His approach in dealing with the creature had been wrong. Rather than embracing an ally he could manipulate, he'd alienated a particularly venomous enemy.

The changeling — when it wasn't amusing itself goading Marcellus — had proven useful. It had discovered a spy among them. Jorge Pacarro was the miscreant tattling to the Lords of Valdeon. He was solely responsible for every botched intrigue and failed mob.

Deeper into the catacombs, they came to an antechamber. More torches lined the room. Bits of fabric and discarded boots had been haphazardly thrown along the tombs. This was Zoya's playroom. He couldn't understand why a man would stay and play her games rather than turn tail and run after seeing those who'd come before him. He shifted his eyes away with a mixture of disgust and familial pride.

Bright light from the chamber beyond beckoned him. The Dirge had taken up residence within the tight crawl spaces between bodies. Their own emaciated features were perfectly suited to their new chamber.

They slept now. All five of them were in hibernation, silent as the graves about them.

Zoya sat cross-legged upon the tomb of a long-dead queen. Marcellus leaned beside her, careful to keep his eyes away from the tombs. Julian smirked. Zoya and Marcellus were uneasy around his grotesque pets.

"There you are, Brother, and you have brought Armando with you." Zoya gave him her wicked little grin when Marcellus pushed angrily away from the tomb.

"I wish, my sister, you would spend more time aiding me in my efforts to save Valdeon. It seems you are more intent upon playing your frivolous games. And you, Marcellus. What of the barbarian? Why is his blood not upon your sword and the Regent Medallion in my hand?"

The precious symbol of power would end all of Wolf's barking. He'd sent his best men after the medallion. All they had to do was take it out of a glass cabinet. A barbarian from the west had bested them. Jorge Pacarro may have retired from his service as legion squire, but he still remained loyal to the rangers.

"We've tried to find him, my lord prince. It is as if he has disappeared again." Marcellus gave Julian a nervous glance. "I have told our allies about the bounty you've placed upon his head. It doesn't seem to be motivating them."

"Perhaps it is not money that I must offer. Tell them I will grant a position in my court for the man who brings me Jorge Pacarro's head."

The changeling drifted past him to lean next to Zoya on the tomb. Shaking its head, the borrowed features twisted in a sneer. Zoya rested her hand upon its arm and smoothed her fingertips upward. The changeling caught her hand, twisting it sharply until

Zoya cried out. Then it threw her touch away with a laugh.

Her eyes sparked with angry fire for a moment. The spark within their depths began to smolder. She had chosen her game. This time the prey was refusing to play. Marcellus's sharp steps hurried to the tomb. He grabbed Zoya's arm and pulled her away. The changeling laughed. Clever creature. The prey was playing his own game. Perhaps there was a way Julian could use it to his advantage.

"Those bumbling fools won't find him. You'll have to draw the barbarian out of hiding." The changeling's sharp grin stretched toward Marcellus.

"How? We've tried everything to bait him." Marcellus folded his arms, staring dangerously at his rival.

"Not everything. What would you do if someone threatened to harm me, Marcellus?" Zoya pressed her body against him. "Would you hide away in a storeroom? Or would you defend me?"

He put shaking fingers under her chin. "I would kill them to save you, of course."

"Of course," the changeling snickered.

"Don't you think this barbarian would do the same? Threaten the friend he holds most dear and watch how quickly he rushes into the light." Zoya pulled the small dagger Julian had given to her and began plucking at her fingernails. "I wish it could be Fausto De Quintaro. His death must be another day. We need to draw western blood. Who better than Xavier the Wolf's mentor?"

Marcellus stared at her, his eyes twitching madly. "Killing Cesar Santiago is a death sentence for the man holding the assassin's blade. Even if he could get close enough to try the deed, Wolf would stop him before he could reach the old man."

"We must see this done at a time and place the Wolf will not expect. If the Lords of Valdeon are otherwise occupied, our assassin will do his job and our friends will hide him. The man who does this for me will go down in history as a true patriot!"

"I would be your logical choice, of course." The changeling tilted its head with a shrug. "I am, after all, the most skilled among your men."

"You? Always skulking in the shadows like a coward." Marcellus lifted the sleeve of his shirt. Several cut marks sliced his skin. "These represent all the lives I've taken. What do you know of killing and death? If the deed is to be done, then I'll be the man."

Julian went to him then and put a hand on each shoulder. "You are my greatest ally, Marcellus. Your future king will never forget the courage you show today."

The mad fool gave him a proud smile. Julian returned it. Marcellus should have listened to his own counsel. He'd been right about Wolf. The ranger would cut him down before he reached Cesar. No matter. The barbarian would be drawn out into the open. Then they would have him and the Regent Medallion. It would be his greatest pleasure to wave the golden necklace in Lord Gorman's hideous face.

Chapter Twenty-Four

The Great Hall within the Palace of Kings had seen war and destruction in its centuries-old existence. Rebuilt many times, its walls were a patchwork of old and older. Jorge found inconsistencies in its brickwork convenient. Discreetly covered by tapestries, they offered an abundance of hiding places. He'd used them frequently in the past few weeks to spy on Julian and his treacherous band. Many plots had been stymied by the Lords of Valdeon due to the information he'd overheard.

He kept watch now as the prefects assembled to bicker again over the future of their country. These meetings were tiring for men of action. Even the eastern prefects, dressed in their colorful plumage, seemed strained with temper. Many times their eyes would shift from the Lords of Valdeon to the bastard prince. A few of the eastern lords — Fausto De Quintaro for one — kept their gaze firmly on the chancellor as he spoke. Those faithful to the Altar would not be enough to stand against Julian's supporters.

Their dark prince sat upon the small dais beside the chancellor. He was a hand's breadth from the king's seat. His covetous fingers stretched absently toward it while his eyes remained upon Wolf. Open contempt was in their depths.

Jorge shifted his attention to the twitching man beside Julian. He'd made the mistake of passing too close to the beast once. The faint odor of rotting blood mixed with cherry blossoms and spice wafted around Marcellus De Costa. He was the breath of death and the hand of madness. The killer warranted close surveillance, but he was not Jorge's target today.

A man approached Julian, carrying a tray with spring water and fruit upon it. The prince waved the tray away without acknowledging his new valet, Armando. Jorge had witnessed Julian's resentful behavior toward his attendant before and had grown curious about the man. His face was a familiar one, though Jorge hadn't placed him at first. Then he remembered their last meeting many years ago. Armando had been one of Leo's lion friends.

Why would a lion friend offer himself into service to the king's bastard son? It was a mystery Jorge was determined to solve. He'd spent the past few hours following the man, hoping to gather clues as to his purpose. Armando's behavior was peculiar for a man in service to the prince. He wasn't a subservient domestic when they thought they were alone. Rather he behaved as an equal to Julian. One who enjoyed toying with his irritable employer.

Julian may not have craved refreshments, but the chancellor certainly did. Benito stepped away from his position on the dais and took up a glass of wine offered to him by the servants patiently waiting at the side of the room. Wolf and the other members of the Sacred Guard followed. Their emotionless faces revealed nothing about their moods, but Jorge knew them well enough to know rangers weren't immune to impatience.

Conversation and ambient noises rose into a loud buzz. The room was in movement. Prefects mixing with one another as they took refreshment under the lights of the Great Hall. Jorge kept his eyes focused on

Armando. The valet stood quietly against the wall, outside the chaos. Jorge grinned at his good fortune. Armando had chosen to stand beneath one of his hiding spots. Finally, a chance to get a close look at the man.

He slipped from behind the tapestry to crouch low on the floor. Jorge crept along the wall unnoticed. Lifting the edge of the next massive tapestry, he crawled along the small ledge the cloth was designed to hide. The dust of many years puffed into the air before him. He swallowed the cough trying to escape his throat and took a slower pace. Better to show caution than risk attracting the attention of an observant onlooker.

Counting the paces, he calculated Armando's location. Jorge stopped and pressed his fingers on the age-worn material. Heaven forgive him, he pierced the antique tapestry with his dagger. The blade sawed down a few inches until he had an unobstructed view of Armando's head.

Obviously bored, the valet took an easy stance. Dark hair peppered with age fell straight against his ears. A meager mustache lined thin lips. He looked a few years older than the last time Jorge had seen him, but nothing out of the ordinary leapt to his attention.

Warmth began to radiate from his skin where the Regent's Medallion had touched him. Jorge put his hand upon the spot. Nothing met his touch, only the skin he'd been born with. He smoothed at his side. The sensation was coming more often. Why now?

Suddenly, Armando's tray flew upward a few inches as if something had bumped it. Water and fruit spilled on the sleeve of his left arm. He set the tray down upon one of the chair seats and squeezed at the fabric of his sleeve. Armando was careful to pull the material back down over his arm, but Jorge had seen the skin beneath. Leo's Lion Friends were known by three deep claw marks slashing across the left forearm. Armando's were strangely absent. The Jalora's magic could not be faked. This imposter was pretending to be a lion friend. The why and the how of the pretender's performance was for Xavier the Wolf to uncover.

Jorge backed down the narrow ledge toward the edge of the tapestry. Cesar was standing, face red with fury, in the center of a handful of eastern prefects. One of them was the butcher De Costa. Julian had let his rabid pet off his leash. De Costa leaned against the table grinning insolently at Cesar. Alberto, Fausto, and the Lords of Valdeon stood beside the chancellor, speaking in low tones. They hadn't noticed their old friend had been surrounded by a dangerous crowd.

"How do we find what the Dragon cannot, My Lord Santiago? It would be as difficult as finding civilized conversation in the west." De Costa's insult drew a nervous laugh from Julian's other lackeys.

Cesar bristled at the young man's rudeness. Jorge recognized the look upon his lord's face. His temper was up again. Rather than showing caution and remembering his advanced age, he would try to teach these young men manners.

"As I have said before, we must urge the Dragon to return to the Altar of Providence. He must bring all the bishops with him. Perhaps the combined strength of these rangers along with the Lords of Valdeon can ascertain the ring's whereabouts."

Foreign interference of any sort wasn't a popular idea among Julian's supporters. The legion's presence would squash Julian's lusts for the throne in short order. Emboldened by the bitter grumblings of his friends, one of the young men broke away from his circle and advanced upon Cesar.

"We don't need foreign rangers on Valdeonian soil. Would you have rule over San Leonora handed over to them?"

"Don't be a blasphemous fool! The legion will protect the Altar for all of Andara's sake. It is their duty in such times to follow the Lords of Valdeon. Do you not trust in the Sacred Guard? They are Valdeonian after all and follow the Jalora without question."

"That is a feeble old man's wisdom."

"No, that is a sober man's wisdom. Your mind is still awash with drink."

He turned to walk away. Jorge's tension eased until the young men crowded around Cesar to block his escape. De Costa took a step back, standing outside their circle. A sick smile of anticipation twitched upon his lips. What game was he playing?

"Tell me, old man, do you honestly think anyone will miss a relic like you?" The young man lifted up onto the table and sat down, dangling his legs.

Jorge pulled his hatchet and let it fly in one practiced movement. It split the table, stopping a few inches from the young man's groin. Wetness spread across his britches. The dark spot grew as Jorge yowled the infamous Pacarro battle cry.

"How dare you, treacherous vermin! Do not speak ill of your betters when you spend your days looking for discarded scraps from Julian's table."

Jorge stormed into their numbers. He threw a few well-placed strikes into the others, sending them all to the floor. Turning slowly to face Julian, he lifted his chin. The bastard prince's dark eyes were swimming with amusement. In that moment, Jorge understood he'd made a mistake. The prey hadn't been Cesar. Their performance was meant to flush out Wolf's spy.

Chancellor Benito pushed through the murmuring prefects. His purple robes ruffled when he took in Jorge standing in the center of the fallen men.

"Stop this. You're behaving like a savage. Leave us until you can conduct yourself like the nobleman you claim to be."

"Now, see here, Benito. De Costa goaded the fight."

"You'll not sway me this time, My Lord Santiago. Weapons and skirmishes in the Great Hall? These men have no respect. They are all banned until I say otherwise."

A familiar touch brushed across Jorge's consciousness. Lucio the Ferret stood at his shoulder. De Costa's face twitched with agitation as the young lord of San Lucida headed toward his group of followers. Lucio, never breaking eye contact with Julian's lackey, yanked the hatchet from the wood. He whispered something low to the young fool who'd insulted his father. Eyes wide with fear, the idiot cowered away. Lucio turned his back on him and joined Jorge. His bright eyes sparkled with amusement.

"You spared his life, Jorge." Lucio handed him the hatchet.

He grinned slowly and tucked the hatchet into his belt. "No, little buck tail. Time passes, and my arm has aged."

"You will never be too old to hunt, my friend."

Lucio gave him a nod and came to clutch at his father's arm. They moved through the crowd to join the Wolf. The Lords of Valdeon had not been idle. Two men Jorge didn't recognize were kneeled before them with hands raised over their heads. Jaguar and Raven held their confiscated bows and quivers of arrows. Jorge's suspicions were confirmed. A larger conspiracy had been at work this day.

He'd underestimated Julian's gifts for strategy and manipulation. Hoping to get Wolf's attention, Jorge looked over his shoulder as he was escorted out of the Great Hall. The Lords of Valdeon were occupied breaking up fights instigated by his brief encounter with De Costa. He lifted his chin and marched steadily away from his palace guard escorts. The western prefects offered encouraging words as he passed. Well, at least they weren't annoyed with him.

A shimmer of gold upon the horizon caught his eye through the atrium windows. The museum of San Leonora beckoned. Though he'd been to the city many times, duty always seemed to keep him from its treasures. Restless in his frustration, he headed down the stairs into the courtyard. A long walk in the city would cool his temper.

Stares of curiosity from San Leonora's citizens followed him as he left King's Row to enter the cultural district. The Museum of San Leonora stood like a mighty, ancient temple. Its golden roof shimmered in the sun, a beacon for all the great art ever created in Andara.

Jorge took a deep breath and moved to the stairs. He was struck dumb by its magnificence. The hours flew by as he wandered along the marbled statues lining the halls. Paintings of past kings, historical events, and beautiful women with faraway looks captured his imagination. It was the most beautiful place he had ever been.

Stepping out of the museum, he found morning had passed into afternoon. He hurried to the next treasured building. This was a rare chance to see the most famous library in all of Andara. A sudden warmth along his side made him pause at the door. Then the sensation left him to be replaced by another. Prickles along the back of his neck told him he was being watched. He casually pulled open the door and twisted his face briefly to scan the street behind him. Nothing.

Inside the library's marble foyer, his attention was pulled into the aisles. Each shelf was lovingly loaded with leather-bound books and parchments. Three stories of precious information, which could not be found anywhere else on Andara, awaited his hungry mind. Where to start? His fingers lightly touched the leather as he passed through the first book-lined shelf.

Hours passed as his active mind raced over the volumes. Jorge finally settled on a book called *The History of Valdeonian Wine*. Perhaps it would help him to discover the ailment of his vines on the far north of the vineyard. He found a comfortable chair in the reading area of the library's second-floor atrium. Leaning back in its comfortable upholstery, he began to read. Movement over the top of the pages alerted him to someone else's presence. A man stood within the shelves pretending to examine the parchments. His eyes periodically darted toward Jorge.

Sweet Erthe Mother! Was he to be denied a moment's peace? Snapping the book closed, Jorge lifted out of the chair and walked into the shelves opposite the man. His shadow waited a few moments and followed. Jorge kept to a steady pace, zigzagging slowly between the shelves. The man kept at a good distance, pretending to casually browse. He didn't seem to realize Jorge had spotted him. Good. The man was a fool. Losing him shouldn't be too difficult.

He tucked the book carefully inside his waistcoat and stepped into the next aisle. Rather than keeping to his customary zigzag pattern, Jorge skipped two aisles. The man walked past his position, noticed Jorge was not where he should be, and began to spin around. He hurried to the next aisle in the wrong direction.

Chuckling, Jorge moved several aisles over in the direction of the staircase. He found a position close to the top stair and stood listening for his opportunity. It finally came in the form of two young men loaded down with parchments and books. They were slowly making their way up from the first floor.

Jorge stepped out of his hiding place and into an open aisle. He coughed loudly, drawing the attention of several patrons, including his shadow. Pretending to examine a pile of parchments, Jorge let the man draw closer. Then he jumped back into his hiding place the same moment the two students reached the second floor and continued up the stairs. Their boots stomped loudly upon the marble. They disappeared from view just as his shadow reached the staircase. He did exactly what Jorge hoped he would do. Taking a careful pace, the man moved up the stairs after the two students.

Descending to the first floor on silent feet, he kept to the walls in the event the man realized too soon what had happened and decided to look over the balcony into the foyer. The book grew heavier under his waistcoat. Books were rare, and those within the largest of the four great libraries of Andara were irreplaceable. Taking them outside the protective walls of the building was not allowed. He couldn't spare the time to read his find now. No choice was left to him. He'd have to temporarily borrow the book until he could return it in a few days.

He nodded to one of the stately librarians and exited the building into the fading light of late afternoon. A light rain trickled from the sky. He put a protective arm over the book. It was best to take the quickest route back to the palace in case his shadow had friends. Jorge walked to the curb to summon one of the carriages for hire. One look at his braids and the driver prodded his horses quickly past.

Two men standing under a streetlamp were watching him with an unhealthy interest. Jorge walked slowly to one of the shops jammed with people escaping from the rain. His shadow from the library joined the two men beneath the lamp. They began speaking low together and casting quick glances in Jorge's direction.

Jorge kept his steps unhurried as he merged with the crowd upon King's Row. A bakery stood upon the corner. It was bustling with shoppers, eager for the evening's bread. He peered into the window, pretending to eye the pastries. The three men appeared within the reflection. They were moving closer to him. He entered the bakery, pushing his way around the busy shop. Moving closer to the counter, he lowered himself slowly to the floor. Twisting his body through a swinging gate separating the clerk from his customers, he crept into the kitchen.

Ignoring protests from the baker, he flew out the back door into a deserted alleyway. Two young men with clubs were standing at the far end of the alley. He gave them an evaluative glance. Richly dressed, lazy, he guessed from the way they aimlessly searched the alley. They were probably fresh off their father's estate.

"There goes the Pacarro barbarian!"

He shook his head as they slapped their clubs against gloved hands. Mustering a fierce Pacarro warrior cry, he flew at them. Their eyes grew wide with fear. One of them dropped his club. Jorge slammed a fist into his jaw, laying him out upon the ground. He struck the other man's head with the butt end of his dagger. They both groaned helplessly upon the dirt and trash littering the ground.

Shadows darkened the alley as he moved further into the heart of the city. Soon one alley looked the same as another. He'd lost his bearings. Climbing the nearest wall like a ram in the mountains, he straddled his weight upon the top. The Palace of Kings came into sight. He would find rangers on duty there. Unlike the city constables, a ranger could not be purchased for any price.

A neighborhood open space awaited him on the other side of the wall. It was a large, main hub connecting alleys. Several options awaited him, but none seemed to lead directly to the palace. He sprinted toward the nearest alley. A sharp sting at his side threw his body against the wall. Gunpowder. Its distinctive smell struck his nose. The musket's bullet missed him by inches as it struck the far wall.

Armando, Julian's valet, stepped out from behind a pile of crates. His men moved in to form a half circle at his back. The false Lion Friend nodded with a smile.

"I must say this has been a worthy hunt. You have proven to be more challenging than any animal I've hunted, Pacarro."

Black chased away the brown of Armando's eyes. Inhuman orbs stared down at Jorge with murderous intensity. Points formed on his canine teeth as a beastly hunger crossed his features.

"What are you?"

Jorge clutched at the medicine bag he'd made before the trip. It was a Pacarro tradition to ward off evil spirits. He'd made it out of sentiment, never really believing in the myths of his people. Looking upon the creature standing before him, he knew he'd been foolish to dismiss centuries-old wisdom.

"You'll never know." The thing of evil's face undulated as it assumed human form again. "Kill him and make sure you leave the body in a place the Wolf will find it."

It gave Jorge a nod and then disappeared into the shadows of the alley once more. Jorge kept his eyes upon the creature for as long as he dared. Escaping this trap and returning to the palace had just become a matter of utmost import to his country. Wolf had to be warned about the creature as soon as possible before it could exercise any more evil upon Valdeon.

Chapter Twenty-Five

JULIAN HURRIED AWAY FROM THE Great Hall, skirting the crowds of murmuring onlookers. Cesar was still alive, and the men Marcellus recruited for their diversion had been captured. Minor annoyances. The plan had worked. Jorge Pacarro was out in the open with the changeling in close pursuit. As insolent as it could be, the changeling's skill for espionage was impressive.

A palace guard matched his hurried pace and bolted forward to block him. "My lord prince, Wolf and Chancellor Benito wish to speak with you."

"I am otherwise engaged."

"Forgive me, Highness, but My Lord the Wolf says if you do not come this very moment, he will send a ranger guard to fetch you."

"Fetch me? I will not be fetched like a stray dog! Get out of my way."

The guard gasped, clutching wildly at his back. Marcellus's gleeful face appeared over the man's shoulder. Twisting the dagger deeper into the unlucky victim's back, he caught his dying body as it sank to the floor.

"Hide the body quickly. We must hurry to my chambers. Armando may be awaiting us now."

Marcellus gave him a quick nod and dragged the guard behind a statue of Mikel D'Antoiné. He was sweating profusely when he rushed to Julian's side. Tiny flecks of blood covered the sleeve of his shirt. Marcellus quickly rolled them up when he noticed Julian's look.

"Where is Zoya?"

"She awaits us in your chambers, my prince."

"Good. I won't have her harmed by any western bumpkins out for revenge."

A small body rammed into Julian with a thud. He grabbed at the boy's arm before the little devil could get away. Rather than showing fear at being caught, the boy — to Julian's surprise — pulled out of his grip and put a small fist on each hip. Hard eyes glared at them above a sharp nose and square jaw. He could be no other than the son of Xavier the Wolf.

"One of the De Vincente pups." Julian kicked at the boy and missed. "Go back to the Wolf bitch that bore you, whelp."

"Don't you talk about my mama that way!"

Dark eyes stared up at them in defiance. The scowl on his face was a familiar fixture of the family De Vincente. Even at his young age — Julian guessed about five or six — he still held the famous temper.

The little brat flew at him and kicked Julian's shin as hard as he could. Leather boots didn't guard against the well-placed strike. He rubbed at his leg with a yelp of pain. Marcellus grabbed the boy by the hair, pulling him away from Julian. Terror ripped anger from the boy's face. Little hands pushed at the unyielding fist holding his locks. His breath came in haggard wheezes. Marcellus pulled the boy's face roughly up to look at him.

"You must be the sickly little pup Wolf was too weak to drown in the river. I'll do him the great favor of cutting your throat."

His blade lifted toward the tiny neck, its point pushing into the skin. The fool was courting certain death. He'd have the entire De Vincente family hunting him and any who named him ally. One slash of his blade and every hope Julian had of ruling Valdeon would be dashed.

"Leave him, Marcellus. We've no time for this!"

Julian's words were lost within the bloodlust filling Marcellus's heart. The warning came too late. Streaks of ash raced toward them. They circled in a blur around Marcellus. He fell flat on his back with an angry cry. His knife slid along the tile to the other side of the atrium. Something slapped against the back of Julian's knees. He fell upon his backside, joining Marcellus upon the ground.

Two rangers stood before them, weapons drawn, bodies ready to strike. Chestnut curls framed young faces. Firm, intense eyes held their prey. Julian exchanged a warning look with Marcellus. Good. He knew better than to move. Their captors may be in their teen years, but they were still rangers with full power.

The little De Vincente boy wheezed behind his rescuers. His head rested in the lap of a slightly older boy. Both children glared at Julian. Mockery shimmered in their eyes. Two more soldiers in the D'Antoiné and De Vincente feud.

"Well, Rabbit and Otter, what wonderful nannies you make. Does the Wolf have you watch his litter often?"

Rabbit, the youngest member of the Sacred Guard, turned his perfectly calm face to Julian. "Why don't you ask him yourself?"

Marcellus screamed in a sudden burst of pain. The bloodied tip of a sword pulled away from his right hand. He covered it before Julian could determine what wound had been inflicted.

"I mark you as the killer you are, butcher of children." Wolf's voice thundered behind them. "Allow one of your pets to come near my little ones again, Julian, and I will carve the same symbol upon your beating heart."

Julian rolled onto his knees. This was inexcusable! Lord of Valdeon or no, Wolf had no right to abuse a companion to the Prince of Valdeon. The flat of a blade rested upon his cheek. The cold steel tip twisted in a caress against Julian's skin. Fox, a deadly favorite among their numbers, held the blade's handle in a practiced grip.

"You were not given leave to rise, bastard prince."

Julian spun around, slapping the blade away. They were all there, the Lords of Valdeon. Each regarded him with their serene faces and burning eyes. They were inspecting him as if he were an insect.

"I am a Prince of Valdeon. How dare you!"

"Do you hear the clucking of a crow?" The Jaguar lifted a set of irons and let them swing in his grip. "We are within our right to take this killer for the attempted assassination of Lord Santiago."

"I saw the entire incident. Marcellus was trying to stop the attack. Do you doubt the word of a member of the royal house?"

"Lord Pacarro is a witness to his crime."

"And where is this barbarian, Jaguar? I don't see him here making his wild accusations in person. Perhaps he lacks the courage to face the victim of his lies?"

Julian clutched at his ring as their probing began. Without its protection, the rangers would know Marcellus had just killed a man. The Sarcion slapped their powers away, but its strength would not hold for long against the entire Sacred Guard.

"We will have the truth when Lord Pacarro returns. Take your pet and go." Wolf's hard look burrowed into them. "And De Costa, when next we meet outside these walls, you will answer for what you've done to my son."

Julian pulled Marcellus to his feet and hurried him down the corridor. How dare they insult him, and in his own palace! He regarded Marcellus, clutching at his bleeding hand. The bloodthirsty fool had almost killed them both. It was a great pity Wolf had been bound by his respect for the Altar. He might have relieved Julian of his mad burden.

"I will see you avenged, my friend." Julian forced sympathetic outrage to his face. "The Lords of Valdeon will be sorry they ever returned to San Leonora."

Marcellus nodded and followed his lord to Julian's private chambers. The curtains had been drawn, and the room was illuminated by a single candle. Zoya was strapped tightly to a chair. Her head hung forward in what Julian hoped was sleep.

"Leave her." An unfamiliar voice had come from the darkened corner of his personal chambers. Many guarded the corridors between the public areas of the palace and these private rooms. Whoever the stranger may be, he had shown an excess of brass.

Marcellus drew his sword, but Julian stopped him. The stranger could be an enemy or worse — one of his allies. Either one of them would delight in killing Zoya to hurt him.

"I won't ask the typical trite questions, but rather I will get to the point. What do you want?"

"Your family is having a run of misfortune, Julian. Both your brothers were killed in accidents, and now your father has gone missing.

"Tragic."

"If it pleases you to pretend so, but I would call it advantageous."

Their visitor's shadow moved along the wall to the wine cravat. Spice wine gurgled as it filled an unseen glass. The sound grated upon his nerves. Julian bit his lip. This intruder visitor was bold and obviously delighted in expensive treats belonging to others.

"Advantageous. I wouldn't think my father's many admirers would agree. We share opinions, sir. I would ask you to get to the point."

"Very well. I know the circumstances surrounding your father's disappearance. He has been running for these two years from a foe capable of besting his Lion Ring. The king remained in hiding, but never in safety. His pursuers caught up with him in every town and every inn in which he hid. He finally reached a place of safety, but left soon after receiving a letter."

"Letter? How do you know Leo's comings and goings? Better still, how do I know you speak the truth?"

"It is best for you to trust my word. Let us say I have intimate knowledge. He received a very special letter from the Grey Cliff Isles."

Julian forced the new surge of hope out of his voice. "Why tell me?"

"Let's just say I'm a Patriot."

The voice came from behind them this time. Julian spun around. How had the man moved so quickly? He waited. Soon a demand for money or royal favors would come.

"Do you have a specific location? Those Isles would take a lifetime to search."

Their visitor gave him a condescending sigh. "Surely you have spies to help you, Julian. You must hurry if you wish to take the throne. The ring goes to find its heir."

"I am its heir! I am the last son of Edmund D'Antoiné."

Julian gritted his teeth, angry with himself to have allowed his emotions to escape. The D'Antoiné family was fresh out of cousins and distant relatives. He was the last. Esteban the Hawk, the king's brother, had disappeared long ago. He wouldn't have any interest in the Lion Ring or anything else to do with Valdeon.

"You know Edmund had rather dangerous tastes in women." The stranger's voice took on an amused purr. "His interests drifted over the border to Tslavia. Think, Julian. How long has it been since the king took himself a queen?"

Julian glared into the darkness. "Well over fifteen years."

"Sixteen. I believe this is the length of time Princess Anne Von Wolkhurst of Tslavia has been missing." The stranger paused, letting this information drift upon the silent air. "You didn't murder all the sons of Edmund D'Antoiné. Leo will favor this half-breed, no doubt, because he is their child together — leaving you once again, the unwanted son."

"How dare you! Let me dispatch this worm, my lord prince."

"Keep silent, De Costa, or I will give you a mark upon your left hand to match your right! Beware the Lord of San Rudalfo, Julian. He has great power and many friends. They would put the Crown of Sorrows upon his head."

Stone scraped against stone. He hurried into the shadows. The stranger disappeared through the wall, leaving Julian seething in his wake. He slammed his fist against the hidden entrance. How had a stranger to the palace been able to navigate long-forgotten passageways?

"Marcellus, contact the Amity raiders. I have need of their services."

"You trust him enough to risk doing business with raider scum?"

"I have to believe him, fool! He knows more about my father and my home than I!" Julian turned violently on him. "I will have the Lion Ring no matter the cost. Now go prepare my ship. We leave at once."

"What of the Wolf?"

"Have him followed. We can't afford to let him run loose."

Julian smoothed his fingers over the cold surface, but their probing found no latches or loose stones. He struck his fist against the wall. Nothing! The stranger must be a member of the Valdeonian Court, but who would be so brazen? He rested his forehead against his stinging hand. A new player had joined their game, but whose side was he really on?

Chapter Twenty-Six

WOLF SANK TO THE MARBLED floor of the atrium and picked up the struggling body of his little son. Cradling Gaspar, he reached inside his waistcoat for the emergency kit he always kept ready. Grasping a tiny flask of water, his fingers tugged upward. A soft cloth fell upon his lap as the flask worked free.

"Come now, my son." Wolf patted the wet cloth on the back of Gaspar's neck. "Calm down for Papa. They've gone. I am with you now."

The little body shivered in his lap. Short gasps of air wheezed between pale lips. Wolf continued to pat Gaspar's neck with the wet cloth. It had been many months since the breathing illness had viciously attacked his son. Julian and his pet were to blame. He hid his anger. Gaspar needed him now. A father's justice would wait.

Otter sheathed his sword and came to join them with Rabbit in tow. Wolf regarded the two young men kneeling down beside him. They were no more than boys themselves, not quite a year out of their apprenticeship. Both were becoming fine men and brave rangers.

Lifting a hand toward Gaspar, Otter hesitated and let it fall again. "I didn't mean to leave him. We were playing. Will he be alright?"

"He'll be fine. Thank you both for saving him."

Wolf rubbed Gaspar's back and began to sing.

*"Sailboats made with candle wax, sailing to the shore line.
Wave your little arms, help them find you.
Carry my little one to the distant shores of dreamland
And back again to Papa's arms come morning."*

Gaspar's breathing finally calmed. Wolf kissed his cheek. Danel, his oldest, moved to them. Wolf pulled him into his arms as well, sitting both boys upon his lap. He projected comfort and protection, wrapping the power around his little ones. They'd lived their short lives under the protection of Wolf's title. None dared to threaten the family of one of the Sacred Guard until this dark day. It was considered an act of treason. These troubling times meant new dangers for his family.

Wolf cupped Gaspar's quivering chin gently in his hand and lifted his son's face toward his own. Tears spilled from the dark eyes, wetting his little cheeks. Wolf swore an oath in his heart as he looked upon the innocent face. He would collect a bucket of blood from Marcellus De Costa for each tear his son shed. That butcher would die the death he gave others.

"You are both my blessings from heaven. The Creator made you both special just for me and Mama. Others like De Costa or Julian can never understand how wonderful you are. I pity them for it."

Gaspar threw his arms around Wolf's neck and favored him with a wet kiss. "You scared Julian and his pet. Didn't you, Papa?"

"Of course he did. I think De Costa wet himself." Danel grinned when Gaspar started to giggle.

"Prince Julian called Mama a bad name, Papa. I kicked him in the shin as hard as I could!"

Gaspar's eyes glowed with pride when the Lords of Valdeon burst into laughter. He was a brave little man despite the illness. Wolf sometimes imagined his fierce little son as a man full grown, wearing his father's ring.

Alas, it was not meant to be. The Jalora chose its rangers. Neither of his sons were born with the golden aura of power marking them as heir to the Wolf Ring. Another destiny awaited Gaspar and Danel. Their father would help them find their futures in a peaceful Valdeon.

"You mustn't look so pleased with yourselves when we tell Mama. Promise me, children. If Julian or De Costa come near you again, run to find me or one of the Lords of Valdeon."

"We promise."

"Come, we'll see you back to our quarters." Wolf pulled the boys up and took their hands. "Papa must meet with the other rangers."

They made their way down the ornate corridors lined with tapestries toward the guest wing of the palace. Wolf and his family were given a floor of their own, while the young Lords of Valdeon had been housed above them.

"Playing hide and seek in the Palace of Kings. Jalora spare me from fools!" Jaguar slapped his younger cousin across the back of the head. "Have you no respect, Otter? The Altar of Providence is just down the hall."

"It was a game. Don't be so stuffy. Your father isn't, and he was a general in the Valdeonian Army."

"Papa?" Danel tugged on Wolf's sleeve, drawing his attention away from the Mendoza cousins. "What did you carve on the man's hand?"

Wolf ran his thumb gently along the smooth skin of Danel's little fingers. "Do you remember when you went with Papa to ride among our herd of horses last year? We had a stallion who had turned bad and hurt some of the other horses."

"Yes, I remember. The stallion kept everyone away, but you walked right up and roped him."

Wolf chuckled. He was their hero. Creator willing the day would never come when his sons replaced him with another.

"Yes. We marked him with a 'C' to warn everyone he was bad and must be culled to protect others. I gave De Costa the same mark."

"No one is more deserving of such a mark than that butcher." Bitterness hung heavy in Ernesto the Raven's words. De Costa's crime had been committed on De Quintaro land. The rangers would never forget the horror they found as they helped their comrade deliver justice. Wolf pushed such things from his mind as he looked down into the innocent faces of his two little ones. No such thing must ever happen to them.

Soldiers of the San Rudalfo Army snapped to attention as they approached. The forest green and black of their immaculate uniforms appeared harsh against the golden walls of the palace. Good. Wolf wanted the strong presence of his army felt in San Leonora during these troubling times.

The men he brought with him were well trained and not prone to panic or other breaches of discipline. Their lieutenant unexpectedly stepped away from his post to meet them. His eyes were troubled. Something had happened. Anger, shock, and concern swirled around his body. Wolf probed his memories and saw the unthinkable there.

"Double the guard around my family and keep a wary eye open."

"It will be as you say, my lord. No friend of the bastard prince will set foot within this wing."

Fox gripped his shoulder, questions burning in his eyes. Wolf shook his head and looked down at the children. Such things were best discussed when little ears could not hear them. The innocent nature of children allowed them to see through a ranger's mask to the true emotions hidden beneath the Jalora's magic. He forced a smile for his sons.

Two servants bowed low and opened the doors for them. Wolf gave them no notice. Dulcina had insisted they bring along half the household to San Leonora. It wasn't her normal practice, but Lady De Vincente would not see her husband and family lowered in the social circles of Court. Wolf left such things to his wife. Dulcina had a gift for politics.

"What high adventures have my men been up to today?" Her melodic voice called from the settee. Dulcina stood to greet them. Wolf's breath caught in his chest as his lovely wife smiled. After all their years together, she could still command his heart with a look. Her eyes sparkled as they found his.

"Mama!" Gaspar ran to her arms. "Julian and his pet tried to slit my throat, but I kicked him in the shin as hard as I could!"

"You kicked him before he had the knife." Danel stuck his tongue out.

"You weren't there!"

They began to shove each other about. Danel may have been older and taller, but Gaspar had the De Vincente temper. It was an equal match.

"You aren't helping yourselves, my sons." Wolf pointed to their Mama who had her arms crossed before her.

"Children, you must leave such things to your Papa. It is his place to protect our family. One day you will join him, but not until you are as tall as he." Dulcina came to stand beside Wolf and wrapped her arm around his waist.

Shock. Rage. It pulsed from the rear of the room. The Wolf's squire stood with his hand clasped upon the hilt of his sword. His eyes were alight with fury. Basilio was fiercely protective of his adoptive family. He would never go against his ranger's wishes or speak out of turn, but there would be danger of him provoking De Costa into a fight.

"Here you are, Little Sirs. Your bath water grows cold."

"Basilio, must we bathe now?" The boys began to shuffle.

"I'm certain your good father wouldn't want his sons going to their beds dirty."

"Indeed not, my sons. Go prepare for your baths. Basilio will join you in a moment."

Two curly little heads drifted down the hall, dragging their feet. He waited until they were safely out of range. Then Wolf turned to Basilio. He held out his hands. Basilio put Dulcina's burgundy hair ribbon in one hand and a plain white handled dagger in the other.

"They were found driven in the door of your bedchamber." Basilio relaxed his mind, allowing the rangers to probe his memories. Wolf was grateful he'd thought to pluck the dagger from the door before the children came home.

"Your apartments are well guarded." Fox ran his finger along the hole in the wood. "This had to be someone with access to the chambers. A maid from the palace staff, perhaps?"

Dulcina took Wolf's arm and squeezed it gently. "Someone has made a foolish mistake, Husband. This was simple mischief."

Wolf smoothed at her face gently. "You attempt to put me at ease, my love. Mischief or no, the person who did this will face my justice. Any who threaten my family must expect their time in this world to be very short."

Run to the streets of San Leonora, Lord of Valdeon! The Jalora's command held Wolf in its grip. *Help our ally who faces treachery!*

A sharp stab of apprehension pierced his chest. The Jalora stirred, its anxiety compounding Wolf's own. As with most rangers, the Jalora warned him in times of great trouble. It normally communicated in images and impressions, but not since he first put the Wolf Ring upon his finger had he heard its voice so clearly.

"Squire! Guard my family with your very life!"

Wolf spun toward the door, halting only to wait for his fast-approaching squire. The Lords of Valdeon were beside him, ready to follow their commander into the fray. Basilio marched out into the room with bubbles up to his elbow. A look of understanding passed between them.

"Lieutenant! Kill anyone trying to enter these rooms. I don't care who they are!" Basilio barked his orders past Wolf's shoulder to the guards shrinking away from the powered-up rangers.

Wolf raced past the soldiers with the young Lords of Valdeon right on his heels. They flew through the glass patio doors, through the gardens and into the main courtyard. A mounted patrol heading toward the gates cantered through the yard. The Lords of Valdeon swept between their horses, outpacing the beasts.

Two long buildings housing the barracks of the palace guards on one side and visiting Valdeonian rangers on the other, boxed in the yard on either side of the palace steps. Rangers and soldiers alike came out of their chambers as the alarm bell's clang sounded. Wolf breathed a little easier. The Jalora's warning must have reached other rangers as well. His family would be safe for the time being.

The Jalora drew them down King's Row and forward toward the busy shops of San Leonora. Darting between the townsfolk, they were streaks of ash on a gusty wind. An urgent prod of power directed Wolf down a small alley. The San Leonora Library's ornate roof peeked over the top of the other buildings. He knew now who they were rushing to save. Jorge Pacarro. The urgent prodding of power was understandable now. Jorge's body was the hiding place for the Regent's Medallion. If he were in danger, it was also.

His keen ranger sight could make out several blades flashing in the distance. The alleys intersected into a small open space littered with trash and discarded crates. The attackers were circling their prey slowly, gauging his strength. One of them cried out as a hatchet sunk deep in his chest. A head of war beads twisted around as its owner yanked the blade out of his kill and brought it up to meet a new opponent. Jorge was bleeding, but still not beaten. His attackers had made the mistake of misjudging their prey. They were discovering how deadly a Pacarro warrior could be in battle, especially when he was cornered.

Beware the high ground!

Wolf stopped at the entrance to the open space, scanning the roof tops above them. Something was suspicious about the scene before them. The men attacking Jorge hadn't bothered to post lookouts to watch for patrols or the Pacarro tribesman's allies. They were leaving their backs completely unguarded. Their confident strikes directed at their victim appeared experienced. These were no amateurs.

Lucio the Ferret bolted forward, racing into the open space. Wolf thrust an arm out to slow the impetuous youth down, but it was too late. The trap had been sprung. An old crate smashed to the ground a few feet to Wolf's left. He chanced a look around the building's corner, turning his gaze upward. A man waited at the top of iron rod stairs attached to the back of the building. In his hand was a musket aimed at Lucio's head.

Jorge's death would please the black-hearted prince holding their leash, but the assassins' true targets were the Sacred Guard. Such disrespect and open treason could only mean one thing. Wolf was losing the fight for Valdeon's stability.

Chapter Twenty-Seven

A MUSKET'S BOOM ECHOED AGAINST the building walls. Stone chips exploded at Lucio's feet. He twisted his body, putting one of his attackers in the sniper's line of sight. Wolf sheathed his weapon and crouched at the corner.

"He has us pinned down, sir." Berto knelt beside him, growling with frustration as another shot struck close to Lucio.

"The gunman couldn't have reloaded so quickly. They have another hidden somewhere." Wolf stretched the Jalora's power out into the rooftops. "Berto, across from us. The other gunman has taken up position in a rear window on the third floor of one of the shops."

Berto nodded. Pulling the hood over his head, he disappeared against the backdrop of brick and wood. The others waited for Wolf's next order. Their two youngest fidgeted slightly at the prospects of their first real battle. Wolf turned his gaze upon them, capturing their attention.

"We aid a friend today, but this battle is larger than such things. Traitors strike at the heart of the Jalora's home. They threaten Valdeon. No mercy will be given to these traitors." Wolf's look was hard. "Attack when you hear Berto's signal for the all clear. I will take care of this gunman."

He bolted forward, staying low against the wall. Above him, the gunman was reloading his musket.

Their eyes met. It had just become a deadly race. Wolf gripped the iron rod with both hands and summoned the Jalora's power. His advanced rank in the legion gave him stronger powers than most. He pulled with all the might he had, ripping the iron away from the wall. It crashed to the ground sending the gunman rolling across the stone. He reached for the musket, but Wolf's boot slammed down on the weapon. It broke in two with a loud snap. His blade arched upward, severing the traitor's head from his shoulders.

Glass exploded into the open space as Berto's prey flew through the air. His broken body fell into the midst of the attackers surrounding Jorge. The fighting stopped. Jorge's opponents stood motionless when they noticed the Lords of Valdeon. Fear was on their faces.

"Protect the innocent. Punish the guilty." Wolf's voice thundered around the walls.

The Lords of Valdeon swept into the group of men. Their blades moved with deadly speed, cutting through bone and flesh. Weapons swinging at empty air, the traitors failed to strike the untouchable blades. In moments the battle was over. Only the Lords of Valdeon remained standing.

Tulio the Rabbit stared at the dead as he wiped blood from his blade. Something was missing from his eyes. Wolf regretted Tulio's loss of innocence. He would never be the same again, but he was a ranger tasked with a sacred duty. It was not an easy life sometimes.

"We have seen the Jalora's will done this day. You honor your ring."

He gripped Tulio's shoulder and nodded to Otter. Pride replaced their somber reflections. They sheathed their weapons and joined the other, more experienced rangers keeping careful watch on the rooftops above them.

Jorge wiped his hatchet clean upon one of the dead men's waistcoats. "My eyes are glad to see you, my lords! I thought I was a dead man."

"You very well might have been." Wolf helped him to his feet. "Why were you wandering the streets alone?"

"A man may wander if the mood strikes him, my lord." The beaded head tilted to regard him. "It is the very young and the very old who need show caution."

Wolf grinned reluctantly. "And the very outspoken. You've made many enemies in San Leonora."

"One more vengeful than the rest, I dare say." Fox kicked at one of the bodies. "Julian has many pets."

"His valet, Armando, is particularly deadly. It cornered me like a bloodhound."

"It?" Fox lifted a fine eyebrow.

"Julian has brought a creature of evil among us. I knew the man, Armando. He was one of Leo's Lion Friends. No marks appear on this creature's arm. I believe we are dealing with a changeling. It showed me its true nature a few moments ago. Some magic hides its sharp ears and inhuman black eyes."

"Are you saying a mythical creature is running around the Palace of Kings?" Otter's youthful face struggled to hide his skepticism.

"Not for long." Wolf eyed the rooftops uneasily. "We'll take care of Julian's valet soon. Right now, we must meet with the other rangers. Jaguar. Take point. Ferret. You're with me."

Wolf pulled Lucio aside. He was furious with the young man. His impetuous act had almost gotten them all killed. He folded his arms and gave the young ranger what many subordinates had come to call Wolf's "I'll make you wish you were back home" look.

"Jumping into a circle of blades without a plan was foolhardy."

"But, Jorge was in trouble." Ferret's words faded when he looked into Wolf's face. "Yes, Wolf."

"You're a leader of men now." Wolf tapped on the dark green crystal of Ferret's Heart of the Warrior Ring. "The men who follow you will watch your every move. If you're impulsive, they'll fear your actions. Take time to make a clear-headed decision and they'll respect you, because they know you respect their lives."

Ferret nodded and looked down at his boots. Wolf noticed Jorge had turned his head and was listening. The tribesman nodded his thanks to Wolf.

"Well, Jorge. I think young Ferret's skill with a blade has already surpassed his father."

The young ranger looked up with a mix of surprise and pleasure. Flattery and other such sentiment were not easily pried from Wolf's lips. Such nonsense served only to distract men away from the pursuit of bettering oneself.

"My young lord is impressive." Jorge nodded sagely. "It is a pity his father was not here to see him fight. Cesar will burst his buttons with pride!"

"You'll have your chance to tell the tale. We'll take you to the ranger quarters where it's safe."

"Yes, well I had better tell the tale well. I'm sure I'll have more than one proud father listening."

The other young rangers began to swagger up the alley, pretending Jorge's compliments didn't please them.

Wolf took the lead as they moved through the backstreets. Anxious to avoid more traitors, they used their cloaks to move about unseen. Jorge managed to match their pace though he was wounded. Sending the Jalora's power of sight and perception before their path, Wolf found friends rather than foes awaiting them. Two rangers stepped out of the shadows and saluted as their group approached Stallion's Gate.

Owl stepped forward. "We've put the palace guard on high alert, sir. What has happened?"

"My Lord Pacarro was ambushed by friends of the bastard prince. Have a guard put on Armando, Julian's new valet. Tell them to show care. He's dangerous. Come, we must go to HQ."

"Owl, fetch the legion doctor. I will escort the Lords of Valdeon to Headquarters." The other ranger, Griffin, pulled his blade.

"Yes, sir." Owl saluted and then hurried toward the infirmary.

"The others await us in the hall." Griffin led the way through the palace gates.

Headquarters was located in an elegant three-story villa just inside the gates. It had housed the Valdeonian rangers and their families for centuries. Squires on sentry duty pulled open the doors for them. The building was no less elegant on the inside. Ancient stone halls were lined with drawn images of animals and murals of the Valdeonian countryside. Hardwood floors made from the ancient forests outside Varianne stretched along the corridors.

Griffin eased closer to Wolf. "You have a guest waiting for you in your office, sir. It is a matter of great importance."

The elaborately carved wooden doors of the dining hall stood open as they approached. Several conversations halted abruptly as the Lords of Valdeon entered the room.

"What's happened?" Cesar's voice thundered up to the ceiling.

"Jorge was ambushed by friends of Julian." Wolf rested a hand upon his mentor's shoulder. "We have sent for the doctor."

"They dare touch the squire to a Lord of Valdeon!" Cesar turned purple when he saw his son who now held the title. "You know what I meant. And what were you doing wandering about by yourself, Jorge?"

"My lord need not fear. His son and the other Lords of Valdeon were victorious." Jorge came to stand beside his lord, maneuvering him toward a chair.

"Get the duke some strong drink!" Fausto clapped his hands together and winked at Wolf. "You'll need a wet throat to tell us this tale."

"Berto." Wolf leaned closer to his second. "Take the Sacred Guard and make sure we weren't followed. Meet me back here in ten minutes."

He followed Griffin to his office. The lights in the hall surrounding the door had been extinguished and the surrounding rooms deserted. Griffin opened the door for him and then pulled his sword to take a guard position in the hall.

A fully cloaked ranger stood behind Wolf's desk. He'd drawn the curtains in the office, casting it into darkness. Wolf closed the door. When they were alone, the ranger lighted the lamp. Violet glowed from his Falcon Ring as he threw the hood from his head. Gray curls had overtaken his darker hair. Though he was in his middle years, no man dared push Bishop Falcon's temper. He was one of the most powerful rangers in the legion.

"I bring words of warning from Dragon, Xavier the Wolf." Falcon stepped from behind the desk. His trousers and boots were covered with filth. A weary face took up his glass of bourbon and he gulped it down. This ranger had traveled hard.

"Why has Dragon not answered my pleas for aid?" Wolf's heart constricted. He feared he already knew the answer.

"We have received no messages from you, ranger." Falcon lowered the glass with a frown. "We'd begun to fear the worst. News of Leo's death and the Lion Ring's disappearance has begun to spread about Andara. The legion has its hands full squashing panic in the United Realm. Our powers have begun to fade, Wolf. Many of your comrades have faced ambush and injury. I was sent here in order to bring hope back with me."

"I have none to give, Bishop. The Jalora has closed the golden doors to the Altar of Providence. The bastard prince of Valdeon and his murderous pet have lain violent hands upon my son. A few hours ago, Julian's allies set a trap with the purpose of killing one of the Sacred Guard. Evil attacks us."

"I'd hoped to lend aid for a few days, but this news must be taken back to Dragon." Falcon slammed the glass upon the desk. "I've left a special request for Lucio the Ferret's assistance on your desk. Under the circumstances, I will understand if you cannot part with him right now."

He moved to the window and unlatched it. Turning to Wolf, he extended his hand and they shook in farewell. "San Leonora isn't the only Valdeonian city in peril. I came on horseback from the north. The inns and byways are full of strange men spreading discontent. Be careful."

Wolf joined the others and moved to the podium at the head of the mess hall. A long table stood behind him. The Lords of Valdeon traditionally took their meals upon it. A chair at its center stood empty. Leo.

His memory was another fixture in the room. Wolf looked out over the dozens of faithful lords. All eyes turned upon him as he waited for them to quiet down.

"I go to meet with the rangers now; you will wait here until we return. I warn you, don't try to pass through the doors into central headquarters. The Jalora only allows its rangers and their squires within those walls."

They bowed low as Wolf moved through their numbers toward the doors to central HQ. Gasps of amazement and whispers of awe filled the mess hall when the great doors opened by themselves. The Lords of Valdeon, with Wolf at their head, went inside to join the rest of the Valdeonian rangers.

He marched the Sacred Guard past the ancient drawings depicting the animal rings of Valdeon. White marble, of a lesser grade than the throne room, stretched across the floor, pulsing with the magic of the ancients. Being in this legion haven always renewed Wolf's strength and faith in the legion. He wasn't alone. The young lords of Valdeon too breathed in the power. They looked strong and confident. Good. They were ready to stand before their countrymen and legion comrades.

The twenty-two rangers of Valdeon stood at attention and saluted the Sacred Guard as they entered the room. When a Jalora Master sat upon the Altar of Providence, these rangers would act as the Altar Guard, taking up the duties normally held by the Lords of Valdeon. The elite Sacred Guard's duty shifted to a more important role, guarding the Lion who was the living embodiment of the Altar and the Jalora itself. Though that had not happened in more than a hundred years, the Valdeonian rangers kept themselves at the ready. Only the Jalora knew when it would walk upon the earth.

Jaguar gave the order to stand at ease. They obeyed with solemn faces. Wolf had briefed them about the Lion Ring's disappearance and Leo's death when they'd first arrived. Shock and fear had been their response. Now they waited with acceptance.

"I have had a message from Dragon. News of Leo's death and the Lion Ring's disappearance has begun to spread about Andara. The legion has its hands full squashing panic in the United Realm. Many believe the legion's days are over. Evil prepares to spread across the land. We are all that stand between the Altar of Providence and disaster." Wolf paused, allowing his words to reach their hearts. "We must help the government continue to function. Evil must be kept at bay."

"Yes, Wolf." Commitment was in their voices, but very little hope.

"Since Leo's disappearance, times have grown hard for Valdeon. The dangers will be much greater now that the Lion Ring has been lost. We have no lion heir to lead us. Already factions lusting after power are plotting to take the throne. Beware, rangers, of plots against the throne and against the chancellor." He met each of their troubled gazes. "Be strong in your dedication to the Jalora. Do not listen to the men of Valdeon. Only the Jalora's wisdom will see us through these times."

Devotion radiated from their numbers. Wolf nodded, letting the knot in his stomach ease. The rangers were of one mind at least. That would make things a bit easier in the coming days. He turned and led the rangers down the corridor and into the mess hall where the prefects loyal to the throne waited.

Wolf took his place upon the dais with the young Lords of Valdeon standing behind him. The other rangers moved into the crowd, mixing with the landowners from the west and those loyal from the east.

"You can see how dangerous San Leonora has become." Wolf pointed at Jorge Pacarro. "Earlier today my sons were threatened by the butcher De Costa."

Wolf waited for their cries of outrage to die down. "The bastard prince has grown brazen in his contempt for the Jalora. Mark me, my lords. He will try to take the throne by force."

Several of the landowners began to murmur anxiously amongst themselves, but the rangers remained silent and stoic. They knew he wasn't exaggerating for effect.

"What should we do, My Lord De Vincente?" A young man dressed in the garb of the southwest stood at the back of the room. "Would you have us make you our new king?"

"Yes! Wolf is the only man to save Valdeon from civil war!" One of the minor eastern prefects jumped to his feet at the center of the crowd.

"But what of the Lion?" Another voice joined the banter. "Xavier the Wolf doesn't bear the Lion Ring!"

"Perhaps the Jalora has decided to replace the Lion with the Wolf?"

Blood drained from Wolf's face as he stared in shock at the group of men. They had no idea of the dangers they were bringing upon Andara. He beat his fist upon the dais to settle them. Sweat was dripping from his hair. He wiped at the wetness on his forehead with a shaking hand. If these great fools hadn't the sense enough to be frightened, Wolf was terrified for them. What had he done to make them speak of such blasphemy?

"Stop this talk of treason!" He looked out across their sea of faces. "Are you mad? Will you bring down the wrath of the Jalora upon our nation?"

Oath breaker. Memories of Leo's disappointed face, their harsh words, and his own failure to stem the tides of unrest filled Wolf's mouth until he thought he'd vomit.

"You are modest, My Lord De Vincente! Everyone knows the Jalora favors you. It has given you great honor and the devotion of the Valdeonian people."

"I will hear no more of this! I am a servant of the Jalora. Never will I conspire against it!"

His body went rigid as the Jalora's great power wrapped about him. Its presence invaded Wolf's nostrils and mouth until he thought it would suffocate him. Blinding light assaulted his eyes and then suddenly dimmed. The Jalora had come among them and it had chosen Wolf as its temporary vessel. The rangers fell upon their bellies, faces to the ground. The other men backed away in terror.

"Look at his eyes! They glow with power."

"On your knees, men of Valdeon!" Jaguar motioned to the stunned men in the crowd. "The Jalora has come unto us."

"In Wolf, my servant, I am most pleased." Wolf 's mouth opened and the Jalora's power flowed from his lips as it took over his body. He did not resist. He was its servant and would give himself in any way it needed.

"War is coming. Prepare yourselves as best you can." Then its voice turned inward for Wolf's ears alone. *My sheep need their shepherds. Keep those you need with you. Send the rest back to their homes. You must also ensure Jorge Pacarro is protected.*

"Yes, holiness. It will be as you say." Wolf kept his eyes closed and waited for the room to stop spinning.

I am most pleased with you, Xavier the Wolf. You have earned my complete trust. Soon I will give you a very special gift. Hold on to the hope you have, child. You will not be disappointed.

Then it released him as abruptly as it had come. Wolf leaned against the dais, exhausted. Jaguar hurried to help him into a chair. The unflappable young man was pale with fear. Neither of them had experienced the Jalora's full presence with this much power.

"Rangers and men of Valdeon, the Jalora commands you to return to your homes. Prepare for war."

Wolf turned to face three faithful men kneeling a few feet away from him. Cesar, Fausto, and Jorge stared at him, open mouthed. They well knew what had just happened was rare.

"And you, Jorge Pacarro, will stay close to me."

Chapter Twenty-Eight

JORGE TURNED THE PAGE OF his book. He'd read it twice and was ready for a new piece of literary treasure. Wolf, however, wouldn't allow him to go into the streets of San Leonora on his own. The ranger had in fact forbidden him from, as Wolf put it, "wandering, spying, or otherwise putting himself in danger." The Lords of Valdeon had been overly protective of him since the Jalora had come among them through Wolf the day before. The sudden disappearance of Julian's valet didn't help matters. The creature of evil was hiding somewhere, waiting for its chance to cause more mischief.

Giving up on the book, he closed it and tucked it inside his waistcoat. Jorge extinguished the crystal lantern. Moonlight flowed into the gardens, enveloping him in its silver light. San Leonora was known for its romantic atmosphere. No location offered a more breathtaking, dreamlike ambience for lovers than the gardens surrounding the Palace of Kings. It was his great misfortune to be without wife or frivolity this trip.

The aching in his arm reminded him such youthful pursuits were best left to others for a time. He stretched his wounded arm. He'd had worse injuries, but Cesar made it a point to bring up Jorge's reckless foolishness. With so many nursemaids scolding him, he'd been grateful to sneak away on his own for a bit of reading in the gardens.

Moonglow, pale and delicate, fell upon his out-stretched hand. Tiny sparkles of white winked against his skin. More of the glittering white fell upon the grass and foliage about him. Then a powerful presence entered the garden. It brushed at the hairs on his arms. Jorge recognized the presence from his many years of service as squire. The Jalora walked its garden this night.

His keen eyes lifted toward the path winding among the foliage. Xavier the Wolf's body walked toward him in the moonlight. The ranger was complete-ly nude, even his boots were missing. Wolf held his sword outstretched before him. His eyes were ablaze with the power of the Jalora.

"Wolf?" Jorge carefully approached him. It wasn't wise to test the ranger's patience, especially when he wasn't sure he was actually speaking to Xavier De Vincente. "May I assist you in some way, my lord?"

"Behind me, squire." Wolf's grip tightened upon his sword, sending the blood rushing from his knuckles. "We must find him! His enemies draw closer and he is without protection."

Jorge came to stand at his elbow. He'd known Wolf long enough to read the fury upon his face. This ranger was ready to kill. Wolf shouted a fierce battle cry and dove into the trees. Sweet Erthe Mother. It was no easy task to keep up with a ranger at his top speed, but Jorge had been a squire. He knew his limits and how to push himself. Bolting in amongst the broken branches, he followed as best he could.

Breathless, Jorge stumbled to a stop at the garden's cherry orchard. The ranger's body was a glowing outline among the thicket of cherry trees. Swinging the sword's tip along the treeline, he growled incoherently at the shadowed branches. Wolf was growing agitated, and in his current state, it could only mean death for anyone in his way — friend or foe.

"Seth! Where are you? Come out. I'll protect you. This I swear!"

Five armed men came out of the thicket. They began to circle the disoriented ranger. Jorge threw off the sling on his arm. He burst into their path, drawing his hatchet as he put his back to Wolf. A storm of confusion and treachery was descending upon Jorge as his country began to crumble about him. Its salvation rested upon one man. Xavier the Wolf must be kept safe to lead their people out of this turmoil. He was willing to give his own life to ensure it.

"Stay away from him, traitors! On the ground, Seth! Hurry."

Then the impossible happened. Xavier the Wolf swung his sword at the trees, their trunks falling in an explosion of bark and power. Jorge had just enough time to throw himself to the ground before the debris and blade came his way. Half of the men attacking them weren't as fortunate. Their bodies fell into bloodied pieces upon the ground.

Jorge stared up at the Wolf as the great power left his eyes. He'd never seen anything like the strike Wolf had just used to demolish the orchard. Even Cardinal Dragon didn't possess such power. The Jalora had changed the ranger standing before him. It had given him more power in an uncertain world. The realization gave Jorge hope.

Wolf staggered. Jorge hurried to his feet and helped the ranger stand. A shout to his left was a reminder they'd had company within the gardens. One of the fools, still covered in tinder, leapt forward to attack them. Jorge let lose his hatchet, striking the man in his throat. His friend turned tail and ran through the trees. Jorge didn't follow. He stayed beside the stunned ranger instead. The traitor's death would wait for another time.

"Wolf?" Jorge gripped the ranger's chin in his hand. "Can you hear me?"

Wolf lowered his sword and stared about him. "Jorge? What has happened? Where am I?"

"You are in the gardens of the Palace of Kings." Jorge stepped away when he was satisfied his words were getting through. "Yes, you have come back to us." He yanked his hatchet from the dead man's throat. "I was reading when I saw you charging as if you were in a great battle. These fools took advantage of your…dream to attack you."

"Dream? It seemed so real, as if I were really there."

"You were calling for someone named Seth. Who is he?"

Wolf shook his head, blankly staring into the ruined stumps of the orchard. "I don't know."

Well, whoever this Seth may be, it sounded as if he was in great peril. Jorge took Wolf's blade from his shaking hand and rested it against a broken tree trunk. If this Seth was important to Wolf, then he was important to Valdeon. Perhaps time would restore Wolf's memory.

Jorge whirled around when other bare feet stomped into the garden. The young Lords of Valdeon and several landowners from both sides stared at the scene. Wolf's squire came behind them, carrying a robe across one arm. He helped Wolf into the garment, picked up his lord's sword, and guided his disoriented master back toward his bedchamber.

"Get back to bed, all of you!" Wolf's squire nodded to Jorge. It was as close to a "thank you" as Basilio would ever give.

The Lords of Valdeon circled around him. Though the Jalora masked the countenances of its rangers, nothing could keep raw emotion out of the eyes. These young men looked to Wolf for leadership and guidance. Seeing him in such a helpless state had shaken them. Jorge shook his head as the anxious young men asked their silent question.

"Very well, probe as you will. It is important you see what has happened."

Their prodding began, gently at first. Jorge gripped at his poor head as their touch took on a more urgent need. A dull ache was beginning to form. Finally, they stood away when they were satisfied they'd seen everything.

"Come, we must stay close to Wolf this night." Jaguar kept his weapon at the ready and took point as they headed toward the palace.

Lady De Vincente stood in the double glass doors opening onto one of the garden's many patios. She was a vision in burgundy robes, her long hair falling to her waist. A lovely hand stroked her husband's arm as Basilio helped him inside their rooms. She clutched at the neck of her robe and turned to face the Lords of Valdeon.

Jorge heard a low whistle of appreciation behind him. He turned, realizing the landowners had followed. One of them, a young man with wandering eyes, took in Dulcina. Jorge stepped between them, blocking the young fool's view. Xavier De Vincente was a jealous man. He would not tolerate any disrespect or improper admiration of his good lady.

Dulcina swept before Jorge and gripped his hand. "What has happened, Duke Pacarro? I understand from Basilio you protected my husband this night."

"My Lord the Wolf has had another vision from the Jalora, my lady." Jorge shared a smile with her when the landowners started their excited whispering.

"He will be angry with you, Jorge." She gripped his arm fondly. "But, I can only thank you and will help pass along this news of another miracle. He cannot be angry with us both for long."

She was absolutely right. Word would spread quickly of Wolf's miracle. The ranger wouldn't like it, but they couldn't afford talk questioning his sanity. Jorge turned his attention to the giddy landowners. If they were not in awe of Wolf before, they certainly were now.

Chapter Twenty-Nine

Sunlight pierced through thinning branches to illuminate the damage within the palace gardens. Wolf's ranger eyes took in the snarled trunks and bits of human remains. Several soldiers stomped around the ferns conducting their gruesome duty. He gripped his belt tightly. The incredible destruction had been done with a flick of his blade, and he didn't remember any of it. Was he losing his mind?

"My Lord De Vincente?"

He turned from the window with a restrained sigh and waved away the drink Basilio offered to him. Jorge, Cesar, and Fausto stood to one side of the room. The Sacred Guard had positioned themselves close to the wall in a discreet half circle. His gift of discernment came unbidden to surround the men in the room. A mixture of awe and concern swirled about their bodies. He forced the sudden surge of fear from his own energy. The Jalora's power had grown stronger within his body over the past few days. Such increase usually came when the Jalora granted a ranger a higher rank among the legion, but Wolf was certain this occasion was different. He was gaining power while other rangers among them were losing their gifts. The bearer of the Mongoose Ring, a low-ranking young man from central Valdeon, had been taken to the transport ship's infirmary after his powers had been almost completely drained. He'd have a miserable trip home.

"As I was saying, my lord, tensions run high in San Leonora. Rumors had to be managed." Jorge lifted his chin, sending his warrior beads rattling. "I did what was necessary."

"You told a blatant lie." Wolf paced before the disturbingly calm Jorge Pacarro. "And you used my wife to spread it."

"Such dreams experienced by a member of the Sacred Guard are best heeded, my lord. You must admit there has been a change in you since your, um, experience with the Jalora in HQ."

Wolf couldn't deny the changes in his body and the strengthening of his ranger powers. He was ashamed to admit it, but Wolf was unsettled by these changes. He'd asked for guidance before the doors of the throne room, but the Jalora hadn't answered the respectful pleas. His trust in the Jalora was absolute of course, but he wished it would explain what was happening to him.

"Yes, My Lord Pacarro, I don't know the extent of these changes. Last night's dream has forced me to take action."

The attempts on their lives and the threats to his family were symptoms of a larger problem. Valdeon was no longer the country he'd known. War was coming. Nothing would be the same for any of them again.

"The Jalora tasked me with your protection, Jorge. I can no longer do so here within the Palace of Kings."

Wolf raised his hand in warning. As a former squire, Jorge understood the risks of questioning the Jalora's wisdom or its commands. The Pacarro tribesman wasn't going to like being treated as a sacred Valdeonian artifact. He must be kept safe. If it meant sending him away, so be it.

He turned to his squire, Basilio, who had been trying very hard not to comment on their conversation. "Send the captain of our small schooner to me. Go to Duke Pacarro's rooms and pack his belongings. Take Ferret's squire with you to help. Jorge and Cesar leave for San Lucida tonight."

"What?" The rust hue of Jorge's face turned into a deep shade of purple. "I want to stay beside you, Wolf. You'll need help!"

Cesar Santiago remained where he was, arms folded and face calm. He'd anticipated this, though Wolf had not breathed a word to anyone about the Regent's Medallion. His old mentor was not easily fooled. He'd most likely seen the changes in Jorge's energy and guessed the rest.

Fausto hurried forward to rest a hand upon Jorge's shoulder. "I don't like leaving Wolf here alone either. You must trust him, Jorge. He does this for good reason."

"Xavier De Vincente has always had and will always have my trust."

Jorge nodded to Wolf and joined Cesar beside the door. They followed Basilio out into the hall. Wolf grew troubled when he noticed the twinkle in his old mentor's eyes as they left. Cesar had accepted the command to return home a little too easily. He'd been suspiciously quiet during their conversation.

"I can see the wheels turning in your head, Wolf." Fausto came to stand beside him. "Our old friend will not be sent away so easily. I can take him back to San Lucida myself if you'd like."

"I have another task for you, Fausto, if you will see to it. Dulcina and the children, they must join the rest of the family in San Rudalfo."

Fausto nodded and gave him a troubled smile. "Have no fear, my friend. I will see them home safely."

"I wonder who Seth is and if he escaped those men?" Otter's young face puckered as he gave voice to the question Wolf had thought about most of the day. He and the other rangers had remained close to Wolf since they'd found him with Jorge in the garden. Anxious to make sense of such troubling things, they'd speculated on various theories all morning until Wolf's head ached.

"Have I not said I don't remember!" Wolf shook his head and gave the young man a quick smile. "My apologies, Otter. I hadn't meant to take my frustrations out on you."

He'd gone to bed holding his wife. One moment he'd just closed his eyes. The next moment he was standing naked in the garden with Jorge holding his chin. Seth. Jorge told him he'd been searching this person out to protect him. His unsettled mind remembered the vision of the young man he'd seen before the Orb. Could they be one and the same?

"San Leonora has grown dangerously unstable. I fear we cannot stop the violence headed our way. The Jalora has sent the other rangers to their homes to lead their armies against uprising. We don't have enough rangers to patrol all of Valdeon. I must try again to send word to Dragon. We need the legion soon whether or not the rest of Andara grows restless. The Altar must be protected."

War. This was Edmund D'Antoiné's doing. If he hadn't run away from his duties, that dark-hearted offspring he called son wouldn't be running wild. Wolf's thoughts turned to his own family. San Leonora had grown dangerous. He must send Dulcina and the children to safety. His wife hated to split up their family, but she had to leave him this time.

Raising the subject with his wife had proven harder than he'd anticipated. She'd planned a picnic with their sons to cheer him. They'd found a grassy spot in the gardens and spent the afternoon watching their children play. Twilight turned to night. Still the words would not come. In their chambers, he held her. Their parting would not be an easy one.

Orange bands of gentle morning sun peaked through the window to stretch across their bedchambers. Sunlight fell upon his wife's sleeping body. He was a blessed man. Out of all her suitors, Dulcina had chosen him. Many a maid had thought him handsome, but his disposition chased them away. His family was fond of teasing them. The mighty Wolf had finally been tamed by a gentle soul like Dulcina.

He stroked her hair gently and kissed her. "I love you."

"My lord rises early this morning." She yawned, rubbing a soft cheek against his stubbly one. Dulcina opened her eyes and frowned when she noticed him dressed in his uniform.

"You and the boys must return to San Rudalfo this morning, my love. Tempers grow heated in San Leonora. I'm no longer confident the chancellor can maintain order within the city."

His wife brought her hand behind his head and pulled him in for a kiss. "We go where you go, and we stay where you stay, my darling." Dulcina breathed a kiss in his ear. "I'm not afraid."

Wolf pulled her to him. "I'm afraid for all of you. Please go home to San Rudalfo. The family will protect you for me. Think of our future."

He rested a hand on her small belly. It would grow larger soon. Their other sons had been born in outpost infirmaries by legion doctors. He wanted her home when the baby arrived this time, with family and friends nearby.

Wolf rested his head beside her on the pillow and cast a glance at the Wolf Ring. Xavier loved his sons with all his heart, but neither had been born as heir to the Wolf Ring. Perhaps this child would have that honor. He could think of no prouder moment then seeing the Holy aura of the Jalora glow around the babe.

"You and the children are my heart, Dulcina. I couldn't bear life without you."

Her lips found his in hungry kisses. Fingers unfastening his uniform, she moved her hands inside. Wolf brought his mouth down the length of her neck, letting his own hunger kindle. He touched Dulcina's mind gently with his power, using what he found there to anticipate her desires. Joining as one, they moved to a rhythm belonging only to them. Wolf moved his body, touching, feeling, probing until Dulcina cried out and trembled beneath him. He followed her, releasing in contented euphoria.

Dulcina lay across his chest, her long, dark hair cascading across his skin. "You must come home to me soon, my Wolf."

"I am already home with you in my heart."

Home. Wolf closed his eyes, smoothing his hand along Dulcina's back. Their villa rested in an orange orchard. The sweet citrus smell filled the air on summer afternoons as the breezes of San Rudalfo brought the scent of the orange blossoms to their shady veranda. He loved watching the sunset with Dulcina by his side. Their children often played on the warm stones, catching fireflies with their little hands. One day, Jalora willing, he would be released from his duties and would place the Wolf Ring upon his son's hand. He and his wife could spend their remaining years tending to the orchards, riding their horses, and fussing over the grandchildren.

His thoughts drifted to their estate and the work waiting for him. Their herds must be moved to the far pasture. The horse master had reminded him that he'd already missed the branding of the yearlings. The De Vincente clan boasted the largest and finest herd of Thunder Stallions in all of Andara. Their midnight color shimmered with tints of blue. They were the fastest creatures on four legs. Wolf smiled. Perhaps he would challenge young Jaguar to another race. Berto's family was famous for the gigantic San Marimosa Stallions, war horses that stood taller than a man. Young Jaguar had challenged him to a race and had been soundly beaten by Xavier's favorite mount. Jaguar still maintained Wolf had won because he had the home advantage.

He drifted into a light sleep, listening as the servants began gathering their possessions. They were well practiced in quickly packing the family De Vincente. As a ranger, Wolf could be called to action at any time. He smiled and kissed Dulcina's hair. This time their bedroom would be the last to be put away.

The hours passed too quickly. Wolf stood upon the docks of San Leonora, waving up at the airship hovering above them. Fausto held Danel and Gaspar up so they could see over the railing. Their little arms waved frantically to Wolf as the ship began to rise. He kept his hand in the air until they disappeared into the skies above the Valdeonian countryside. His heart ripped out of his chest as it went with them.

He turned and hurried away from the docks. The young Lords of Valdeon waited atop their horses, their squires sitting quietly upon their own mounts behind them. Wolf took the reins of his stallion from Basilio and mounted. Sensing his mood, the horse fidgeted beneath him.

"We go for a ride in the country. I suspect Julian's allies have not finished searching my rooms."

They rode toward the eastern border of Valdeon. Heat rose off the clusters of large boulders dotting the drying prairie grass. It was abnormally hot for late autumn. Legends gave warnings surrounding the death of the king. If his Lion Ring died, the land would die with it. He hoped the legends were nothing more than tales to frighten children.

A few miles outside the gates of San Leonora, Jaguar tapped Wolf's arm and motioned slightly to their rear. He held up a finger, indicating one man was following them. Wolf prodded his horse into one of the rock formations. Dismounting quickly, he tethered his horse on an old tree stump.

"Tether your horses and wait here. Come, Fox. We have a bloodhound to deal with."

Wolf and Fox raced around the formation and hid in its shadow. The horseman was riding hard to overtake them. Ranger eyes focused in on the rider. It was a familiar and unwelcome face. What bangtail mischief was this?

"Well, well. It would appear Prince Julian has taken an interest in our leisure time activities. I feel deeply honored he's sent one of his favorite pet prefects after us. Are we to kill our tagalong, sir?"

Wolf shook his head slowly. "No. Let him keep riding. I'm sure his lord prince will be pleased when he finds his spy has lost us."

The rider spurred his horse on faster as he passed the rocks. Making for the south, he hadn't realized he'd lost his quarry yet. Chuckling, they climbed down to join the others and found them taking an easy stance among the stones. Jaguar, Raven, Ferret, Otter, and Rabbit. They were being asked to carry more responsibility than their fathers before them. Each was loyal to his duty, but would they be enough?

"It is a fine day for a ride in the country, Wolf, but I don't think that's why you've brought us here." Fox, their eldest at the ripe age of twenty-eight, joined the others.

"We can no longer speak freely within the walls of the palace. I fear the Eastern prefects — those not loyal to the Lords of Valdeon — will soon urge Julian to take the throne by force."

Jaguar spat upon the dirt. "I'd say he doesn't need any encouragement."

"The chancellor still is not convinced Julian has completely turned to evil. He feels I am overly hard on the prince, because I am a De Vincente."

"Chancellor Benito is a fool." A long-forgotten voice reverberated from the rocks. "He's allowed Prince Julian to leave San Leonora in the night like a common thief."

Wolf pulled his sword. The other rangers took a guard position at his back. Their squires made a half circle behind their lords. They waited, weapons at the ready for the ghost to come before them. He stepped slowly into the opening and threw back the hood of his ranger cloak. Violet glistened within the stone of his ring under the afternoon sun. Esteban D'Antoiné, Hawk Prince of Valdeon, stood before them. He was the last person Wolf expected to see haunting Valdeon. His emotionless eyes regarded their naked swords.

"Well, Wolf, you have the Lords of Valdeon hiding like sniveling dogs, I see. It is time I took control of the Sacred Guard, before you have them kissing the boots of the old fool you've left in charge of our homeland."

"And how will you protect the altar, Hawk Prince? You haven't been welcome in its presence since you bedded your brother's queen and tried to usurp the throne." Wolf gave him a bitter laugh. "You expect us to trust you now? Tell me, where were you while Leo was missing?"

"I am a Prince of Valdeon and bishop in the legion. I won't answer to those beneath me. You ache to cross swords, Wolf. Come at me! I'd love nothing better than to see the Jalora strip you of your powers."

"You'll have to fight all of us, adulterous bastard." Jaguar came to Wolf's side with the others close behind.

Hawk flew at Wolf, stopping a few inches short of his sword tip. Even with his ranger sight, Wolf had not seen the rapid splitting of air and time as the ranger moved. The scar stretching from Esteban's chin to the corner of his right eye turned a pale red with his fury. Edmund had given Hawk the scar as a warning never to return to Valdeon. Apparently, Hawk's courage had returned upon the death of his brother.

"You poisoned them against me, I see."

"We can judge your actions for ourselves...bishop." Raven spat at his feet.

"Indeed?" Hawk took a parchment from his belt. He threw it at Wolf. "I bring orders from the Dragon. They are very clear. You must return to your homes and seek out any traitors hidden there. This is a direct command from the Dragon. He wants you to leave today."

Wolf opened the orders and scanned through it hurriedly. They seemed genuine. Hawk was watching him as he read. Strange the Jalora hadn't mentioned these orders when it spoke to him at HQ. He didn't trust Hawk, but he could not disobey a direct order, either.

"And where will you fly off to next, Hawk?"

The bishop turned and put the hood back on his head. "I have my own concerns. Don't worry, Wolf. I will not seek aid from your young whelps. I can see they are inadequate for the task."

Wolf threw his arms out to stop Jaguar and Fox from charging at the Hawk. Esteban raced away at ranger speed, leaving them confused and seething with anger.

"What do we do, Wolf?" Jaguar slammed his sword back into its sheath. "I don't trust Esteban."

"Neither do I, but these orders look genuine."

Wolf shook his head. He wasn't about to leave the Altar unprotected at the Hawk's word, but he wouldn't let the others follow him in his disobedience. "You will return to your homes."

"And what of you, Wolf?" His second searched Wolf's face with troubled eyes. "Do you also return to San Rudalfo?"

Wolf shook his head. "I stay in San Leonora beside the chancellor. It's here trouble will begin."

Ferret bounded forward, ever ready to argue. "Alone? I can stay with you, Wolf. Father will see to San Lucida…"

Wolf rested a hand on Ferret's shoulder and gave him the parchment Bishop Falcon had delivered from the Legion Headquarters. Odd Hawk hadn't asked about it. No matter. Someone must get word to Dragon. Lucio was a skilled tracker and knew the northern woods well. He'd have a better chance than most to cross the border into Andara unseen.

Ferret unrolled it and frowned as he read. "I'm to leave for the Buells immediately. I don't understand! How can they expect me to leave while Valdeon is so unstable?"

"The Eagle wouldn't request you if it wasn't critical, Ferret. Don't worry. Your father and Jorge will see to San Lucida." Wolf handed Lucio another parchment he'd written while his family slept. "I need you to take this to Dragon. Hand it to him personally."

Lucio nodded reluctantly. The constant smile upon his face was missing. He tucked the parchment into his waistcoat and headed for his horse. The others waited solemnly as he mounted.

"Falcon warns of dangerous men upon the road. Head straight for the Temple Cave, Ferret. Do not stop within the borders of Valdeon for any reason."

In the northern mountains bordering Valdeon and Tslavia, a cave of rare beauty had been formed at the edge of the forests of Varianne. Its walls were encrusted with rare heart crystals. Pure water from the mountain peaks ran through its center. The Jalora's magic kept it hidden for many a century. It was a haven of safety and renewal for the Sacred Guard.

Ferret gave them one last look and then spurred his horse toward the north. Wolf sent all the hope he had with the young ranger. Silence fell upon the rocks as Ferret and his squire disappeared into the horizon. Chaos was at their door. Nothing they could do would stop it from breaking in.

"Listen to me, Lords of Valdeon. We live in a perilous time. Our king is dead and the Lion Ring is missing. Traitors plot to take the throne as the legion's power fades. If the worst should happen, go to Temple Cave. The rest of us will meet you there."

He rested his hands upon their two youngest. Sending them back to their homes alone was the last thing he wanted to do, but Dragon had been very clear. Wolf gave them a reassuring nod. Ready or no, they must take up their duty, no matter how difficult.

Chapter Thirty

Seth rubbed at his tired eyes. He'd spent hours working on the parchment before him, carefully reading the sentences written in the Geltic language. The trade agreement with Heidelbreckt was important for the farmers of Marianna. Their profits would increase twofold. Of course, Elder Newcastle would get his share as well. Perhaps his help in obtaining the additional monies would finally earn Seth forgiveness from his neighbors. Leo assured him it would.

They'd spent the last few weeks together. Father and son worked side by side each morning before sunup on the farm. Then Leo would teach Seth the sword in the afternoon. It was his favorite time of day. His father was a gifted swordsman and an inspiring teacher. Leo's pride in Seth's natural abilities with the sword motivated him to work all the harder.

Then Leo had done something unexpected. He'd lined up Seth's evenings with several odd jobs. He didn't mind, especially when Leo had told him he was clever enough to do any job on the island. Though he was secretly pleased, Seth wasn't fooled. He knew Leo was trying to keep him busy so he wouldn't go looking for Sandor. Unfortunately, Leo's plan was working. He hadn't been able to spare any time to search for more clues.

"I'm for bed, Cub." Dante yawned. "Leo has already gone to his rest."

"I'm sorry to keep you up so late. I'll lock up."

Dante waved at him, muttering something about foolish apologies. Seth smiled as the old man shuffled to his bed. Dante was a surprise. He cooked, cleaned, and helped around the farm. Seth had assumed he was a simple servant until the man had surprised him with a series of tests on complex mathematical equations and advanced language skills. Seth had managed to keep up, but he'd been challenged. Dante, he discovered, had been educated in the most famed universities on Andara. It was his courage, however, which had won him a place as Leo's companion.

The letters on the parchment began to blur. He closed his eyes and rubbed them again. His translations were due first thing in the morning. The elder wasn't a very patient man. One page left. Reaching for the cold tea he'd left unheeded upon the table, his eyes strayed toward the candle's tiny flame. It flickered in several short bursts as if someone or something were trying to blow it out.

Across the kitchen table, a massive lion stared back at him. Its large mane of pure energy spanned the length of the table. Gigantic jaws parted, revealing sharp teeth. The beast's presence filled the entire kitchen. Large green, ethereal eyes held Seth in his seat. Ageless and wise, they saw through his being into his very soul. No thought, no pain, no desire was hidden from the beast. He remained helpless and completely naked under its gaze.

I call you to me, Bearer. Its voice whispered in his mind.

Spellbound, he remained motionless as the beast moved closer. It came up beside him, close enough to touch. Sparks of energy raced through the space between them. His hair and skin prickled with tiny flickers of power. The lion regarded him for a moment. It was waiting. Then the beast gave him a short grunt and began to leave. Seth's body stood of its own accord and followed. His feet moved clumsily as they directed themselves after the great cat.

The little farmhouse faded away. Haze and mist swirled about his body as he followed. The skin on his face and forearms numbed at the light touch of misty fingers. It was like walking on the verge of a dream. Then brightness pierced the dark. Sunshine greeted them as the haze parted. A lovely green meadow blanketed with bright yellow spring flowers stretched out before their feet. In its center was a brilliant green knoll. The lion pounced up the hill, leaving him at the bottom. It turned and waited for Seth to follow.

Come to me, Son of Lions!

Seth hurried forward. An iron rod gate sprang up from the ground to block his path. He gripped at the bars and shook them, but the gate wouldn't move. Panicked, Seth looked up with pleading eyes to the beast. A burning desire, strong and urgent, took hold of him. He must join the lion! Shaking the bars of the gate, he pulled with all his might.

The Lion growled impatiently. It lifted its mighty head and let loose a powerful roar. The might behind its call shook Seth to the core. He began to ram the gate with his body, then his head.

"Hold him, Dante!"

Arms pulled him away from the gate. He thrashed his body about, trying to break free of their grip. A sharp rap struck his shoulder. Pain pulled him out of the meadow and back to the farmhouse. His legs betrayed him and he sank to the floor. Leo and Dante stood over him, dressed in their nightshirts. They were in Leo's bedchamber. The heavy wardrobe had been thrown on its side. Several marks on its doors looked as if someone had tried to beat their way in.

Warm fluid trickled down his forehead. He reached up with shaking fingers and brought back blood. Leo and Dante helped him to his feet. Guiding him back into the kitchen, Dante saw to his bleeding head.

His father put a glass of spiced wine to Seth's lips. "Tell me what you saw. Leave nothing out, no matter how farfetched."

"I dreamed I saw a lion standing right there beside the kitchen table. It took me to a meadow. I couldn't help myself. I was compelled to follow it."

He hesitated, feeling the fool. Seeing a lion on Marianna would earn most a trip to the doctor. It was absurd. Most Islanders had no knowledge of the exotic beasts inhabiting the eastern deserts of Andara. Seth had been fortunate enough to find a book of animals in the school's library. He'd gotten through all the pictures, before the headmaster had found out and threw the book off the cliff. His tired mind must have conjured up the memory of those mighty beasts and brought one to life within his dream.

Leo and Dante leaned toward him. The anticipation he saw in their eyes was unnerving. He didn't see the slightest hint of humor or disbelief upon his father's face. It was almost as if they'd been expecting something like this to happen.

"It called me a bearer and told me I was a son of lions. What does it mean, father?"

Leo breathed deeply and relaxed his grip. Offering Seth a fleeting smile, Leo kissed him on the forehead in the Valdeonian fashion. He stood and moved to the window. Staring out into the night, his father said no more. He remained before the glass, rigid and motionless.

"That's enough for tonight. Off to bed with you, Cub."

Dante pulled Seth to his room and helped him into the little cot. He fussed over the bandage, before patting Seth's arm and giving him a rare smile. Dante left, closing the door behind him. Something important had happened, but what did it mean? He hadn't been exposed to many miraculous occurrences in life, but Seth knew in his heart the lion had not been a dream. It had been real.

Muffled voices from the kitchen brought him wide awake again. He eased off the cot and crept along the chilly floorboards to the door. Pressing his ear against the small crack, he strained to hear their conversation.

"I've never seen the draw so strong. He would have ripped the doors off that wardrobe."

"It calls to him, Dante."

"Why so glum then? This was what you hoped for, wasn't it?"

"Did you hear him speaking the old language? Could he be the one? Perhaps Anne was right to hide him. Am I doing what's best for our son?"

"That choice is no longer yours."

Silence hung heavy in the kitchen. Then Dante's voice came softly, hesitantly. "Will you summon the Sacred Guard then?"

"And what do you think Wolf's reaction will be? He refused to help me when I came to him in my most desperate hour. What do you think he will do for the son I sired with Anne?"

The Sacred Guard? Wolf? More mysteries only his father could shed light upon. Whoever this Wolf was, it seemed he and Leo were at odds.

"Hot tempered he may be, but you know Wolf will protect your heir. Leo, you must think of Seth."

"You're right." His father's voice was soft, regretful. "I know what I must do."

"Take your rest, Leo. Things will be clearer in the morning. I'll need Curl Top here with me."

"I will arrange it. Thomas Logan and I are on good terms after his visit. He is an honorable man. His son will be a fine choice."

Seth hurried back to his bed as light flickered under his door. The candlelight faded, and soon the house grew still again. He looked up at the ceiling above his bed, pinching himself in frustration. Something incredible had happened to him tonight. Leo was not a man to be pushed. He'd have to remain patient until his father chose to reveal the secrets he was keeping.

Chapter Thirty-One

THE NEXT MORNING HIS FATHER had given Seth a rare few hours away from work and training. In truth he wondered if Leo needed the time off more than he. Drawn and tired, his father looked as if he hadn't slept. He'd picked at the morning meal, hardly speaking to anyone. His father had refused to discuss the evening's antics, which only served to confirm Seth's suspicions. The lion had been real.

"I asked you a question, Seth. Did that bump on the head rattle your ears?"

Riley shoved at his arm. They walked among the shops on the Main Row, window shopping and not doing much of anything else. It was a needed break after the relentless training Leo had put him through recently.

"Sorry. I just have a lot on my mind."

"I was saying Leo came to the farm early this morning just as Dad had started the fire. I tried to hear what they were talking about, but Dad caught me listening and sent me to the barn. Next thing I know, here come Dad and Leo. They told me to meet you here after my chores, and that I'd be working on Leo's farm with Dante from now on. He's supposed to train me, but they didn't say on what. Do you have any idea?"

"I don't understand a great many things in my father's house."

Riley shrugged. "Well, at least Dad is happy to have me out from under foot."

Alice came toward them. Her hair was pinned up off the shoulder. A single ringlet bounced beside a rosy cheek. The style made her look a good deal older. She twisted the loose strand of hair and smiled at Seth. Against his better judgment, he smiled back.

"I wish she'd stop her flirting. I grow weary of the beatings."

"I hear she has a crush on you, Seth McCloud. I suppose you are a lover and not a fighter."

The McKenzie boys materialized out of the leather goods shop. Fists raised and muscles bulging, they struck Seth with a warning glare. Mike muttered something low to his sister. She gave him a haughty response in turn. Alice waved at Seth and made her way down the street toward the shops.

"I'm beginning to think she likes seeing me beaten up." Seth sighed and stepped forward to meet the men.

Mike threw his punch first, expecting the familiar contact, but Seth dodged it. He whipped around and buried a fist in the big man's gut. Mike folded onto the row in a gasping heap. Danny came at him next. He swung both fists to meet Seth, but struck wide. Seth grabbed his arms and let them carry his body to the hard ground.

"You just pummeled the McKenzie boys! How in the green, green fields…"

He grabbed Riley's arm and pulled him away. It would be best if they weren't close by when the boys came around. He'd not told Riley about the sword lessons. It was selfish of him, but he'd wanted the time alone with his father.

"Here now, what are we doing?"

"The last thing I need is more trouble with the constable." Seth pulled him along faster. "Let's get out of sight for a while."

They left the town square and headed north toward the Sea Steps. The morning sun brought welcome warmth to Seth's face as they walked. A ship moored on the docks of the airship port cast a long shadow over Main Row. He took one last stretch under the sunlight and ducked into the shade.

Someone had secured the boards blocking the Sea Steps. Too many eyes might be watching the barrier for them to force entry. They'd have to come back another time when it was dark and empty. Seth shrugged and walked slowly under the port's pillars. The corrals blocked the view from the row. It was as good a place as any to hide out.

Beatrice walked slowly beneath the docks. Her long braids dangled before her as she searched the ground. She gave an excited cry and bent down to pick up something she'd found. Searching the port for lost or discarded treasures was a favorite pastime for Haven Bay youths. Seth had once found a beat-up, old pocket watch with a cracked face. It no longer told time, but he kept it for the etching of a mountain range within the gold.

"What's the pest up to now?"

"Why do you hate her so much, Riley? She liked you well enough."

"I don't hate her. She just annoys me."

"Ask yourself why." Seth raised his hands and laughed. "I'm just saying maybe you like her a little."

Riley put his fists on his hips and glared at Seth who was beginning to laugh harder. "She's just a child."

"Great gulls!" Seth wiped at his eyes. "Beatrice is a year younger than us."

She stood, holding a treasure to her heart as they approached. Beatrice gave Seth a curt nod. Riley was favored with a frigid scowl. She lifted her chin and pushed the beaded bracelet she'd found upon her right arm. Bright blue beads tinkled upon her wrist.

"Well, Riley Logan, what do you want?" She wagged the bracelet at him. "I have much more important things to do than stand here and waste time with you."

"Plainly she does not want to speak with me." Riley shook a finger at Seth. "Now you know, don't you. She's the one who's rude."

Seth stepped between them as Beatrice took an angry stance. This would soon turn into a shouting match. They'd come here to hide, not to draw a crowd. Movement beside one of the far pillars drew his attention. Their audience was already arriving.

"Hide! It could be the dock master or the constable." Seth prodded them closer to the ramp. "Start climbing. We'll lose them on the next level. Hurry!"

Riley gripped Beatrice's hand and pulled her to the underside of the ramp. He lifted her up and pushed her feet until she was safely on the first level. Seth gave him a boost and climbed up after them. He leaned down and saw two cloaked men coming nearer. They were strangers to Haven Bay, which under the circumstances, made them potentially dangerous.

"We have to keep moving. They'll see our boots."

He crept along the boards of the ramp until it evened out onto a platform. They were at the back of the port where the dock workers kept their loading gear. This wasn't a good hiding place either. They were in the open. Seth moved along the platform until it took a curve. Steps leading to the next level were anchored upon a pillar at their left. He raced up them with Riley and Beatrice following.

It was another storage area walled up on all sides. Great gulls. He'd just brought them to a dead end. Boots pounded on the platform below. They couldn't go back the way they'd come. He ducked behind some crates while Riley pulled Beatrice against the wooden wall on the other side of the steps. He held his breath as the two men stopped at the bottom of the stairs.

"You take great risks to call me here in the daylight. What do you want?"

Seth recognized the man's harsh accent. It was Pavel Sandor. Fists clenched in impotent frustration, he ached to dive down the stairs and attack his mother's killer. Unarmed, he wouldn't stand a chance against a deadly butcher like Sandor. He had to be smart this time.

"I've come on urgent business. A certain party will pay well if we kill the boy now." A man's voice, one Seth didn't recognize, rose up from the boards. Judging by the halting common tongue, he was most likely an Amity raider. How were they sneaking into Haven Bay so easily?

"Who is this party?"

"He prefers to remain anonymous. What does it matter? His money's good."

"We have a little problem. Edmund has taken notice of his son. He is here on Marianna watching over his heir like a nervous mother hen."

Seth chanced a glance over at Riley. He was holding a terrified Beatrice in his arms, stroking her hair to calm her. She squeezed him tightly as brutish laughter barked beneath them.

"You worry about a toothless old lion when so much money is at stake?" The raider spat an Islic curse.

"I am not a man to trifle with, raider scum!"

A body struck the wall beneath them. Beatrice let out a small cry. Blue beads fell to the floor, bouncing and clanging like thunder on a tin roof. Seth motioned for Riley to hide, but there was nowhere to go. He ducked behind the crates, but there wasn't room for all three of them. Riley twisted his back toward the stairs to protect Beatrice.

"Quiet. I will see to it." Sandor's voice was close. They'd run out of time.

Preparing his body to attack, Seth waited for Sandor to come up the stairs. It would be another life and death struggle. This time, Seth would have the element of surprise on his side. The fight, however, didn't come. Sandor chuckled softly a few feet away from Seth's head.

"Well?" The raider spat another Islic curse. Steel scraped against leather as he pulled his sword.

"We interrupt young lovers."

"Aren't you going to kill them?"

Seth held his breath. He was unarmed, but Leo had taught him several defensive moves. Riley was no stranger to fighting either. They might have a chance of defeating Sandor together.

"Have you forgotten what it is to be young? I doubt they know what time it is the way they carry on." Sandor's voice retreated a few paces. "The runt of the litter among woolie farmers isn't a great threat. If I kill him now, I might tip my hand too soon."

Seth popped his head carefully around the crates. Riley and Beatrice were engaged in a passionate kiss. Her fingers had moved up to Riley's red curls, wrapping around them as he pulled her tighter.

The boots beneath him began to walk back toward their entrance onto the docks. Seth crept down the steps, carefully following the cloaks as they took a slow pace.

"What shall I tell this interested party? He does not know the exact island in the Grey Cliff Isles yet, but that could change soon and we could lose out on our payday."

"You forget the other interested party. He is a powerful ranger. The money will have to be very good in order for me to risk double-crossing him. Let me think on these things. In the meantime, tell this benefactor our answer is yes."

The two men dropped down under the docks once more. Their voices faded in the darkness. Seth hesitated. He desperately wanted to follow Sandor to his hiding place. The desire to uncover his true identity was overwhelming his reason. He had to get back to the farm and tell Leo about what he'd heard. They were about to be visited by unwanted guests.

Seth stood and headed back toward the storage area where he'd left his friends. He walked up the steps and stopped abruptly. Riley and Beatrice were still wrapped together, lips pressed in a kiss. He put a hand over his mouth to hide a smile and cleared his throat loudly.

"They've gone."

Riley pulled gently away from Beatrice's lips at last. "Poor little Honey Bee. You're trembling. We need to get her home, Seth. She's been frightened out of her senses. You mustn't tell anyone what happened here today. Promise?"

"Yes, Riley." She put her cheek against his shoulder. "Father would be very angry."

"I can understand." Riley stared down the steps at the memory of the strangers.

Seth shook his head, watching the happy face of Beatrice McFadden as she snuggled against her hero. Once again, Riley Logan had missed the point.

Chapter Thirty-Two

A BUBBLING MIXTURE OF GREEN slime simmered slowly over the low flame. Riley leaned over the pot and took a sniff. Gagging, he turned his face away. It was almost worse than mucking out Bluebell's stall. Almost.

"It smells terrible."

Dante hurried to the stove, eyes sparkling. He leaned his white grizzled head over the pot and took a deep sniff of the green mixture. Slapping his hands together, Dante nodded in appreciation.

"Good work, Curl Top! You'll make a fine healer or at least an apothecary when I'm done with you."

Dante dipped a finger in and tasted the mix. The Valdeonian motioned him to do the same. Riley stuck his little finger in the mixture and put the hot liquid to his mouth before he lost his nerve. It tasted sweet, like meadow grass with the tang of wildflower petals.

"That little bit of sour tells you when this concoction is ready. We just add some ground barley to make paste, and you have an ointment that will keep a wound from festering."

Yesterday they'd made a powder that reduced fevers from trees. Earlier this morning he had helped Dante make bandages and tourniquets out of old fabric. Now he was learning how to heal wounds.

"Are you expecting an invasion, Dante?"

"I am expecting to give these things to that over-worked doctor of yours. And to teach you a thing or two. Any objections?"

Riley shook his head. "No, sir. I suppose I didn't expect to be doing things like this when Leo hired me off my dad's farm. I'm not complaining, mind you."

"I hired you, and for my own reasons. Now, go knead that mix I have in the bowl."

Riley pounced over to the large bowl on the counter by the kitchen window. He was still learning his boundaries with Dante. The old man was as prickly as a thistle. He had to admit he was growing fond of listening to the Valdeonian man's teachings. They were interesting, and Riley was surprised at how much he remembered them from day to day.

He looked over at the bandages they had made. Would it be so farfetched if he were to become a healer? His dad and brothers would think he had gone off his head, but Riley didn't care. He'd see how this played out.

"And what is this for, Dante?" Riley asked, deciding to get in the man's good graces again.

"It's for supper. And at the pace you're going, it will be done about sunup tomorrow."

Riley bit back a comment and looked out the small kitchen window. Seth and Leo were walking in from the fields. They were deep in conversation about something. Riley shrugged. It really didn't matter what the subject was, Seth was always eager to listen to anything the Valdeonian had to say. A little too eager.

He rubbed his chin with the side of his arm and kneaded the bread dough harder, watching their easy conversation. It was true Leo had saved Riley's life, but that didn't mean they could trust him without question. His claims about Anne McCloud hiding her son away from his father didn't set well with Riley. She'd been an uncommonly kind woman. Such a thing was too cruel for her gentle soul.

"They look so much alike," he muttered.

"What's that?" Dante huffed from the stove. His self-proclaimed teacher joined Riley by the window. "That they do, Curl Top."

Dante lifted the bread dough out of the bowl. Practiced hands twisted it into a rope-shaped loaf and set it on the window sill to rise. The loaf joined other tantalizing cakes and pastries Dante had prepared that morning.

"You're a better cook than my mum."

"Oh yes?" Dante snorted.

"Aye. But, I'll deny I said it if you tell her."

They both chuckled. Mrs. Logan had marched to the McPherson farm after she'd found out Leo hired Riley. She was furious with her husband and wanted Riley back, but Leo had managed to convince Mrs. Logan her son would be treated well. It was only after Dante bribed her with a Valdeonian pastry that she finally relented.

"It's time for you to practice the sword with Leo."

Outside in the farmyard, Seth began to stretch, holding his blade straight ahead. Riley grinned. If someone had told him a year ago that Seth McCloud could use a sword as well as anyone on the island, he would have called them a liar.

"I don't think I'll ever be as good as Seth."

Riley didn't really mind. He was just happy to be included in the lessons. It wasn't as if he would ever use the sword. Muskets were better for fighting off Amity raiders.

"You can't compare yourself to Seth, Curl Top. He is meant for a different fate than you are, though your paths will be bound."

"Riley Logan! Must I wait all evening?" Leo's call thundered from the barn.

He exchanged a knowing look with Dante. Leo had been growling at everyone for days. He didn't know the man well, but his surly mood seemed out of place for the charming man who'd won over his mum. Riley pulled off the apron before Seth could see him in it and raced out to the barn.

Leo helped him into a heavy leather vest with gloves to match. Seth had managed to put his own gear on without any help. His tall frame twisted and stretched to adjust the leather. Heavy work on the farm had given Seth strong muscles and a hard torso. He seemed so different, calmer and more confident. Seth had been lost before Leo had arrived. Now Riley's best friend spoke about his future with growing excitement and hope.

"Tonight we use steel, my pupils. You wear the leather for protection."

Seth gave Riley a reassuring wink. He had already fought the wooden dummy with a real sword, but it was Riley's first time using steel.

Leo handed Riley the hilt. "It will only bite you if you let your defenses down."

"Seth and I will show you first."

Leo's tall frame remained perfectly straight as he moved to the center of the barn. He pulled his sword and flourished it elegantly in the air before them. Taking his stance, he motioned for Seth to strike.

"Shouldn't you put on the safety vest, Leo?" Seth lowered his weapon.

"Do you think you have advanced far enough to wound me, boy?"

Leo turned flashing eyes upon Seth. Riley stepped back a little, watching the two men. What had happened in the field today? Seth practically worshiped his father.

He hung on his every word. It didn't seem possible he could have offended Leo in some way.

"Strike me."

Seth lifted his weapon and came at Leo's chest with a fast thrust of the blade. The Valdeonian warrior dropped to the ground and spun with his leg outstretched. The leg swept Seth off his feet and onto his back before he could complete the thrust. Leo came out of the spin in an upright position. He rested the sword by his side.

Riley held his breath as the tension grew heavy in the barn. Seth looked up slowly from the ground, his eyes flashing with amber. A thin trickle of blood dripped from his lip. Riley hurried over and helped his friend to his feet.

"Cold water is what you'll need, Seth."

Riley pushed him out the barn door toward the farmhouse, before real blows were thrown. It was growing dark, and the fog was beginning to creep toward them. A warm glow from the kitchen's window promised good food and the comfort of a warm bed. Too bad they had to get through the evening before he could lay his head upon his pillow.

"Did he cut you on purpose?"

"I must have bitten it."

Anger, hurt, and confusion were in Seth's eyes. His face remained calm, but Riley knew him better than anyone. He knew how much Leo's attack had hurt. Seth turned away.

"Did something happen today in the fields to make him angry, Seth?"

His friend wouldn't look at him. "No. He has been this way since…I should be getting to Paddy's. It's my turn to tend bar."

Seth pushed his leather vest and gloves into Riley's arms. Then he ran up the path and disappeared into the fog. Riley spun toward the barn and marched in through the doors. He threw Seth's leathers down on top of a bale of hay and began removing his own.

Leo was standing with the naked sword in hand, eyeing it casually as he extended its tip toward the hay. The warrior had the same calm, unemotional expression he'd worn when he'd killed the two Amity raiders.

"The lesson is ended, it seems." Leo swung the tip in short swipes across the hay. "He must learn to overcome childish slights."

"Childish slights? You should take your own advice, sir. Seth meant no slight to your wounded pride."

He took a step back when those amber-flecked eyes turned angrily upon him. It was dangerous to provoke a man like Leo, but Riley didn't care just then. Seth wouldn't tell Leo how much his slight had hurt him. It wasn't his way.

"Seth looks up to you, Leo. He needs you. What he doesn't need is you slapping him down. He gets enough of that at home with his uncle."

Riley walked out of the barn before Leo had a chance to respond with a sword in his belly. Moving at a good pace toward the farmhouse, he didn't stop until he reached the door. Swinging it open with a hard shove, it slammed against an unlucky chair and shuddered back toward the jamb. Dante jumped and turned from the pot he was stirring.

"You can't be done already? I haven't finished the meal yet."

"It will be just you and Leo tonight. Thank you for everything you've shown me. Tell Leo I'll get the money he paid for my labor back from Dad." Riley pulled his cloak from the peg by the door.

"That won't be necessary."

Leo stood in the doorway. His sword was sheathed at his side. The warrior's manner was calm and cold again, as if Riley's words hadn't affected him at all. He regarded Riley with probing eyes.

"I won't keep money I haven't earned. You certainly don't expect me to stay if Seth does not."

"What's this?"

Dante turned a puzzled face from Riley to Leo. His impatient gaze finally rested upon the Valdeonian. Some unspoken agreement passed between them. Well, their reasons for wanting him on the farm were no longer Riley's business. He fastened the clasp on his cloak and started toward the door. Leo still blocked his way.

"Let me pass. Seth will need his real friend to talk to after his false one has stabbed him in the back."

Leo grabbed the front of Riley's cloak. "He has gone then?"

Riley folded his arms across his chest. "What did you expect after the way you've been growling for the past few days?"

"You don't understand." Leo towered over him with those intense, angry eyes. "Tell me where he has gone, boy!"

Shaking his head, he pulled his cloak from Leo's fists. "I'll not let you harass him anymore tonight."

"It's near week's end. He should be on his way to Paddy's by now."

Dante tossed Leo his long, ash-colored cloak. The hem slapped Riley on the cheek as it flew past his head. Leo wrapped the cloak about him and stepped back out into the darkness. Dante shoved Riley to the side and closed the door.

"You'll help me with this elixir until Leo returns."

Dante took supper off the stove and began to bang pots about. He'd never seen the old man mistreat his kitchen equipment. Riley folded his arms and leaned against the table. Dante was in a mood, and Riley didn't fancy listening to him grouse all evening. He moved to the kitchen window, looking out into the darkness. Leo was disappearing up the path to follow Seth, no doubt. Riley gave a last look at Dante's back and tiptoed to the kitchen door. He quietly turned the knob. He was out the door and down the porch steps without a sound.

Leo stopped at the top of the hill and pulled on his hood. If Riley hadn't been looking right at the man, he wouldn't know Leo was there. A slight shimmer against the gray of the fog told him Leo had moved toward town. He pulled the hood low to cover his face and followed, keeping close to the trees.

The Main Row waited at the end of their path. Leo's cloak pressed flat against the wall of stone lining the row. His attention was firmly fixed on the signpost for Main and Farm Rows across the way. Seth was there, lighting his lamp. Riley threw himself on the damp ground when Seth turned around.

Something hard jabbed into his side. The hilt of his sword poked out from under his cloak. He'd forgotten to take it off. Enduring the discomfort, he held his breath as Seth lifted the lamp and stared out into the darkness in their direction. The moments ticked by until Seth shrugged. He turned and headed down the path toward Paddy's. Riley struggled to his feet and noticed with a curse Leo had disappeared. No matter. He knew exactly where the Valdeonian was headed.

Chapter Thirty-Three

RILEY CRAWLED THROUGH THE DRIED grass on the roadside a fair distance behind Seth. Down the row to the left were the bright lights of the airship port. Thick fog blanketed the ground beneath, giving the allusion of disembodied fire. Several large rock fire pits lined the row on either side of the port. The militia had them burning bright to guide landing ships in harsh weather. Unfortunately, they hadn't been placed all the way to Paddy's. He'd have to stumble in the dark as he followed Seth's lantern.

A dark shape ran through the fog between his location and Seth's back. Leo. Riley grinned. He'd expected the Valdeonian to show a little more stealth. Seth wasn't a fool. Then Riley saw a second shape — coming from the same direction — run across the road behind Seth. A third followed a few heartbeats later. Great gulls! They weren't alone in the fog.

Four sets of eyes watched Seth's lantern bob up and down in the thick banks of fog. One of the cloaked men had to be Leo. Two of them had an unhealthy interest. Did they mean to do Seth harm or were they just following? For all Riley knew, one of the men could be Jamie Newcastle out for a joke. No. Jamie wouldn't have the guts to stand out in the middle of a thick fog even around the comforting flames of the pits.

Amity raiders would have the brass and the skill to sneak about without being heard. Riley gripped the hilt of his sword. He could attack and raise the alarm, but he'd never so much as held a steel sword in his life. They'd strike him dead before he could scream. He rubbed the back of his neck and looked from one side of the road to the other.

The second man reached into his cloak. He held his arms over his head and appeared ready to strike the first man. Riley ran as fast as he could and dived at the figure. Something long, a sword, flew onto the side of the row. He yanked off the man's hood. A black mask with a white dagger drawn down the center stared up at Riley. It had to be Pavel Sandor.

Harsh words in a strange language spat out from under the mask. Sandor pushed Riley off and dove toward his sword. Riley yanked at the hilt of his borrowed blade, but it was caught under his body. Sandor reached for his fallen weapon. A dagger flew through the dim light and jutted from the space within Sandor's sword hilt. Another shape appeared from the fog. It was the third man. In his hand, another deadly sword glistened in the flames of the fire pit.

The third man pulled his hood away from his face. A white dagger hung in the black fabric. Two Sandors? Riley froze upon the ground as the two assassins stared each other down. The killer he'd disarmed spun on his heels and was over the short stone wall without a sound. His dark cloak disappeared into the fog as he crossed the row. Riley began to rise, hoping to chase after him. Sandor's twin stepped in his path. He pointed a finger at Riley, pinning him in place. Then the assassin snatched up his dagger and hurried into the night after his twin.

Gravel crunched to his left and the first man threw back his cloak. It was Leo. He helped Riley to his feet without a word and picked up the other man's fallen sword. The symbol of a dagger was etched upon the hilt. Leo fingered it, deep in thought.

Riley grabbed his arm and motioned across the row. He couldn't explain why there were two Pavel Sandors or why they seemed to be enemies, but he did know they were keen about following Seth.

"How many?" Leo mouthed.

Riley lifted two fingers. Leo nodded. They both moved slowly toward the opposite side of the street, but there was no sign of either man. He gripped Riley's shoulder in warning. Putting a finger to his lips, the Valdeonian shook his head. He pointed toward the center of the street. Another dark figure was a dagger's throw from Seth's back.

Leo moved with incredible speed. He grabbed the man from behind and lifted him to the side of the road without a sound. Riley rushed over as Leo pushed his blade into the Amity raider's throat. He turned away from the gushing blood in time to see a charging raider headed for Leo's back.

Riley stepped between the men and thrust his arm out. The raider fell against him. His eyes captured Riley's gaze as the life faded from them. Blood gurgled from his gasping mouth. He sunk to the ground. Riley looked dumbly at the sword he held in his hand. It was still sticking in the man's heart. Bright red blood looked obscene against the dead man's painted face.

A thud followed by death's cry sounded behind him. He turned to see another raider drop at his feet with a dagger sticking out of his throat. The world had suddenly gone mad, and all Riley could do was gape like an idiot.

Dante came up beside them. "That's the last of them, Leo. Where are the rest of the bodies?"

"The other five are behind the wall fifty feet back. I must see Seth the rest of the way."

Dante came to stand close to Riley as Leo disappeared into the fog. He bent down beside the two dead men and rifled quickly through their pockets. Collecting two more golden gargoyle coins, he held one of them up to show Riley. The old man tucked them into his pocket and stood away. Dante slapped at Riley's arm.

"Come, boy." Dante rested a hand on Riley's shoulder. "The backwater militia is coming. We can't be found with the bodies."

Stumbling like a half-wit, Riley stayed close to Dante as they ran along the side of the row toward Paddy's. Several torches pierced the fog seconds after they bolted from the scene. Dante grabbed his cloak and propelled him into a clump of trees. He leaned against a tree trunk and tried to sheath the bloodied sword. It was no use. His hands were shaking too hard. Would they ever stop shaking again? He had killed a man without hesitation. How in the green, green fields would he ever erase the dying eyes of the raider from his memory?

Twigs scraping against bark shook Riley out of his stupor. A slim band of light burst into their center, illuminating their faces as the rest of the grove stayed dark. Leo threw off his hood and lifted a strange little lantern before him. Tom had brought back a similar one from his time with the UR army.

"Seth is safely inside. Come, we can go to the usual spot until he has finished work."

The usual spot? They'd watched Seth before. What other secrets was this Valdeonian hiding from his son? Riley forced his body upright and raised the sword again. It seemed to be glued to his hand now.

"Who are you?"

"I've told you all you need to know."

Riley shook his head and raised the sword tip toward him. "You owe me a better explanation, Leo! I killed a man for you!"

Saying the words aloud brought fresh images of blood and death to his mind. Riley fell against the tree again and put a hand on his forehead. No good deed could erase what he'd done.

"I killed a man."

Dante gently pried the sword hilt out of his trembling hand. He wiped the blade with a handkerchief and put it back in the sheath at Riley's side. Words of thanks wouldn't come. His mind was in a haze of shock and horror. What had happened to his dull life upon his quiet island home?

"You showed courage tonight." Leo's words held a hardness to them. "The time draws near when both you and Seth must hold on to your courage."

"Have you told either of them why, Lion?"

Someone moved in the shadows. Leo turned his lantern beam toward the voice. A white dagger glowed in the low light. Gloved hands pulled at the fabric until it came away from a face Riley recognized well. Her graying hair was pull tightly against her head. Gone was the gentle face who'd spent many an hour telling him and Seth bedtime stories to coax them to sleep.

"Emma?" Riley pushed away from the tree to stand before her. "Why are you dressed like Pavel Sandor? I could have killed you."

"Don't be foolish, boy." Emma shook her head, but her eyes stayed fixed upon Leo. "I saved your life tonight. How would I ever look your mother in the eye again if I'd let you be killed?"

"You are the one who's been watching our farm. It is a great pity you've chosen to remain silent all these years. You've kept me away from my son."

"I swore an oath to my lady Anne. It was she and now Seth who have my loyalty. I've watched you with him, Leo. This is not the life Anne wanted for her son."

"That was not her choice to make, and you know it, Emma."

Her harsh features softened and she nodded. "I know, and I think deep in her heart she knew too. We planned to leave for Carlotta, to join the world again."

The tears began to form in her eyes. She wiped them away quickly. "I'm certain there is much you must want to know, Leo. I will come to you soon when Seth is away from the farm. Riley, I saved your life. In return, I want a favor. You must never tell Seth about me and what I've done tonight. I cannot bear for him to know what I once was. In my heart, you will always be the two small boys catching crickets in your little hands." The sad smile left her face, and she was Sandor's twin once more. "Listen well to your mentor. Your life may depend upon his teachings."

"What of Sandor?" The cold hatred in Leo's voice stopped her as she turned to go.

"I've more right to his blood than you, Valdeonian."

Then she was gone. Her body disappeared back into the darkness, and she passed through the trees without a sound. Riley stared into the shadows, trying to make sense of the night. Emma was an assassin, just like this Sandor. The realization made him question the memories of his childhood.

"We'll meet you in the trees across from the pub entrance, Leo. Riley and I need a moment," Dante said.

"Never forget. I have entrusted you with my son's life, Riley Logan." Leo pushed through the branches headed in the opposite direction of that in which Emma had gone. His disturbing words faded, leaving Riley with the sudden desire to bolt toward the northern farms.

"Well, Curl Top, the Jalora chose wisely when it chose you! I think you'll make Seth an excellent squire." Dante gave him a pleased nod and folded his arms. "A squire keeps his ranger's secrets for him. Will you do as much for Seth?"

"You mean Seth is to be a ranger?"

Dante looked back out into the darkness where Leo had disappeared. "It's a hard life you have ahead of you, Curl Top. The ranger needs his squire as surely as Andara needs the ranger. You must see he stays fed, clothed, and bandaged when he bleeds. It is your solemn duty to protect his back in a fight, even if it means you must give your own life for his." The old squire gave him a strange smile. "And you must carry your ranger's legacy to his heir when he falls. Only then are you free from the oath you swear upon your lord's ring."

Squire to a ranger. Riley sucked in a breath and clasped at his hilt again. This Jalora had thought he was brave enough to do the job, but was he? Riley squeezed his fingers together harder. Nobody had mentioned death when they started teaching him the sword.

"What if I can't do it, Dante? What if I'm not brave enough?"

"You heard the call tonight, and you answered it like a true squire. When the time comes, I know you will kneel before your ranger and swear the oath to serve the Jalora just as I did."

"How is Seth to join these rangers?"

Dante lifted his chin up proudly. "Leo will teach him, of course. You mustn't be too hard on my ranger,

Squire Logan. It is very hard for a man to be parted from the Jalora once he has been joined. Leo was a ranger for many years. A lesser man would have died being parted so. He only wishes to help Seth and prepare him for what he must become."

These strange events were happening too fast for him. He wasn't resilient to change like Seth was. Here he was about to promise his loyalty to the Jalora and he had no idea what it was. He'd heard the tales of its magic, of course, but such mystical things didn't stray out to Marianna.

Leo waited patiently for them beside the row across from Paddy's common room. He stepped out to block Riley's path and pulled him into the trees away from the warm glow of the pub. Swift hands brushed grass and dirt off his clothing. Leo held him at arm's length and examined him closely.

"Seth mustn't know anything about tonight, Riley. You must give me your word on this."

"Why? I would think you would want him to know, so he could be careful."

Leo lifted the sword Riley's strange-speaking attacker had dropped. It was a deadly looking sword with a thin blade and a midnight hilt.

"This blade belongs to Pavel Sandor, the assassin. You have bested him. Sandor won't let such a slight go, yes? We don't know how Sandor disguises himself. He could be anyone. If he believes his identity is in jeopardy, he may attack Seth when I'm not there to protect him."

"Very well, I give you my word. But you seem to know this Pavel Sandor, Leo."

"Yes, I know him." Leo's words escaped through gritted teeth. "And when I find him, I'll kill him."

Chapter Thirty-Four

SETH PULLED ON HIS BOOTS and stretched with a yawn. He'd managed a few hours of sleep after closing up the pub. Dante had knocked on his door, muttering something about his father awaiting him. Extra sleep was not in his future this morning. After Leo's unexpected show of anger last night, he didn't want to press his temper further. He shuffled down the short hall toward the kitchen. Leo and Dante were already sitting at the table. Riley was asleep in the rocker by the hearth. They all looked as if they'd spent the night out in the fields.

"It appears I missed something while I was tending bar."

Seth sat down at the table across from Leo. He took the tea Dante handed him and sipped it slowly. His eyes were struggling not to meet his father's amber gaze.

"I apologize for my harsh actions last night, my son. You must understand. I have reasons for the methods I use and how hard I've driven you."

"Do your reasons include my visit by the lion? Or this strange power which comes when I'm angry? What is happening to me, Leo?"

"What lion?" Riley groaned from the rocking chair.

Dante poured another cup of tea and leaned over to hand Riley the cup. "Hush and drink your tea."

Leo leaned back in his chair. He seemed to be preparing himself for a difficult task. The kitchen was absolutely still as everyone waited for Leo to speak. A strange chill of expectation raced along Seth's arms. His father lifted his chin and began to share the secrets he'd kept from his son.

"I think you have guessed I am much more than a farmer, Seth. I once had the honor of being a ranger in the Jalora Legion. Dante was my squire. Each ranger has a unique Heart of the Warrior Ring, which is passed down for centuries from father to son. I bore the Lion Ring."

Seth sat his teacup down unheeded. Edmund's friends had called him Leo. It was a star constellation in the shape of a lion. Then there was the visit from the ethereal beast a few nights before. The sense of anticipation spread throughout his body.

"You have been called by the Jalora as the new bearer of the Lion Ring. You are my heir, son. This is why you received a rare visit from the animal spirit which represents the ring. This is why your body is changing, and the power comes unbidden to you." Leo watched his face for a moment and then continued. "All young heirs experience such things in their sixteenth year. They are called to service by the Jalora. It is Andarian tradition for the father to place the Heart of the Warrior Ring upon his heir's finger. A father dreams of such moments with pride. You have been called, Seth. It is your time now."

Leo reached inside his waistcoat next to his heart and pulled out a small bundle wrapped in fabric. He set it on the table and gently unfolded the cloth. A silver ring glistened in the morning light. Metal wrapped around a black stone. The image of a lion's head was etched in white at its heart.

Riley leaned over Seth's shoulder and frowned down at the ring. "It doesn't look like much."

"It sleeps. Many covet the power dormant within this stone. Men of evil would take the ring and use its power to bring harm to the people of Andara. For two years I have been hunted, hiding in long-forgotten fortresses to protect the Lion Ring." Leo looked down at the stub on his left hand where his finger had once been. "I did what I had to do to keep it safe. We must see you to the Obsidian Citadel in Lea, my son. We will find friends there. They can train you to protect yourself."

Leo's words drifted across the table. They reached Seth's ears through a haze of growing desire and urgency. His father's message was still clear despite the pounding in Seth's ears. Danger would follow if he dared put on the Lion Ring.

"Will you take up the ring and be its bearer? Will you follow the Jalora's command as its ranger and servant?" Leo raised a hand before Seth could speak. "Before you answer, be warned. The ring must accept you as my heir. If it does not, there's a possibility it will kill you."

Seth ran his eye along the ring's surface once more. Power reached out toward him in invisible tendrils. It called to him. The draw to touch the ring's surface was irresistible. His fingertips brushed lightly along the silver. Then the white lion trapped within the stone turned its head to look at him. Seth jerked away.

"You've seen it, yes? The spirit of the ring." Leo came closer to him. "Stand with me, my son. Stand like the man of honor you are to become. Take the ring."

Seth lifted to his feet, still watching the ring as his father held it before him. Leo slid the Lion Ring upon Seth's left middle finger. Searing pain raced up his arm, into his chest. He fell backward as the strange sensation moved into his brain. Flashes of color and light exploded around him. Then everything grew still in one last pulse of brightness.

I have waited a very long time for your coming, Child. The voice was neither male nor female.

"You know me?"

Its ancient power surrounded him, brushing at his curls. It was soothing and intimate. Seth gave into the embrace as the presence entered every pore of his body. His loneliness faded. The deep wounds wrought by his mother's death and the cruelty of Fergus McCloud were healed, but not forgotten.

There is great strength of heart within you, but also there is emotional control. The voice surrounded him with soothing tenderness. *You will be great. Your name will live on throughout the generations. I have called you to me, Lion. Serve me with honor.*

Seth tentatively opened his eyes. He was lying on his bed in the farmhouse. He'd survived. A new sensation pulsed from his left hand. He lifted his arm and saw the Lion Ring sitting firmly upon his middle finger. Gone was the black of death. Now the stone sparkled clear iridescent. The lion's head, now black, regarded him. Then it turned to stare into the nothingness to his left. Inside the belly of the ring, his blood pulsed in time with his heartbeat.

Muffled voices came from the kitchen. Seth turned toward them. Instantly, the voices grew sharper as if he were standing next to them. Dante was grilling Riley on packing some sort of bag. Riley, to his credit, was answering with patience and respect.

Seth stumbled a bit as he moved down the hall toward the kitchen. The ring was bringing everything into sharper focus for him. It was as if he'd been blind and deaf his entire life. The Lion Ring had restored his senses.

Leaning against the wall, he looked upon the crisp images before him. Water droplets rolled down the newly cleared luncheon plates. Riley's shirt freshly laundered, but cuffs still speckled with faded red stains. His gaze was drawn outside and into the fields beyond. Early morning sun had left them and dusk had come.

"Well, awake at last!" Dante had a look of pride and hope in his eyes. "How are you feeling?"

"I feel fine. Different."

Leo came into the house, wiping his hands with a cloth. A flash of images crossed Seth's vision. He saw his father in the barn. Leo had been building something. It was a contraption for Seth's training. What manner of magic was this? He hadn't known what to expect when he'd put on the ring, but this was beyond belief.

"You seem well." Leo gripped Seth's arm with a pleased smile. "The odd feeling you have now will soon pass as you grow accustomed to the ring. It is a part of you now. The sickness will fade in a few days."

"I don't feel ill, Father."

"Of course you don't!" Dante's assurances came a little too quickly. "He has his father's strength."

"Come, Dante! Break out another bottle of wine. My son bears the Lion Ring. We must celebrate!"

Riley gave Seth a fierce grin and began taking glasses from the cabinet. Dante took down a dusty bottle of wine from behind his spices and put it on the end of the table. He pulled the stopper with a loud pop.

Leo brought two long bundles from the corner of the kitchen. Careful to avoid the wine, he laid them on the table. He unwrapped the first bundle and handed it to Seth. It was a sword. Several roaring lions growled from within the strong Valdeonian steel. Gold inlay twisted cord-like around the hilt. The exquisite blade was perfectly balanced.

"It's beautiful, Father!"

His father strapped a sword belt and sheath around Seth's waist. Leo stepped back and smiled. Hope. Pride. Love. They all shone in his eyes. Standing before Leo, knowing without a doubt he had his father's respect, was the best moment of Seth's life.

"In Valdeon, a boy's seventeenth birthday is an important event, yes? He becomes a man. And a man needs a good sword at his side." Leo placed both his hands on Seth's shoulders. "A ranger must have the finest of weapons."

He reached for the second bundle and took it out of the cloth. It was another sword made with fine Valdeonian steel. The hilt was solid silver. A single lion head roared from the leather.

"Come here, Riley Logan! A squire must have a good blade at his side while he serves his ranger."

Seth bumped Riley with his shoulder and grinned. "I wouldn't have anyone else as my squire, Riley. You've earned that blade."

"Thank you!" Riley smoothed the fine blade as Leo put the belt around his waist.

Seth gripped at the hilt of his sword, enjoying the twist of gold upon silver. It was perfectly balanced and must have cost his father a small fortune. He just hoped his skill improved enough to be worthy of such a weapon.

"Come to the barn, my son. I can see your eagerness to test your blade." He marched out the door, his own excitement quickening his pace. "Bring the wine, Dante!"

Inside the barn, Leo had built a large structure of gears and wheels. The contraption was made entirely of wood and stood taller than a man. Scents, grease and freshly cut wood, filled the air. Their odor was made all the stronger by his new senses. Riley elbowed him when Leo slapped at the contraption, causing it to spin around.

"Leo calls it a sword dummy. He let me practice on it this morning. My backside and shoulders will never be the same, I can tell you."

"Come have a glass of wine, Curl Top." Dante handed Riley a glass. "You're about to see what a ranger can do."

Leo motioned for Seth to take a seat on a barrel. He walked to the center of the barn. Moving slowly for Seth's benefit, Leo placed his feet into position. The right toe pointed toward them. The left foot moved to the side, touching his right heel. Leo drew his sword and held the tip before him, a hair's breadth from the ground. It remained perfectly still.

"I'm about to show you the first stance in the Dance of Death. It is a technique only given to rangers in service to the Jalora, for it takes the Jalora's power to execute these moves. We do not move upon the ground as we fight, my son. Here, I believe I may have enough residual power to teach you, yes?"

Twisting his body in a sudden burst of speed, Leo performed the first stance. He was impossibly fast. Seth couldn't keep pace with his eyes. It was incredible. Leo's boots made no imprints upon the dusty barn floor. He really had left the ground by the Jalora's magic.

"Watch as I move into stances two, three, four, and five."

The dance, though intended to be violent, was beautiful. He was enthralled by his father's skill and mastery. Leo must have been a powerful ranger before parting from the Lion Ring. Seth's fingertips stroked the crystal upon his own finger. They'd been joined for a short while, but already he couldn't imagine a life without its gifts.

"It's beautiful, Father."

Leo came to a stop in the first stance. Loss haunted his eyes, but it was quickly replaced by pride as he smiled at Seth. "Yes, but it is also a horrific site for your enemy."

Leo moved through the five stances, twirling toward a bale of hay. His sword passed through it, not disturbing a single blade. He pushed the top half to the ground. Hay rolled along the barn floor, finally falling apart when it came to a stop.

"Now you try, my son."

Seth leapt to his feet and looked down into his ring for a moment. He did feel different, but had he truly changed? Seth pulled his sword out of its scabbard and took the first stance. The sword whipped around and he fell into the second, third, fourth, and fifth positions. His movements were sharper and more fluid. The sword seemed to be attached to his body, almost a part of him. He brought it forth, striking at his target. The second bale of hay exploded into ribbons. Covered in yellow strands, Seth wiped at his hair and clothes.

Leo laughed and came to join him. "Excellent start, Seth. It will take practice, yes?"

"And your teachings, Father."

Their eyes met. A blurred image flickered past Seth's consciousness. He couldn't quite make out the distorted scene, but in Seth's heart he knew time alone with his father would not last much longer.

Chapter Thirty-Five

WOLF LOWERED HIS TIRED BODY to the foot of the bed and pulled off his boots with a groan. The past few days had been filled with endless tactical meetings for the defense of the city. He had sent his squire to bed ages ago. A ranger's strength was fed by the Jalora, but it didn't extend to those serving with them. He'd worked everyone to their breaking point, including himself. The Jalora's gifted energy wasn't without its limits.

He collapsed back upon the mattress with no energy left to take off his trousers. Closing his eyes, he listened to the faint sounds of night outside the window. Cricket song from the gardens drifted over him upon the cool breeze. Sleep reached out for him, but its hands remained at bay. Then a soft touch brushed at his ear. He began to chuckle as the delicate strokes moved to his hair. Rolling over, he stretched his arm out to pull Dulcina to him. Empty blankets met his touch. What bangtail mischief was this?

Blazing light broke through his sleepy haze. Straining against the brightness, he blinked his eyes open. Standing at his bedside inches from his face was a mighty lion. Energy glowed around its body, forming a massive mane of brilliant light. He recognized the great beast. This was the spirit of the Lion Ring. Its image spanned the ceiling of the Obsidian Fortress in Lea. Legends claimed the Emperor of the Luminawni,

Ancients as they were sometimes called, had painted it in honor of the last Jalora Master. Fierce jaws and an eternally watchful gaze had guarded Ranger Headquarters for a century.

Ethereal green eyes bore into Wolf's soul, pinning him to the bed with their power. Then the great beast turned and moved to the door of his bedchamber. Its short growl shook the very room. Wolf's body rose instantly. Muscles and bone took on a life of their own. Wolf's conscious mind followed as an uneasy passenger as his feet fell onto the cold, tiled floors. Taking a slow pace, his body moved closer to the waiting beast. A puppet hand stretched out and opened the door.

Massive paws moved soundlessly into the palace corridor. The lion paused and turned its intense eyes upon Wolf. Dressed only in trousers, his body followed obediently. He didn't resist as the beast drew him onward. Passing between patches of haze and solid objects, they skirted the realm of dreams and mist. The everyday world of man moved past them in distorted, faraway pictures.

The haze released them from its willowy body. Lion and man stood together under the glass of the Grand Atrium. Rumbles of metal against metal thundered before them as the golden doors of the throne room opened. The veil of night parted, throwing Wolf into brilliant white light bursting into the atrium. The incredible power of the Jalora stretched out around his body, pulling him onward. Bounding past him, the lion ran toward the Altar of Providence. Its giant form stopped before a figure made entirely of light. A glowing bulbous head tilted downward. The great beast, once wild and fierce, tamely rubbed against the being. A fingerless hand petted the lion fondly.

Come forward, Xavier the Wolf.

He staggered toward them. Suddenly released from the bonds of energy, he fell to his knees. The Jalora's power was everywhere, pulsing into Wolf's very soul. Gulping in air, he struggled to breathe. He was drowning in its presence. Then the crushing power withdrew from inside his body, allowing Wolf to speak.

"I am your servant, Holiness."

The being of light turned its featureless face to him. *Yes you are, Child. I call you to service. You wonder why I come to you in full power, Xavier the Wolf. You wonder what the changes to your body and powers could mean. The people of this land have forgotten me. Many have grown blasphemous and arrogant. They have allowed my age old enemy into their hearts and minds. The Sarcion revels in their disrespect. It has gained a foothold in Andara. War brews.*

"Is there nothing you can do to stop it, Holiness?"

I have given Andara a great weapon. This I share with you now. The being pointed its hand to the Orb. *I give you hope.*

The Orb of Valdeon swirled wildly with light and color. In its belly a form began to take shape. Wolf came closer, unable to resist his curiosity. The image of a curly haired young man with bright, amber-flecked eyes came into sharp view within the depths of the Orb. It was the same young man he'd seen when the Sacred Guard had first returned to San Leonora. Wolf's heart pounded in erratic beats as the image in the Orb raised his left hand. Then a ghost appeared in the scene. Edmund D'Antoiné took up the young man's left middle finger and slid the Lion Ring upon it.

"Edmund is alive? When did this happen?"

Moments ago.

Wolf stared at the faces of father and son. How could Edmund be alive and another bear the Lion Ring? Never in the history of the legion had the Lion been released by the Jalora. Death was the only way the Lion Ring came off its ranger's finger.

A thousand questions competed for Wolf's tongue. He settled upon one. "Who is the boy's mother?"

Can you not guess?

"Anne Von Wolkhurst, Princess of Tslavia."

Edmund, the great fool! This child of mixed blood they had made would not be accepted by either of his people. Their old hatred ran deep. It was the ancient tradition of both countries to kill the babes of mixed Valdeonian and Tslavian blood. What hope did this new lion have of bringing peace to Andara? No. It wasn't for him to question the Jalora or its choice. Faith. He must keep his faith.

"What do you command, Holiness?"

Edmund plans to bring his son to Andara in the hopes he will take his proper place. We both know the opportunity has passed. Journey to the little island of Marianna in the Grey Cliff Isles. Find the Heir and take him to San Lucida. He will be safe with our faithful western Lords. The being moved to stand before him. Its shimmering body flickered with bursts of yellow and red. *You must be swift, Child. The bastard prince and his allies have already set sail. Beware the agents of the Sarcion. They go to find Edmund, but I fear they will discover the Heir. Protect him at all costs, Right-Hand.*

A jolt of energy struck Wolf's forehead and raced down through his body. Flying backward, he landed on the golden seal within the floor at the center of the throne room. The being and the lion were gone when he opened his eyes. Beside the golden throne, the Orb of Valdeon pulsed softly in time with the Heir's heartbeat.

Wolf slowly rose to his feet once more, wrapping his arms about his body to stop himself from shaking. Right-Hand. He shook his head. The Bearer of the

Wolf Ring always came after the Hawk in service as a member of the Sacred Guard. It was the Hawk Lord of Estabelle who bore the terrible responsibility of Right-Hand to the Master. Books and songs were filled with accounts of the Lion's rage turning against his second-in-command. A gruesome death awaited those fated souls who bore the title of Right-Hand. Xavier gripped his arms tighter, shaking his head at the implications.

"My Lord De Vincente? Something woke me and I felt drawn here."

Chancellor Benito shuffled toward him. He'd hastily dressed in a garish crimson robe. The garment's belt trailed behind him as he walked. Still struggling with one of the sleeves, he came to stand beside Wolf. Sleep-filled eyes saw the Orb of Valdeon alive again. Benito lifted a hand tentatively toward the Orb's surface and then let it fall again. Tears, ignored in his shock, fell down old cheeks.

Boots, headed to join them at a much quicker pace, echoed against the walls of the throne room. Basilio froze beside Wolf. His shock mirrored Benito's stunned silence. He'd had the presence of mind to dress in full uniform and bring his weapon. Ever faithful, Basilio had never let him down before. Wolf was doubly grateful for his service now.

He gripped his squire, spinning him around. "Cesar Santiago has remained in San Leonora against my wishes. Go fetch him at once. Beat him with your boot if you have to! Tell him I call him to service. Then hurry to my ship and tell the captain to be ready to sail within the half hour. Go now!"

"Hope has returned." Benito's voice rose above the stomping of running boots.

Hope. It was something he hadn't expected to feel again. A special lion born once in a hundred years had come among them. And Wolf was to be his Right-Hand. The knot in his stomach squeezed harder. He'd find this young man first, then worry about the rest of their challenges when they were safely in San Lucida.

"What are you about, Wolf? Telling your squire to beat me with his boot? I couldn't sleep and was halfway to the atrium…" Cesar's thundering stopped when he saw the Orb. "Am I dreaming? Is this true?"

"Listen carefully, Cesar. I have little time and can only say this once." He took the older man's face in his hands. "I leave this very moment to join the Heir. We will come to you in San Lucida within a few days' time."

"San Lucida?" Chancellor Benito turned sharply toward them. "Why?"

"The Jalora commands it. Tell no one of plans for his return to Valdeon, my lords. This is a matter of greatest secrecy. Cesar, you must make a believable excuse to return home. No one can suspect we bring the Heir to you."

"I will leave before sunrise."

Wolf raced to the door. He'd burst the sails reaching Edmund and the boy before Julian could find them. Above all else, he must keep this fragile bit of hope alive. Valdeon's future depended upon it.

Chapter Thirty-Six

"LET THE JALORA'S POWER guide your body, Seth. Don't resist it." Leo twisted the sword dummy, setting it back into position.

Seth smoothed a hand along one of the peg arms, admiring his father's cleverness in building the contraption. The wooden surface was holding up well under the beatings from his strikes. In the early days of his training, the dummy had found its mark more often than his body would have liked. The Lion Ring's power had definitely given him the upper hand on his spiky opponent.

He joined his father beside the water bucket and drank deeply from the ladle. Their times together had developed into an easy and comfortable rhythm. Leo spoke often of Valdeon. His love of home and country shone through with every word. One day, they would journey across its wide open spaces. Father and son.

Danger. The Lookout.

The sudden warning reverberated urgently inside his mind. Images of bloodshed and fire flashed before his eyes. Pain. Fear. The innocent victims shared their terror with him from across the fields.

"What is it?" Leo's words came from a great distance, piercing through the rushing waves within his ears.

"Something's wrong. We need to get to the Lookout."

Leo took Seth's face in his hands and held it. "You have learned to listen to the Jalora quickly, my son. Come, we must run hard."

Evening was upon them. Darkness brought thieves in the night. The voice had told him so. He pushed on faster, vaguely aware of Leo calling as they passed the farmhouse. Other boots followed them now. Bouncing light dotted the ground beside him. Seth kept his attention forward as they came to the end of the path. He jumped over the small stone wall running along the row and led them through the fields. The shortcut should save a few minutes, but would they be in time?

Seth came to the top of a knoll. The torches along the Lookout danced upon the horizon. It was a peaceful Marianna night. Had he been wrong? Was the warning a daydream? He gripped the Lion Ring. Perhaps it had reconsidered accepting Seth as its bearer?

Then the alarm began to wail. He released his breath in a puff of guilty relief. Spurring his boots forward, he ran toward the Lookout. The alarm clamored louder. Raiders. They'd come in great number this time. Torchlight circled around the base of the airship port. He couldn't be sure if their light belonged to the militia or unarmed townsfolk trying to help. Protect. He must protect the innocent. In his urgency, he allowed the gap to widen between him and his father. Leo called to him, but the words were lost among the pealing bells.

The last rays of sunlight sank into the ocean behind fast-approaching storm clouds. Droplets struck his face and hands as he drew closer to the cliffs. Approaching the battle, shapes turned into recognizable neighbors. Tom Gunn tugged frantically at the warning bell's cord. Two of his volunteers fired muskets into the darkness. Were they mad? The airship port was a short distance away. They could inadvertently hit someone.

Then he saw their targets. Several dark shapes stalked across the ground. His vision adjusted sharply until he could make out clothing, hair, and even eyes. It was as if Seth was standing next to the men under a noonday sun. The handful of Amity raiders circled around the Lookout. The musket fire stopped abruptly. Tom Gunn and his friends were dead before they could turn around. Haven Bay was left vulnerable for pillaging.

"Marianna!"

Seth charged into the crowd of men with drawn sword. Rather than strike at him under open skies, the rats scurried into the darkness and the cover of the airship port's pillars. He followed with a burst of speed, jumping ahead of them to cut off their escape. One of the raiders lifted his fist above his head. It was a signal. Others, ten strong, crawled out of the darkness. They swung jagged blades toward their prey as they circled about Seth.

A lion cannot be trapped by rats. Protect the innocent. Punish the guilty.

Seth stood in their center, waiting in the First Stance. Brandishing their weapons, they came at him in a rush. Then his sword cut through the air. Precise, well-practiced movements sliced along the throats of the first two men. He lifted higher above the ground, dancing through their numbers. Faster and faster he twisted. Pink mist and dark blood painted the pillars about them. Seth did his dance of death until all the rats had fallen about him. His body came to rest in the First Stance.

Other swords clashed to his side, but he ignored the exchange. His focus rested on the entrance to the

Sea Steps. Another surge of raiders streamed out of the opening and flooded the underbelly of the port. They approached him warily as the rain began to pour.

Seth slowly raised his face. A new kind of power came to him under the pillars of the airship port. His senses extended out past the docks, over the fields and into the stars. Then they fell back into his body, capturing the agelessness he'd found outside himself. Torchlight exploded under the docks as his energy extended outward once more. The raiders fell to their knees before Seth, screaming and holding their hands before their faces.

"Ranger! Mercy, my lord."

Seth stood over them, emotionless and indifferent. His memory flashed to the evening when these raiders had tried to steal away an innocent girl. Other nights they'd snatched children away from their parents and harmed the livelihood of the innocent. His fist tightened on the handle of his sword. It would be easy to kill them all. Marianna would never fear its neighbor again.

A soft memory touched his heart. It was his mother's wisdom he remembered now. She'd told him many times mercy was a gift from the Creator. It made the difference between a man of honor and a common killer.

"Go and never return. Be warned. The Jalora Legion knows of you now."

The raiders scrambled to the Sea Steps. Their boots pounded down the woodened planks toward the ocean. His heart hardened as the last one disappeared into the darkness. He hoped for their sake they would not try to exact vengeance on Haven Bay. He prayed his warning had been enough.

"Seth!"

An insolent touch upon his arm brought Seth spinning around. Sword tip inches from the curly redheaded creature's throat, he hesitated. The mortal creature fell to the ground and covered its eyes with trembling arms. Seth heard the horror in its screams, but couldn't feel pity for the mortal writhing on the ground at his feet.

"Seth, listen to me." Another mortal approached him with his cloak covering his eyes and his face turned away. "Remove the mask."

Mask? He touched his face with tentative fingertips. His nose, mouth, and every other defining characteristic had been replaced with a smooth, featureless surface. The magic he'd joined with earlier had taken his face. Fear loosened the hold he had upon the new sense of oneness. The surface of the mask evaporated. His nose and lips returned. Relief brought nervous laughter with it as he poked and squeezed his face. Then he remembered the mortal on the ground. No, the person.

"Riley?" Seth knelt down beside his friend, pulling Riley's arms from his face. "Look. It's me. I'm back."

Peering under his arm, Riley dropped his hands when he was satisfied Seth was indeed real. "What was that horrible thing? It was like looking into the face of death."

"Indeed it was." Leo helped Riley to his feet and ushered him into Dante's care.

He gripped Seth's arm and pulled him away from the crowd of Islander men beginning to gather. His father took up Seth's left hand and stared at the lion's head within his ring. "This is very important. When I put the ring upon your finger, what did you hear?"

"The Jalora said it had waited for me a very long time. It told me I'd be great and my name would live on for generations." He regarded his father's troubled face. "Is something wrong?"

Leo's words came in soft Valic. "Seth, you formed a death mask during the battle. Very few rangers are able to achieve this until they have completed their apprenticeship. Did you notice you were able to go up to the tenth movement? I only showed you five, my son. We leave this very night for the Obsidian Citadel where you'll be safe."

"Tonight? No, Father, I must find my mother's killer."

"You have a rare gift, Seth. Many people want what you offer. We must make sure your gift is used only for good. Sandor will wait for a time. You have my word. I will request rangers be sent here to hunt him down."

Inarguable truth added weight to Leo's words. His time on Marianna had come to an end. The yearning for adventure was dwarfed by a new sense of duty and purpose. Now he understood the unknown ranger's words. It was his time. He scanned the faces of the remaining militiamen, watching him in wary silence as he passed them. They were men he'd known all his life. Deep in some instinctive part of their mind, they knew Seth wasn't a part of their people and had never belonged on Marianna. A new element of fear shone in their eyes. He hated seeing it there.

Leo placed a hand upon his arm, guiding him toward the bench where Dante and Riley waited. His friend was still trembling. What must he have seen when he looked upon the ancient magic? Seth sat down beside him and bumped his shoulder. Riley nodded wordlessly. He kept his eyes on the ground at his feet.

"Do you still want to be my squire?"

"Now more than ever. You need me."

His best friend slid off the bench and kneeled slowly before him. Riley lifted Seth's left hand and lowered his head toward it. He tumbled backward as the lion's head turned to regard him. Then it floated back into its resting position. Seth guessed the animal spirit approved of its new squire.

Riley came back to a kneeling position and pressed his lips against the stone of the Lion Ring. "I swear to serve you faithfully as your squire, my lord."

"I accept you, Riley Logan." Seth smiled down at his solemn friend. "Rise, squire. Rise and serve your lord."

Dante gave a great sniff and nodded with pride. "I knew this day would come, Curl Top. Now, don't shame me."

Constable McTavish came down from the docks. His uniform was soaked in blood. One of his sleeves had been torn, and the skin beneath it was raw and bruised. Eyes filled with triumph took in Seth standing beside his father. They dropped to the Lion Ring upon Seth's hand.

"We've driven the raiders back to the Sea Steps, Ranger. Thanks to you."

"The Lion is honored to fight in your company, Constable." Leo stepped between them. "You served in the UR Army, yes? I call you to service now. The Lion must be taken to safety. You will tell no one of his whereabouts tonight until we are safely off the island."

"You have my word." Constable McTavish bowed again. An odd sense of devotion rather than fear was in the constable's countenance. He gave Seth a quick grin and then left them.

Devotion or fear. The Lion Ring certainly polarized people. He touched a fingertip to the lion's head within the stone of his ring. He'd hoped all the answers he'd sought would be revealed after he became the ring's bearer. Each answer, however, fostered more questions.

The euphoria of battle faded, leaving Seth drained and somber. The others joined him in his silence as they walked back to the farm. They would be traveling soon, the four of them. Seth had a thousand questions for his father, but they would wait until sunrise. Perhaps he could convince Leo to wait until the morning to leave Marianna. He just wanted to sleep in the comfort of a real home.

The farm was engulfed in rain and darkness when they reached the top of the little hill. A cheery fire and warm food would soon chase the damp out of their bones. They crossed the muddy yard, and Seth hurried up the wet steps onto the porch. He reached for the door. Leo gripped his wrist. He lowered the small beam of lantern light, exposing muddied boot prints disappearing under the door. A stranger awaited them in the dark emptiness of the farmhouse.

Leo's sword pulled free from its scabbard. He nodded, and Dante swung the door open. It struck the wall with a boom. Wet and stray bits of leaves blustered inside. Some of the rolling leaves fell upon a man's boot. A candle flashed to life. Fergus McCloud's face glared at them in the low candlelight. Raw hatred burned within the headmaster's eyes. Gone were the walking stick and the limp it once pretended to aid. A lean, agile body with two good legs stepped forward to meet them.

"Edmund D'Antoiné, you should have stayed dead."

"Fergus McCloud, so you call yourself now." Leo spat at the headmaster's boots. "Time and weather have scarred you, Pavel Sandor, but hatred has made my vision clear."

"Your slow wit finally serves you."

Fergus's perfect articulation had transformed into a heavy Tslavian drawl. Who was this man Seth had spent his childhood fearing? He'd slept under the headmaster's roof, eaten his food, and listened to him read lessons many a night. How could this same man be a murderer?

"You have put the Lion Ring upon your half-breed finger, I see, whelp." Sandor shook his head. "It was a foolhardy decision, I'd say. The bastard prince will come for you now."

"Speak to my son again without my permission, and they will find the pieces of your flesh scattered in the fields!"

"The famous Lion temper." Sandor let an ugly grin spread across his face. "Do you not have the slightest curiosity which of your loyal rangers turned traitor to hide this boy on Marianna? He is Valdeonian, naturally. I'm sure he'll be in touch soon."

"My son is with his father now. This traitor will answer for what he has done." Leo gently pushed Seth away and lifted the tip of his sword toward Sandor. "Let's finish this, Sandor, I grow weary of you."

Sandor stood slowly to meet Leo. They stared at each other for what seemed like an endless and bitterly cold age. Then Sandor pulled his sword in a deadly burst of steel. Leo anticipated him and raised his blade to block the death blow.

"Out of the way, boys." Dante gripped Seth and Riley by the arm. "This has been a long time coming."

Dante hurriedly ushered them toward the corner of the kitchen. The old squire put his hand firmly on Seth's chest in warning. He grabbed the kitchen table and overturned it. Riley helped him slide the table to the corner. They placed it in a barrier position. Dante drew his sword and stood between Seth and the fighting men. They were treating him like a helpless child when less than an hour hence he'd sent the Amity raiders scurrying back to the sea.

Steel slammed against wood as another deadly attack from Sandor missed its mark. He was skilled with a blade and nearly a match for Leo. Seth gripped at the stone glistening on his finger. The battle would have been over before it began if the Lion Ring were still upon his father's finger. Spinning and lunging, their deadly dance drew blood from both combatants. Seth could do nothing but wait for the outcome.

Sandor lunged. Leo twisted into his body, slapping the blade out of his hand. Stabbing his enemy in the shoulder with a short thrust, his father came back into the First Stance. He pressed the sword's tip against Sandor's throat.

"You won't murder me in cold blood, Ranger."

Leo leaned closer to Sandor. His words were slow, deadly. "I am no longer a ranger."

Terror grew in the assassin's eyes. Death was coming for him. Seth leapt over the table and pushed past Dante. He stood beside his father and placed his hand carefully on Leo's sword arm.

"No, Father." Seth moved between them. "I know you have the right to kill him after what he's done, but he is known as another man here. You won't find justice on Marianna. I don't want to lose you again. Let me take him to the constable, or we can see him to the high court in Larkspur ourselves."

"You show your weakness, half-breed filth." Sandor spat at Seth's boot.

"Weakness? No. It's taking every last bit of will I have not to kill you myself, murderer. You took my mother from me, but I won't stand by and let you take my father as well."

Leo's eyes found his own. The anger and hatred melted. He lowered his sword with a smile. Then he twisted his body with a speed worthy of any ranger and slammed a fist into Sandor's face. The man collapsed to the floor.

"My son has spared your life, thief of my happiness. Surrender, before my sword raises again."

Sandor took his hands away from his bleeding nose and lifted them in surrender. Then, with a serpent's speed, the villain rolled onto his feet and bolted out the door. Seth didn't give chase. The man had helped raise him, kept him fed, and educated him. Sparing his life would be payment in full for his past.

"He won't get far," Leo said. "So much like your mother. You have a good and honest heart."

Leo's gaze was drawn to something behind Seth's back. He turned, but saw only empty space in the dark window. His father continued to stare out the glass for a brief moment. Deep loss was upon his face. Clearly forcing a smile, he gripped Seth's arm and led him away from the window.

"Dante, we cannot leave Emma in Sandor's house after all her kindness to Anne and my son. Help Seth fetch her."

"Yes, Edmund, I'll take the Cub in the morning."

"No, you must do it tonight, while Sandor's wounds are still fresh." Leo took Dante's arm with his other hand. "It will be quicker with three. Riley, keep an eye on Seth for me? Make sure he stays safe, yes?"

"Of course, Leo. I promise. Do you think there's time to stop by the farm and say goodbye to my family, sir?"

"Perhaps on the way back."

His father kissed Seth on the forehead again. Gentle fingers lingered upon his cheek. Something was wrong. Seth's heart told him so. Despite his foreboding, he found himself on the lane waving goodbye to his father anyway. He chanced a look at Dante, whose lips had tightened in a frown. The old squire sensed it too.

Chapter Thirty-Seven

DUNG AND DAMP. IN all Julian's wild imaginings of his final moments with his father, he'd never guessed the end of their match would come in such a dreary place. A woolie farm was not the setting for a once great King of Valdeon to meet his end. Then again, Leo had chosen his fodder-filled bed. He could die in it.

A head blocked the light in a corner panel of the kitchen window of the farmhouse. His spy sunk back down slowly into a crouch. Julian's finger tapped impatiently upon the hilt of his sword as the man moved silently back through the shrubs toward his waiting entourage. This was it. The end of his searching and the end of the stinging nettle in his heart. Leo's time would soon be over.

The spy, dropping to his knees upon the ground, shifted his eyes to Julian's boots. "He is there, my lord prince. I could not hear what was said, but there appears to be a disagreement of some sort."

The door of the farmhouse slammed open and a man in black robes staggered out. Julian and his men remained absolutely still as he ran past them toward the backward little town. It appeared some unfortunate woolie farmer had angered Leo and had gotten the worst in the exchange.

Three more figures exited the shack and walked purposefully up the hill. One of them was the Lion's squire. Faithful to the last. The old fool. He prodded two teen boys up the path before him. One was a fiery haired woolie farmer whose pale skin glowed in the darkness. The other was a taller boy with dark hair. Something in his manner seemed vaguely familiar. He didn't carry himself like a farmer.

"It's Dante De Vincente, my lord. Shall we kill him and the boys?" Marcellus drew his weapon with hungry glee.

Julian eyed his butchering friend with a sigh. Marcellus's fetish for bloodshed would bring the entire woolie-dung-infested island to gather at this secluded farm. Nothing must ruin this moment, not after all his planning and pain to stage the raid upon their town.

"No. Dante is nothing. Let him go and settle whatever argument took place tonight. It was most likely a silly disagreement about wages and none of our concern. The Lion's squire will return to their hovel and find he has failed his lord."

Julian stepped out of the trees and onto the path. He didn't bother with stealth. Leo would know he was coming. Motioning for Marcellus and the others to remain where they were, he walked without hiding toward the farmhouse. Years of frustration and waiting had finally brought him to this moment, yet he hesitated at the door.

You lose your nerve now when the Lion Ring is within our grasp? Have you forgotten your desire to bear the crown? Think on your people, Julian. They need their king.

"I have forgotten nothing. You will forgive me for needing a moment. I go to murder my father, after all."

He grasped the handle and threw the door open. Edmund D'Antoiné was standing in the center of the tiny kitchen, sword in hand. The old ranger was still cunning though age had slowed him. Gone was the Jalora's mask of serenity. Raw emotion shone upon his father's face for the first time in more years than Julian had been upon the Erthe.

"Hello, Father." Julian looked around at the tiny farmhouse cluttered with cheap housewares. "Interesting choice of lifestyles. I hadn't guessed you would pretend at farming, nicely done."

"Do not call me father, bastard child. My true son and heir is beyond your reach. He bears the Lion Ring now."

It was true then. Leo had spawned a half-breed babe with his Tslavian whore, and the Jalora had accepted him. He hadn't wanted to believe such a disgusting lie at the word of the stranger in his chambers. Perhaps the Jalora had gone mad out of desperation. No one would accept such an abomination or allow him to take the Lion Seat. If not for Gorman's incessant talk about invasion, Julian was tempted to allow this young Lion to try taking the Crown of Sorrows. The Valdeonian people would assassinate him before the day was out.

"Where is the unlucky young man? I'm afraid I'm rather in a hurry and will be forced to take the Lion Ring from him."

His father's face was stone. "Many warned me against keeping you, my queen's bastard child. I see now I should have listened to them. You've inherited her dark heart."

Keeping his bitter words in check, Julian moved back to the door. Four hungry Dirge hovered upon the threshold, their song already coming in low tones. His fifth Dirge waited upon their ship, keeping any ambitious Amity raiders from betraying their word.

"Don't look so unhappy, Leo. You'll be with your Tslavian cow soon."

Julian hurried out of the farmhouse as the Dirge's song grew louder. Marcellus and his men were waiting for him beside a hovering dinghy. Julian climbed onto the little vessel, turning his face away from the howls inside the farmhouse. Marcellus sat beside him and gave the order to fly.

"You aren't going to watch, my prince?"

"A young Lion bears the ring. Once I find him, we can return to Valdeon in triumph."

Once the Heir is dead, you mean.

"Precisely."

This half-breed boy wasn't a Jalora ranger yet. He wouldn't receive his full powers until his naming and entry into the legion. The creature was practically helpless. He would be easily defeated. Julian's tension eased a bit. The Lion Ring would be his this time. He'd killed two other brothers. One more wouldn't weigh too heavily upon his conscience.

"We have company, my prince!"

Marcellus gestured to the west. An ebony airship sailed low upon the horizon, its hull skipping inches above the cliffs. The sails swelled like storm clouds against the clearing sky. A massive crimson beast bared its fangs from their folds. Julian's new allies from the north — the Jackal — had somehow followed them. It wasn't too difficult to guess who had led them to Marianna. He'd hoped they'd lost their changeling nanny in the streets of San Leonora. Curse the foul creature and may it meet a painful end!

Marcellus shifted uneasily beside him. "Are you certain these men are our allies, my prince?"

"I'm certain of nothing when it comes to Lord Gorman. These Jackal have grown too attentive. Take us in all haste to the fields beyond the airship port. I have a Lion to cage."

Chapter Thirty-Eight

THEY FOUND THE DOOR TO the McCloud home open. Emma, her cloak trailing wet upon the floor, stood just inside the house. Her eyes were riveted upon the closed door of the headmaster's study. Body tense and teeth bared, she kept still like a huntress trying desperately not to startle a thicket of pheasant.

"Emma?"

She turned to Seth, relief swimming in her eyes. Emma came to him. Her strong fingers dug into his arms. Then her gaze was drawn to his left hand where the Lion Ring glistened under the bright lamplight. Shaking her head, she dropped her chin to her chest. Moaning like a wounded beast, she let her hands fall away.

"You have taken up your father's ring then."

Gone was the friendly singsong tone of the woman from Horner Isle. Harsh Tslavic vowels stabbed into his heart just as surely as her lies. She looked at him at last. In her features was stony acceptance. This was a version of Emma he'd never met.

"I cannot say I am pleased, but it is a man's life you've chosen." Her smile was fleeting when Seth made no reply. "You've come for Pavel. He's shut inside his den. Have a care, Seth. He's a cornered beast and as such is more dangerous."

"Riley, will you fetch the constable? Justice is over-long in coming to Pavel Sandor."

Riley came to stand by his shoulder. "Emma's right, Seth. He's a killer. You have a care now."

He passed through the open door and hurried toward the police station across the square. The smart thing to do was to wait until he returned with Constable McTavish. Seth wasn't inclined to wait. Sandor was going to explain a few things or be very sorry he hadn't.

The door handle wasn't locked when he turned it. Seth pushed open the door. A cheery fire burned in the grate, sending shadows dancing upon the walls. The false headmaster sat in his chair behind the desk as he always did during the evenings. Despite his bleeding shoulder, it was almost as if Fergus McCloud had not transformed into Andara's deadliest assassin. Then the man looked at him with the cold eyes of a killer. He lifted a pistol from under the desk and held it toward them.

"Tell me who you really are."

"Not Fergus McCloud, if that's what you mean." Sandor's eyes narrowed as a spiteful grin came to his lips. "Oh, there was such a man. I met him on the airship headed to Marianna. He was thrilled to be embarking on an adventure. I ended his adventure quickly. No one will ever find that body."

"I'll cut the head off this vile snake!" Dante reached for his dagger.

Sandor stretched out the pistol and aimed it in a perfect line toward Dante's head. "Patience, Lion's squire. Your turn will come soon enough. Test my patience further and we will have done with you now."

Seth stepped between them, pulling the killer's attention back upon him. Sandor's laugh exploded in obscene shrills.

"Shocked? You think me a monster? Remember, we're related. I am your Mother's cousin, after all. Stifle your Islander Puritanism, boy. Rest assured, I never touched your sainted mother. Though I wanted her, she would not let me so much as touch her hand." Pavel's eyes grew distant. "I hoped she would learn to love me eventually. How could I compete with you, the Leo's child? You were a constant reminder I was not her lover."

All these years, Sandor had seen Seth as a rival for Anne's affection. His incestuous desire and playacting as another man for decades must have driven him mad.

"If you loved my mother, why did you poison her?"

"Loved? What a child you are. She wanted to leave and make a mockery of all our sacrifices. I gave her a kinder justice than the one she would have found on Andara. Do you know what they do to treacherous women who carry babes of mixed Tslavian and Valdeonian blood such as yours, half-breed?" Pavel gave him a disgusted sneer. "They tie these traitors to a boulder and push the stone into the nearest body of water. If by some miracle the mother escapes and gives birth to such an abomination, the baby is poisoned."

"Tslavians are cruel creatures." He slapped an angry fist against his leg. After all he'd learned about control in the past few weeks, he'd failed to stop the man from goading him.

"My countrymen at least give the bastard children a merciful death. Valdeonians bury the babes alive. Ask the Lion's squire. He cannot deny it."

Dante turned from Seth's gaze. His jaw tightened as he shot Sandor a murderous glare. It was true then. Seth shook his head and took a step back. What kind of a world was he about to enter?

"Our ranger overseer has stopped me from killing you all these years, but even he can't protect you now.

You see, I have new friends. They understand my need to leave these cursed Isles. I will return to my holdings in Tslavia and back to my old life." Sandor's finger tightened on the trigger. "Goodbye, Seth. Give my best to your mother when you see her."

"My father will avenge me."

"I very much doubt it."

Sandor grunted, dropping the pistol to the ground. A knife jutted from his shoulder in the very spot Leo had wounded him. He glared at a point in the room to their right. Screaming with powerless rage, he dove for the pistol. Seth was quicker. He kicked the weapon toward Dante, who picked it up and aimed it at Sandor.

"You always were overly fond of your own voice, Pavel. It is my pleasure to remind you who is really the deadliest assassin in Andara." Emma crouched in a warrior's stance beside the wall, a second dagger at the ready in her sure hand. "Never turn your back on me, my husband."

She moved on graceful feet to stand beside Seth. Taking his hand, she squeezed it fondly. Emma was another soul who'd given her life to protect him. He remembered the cold indifference Sandor had shown her each day. She could have easily killed her bullying husband, but for Seth's sake she endured.

"I warned you what would happen if you threatened him again, my husband."

"This must be a happy moment for you, wife. You turn traitor to your own people for the love of this half-breed!" Pavel Sandor growled like a caged animal. "Will our king forgive you for breaking your sacred oath, my lady? Or will the death you deserve be his gift to you?"

"Silence your lying tongue, Pavel. Do you forget who taught you that game? I stopped fearing death long ago."

Emma lifted her aging hand to touch Seth's cheek. In her eyes, he saw a glimmer of the woman who helped raise him. Gentle fingers smoothed along his cheek. Then she pinched him hard.

"You must forgive your mother, Seth. Pavel's lies kept your parents apart. Our king ordered him to hide her from Edmund until their marriage could be annulled. My husband saw his chance and tricked Anne into coming to Marianna, because he wanted her." Emma spat in Sandor's face. "He fed her lies about imaginary pursuers, pretending to be her protector to keep Anne with him. Pavel had her terrified to leave Marianna."

"And the ranger? I know you have spoken with him, Emma."

"He never revealed his face to me or to Pavel. Be wary of him, Seth. He has his own reasons for keeping you alive."

Riley burst into the room with Constable McTavish in tow. The constable's expression darkened as he took in the scene. Riley, Seth noted, was frowning at Emma. She shrugged and stepped away from Seth. Once again, the little woolie farmer knew more than he let on.

"Fergus McCloud or whoever you are, you're under arrest for murder, fraud, and anything else I can think of." Constable McTavish pulled his prisoner roughly from the floor. "If you behave yourself, I'll let Doctor McFadden treat those wounds."

The constable searched Sandor, pulling another pistol and a few daggers from his clothing. Satisfied he'd found all the villain's hidden weapons, he pulled Sandor toward the door. It was over. Anne's killer had been brought to justice. Now he could live in peace with Leo.

Sandor gripped the door frame, pulling against the constable's hold. Spittle ran down his chin as he fought wildly to face Seth. The constable stopped pulling on his prisoner when Seth nodded.

"You have no idea of the dangers you face if you leave this island, boy! Your mother's people will shun you. Your father's people will kill you. The rangers, well, they will have a far worse fate in store."

Emma move between them. The tip of her dagger poked out of the cuff on her sleeve. Riley came to stand beside her, his own weapon drawn. "Sleep with one eye open, Pavel Sandor. Always remember I serve the Lion."

Dante put a reassuring hand on his shoulder. "Your father would have killed him, Cub. Your head rules your heart."

"Pavel was forced to give his life up for mine by this mysterious ranger. The sacrifice sickened his mind. I can understand his bitterness, though what he did to my mother I cannot."

Emma spun around and grabbed Seth's face in her hands. "How will you ever survive in the world, my little Seth? Pavel is a beast and doesn't deserve your pity!"

Riley regarded her, mistrust firmly fixed upon his face. "If you didn't love him, Emma, then why did you stay?"

"I still saw my duty as protecting my lady Anne." Emma cast a furtive glance at Seth. "I was jealous at first. And yes, I wanted to see them both dead. All my hate left me the night you were born. One look upon your sweet face, I knew I had an important duty. Your mother and I became close friends, tied by the same goal. I swore the most sacred oath I could to protect you until it was time."

Emma began ripping papers out of drawers and tossing them into the fireplace. "Take him back to his father. Tell Leo I stay to erase all trace of Seth and his mother on Marianna."

"One thing troubles me." Dante let go of the hold he had upon Seth's arm once they were outside again. "Sandor was not afraid to kill you. Surely he knew your father would seek him out?"

"Unless he believed there was no reason to fear Edmund. Hurry! Let's get back to Father."

Chapter Thirty-Nine

Dampness from the rain-soaked ground splattered their boots as they ran across the fields toward the McPherson Farm. The speed given to Seth as he'd raced to the Lookout earlier wouldn't come to him now. It was infuriating to have these special powers but not be able to summon them when his need was great.

Bounding onto the lane, they ran to the top of the hill overlooking the yard. Darkness once again had engulfed the farm, extinguishing Seth's hope his father would appear on the porch to greet them. In their urgent rush to find Leo, they'd left their borrowed lantern back at the McCloud house. He strained to see through the night. Dark clouds rolled over them, strangling the few threads of moonlight. Riley came to a stop beside Seth, panting to catch his breath. Dante stood at Seth's other side. He pulled his dagger, listening intently. Something was moving in the darkness below. Seth pulled his sword and stepped toward it.

"Don't rush in like a mad fool, Cub."

Dante grabbed his arm and led them into a clump of trees close to the yard. They crouched low among the trunks and scrub. None of them had thought to grab a traveler's lantern on Main Row. He couldn't see inside the farmhouse. The blackness before them was too dense at this distance.

Then the Lion Ring came alive on his finger, sending pulses of energy through his body. Seth's vision began to clear. Shapes revealed themselves within rays of light. Riley's frightened face came into focus beneath the dying leaves of autumn. The deadly silver of Dante's dagger was ready to kill. Trampled grass and broken branches revealed others had stood in their hiding spot less than an hour before them.

Smashing glass and tumbling kitchen utensils boomed in the night like cannon fire within the farmhouse. Shattered window glass littered the trampled ground at its base. The door flew from its hinges. A shrouded figure staggered through the ruined opening. Blood-like fluid oozed through the cloth hanging from its torso. The creature paused a moment upon the steps, turning its hood toward the clump of trees where they crouched. A low mewing filled the yard. Then it turned away quickly and ran into the night.

"Father!" Seth burst from the trees and raced across the yard.

"No, Cub! It isn't safe!" Dante shouted after him.

Glass crunched beneath Seth's boots as he dove into the kitchen. Shattered dishes and pieces of broken furniture were everywhere. In the middle of the floor a dead body sprawled across the bloody boards. It was dressed in a dark shroud like the other killer who had run into the fields. Seth rolled the body over with his foot and immediately wished he hadn't. An emaciated face with gray-blue skin stared up at him through dead orbs. Thick liquid smelling of rot dripped from its mouth. The flesh from many kills still clung to its dagger-like teeth. What manner of evil had spawned such creatures?

"Father!"

He swung his sword back toward the door as crunching footsteps came into the house. Dante and

Riley stood in the clutter, their own weapons at the ready. Blank faces took in the ruined kitchen.

"What in the green, green fields is that thing?" Riley pointed his blade tip toward the creature at Seth's feet.

"Nothing you want to meet in the dark, Curl Top. Hurry. Come away. It isn't safe here." Dante threw his free hand forward to catch Seth.

"I have to find my father."

He pushed the hand away with a strangled sob. Stumbling on debris littering the hall, he pushed on toward his father's bedchamber. Another dead creature stretched across the doorway. Beyond the corpse was the still form of Leo.

Sword still gripped in his hand, Leo had defended against the creatures of evil to his last ounce of strength. His father's blood-soaked shirt covered the many wounds he'd endured. Rips upon his legs and face spoke of the viciousness of their attacks. Graying strands of sweat-drenched hair fell across his face. Seth knelt beside him and gently swept the strands away.

Leo's amber-flecked eyes struggled open. "Seth?"

"I'm here, Father."

He gripped Leo's bloodied hand. Why had he not been quicker? Why had he left at all? Leo closed his eyes for a moment, body shaking with pain. It seemed to take the rest of his strength and all the will he possessed to open them again.

Leo's hand squeezed weakly. "Don't use the name of D'Antoiné or set foot in Valdeon until the Jalora's will takes you there. It isn't safe. Be mindful of whom you trust, my son. Many will want to use you. Trust only the Jalora."

"I trust you, Father. We can fetch the doctor. He can save you."

Riley sat at Leo's feet, arms tightly about his body. He looked lost and scared. Seth was about to send him to fetch the doctor, when his father tugged at his hand.

"No, my son. There can only be one Lion. It is your time now. Promise me you will fulfill your destiny. Honor the Lion Ring and never take it from your finger." His bloodied grip relaxed as he managed a smile. "Always remember you are my heart. It was worth everything to know you."

Leo lifted his eyes to Dante. "Come, my old friend, there isn't much time."

Dante dropped down beside Leo and grabbed his other hand. "Yes, Edmund. I know what must be done. Just as you've instructed, upon my word it will be so."

His father's face relaxed into a peaceful expression. A deep sigh passed through his lips as if he'd come to the end of a long, hard journey. It was a look Seth would never forget nor understand until it was his time to pass from this life. They stayed motionless as the last breath left Leo's body.

Dante kissed Leo's limp hand slightly above where the Lion Ring had once rested. The old squire struggled to his feet and put a hand gently on Seth's head. Dante opened the wardrobe and pulled out Leo's trunk. He took out the ash uniform of a ranger and reverently laid it across the bed.

"He was one of the greats." Dante carefully straightened his ranger's uniform with fierce pride. "The rest of Leo's things are yours, Cub."

Seth wiped at his eyes and looked inside at the secret life of Edmund D'Antoiné. Daggers, boots, and memorabilia from Leo's travels filled the trunk. He ran his fingertips along his father's possessions, wishing they could revisit all those foreign lands together. A portrait of his mother and father caught Seth's eye. He pulled the drawing out and looked at their happy faces. It was a replica of the one hidden upon the wharf. Anne and her Edmund were together at last.

Dante tossed Seth a coin purse. "Take the money and leave this place. It's no longer safe for you here. I must take your father's body back to our homeland."

"Shouldn't I come with you?"

"No. Valdeon is the stronghold of your enemies. Have you forgotten the promise you made to your father so soon?"

"I don't understand, Dante. Who or what were those creatures, and why would they want to kill me?"

Dante turned to regard Seth with a pained sigh. "They seek you, Cub, because you are your father's son."

The old squire moved back to Edmund's wardrobe and pulled out two pairs of long trousers. He gave them to Seth and Riley. A pair of fine leather boots for Seth and a cloak followed.

"Hide in crowded places. Disguise yourself, Cub. Stay away from Valdeon."

Dante pulled at the long curls of Seth's thick hair and swiped his knife through the strands. The disembodied ponytail fell to the ground beside his father's body. It was the last falsehood tying him to his old life.

"Listen to me, Cub. A ranger will come to find you. His name is Wolf. Your father and he had a falling out, but it was as much Leo's doing as it was Wolf's temper. Promise me you will trust him. Wolf is a man of honor. He can help you."

Dante hesitated a moment, struggling with his words. "Leo kept something else from you, Seth. I must tell you in order to keep you safe." His face contorted with disgust and grief. "Your Father had four sons.

Two were murdered, while another has proven to be a terrible disappointment."

"Are you saying he murdered my other brothers?"

"His name is Julian. You stay away from him. He's no good. It wouldn't surprise me if that devil was in cahoots with Pavel Sandor. Hide from him at all costs. Understand?"

"Very well, Dante. I promise."

Seth exchanged a worried look with Riley. On the run from a murdering brother and foul things of evil. This wasn't how either of them expected to leave Marianna. Now, they faced their unknown future without guidance or protection.

Chapter Forty

Seth worked the tall leather boots over his long brown trousers. Stomping his feet into place, he regarded his unfamiliar image in the mirror. A young man with short chestnut hair and grief-stricken eyes stared back at him. The old Seth McCloud was gone. In his place stood the Bearer of the Lion Ring. He swung his father's gray cloak over the billowing tan shirt. It smelled of citrus and spices. The scent brought memories of Leo. He turned away from the mirror. Pausing at the door of his father's bedchamber, he finished strapping the sword and other weapons to his body.

Riley Logan stood in the kitchen. His friend had removed the simple clothing of a Marianna woolie farmer and pulled on the billowing shirt Dante handed to him. Sleeves meant for a tall Valdeonian hung past Riley's wrists. He tucked the thigh-length shirt into his trouser waist.

"Don't fuss, Curl Top. You'll grow used to mainlander clothes soon enough."

"You've finished then?" Riley pulled on Dante's long, dark green cloak. The color suited him.

His teacher nodded with a sigh. "I've dressed Edmund in his uniform. He rests aboard ship. Chin up, Curl Top. Leo knew this day would come. We concealed a small airship in the trees behind the house. I leave for Valdeon to obey his last order."

Seth gripped at the door frame for support. Leo must have known his attackers were waiting in the darkness. He had sent them away, knowing he was about to fight a battle he couldn't win. His father had sacrificed himself once again to keep the Lion Ring and his son safe.

"You're going now? What about us? Seth will want to…"

"He'll want to tell me where you're going. If I'm captured… You must both leave too, Curl Top. Those killers will be after Seth next. I've passed my legacy on to you. Carry it with honor, Squire Logan."

Dante moved quickly to the door propped up within the opening and paused with his hand on the ruined wood. "Remember the code, squire. Look after your ranger."

Kicking it outside into the yard, he disappeared into the darkness. Riley leaned upon the door frame and stared after his teacher. He looked lost. Seth ran his hands through his short curls. The last connection to his father was gone. It was just the two of them now. A soft touch stroked the skin around his ring, reminding him they weren't entirely alone. He grasped onto it for courage.

Riley glanced over his shoulder as Seth approached. "You look like your father. Dante's gone with Leo's…Leo. He says the murderers will be back. We'll need to be careful leaving Marianna tonight."

"Last chance to change your mind, Riley."

"What's the plan?"

Riley's trusting eyes looked at him through his rain-soaked curls. For his friend's sake Seth wished he really did have a plan. Valdeon was out of the question. He'd promised more than once not to attempt the trip. His father had planned to take him to the Obsidian Citadel in Lea, but it was an obvious destination. His hunters would be lying in wait for him on the road. The obvious choice wasn't the safest. Seth banished his indecision. He was Bearer of the Lion Ring now. It was up to him to see them through this alive. They'd concentrate on getting to Larkspur first where they could catch an airship to Port City on Eastland Isle. From there, they could journey anywhere on Andara.

"It will be safer if we stay off the rows.

Cloaked and hooded, they made their way along the treeline toward the far field and headed southeast. It was slow going in the moonless night, but Seth was sure they'd have an advantage over strangers to Marianna. Riley stumbled forward, catching Seth's legs in his flailing arms. They hit the damp ground with a painful thud. He wished he could summon the strange new ability to see in the dark, but it came at its own pleasure.

"We have to find a way to see where we're going, Seth. If we keep stumbling around, those creatures are bound to hear us."

Several dark shapes sprang out of the trees ahead of them. Seth and Riley hurried to their feet. They pulled their swords as one and stood together in the meadow grass. Tense and ready to strike, Seth's need for revenge knotted in his heart. He swung his sword upward until a thin stream of light pierced the darkness. He stayed his hand. Tom Logan's face floated within the stream. More shapes pressed closer to the little lantern. Riley's brothers stood before them, pitchforks shimmering in the lantern light.

"Riley Logan! What do you think you're about?" Tom opened the shade of his lantern a little more.

"You gave us a fright." Riley's relieved laugh seemed to further enrage his brother.

"And what do you think you've given Dad and Mum? First, you stay away from home without so much as a by your leave, then there is the raid, and we're told you help fight off Amity scum with a ranger. And now Fergus McCloud isn't who he says he is. He's escaped from jail and killed Constable McTavish doing it. What's going on?"

Constable McTavish was dead and by Sandor's hand? Seth squeezed his eyes shut tight for a moment. This was his doing as much as Sandor. He knew how dangerous the villain could be and didn't warn the constable. Better still, he should have walked Sandor to the jail and locked him up personally. Seth couldn't afford more regrets tonight. He moved to the lantern and clicked the shade down, throwing them into darkness once more. Gripping the Lion Ring, he tried to summon the power to him. Nothing happened.

"It isn't safe here. We must move away from the farm as quickly as possible." He stepped around them and began walking toward the east. "I'll explain when we've reached safety."

"Aye, too right you'll explain." Tom hurried after him. "My dad wants to see you."

An explosion ripped through the Marianna night, throwing them to their knees. Flames and debris burst skyward. Hot ash and burning wood rained down upon the empty field. An inferno burned where the McPherson farmhouse once stood. Dante had been right. The killers weren't satisfied with Leo's death. They wanted the Lion Ring and wouldn't stop until they'd found it.

"We'll make for the McKenzie barn. It should be safe for awhile." Tom let a small stream of light escape from the lantern.

He kept the tiny beam low to the ground, shielding its source with his hand. Seth walked beside him, sword at the ready as they made their way on swift feet over the fields. They were out in the open and completely exposed. He tapped Tom's shoulder and pointed to a gully between knolls. It would help keep them hidden to some extent.

Clouds parted slowly, allowing the moon's rays upon the countryside. Hovering like a herald of death upon a distant knoll was one of the creatures who had killed his father. Itching to strike, his hand gripped harder upon the hilt of his sword.

"Get down." Riley yanked Seth to the ground. "I don't want to see one of those things up close again. Dead or alive."

"What is it?" Stephen's whisper was directed to Seth.

He shook his head. "I don't know, but it isn't human. Come on, we've got to keep moving. Stay low."

The McKenzie Farm was on the north side of Farm Row and a short walk from the outskirts of town. Rolling hills dropped down into a small bowl. It was here Mr. McKenzie had built his farmhouse and barn. The yard was full of wagons and single mounts. Bright lights blazed through the windows of the house as men argued loudly from inside. Shadows paced back and forth, their owners gesturing angrily. Many of the crowd were armed.

"Constable McTavish is dead along with half the militia. These men are all that's left to protect Haven Bay and the farms." Tom frowned as he gave Seth a thoughtful look. "Come on. We can sneak in the barn."

Patrick and George muscled the barn door open. Once they were inside, Tom released the light. Their faces were expectant as they looked toward Seth. The world had suddenly gone mad. Murder and evil had come among them this night. He understood their need for answers.

"What I tell you must remain secret, well, at least until Riley and I are safely off Marianna."

"You aren't going anywhere, Riley." Tom shook his head. "You're going straight inside McKenzie's farmhouse and explain this mess to Dad."

"We can't stay here long, Tom. Those creatures are following us. If they find Riley and me here, everyone inside the house will be in danger."

"Explain what's going on, Seth McCloud." Patrick punched down hard upon a bale of hay.

Seth stretched out his left hand. The Lion Ring shimmered in the dim light, drawing the Logan boys closer. George stretched his hand toward it. His fingers hovered over the stone. Tom slapped his brother's hand. George pulled it away again with a yelp.

"I'm the ranger from the raid. Pavel Sandor, or the man you knew as Fergus McCloud, murdered my mother." Seth choked on the words. "My father was killed tonight after giving me this ring. The creatures who attacked him want it. Riley and I have to leave Marianna before they can catch us."

It sounded absurd to Seth, and he wondered if Tom or the other Logan boys would believe him. Tom's eyes were still transfixed on the ring. His knuckles turned white as they clutched at the handle of the lantern. Then the lion's head turned to regard Tom. He and his brothers stumbled away from Seth.

"We'll see you safely along the northern fields above Haven Bay. If we travel quickly, we can make it to the airship port inside an hour."

"This can't be real." George's stare remained fixed upon Seth's left hand.

"Aye, it's all true. I served three years at the Citadel. I know a ranger when I see one." Tom gave Seth a small nod. "Rangers never lie. They cannot. Great gulls. I never thought to see the Lion Ring in my life, Ranger. Imagine. The Lion's son has been here on Marianna all these years right under our noses."

Tom sat back on the hay bale, unaware all eyes were fixed upon him. "I'll do what I can for you, Ranger, but Riley won't be going with you."

"I must go with Seth, Tom. I've sworn an oath as his squire. I must serve my ranger."

Tom sprang up to pace about the barn. "Do you know what you've done?"

"Aye, I've trained these past weeks with Leo's squire."

"Did he tell you what war would be like, Little Whiskers? Did he tell you what is expected of you?

Tom's eyes grew distant. They seemed haunted, as if something scarred his memory. A shiver of foreboding ran along Seth's arm. His future would be full of war and death it seemed.

"Most squires in the Jalora Legion die or are maimed serving their rangers. If by some miracle they outlast their lord, those squires risk their lives fetching the ranger ring off their dead master's hand. I've seen a squire throw himself before a death blow to save his lord. Another leapt off a cliff to try and reach his fallen ranger, only to have them both die. Did he tell you the truth of war, Riley Logan?"

Seth looked at his best friend, waiting with the rest for the answer. What had he done? Accepting Riley as his squire seemed selfish now. Rather than following him into danger, Riley could be with his family, safe and sound.

"Aye, he told me." Riley came to stand beside Seth. "I gave an oath."

Tom leaned against the barn wall and nodded at last. "Aye, go you must."

"You can't be serious!" Patrick spun the eldest Logan brother around. "What if he doesn't come back?"

"We'll come too." George, finally able to tear his eyes away from the Lion Ring, turned to Riley. "That should see you to where you're going."

Their anxious, frightened faces flashed before Seth's eyes in images of death. He staggered back as the power left him. More magic, none too pleasant this time. The Logan boys were no match for the enemies hunting him. He couldn't add their deaths to those lost tonight.

"No." Power surged behind his words. The Logan boys stepped back a little. They looked at him as if he were a stranger. Fear was in their eyes. He couldn't bear seeing it there.

"Where we go you cannot follow."

"Then we'll see you both safely off Marianna at least, Lion."

Tom pushed the barn door open tentatively. He waved them to follow. The Logan boys surrounded Seth and Riley as they made their way south. The familiar sense of safety Seth normally felt in the presence of the Logan boys was absent as they walked. Creatures with skill enough to murder Edmund D'Antoiné could easily crush farmers. Seth had dragged Riley into danger, and now he had inadvertently endangered his best friend's entire family.

"Look." Stephen pointed to the west. "Two more of those creatures."

Their hulking shadows crossed Farm Row a few moments after Seth and his friends had entered the outskirts of town. How many of those killers had been unleashed upon Marianna to hunt him? Not wanting to find out, he kept them behind the stone wall running along Main Row. They stopped just short of the airship port. It appeared to be deserted. Seth scanned the platforms illuminated in the torchlight. No sign of his hunters.

"Riley and I must leave you here."

"You can't risk buying tickets. Best to go up in the cargo lifts." Tom pointed at several bales of woolie wool. "You can stow away. It's a short trip to Larkspur. You'll be safe enough in the hold."

"Listen, Tom," Riley began awkwardly. "Tell Dad and Mum I had to go with Seth."

Tom gave him a troubled smile. "Of course you had to go, Little Whiskers. Logan men aren't cowards. We see our duty and we do it."

"Will you look after Beatrice for me?"

"Anyone bothers her, we'll pound them." George nodded with a hard swallow. "I promise."

No hint of humor laced his brother's voice. Jamie or anyone else who bothered Beatrice would soon regret it.

"Ranger." Tom stood before him, looking much like his father in the moment. "Watch after Riley. Promise me."

"You have my word." Seth gripped Riley's shoulder. "Ready?"

"Let's go."

Darting across the Main Row, they moved into the shadows of the warehouses. Seth didn't look back as they left their past and headed toward an uncertain future.

Chapter Forty-One

Julian adjusted the spyglass until he could clearly see the young Lion's face. Those amber-flecked eyes shot a look directly up at the docks, but he made no reaction. The boy turned back toward his companions, seven farm boys not much older than himself. Julian had guessed right. The young Lion didn't have all his powers yet. He was still vulnerable.

The very thought of the boy curdled his stomach. Their country's most precious sacred object was upon the finger of a dirty Tslavian. The sacrilege made no difference to Leo, apparently. Of course not. The boy looked so much like their father. No doubt Leo had doted upon his heir, lavishing the boy with affection never spared for his other son.

The Lion and a curly headed young man, his squire perhaps, leapt over the stone wall and ran toward the warehouses. The rest of their group stayed behind the wall. They must have meant something to the boy. It was unfortunate their loyalty to him would result in their deaths. A handful of armed Jackal soldiers crept low through the fields toward the weaponless boys. While it would be entertaining watching his barbarian allies cut them down, the farmers weren't his concern. He swept the spyglass back to the young Lion. It was time they met. The boy should know why he was about to die. Julian had, after all, faced his other siblings before their lives drained away.

He snapped the spyglass home in his belt and stood away from the railing. The Dirge could make short work of the Lion of course, but they hadn't returned from disposing of Leo. Julian didn't like to lose sight of them for long. They were difficult to control, but manageable. Perhaps their absence was best for now. He wanted to face this half-breed boy. It was a risk. The Lion Ring may not accept him after he personally killed its bearer, but he was out of time. Gorman was growing impatient.

A man stepped out of the shadows a few feet away from Julian. Black tattoos covered a bald head. Gold rings pierced his brow and cheeks. It was the Amity raider he'd paid to find Leo and the boy. A hungry smile crossed his painted face. Rings jingling as he moved, the raider gestured toward the warehouses.

"You see. We have completed our side of the bargain. Now you must pay us."

"Your payment is aboard my ship. Wait for me there. You'll have your reward once I'm done."

"I wait for no one. Least of all you, bastard prince." A figure cloaked in midnight emerged from the crates to stand between Julian and the raider. His gloved hand threw off the enormous hood. Turning his masked face toward the faint light of a sulking moon, he made certain Julian saw the white dagger running down its center.

"Well, I'm honored." Julian eased his hand toward the hilt of his sword. "Does the Tslavian Court despise me so much they would send their most legendary assassin to kill me?"

"Don't flatter yourself, Valdeonian pig. The prey you hunt is mine." Pavel Sandor grabbed the raider's tunic. "You didn't tell me we were taking money from the sworn enemy of my country. I will not be traitor to my king!"

A dagger sprung into his hand. The tip drew a deep cut across the raider's throat in moments. Though time had aged Sandor, clearly his skill had remained sharp. He pushed the raider's body over the railing and into the dark void.

"I endured years looking after Seth, watching the half-breed child of Edmund D'Antoiné grow into adulthood. My blade was stayed by the deadly promise of an unknown ranger. No more. I will have my justice! My blade and not yours shall slit Seth's throat."

Seth? It was a strange name to give a Lion. And what of this unknown ranger? A great deal of mystery surrounded this boy. No matter. His life would end shortly, and the Lion Ring would be in Julian's hands. The Tslavian scum before him mustn't be allowed to touch it. If he took the Lion Ring to his king, then news of the boy's death would be out. Pavel could prove Julian was behind Leo's death. He had to be stopped.

Sandor readied his body to strike again. He seemed to be favoring his right shoulder. Julian pulled his own weapon. This was an opponent used to killing and no rules of honor or etiquette would hinder him. Injured, he might prove to be even more deadly.

"I am his blood relation. That gives me precedent over you, Tslavian scum." Julian lunged at the assassin with his most deadly attack. It was met with a parry, easily deflecting his strike.

"You have but a distant claim on him, bastard prince." The Tslavian spat with distaste. "I have the tie of blood. His whore of a mother was my cousin. Your king sullied her body and the tainted result of their union runs along the ground below like the pathetic vermin he is." Sandor twisted his sword and disarmed

Julian. "It is a matter of family honor, you see. I must kill the boy and take his head to my king. Only then will my family's name be restored."

The tip of Sandor's sword pressed against his chest, twisting with a hatred which Julian returned. To come so close and be bested by a Tslavian was unforgiveable. He braced for the strike he knew was coming. Then Sandor groaned and fell forward.

"Did you miss me, Julian?"

The changeling grinned as it came to stand before him. Two Jackal soldiers stood beside the crates. One had a club in his hand. He licked at the blood his weapon had caused to Sandor's head.

"Kill him!"

"We've watched him this night. He is a warrior and deserves a warrior's death. Even barbarians, as you call us, have honor, Andarian." The changeling folded its arms. "Come. Our lord summons you."

It gestured for Julian to follow with an outstretched finger, while the two warriors dragged Sandor to the side of the dock and pushed him behind a crate. His allies may have saved his life, but they were ruining his chances to take the throne.

"I will not be summoned like a wayward child!"

Julian walked around them, heading for the last location he saw the young Lion run. They grabbed his arms and pulled him off his feet. He was dragged like a drunk from a tavern. A lock of sticky, bloodied hair fell onto Julian's face. He turned away, disgusted by the stench. Clearly these barbarians didn't believe in bathing. Not in soap and water, at any rate.

Struggling against their hold was futile. They were too strong and too disciplined to disobey their lord. Then a sickly gray-blue face appeared beneath them.

The Dirge stared for a long moment before drifting toward the warehouses and the young lion.

Chapter Forty-Two

FIRE, HUNGRY AND WILD, escaped into the night sky, heralding tales of violence in an otherwise calm sea. Xavier the Wolf clutched at the railing of his airship. Was he too late? The ship had raced from Valdeon at full speed, but their journey to the little island had still taken two full days.

The ship's hull vaulted past the jagged rocks, sending the birds scattering out to sea. They drew closer to the small airship port resting a little to the side of what apparently was the only town on the island.

"Take us directly to the explosion, Captain."

Darkened fields and bleating sheep passed beneath them. They rose on the currents over a cluster of trees and came to an open meadow. It had been a farm once with a tiny house and barn. Everything surrounding the skeletal remains of the farm was aflame. Several men and women were desperately trying to douse the fire. They were fighting a losing battle.

Take comfort, Right-Hand. The Heir still lives.

"The launch is ready, my lord." The first-mate saluted. "Shall I have an armed guard escort you?"

"Let them attack me if they dare. I will have answers."

Wolf leapt onto the dinghy with his squire following close behind. Basilio took the rudder and sailed the little vessel up and over the railing. Heat from the fire came at them in waves. Basilio banked the dinghy sharply to the left and away from the fire.

Giving up on the farmhouse, the crowd of islanders stood watching the blaze. Wolf motioned Basilio to land in their center. Cries of shock rose over the sounds of the flames as they hurried out of the path of the dinghy. Wolf stood, letting his presence and power take their full effect.

A fat, sweaty man dressed in breeches and a coat much too small for him approach their vessel. He was dressed a good deal better than his neighbors. Soft hands with clean fingernails. He was a minor official on the island and no doubt lorded over the others.

"What is your business here, Stranger?" The chubby little man put fat hands upon his waist.

Wolf lowered his eyes, examining the puffed up, petty official. The little man wilted under his gaze and stepped back into the crowd.

"I seek Edmund D'Antoiné and his son." Wolf lifted his voice over the rumble of burning and murmurs.

Confusion and fear came back to him as he probed the crowd. Their quiet world of woolies and seabirds had been tilted on its head this night. Wolf was another stranger to fear.

"You call him by the name, Leo."

A few heads raised. Whispers circled among the islanders. Anyone who had met Leo never forgot him afterwards. Wolf stretched out his senses to the crowd again. It was useless. These people only knew suspicion and fear now. They would not willingly tell him anything, especially after the violence their island had seen in the past day.

Close your eyes, Right-Hand. Concentrate on the young lion.

Wolf did as he was commanded, shutting out all sound and emotion. He was not surprised to feel Basilio come to stand between him and the frightened islanders. Eventually his presence too was blocked from Wolf's senses. Then he felt it. A steady beat of power coming from the southeast. It was the young Lion. He was in trouble.

"Basilio, the Heir is at the airship port! Follow in the launch."

He jumped out of the vessel, vaulting over the heads of a handful of farmers. Wolf ran at full ranger speed toward the structure in the distance. The grass was wet beneath his feet. In his haste, the drops of dew could not touch his boots. The Jalora stirred within him. It was unsettled and angry. Images of murdered innocents were coming at him in a dizzying frenzy. He kept his focus on the Lion's heartbeat, using it as a compass.

The small port stood against the dark horizon. He was fast approaching a short rock wall separating field from road when he saw them. Strange soldiers dressed in unfamiliar armor circled about a group of unarmed farm boys. Swords drawn, the soldiers closed in for a tighter circle about their victims.

"I make necklace from your ears and send to your friend the Lion." Their leader, a hideous-looking man with long, blood-stained braids, tugged at a gruesome necklace of leathery flesh around his own neck. "You see. Just like mine."

The other soldiers moved in perfect unison, sweeping their swords at the boys. These were no mercenaries or common thieves. They were well disciplined and schooled in the art of intimidation. The strange soldiers, however, were not infallible. None of them noticed Wolf standing a few feet behind their line.

The stench of their bodies was horrid. Best to have done with them quickly.

His blade swept through the invader bodies swiftly, not dissuaded by their blood-stained armor. Wolf's Dance of Death didn't stop until he faced the last soldier, the same blaggard who'd made disparaging remarks about the Lion. He flicked his blade twice. The villain's ears fell to the ground. Then Wolf parted his head from his foul shoulders. He wiped his blade upon the man's cloak and sheathed it.

The islander boys, brothers from their shared copper hair and pale skin, stood in a circle surrounded by blood. Casting worried looks toward Wolf, they seemed to be more afraid of him than they'd been of their armored enemies. He listened intently to their conversation as he examined the bodies of the strange new evil which had arrived upon their shores.

"I'm telling you, he's a ranger." The eldest of them hushed his brothers. "If he asks us, we'll have no choice. He'll make us tell him where Seth has gone."

Wolf crossed the distance in seconds to tower over the shorter islanders. "You will tell me of Leo and his son."

"Yes, sir." Their eldest snapped a hasty salute. The young man's hair may have grown and his weapons been left behind, but he couldn't be rid of the military training he'd been given. Clearly, he'd served in the UR army recently. Good. It would save time.

"How do we know we can trust him, Tom?"

"Shut your mouth, fool! This ranger is a Deacon. He can read your thoughts."

It wasn't exactly true. Wolf couldn't read their thoughts word for word, though the legion didn't go out of its way to correct this common belief. Criminals were more likely to confess if they believed a ranger could read their very thoughts. In truth, an individual's images and memories came to a ranger when he probed a person's mind. The gift was invaluable. Wolf stared at Tom and began to probe his memory.

"Why do you reckon this stranger is so interested in Seth?" One of the brothers clutched at Tom's sleeve. "First Fergus McCloud turns out to be Pavel something-or-other, and now this ranger shows up."

"Hush, Patrick! I'll do the talking."

Wolf stopped his probing abruptly and lifted Patrick up by the waistcoat front. "Pavel Sandor was here on the island?"

"Aye!" Patrick kicked and struggled, but Wolf's hold was firm. "He pretended to be Seth's uncle. Constable McTavish had him locked up and was killed for his trouble. Pavel what's-his-name murdered him."

This was unexpected news. The Tslavic court had professed innocence in their princess's disappearance. Dragon had facilitated a meeting between the Sacred Guard and Tslavia's crowned prince, Bearer of the Gargoyle Ring. They'd accepted the word of their enemy, because he was a ranger and a man of honor. Now it appeared they'd all been fooled. Some faction of the Tslavic court knew of the Lion, but why keep him hidden? Why not kill him outright?

"Where is the young Lion? I will not ask again."

The brothers charged toward Wolf, but a deadly force blocked their path. Basilio flicked his lantern open. Bright light burst from the crystal chamber. Dropping it to the ground, he growled a fierce battle cry. His anger could be fierce and his visage terrifying. Fists and legs knocking the young men easily away, he pulled his weapon.

"Stand down, squire. These boys are friends to the young Lion."

The redheads regarded Basilio with keen interest. Wolf probed the young man he held in his grip. Their brother, the youngest of them, had gone off with the Lion as his squire. No wonder they found Basilio so fascinating.

"He and my brother have gone to hide among the wool upon the lifts. They plan to stow away onboard the ship headed to Larkspur." Tom stared at Wolf's hand holding his other brother; his eyes were riveted upon the Wolf Ring glistening in the lantern light.

"You know this ring. You know I am a Lord of Valdeon."

Tom nodded. "We will do as you say, sir."

"Warn the men who search for Sandor quickly." Wolf let the full power of his voice wash over the young man. "Sandor is known as the deadliest killer in all of Andara. A death sentence was placed upon his head years ago. No cell can hold him."

Wolf let the young farmer loose and started toward the airship port. The steady beat of the young Lion's heart was stronger now. He could almost hear it beating beside the warehouse where the boy crouched. Danger was coming toward him. It was unclear if he was aware of the many Dirge about to descend upon his hiding place.

"You'll help Seth, sir. Won't you?"

"It is my duty to do so." Wolf turned to look upon their worried faces. "The Jalora's blessing upon you and your family for your kindness to the Lion."

Then Wolf called to him his full power. He dissolved into the night. One thought. One goal pushed him forward. Protect the Lion.

Chapter Forty-Three

SETH AND RILEY KNELT DOWN behind an empty barrel at the corner of the warehouse. The everyday shouts and bustling upon the docks were absent. Sailors from the cargo ship pulled frantically at the ropes, while one of their armed comrades guarded them as they worked. They were anxious to escape the violence invading Marianna with as much eager urgency as Seth and Riley. Above their heads a large platform carrying bolts of wool lifted slowly up. They used the pulleys to swing the cargo over the cliffside toward the ship's waiting crew. The wool was almost loaded despite the violence that had taken place at the docks. They'd have to hurry if they were to sneak on board without being seen.

"Get ready to run, Riley. We'll have to stay close to the warehouse walls, but I think we can make the closest bundle without being seen."

Riley grunted. His curly head fell upon Seth's back and then rolled to land in the mud. Seth twisted in his crouch and brought his finger to Riley's neck. A steady heartbeat pounded slowly beneath his fingertip.

Strange humming came from the shadows. Soft at first, the hums grew to a painful wail. The sound grated on Seth's ears, forcing his fear to the forefront. Three of the shrouded creatures floated under the flickering light of the port torches. Boney fingers pulled off their cowls, exposing stalks of thinning white strands hanging limply from their gray-blue scalps. Old sores and tainted bits of flesh covered their faces and hands. What evil had created such monsters?

"Riley! Get up. We have to run!"

His words sparked a fresh song from the loathsome creatures. They opened their maws wide. The sight of their hideous mouths froze his blood. Two rows of sharp, jagged teeth lined their jaws. Built for eating flesh and bone, they looked well used. Black orbs fixed upon Seth with fevered hunger.

He stood, pulling his sword. Seth moved between them and his fallen friend. They couldn't run this time. He would have to face these creatures on his own. Seth struggled to keep his fear in check. This was a fight he couldn't afford to lose.

"Stand away from him, creatures of evil!"

A man's voice shook the very walls about them with its power. The barrel they'd hidden behind lifted up upon the waves of sound and energy. It hurled back to the ground, smashing in pieces.

The Dirge turned as one with an angry wail to face the intruder interrupting their meal. His sword was too quick. The blade cut diagonally with a deadly flourish. Pieces of dried fabric and rotting flesh fell to the mud in a perfectly formed line. Standing in the first stance of the Dance of Death was a ranger. The golden emblem of the Jalora Legion blazed from the ash chest of his tunic. Silver peppered his short, dark hair. Intense eyes kept their focus upon Seth.

He was Valdeonian, but was he the traitor ranger? Seth had never experienced such power or seen the skill this stranger used with such ease. It would be impossible to escape him. He wouldn't try with Riley unconscious upon the ground.

"You are unharmed, yes?" The ranger stepped over the gruesome line to stand before Seth. "I am called Wolf."

The ranger slowly sheathed his sword and stretched his hands hip-wide in a calming gesture. He extended his left hand to show Seth his Heart of the Warrior Ring. Movement within its dark blue depths made the Lion Ring stir. The Wolf's head inside the stone swiveled to regard him. It seemed to be waiting for something.

Seth extended his own ring. The Lion's head's reaction was immediate. It looked upon the Wolf. Tendrils of energy reached out from Seth's ring to circle about the ranger. The Wolf's ring returned the energy, drawing their hands closer together. Wolf smiled, and his eyes moistened.

Then the ranger's fingers touched Seth's hand. The Jalora's power sparked between them, pulling Seth into a world of misty images. He saw Wolf lifting two little boys, his sons, in his arms. A beautiful woman with a kind face came to kiss him. The mists shifted. Wolf was marching before a large company of other rangers in a room filled with gold and glass. The assembled crowd bowed as Wolf walked past. The power released them. Wolf seemed as startled by the exchange as Seth.

"The Jalora has sent me to help you, Seth. I am to take you to safety and continue your training."

Seth nodded, knowing without a doubt he could trust the Wolf. Dante had been right. This ranger was a man of honor and someone who could keep them safe. He wasn't the traitor ranger. Seth's existence seemed to have been a surprise for him as much as it was for Leo.

A man moved out from behind Wolf. He must have been waiting there silently for some time. The man was also Valdeonian. He was dressed in a black uniform with a small golden Wolf's head on his collar. Kneeling down beside Riley, he began running his fingers through the red curls.

"This is my squire, Seth. He will help your young friend."

"How is he, sir?"

Wolf's hand came to grip his shoulder. It felt solid, like a strong pillar he could lean against. Calming instantly, Seth's heart slowed into a steady beat. His breathing eased and his fear left him.

"He was struck upon the head, Lion. I see no stab wounds. He will recover soon." Wolf's squire put a strong-smelling vile under Riley's nose. "Stand out of the mud, boy."

Riley grumbled as the Wolf's squire helped him to his feet. He rubbed at his head, but seemed unharmed otherwise. Seth was grateful for their luck. They'd have to be more careful in the future. Danger would follow them now.

"A Marianna squire is not an acceptable choice for the Lion. No doubt my lord will correct this egregious error quickly." The Wolf's squire frowned at Riley. "You will be well fit enough in a short while, boy. It would be best for you to go back from whence you came."

"Here now! I'll not be leaving my ranger. I don't care who says what," Riley grumbled, leaning against the wall. It would turn into a fight in a moment, and this time Riley wouldn't win.

"We will discuss such things later, aboard my ship." Wolf frowned at their squires and then turned to Seth again. "More Dirge coming. We must see you to safety."

Dirge. It was a proper name for the foul creatures. Seth looked into the direction Wolf was facing. He didn't see anything, just an empty row and fields beyond. This ranger must have incredible powers Seth hadn't begun to guess at yet.

Then Wolf swept around Seth, pulling his sword. The low hums of the Dirge was a noise Seth was quickly growing to dread. Ten of the hideous creatures emerged from the shadows. Wolf stood between him and their hungry maws.

"Go! Take your squire and run."

"What about you? I can't leave you to face them alone!"

Wolf pushed Seth forward. The ranger began to draw the Jalora's power into his body. Seth staggered back from its angry wrath.

"I will find you again. This I swear. Now go!"

Seth grabbed Riley's arm and pulled him toward the last remaining palette of wool. They climbed inside, shoving their bodies in between bales. Seth caught sight of Wolf as he lifted his sword to meet the Dirge. Then the palette spun away to face the open ocean. Embers of a large fire glowed upon the sea beneath them. Someone had burned the wharf, destroying his mother's letters along with the portrait of his parents.

"Was he a ranger, then?" Riley tugged on Seth's coat sleeve.

Seth thought back to the bit of Wolf's life he had seen. "Yes. They call him Wolf. I think he was the King of Valdeon."

"Well, he's gotten us safely off." Riley rubbed gingerly at his head again. "I don't much care for the fellow with him. Squire or no."

Beware the darkness!

Seth ducked down behind the bale just as a blade pierced the burlap next to his head. Riley pushed Seth out of the way and grabbed their attacker's arm. A gust of sea breeze blew off his cowl, revealing the white dagger stretching down his face. Sandor brought the hilt of his sword smashing against Riley's jaw. He fell backward and tumbled off the platform.

"No! Riley!"

A hand smacked on the platform next to the edge. Riley's pale face tried to lift up. He was hanging on precariously from the rope steadying the cargo. The palette began to spin out of control over the ocean. Frantic shouting from the crew filled the docks as they tried to steady the load.

"I won't let you leave this island alive, half-breed!" Sandor swung up on top of the bundles, his cloak whipping wildly in the gusty air. "Your head and the Lion Ring were to be my prize. Now I just want you dead in a watery grave."

Seth climbed up the burlap and came to his feet across from Sandor. "You should have left well enough alone. I spared your life for my father's sake. Now it is forfeited."

"You may have a ring upon your finger now, boy, but you are not a ranger yet!"

Sandor came at him with a deadly strike. Seth side-stepped it. His foot caught in the burlap and he stumbled into Sandor's body. The Tslavian smashed a fist down hard against Seth's back. Ignoring the pain, he brought his elbow up to make contact at the center of the white dagger. Sandor staggered backward, stumbling on the bales. He gripped the guide rope to right his body. Diving with the speed of a viper, he thrust is blade toward Seth's torso. Seth knocked the blade away and brought his own down in a diagonal arc the way he'd seen Wolf do with the Dirge. Pavel Sandor's head and shoulders fell to the left. His other half fell to the right.

Seth wiped his blade upon the burlap. He would spare no remorse for Pavel Sandor. Justice had found him at last. He climbed down the guide rope and helped Riley up. They hurried behind the burlap back into their hiding place as the palette reached the ship's hull. The oily rigging of the cargo lift was their last image of home before they were lowered into the belly of the ship.

"We've got trouble down below. Leave the rest of the wool." The ship's captain pushed his first mate toward the railing. "Have those men get their tails onboard. We're leaving this cursed island right now."

He remained still as their palette was secured inside the cargo hold. The captain had been right. Marianna was a cursed place now. Evil had been drawn to its isolated shores as it hunted for the Lion Ring. He smoothed at the stone upon his finger. They were headed to a larger, more dangerous world. He hoped he could master the power of the ring before evil found them again.

Chapter Forty-Four

BLACK SAILS CAST A SINISTER mantle against the Marianna sky. Julian's ambitions chilled under the shadow as they drew closer. The sleek airship's metal hull was reminiscent of a prison. It was an impressive vessel, fearsome and fully armed. Always battle ready. The same could not be said for San Leonora's armada.

"Bring his highness. We don't want him losing his way now, do we?" The changeling bared its teeth between grinning lips.

His foul-smelling guards lifted Julian off his seat and set him none too gently upon the deck. The changeling's black orbs glistened with humor as he struggled against his captors. They kept a tight hold upon his arms as they headed below deck.

Sour odors slapped at his senses. Fermented cabbage mixed with some kind of unappetizing sauce. He recognized the smell from his last disgusting meal with Gorman. Julian's stomach turned. He was being taken to the mess hall where more of repugnant Akkutarian delicacies were being served.

Lord Gorman sat at the head table, eating quietly through the hole in his steel mask. Fresh red linen rose to his metal face. His gloved hand patted delicately at the tiny drops of sauce escaping from his lips. He ate like an old duchess.

In contrast, his men ate like the barbaric dogs they were. Filthy hands grabbed bread and raw meat from bowls at the center of their long tables. They fed in a frenzy, all the while, keeping their eyes upon their deadly lord.

Julian's two foul-smelling guards threw him unceremoniously forward. He managed to right himself, before tumbling awkwardly to his knees at the Jackal lord's feet. Standing defiantly before the hideous mask, he lifted his chin in a failed attempt at dignity. Gorman's laugh was rich, melodious. His voice might even have been considered pleasant if not for the viciousness of his nature.

"I am a Prince of Valdeon." Julian put a threatening hand upon the hilt of his sword. "You are my ally, sent by your emperor to assist me. I will not answer to you or be summoned in such a disrespectful way."

Lord Gorman leaned forward; the skull mask he wore gave no hint of his sentiment. "You are a braying ass. If not for the wishes of my emperor, I would gut you and hang your hide upon the hull."

Laughter filled the hall as the men made merry at his expense. Julian sneered and let his hand drop from the hilt. Their emperor still needed Julian alive. He had a bit of power over the warrior before him. Julian grabbed one of their uncomfortable chairs and dragged it over to the general's side. Exactly equal to his chair. He sat down and leaned casually on the armrest. Angry growls of shock and contempt raced around the gathered warriors. Lord Gorman gripped at his armrest in fury and then let it release slowly. This time his laugh was low and dangerous.

"My forces are in place to strike at Valdeon's strongholds. We go in less than an hour."

Gorman's hideous mask turned to Julian again, gauging any emotional reaction he may have. He wouldn't get the satisfaction.

"Are you prepared to do what you must, Andarian?" Gorman spat through the mesh opening of his helmet. "Are you prepared to see through to the end the betrayal you bring upon your own?"

"I wouldn't have guessed you to be a sentimental man, Gorman." Julian, by force of will, met and kept eye contact with the Jackal's fiercest warrior. "I am prepared to do what I must. Now, I have some unfinished business upon the docks. You will arrange transportation for me."

"Why must you be a fool? I have your vessel and your crew in my power. They are waiting for you a few leagues from here." Gorman gestured to Julian's changeling nanny. "Take the Andarian to his schooner and have it followed until it reaches San Leonora."

"Wait a moment! I must go back to the docks. The Lion Ring rests upon the finger of a boy. It can easily be won. Without the ring, Valdeon's invasion will be pointless."

"You journey to San Leonora, Prince of Valdeon. You must be there when the city falls. They will come to their prince and beg to bestow the title of Regent upon you."

The hunger came to Julian again. He could almost feel the golden medallion of the Regent resting upon his chest. It was very close to being his, but if he wasn't there to accept it...

Taking his silence for brooding, Gorman went on. "It may interest you to know the Jalora's favorite plaything, Xavier the Wolf, has landed on Marianna. I understand he despises you as much as I. We could arrange a play date between the two of you if you'd like."

Julian pushed away from the table in a rage. Wolf! He was always in the way, always there to be the fly in

Julian's ointment. Now he'd come to find the Lion. No doubt, Wolf would hover over the boy like a nurse-maid.

"The Dirge have disabled Wolf's ship," Gorman told him. "He will not be able to return to Valdeon for a few days at least."

Gorman took another bite of food, chewing it with infuriating ease. Amusement hung heavy behind his words. He nibbled while Valdeon's fate was drifting away with the young Lion. Julian didn't know who he hated more, this barbarian or the Wolf.

"Why not order the Dirge to kill him now? Why take the risk?"

"Those were their orders." Gorman's eyes lifted to examine Julian's face. "This ranger has killed thirteen of my Dirge tonight. I will not risk others until more can be made."

Julian shivered and tried not to think about how the Sarcion created its Dirge. He focused his thoughts back upon the Wolf. He'd known the ranger was gifted, but killing thirteen Dirge on his own? Perhaps the Jalora knew about the upcoming betrayal and had armed its servants?

"Can you beat him?" Julian asked.

His host wiped delicately at his mouth and stood away from his table. He didn't answer. Instead Gorman walked up the stairs and onto the deck. Julian followed. He was not willing to give up the Lion Ring despite what these barbarians thought.

"What of the boy? If he is allowed to cultivate his full power, he will be a threat to us. I can still find him and take the ring."

"I grow weary of your constant whining about a useless bobble. Look." He pointed toward a small schooner sailing away from Marianna toward the other isles. "Your Lion has escaped you in a small cargo ship. Captain, ready the cannons."

"Wait! What are you about? We need the ring!"

"If the boy is dead and his Lion Ring is lost at the bottom of the ocean, the Jalora will have no means to protect the Altar of Providence. It will have no recourse but to surrender this time."

"This time? You are speaking in riddles."

Julian moved to the ship's railing, watching as the tiny vessel sailed through the darkness. He didn't like this new turn of events. This ally was turning quickly into an invader. He'd taken a few lives — his brothers', in fact — to see Valdeon restored, but was he so daring as to challenge the Jalora itself by destroying the Lion Ring?

Then something began to form from the mists of the ocean. It was sickly and wrong. A massive wall of green fog rose up, blocking their view of the little vessel. Julian covered his nose to block out the rank stench of the fog. He recognized the Jalora's lust for death. It had come for him once before at the ruins of Sea Point.

Gorman came to stand beside him. His hands gripped the railing until his pale fingers drained of all color. He pushed away from the railing with a bitter laugh.

"Captain, set sail immediately away from the fog bank. Any who touch it will perish." Gorman turned to Julian. "The Jalora protects its pet. It would seem you will have your chance to hunt the young Lion again another day."

"Where are we going, then?"

"We journey to your home, Andarian. My forces are in place. They only need hear my command."

"And where will you be, Lord Gorman?"

"I will remain on the command ship."

"Not with your men? Well, it doesn't seem very warrior-like, now, does it?"

Gorman bounded at Julian with the speed rivaling any ranger. His fingers gripped Julian's throat, lifting him up until his boots dangled off the deck.

"You dare question my courage, betrayer? I do not sully my blade with the blood of the inadequate. Get him out of my sight."

Julian's body rolled roughly across the deck until he stopped at the changeling's feet. Shaken, he struggled to sit up. Gorman's power was more than he'd anticipated.

"You are foolish, prince of nothing." The changeling laughed, exposing more sharp teeth in a leer. "But for our emperor's word, our lord would have ripped you to pieces. You do not want Lord Gorman setting foot upon the battlefield in your country, Julian. None can stand against his blade. Once he draws his weapon, he will not sheath it again until every last enemy is dead at his feet. Remember that before you goad him again."

"Yes, I'll remember well."

Julian kept his eyes on the hideous metal helmet sitting atop a massive body. A killer more powerful than any ranger in the legion had come to Andara. He brought death with him. Would his sword be the end of the Jalora Legion? Only time would tell.

The End

People, Places, Things

People

Grey Cliff Isles

De Vincente, Dante - Leo's Squire

Emma - The McCloud's Housekeeper

Gunn, Sergeant - Head of the Marianna Militia

Leo - Valdeonian Warrior and Seth's Mentor (see D'Antoiné, Edmund)

Logan, Andrew - Woolie Farmer, Riley's Brother

Logan, George - Woolie Farmer, Riley's Brother

Logan, Laura - Farmer's Wife

Logan, Michael - Woolie Farmer, Riley's Brother

Logan, Patrick - Woolie Farmer, Riley's Brother

Logan, Riley - Seth's Best Friend

Logan, Stephen - Woolie Farmer, Riley's Brother

Logan, Thomas - Woolie Farmer

Logan, Tom - Woolie Farmer, Riley's Brother

McBride, Stan - Haven Bay Youth

McCloud, Anne - Seth's Mother

McCloud, Fergus - Headmaster and Seth's Uncle

McCloud, Seth - Heir to the Lion Ring

McDermott, Charlie - Haven Bay Youth

McFadden, Beatrice - Haven Bay Youth, Doctor's Daughter

McFadden, Doctor - The Isle of Marianna's Only Doctor

McKenzie, Alice - Haven Bay Youth

McKenzie, Danny - Woolie Farmer

McKenzie, Mike - Woolie Farmer

McKinney, Teb - Barkeep at Paddy's

McTavish, Angus - Owner of Haven Bay's Mercantile

McTavish, Constable - Haven Bay's Police Chief

Newcastle, Elder - Haven Bay's Elder

Newcastle, Jamie - Haven Bay Youth and Elder's Son

Paddy - Owner and Innkeeper of Paddy's Inn

Sandor, Pavel - Andara's Deadliest Assassin

Valdeon

Armando - Changeling Disguised as Julian D'Antoiné's Valet

Basilio - Squire to the Wolf

Benito - Chancellor of Valdeon

Cristiano, Felix - Usurper of San Angelica

Cristiano, Rafael the Fox - Member of the Sacred Guard, A Lord of Valdeon

Cristobal, Tulio the Rabbit - Member of the Sacred Guard, A Lord of Valdeon

D'Antoiné, Edmund the Leo - King and a Lord of Valdeon

D'Antoiné, Esteban the Hawk - Former Member of the Sacred Guard, A Lord of Valdeon

D'Antoiné, Julian - Prince of Valdeon

De Costa, Marcellus - Minion of Julian D'Antoiné

De Vincente, Danel - Son of Xavier

De Vincente, Dulcina - Wife of Xavier

De Vincente, Gaspar - Son of Xavier

De Vincente, Xavier the Wolf - Leader of the Sacred Guard, A Lord of Valdeon

De Quintaro, Ernesto the Raven - Member of the Sacred Guard, A Lord of Valdeon

De Quintaro, Fausto - Steward of Varianne, Former Lord of Valdeon

Jalora - Embodiment of Good Upon the Erthe

Mendoza, Alberto - Steward of San Marimosa and Father to the Jaguar

Mendoza, Berto the Jaguar - Member of the Sacred Guard, A Lord of Valdeon

Mendoza, Yuli the Otter - Member of the Sacred Guard, A Lord of Valdeon

No Name, Zoya - Sister of Julian D'Antoiné

Orryo - Minion of Julian D'Antoiné

Pacarro, Jorge - Former Squire to Cesar Santiago

Santiago, Cesar - Steward of San Lucida, Former Lord of Valdeon

Santiago, Lucio the Ferret - Member of the Sacred Guard, A Lord of Valdeon

Sarcion - Embodiment of Evil Upon the Erthe

The Jalora Legion

Dragon, Cardinal - Leader of the Jalora Legion

Falcon, Bishop - High Ranking Officer in the Jalora Legion

Akutar

Changeling - Lord Gorman's Spy

The Dirge - Sarcion's Undead Assassins

Gorman - A Lord of Akutar, General of the Jackal Army

Whisper - Emissary of the Akutarian Emperor

Places

The United Realms of Andara

Amity - Island in the Grey Cliff isles

Commonwealth - The Small Circular Space of Land Surrounding Lea, The UR Capitol

Eastland Isle - Located Off the West Coast of Andara

Estabelle - Located in Valdeon, Home of the Hawk

Fort L'Azure - Located in Valdeon, Home of the Rabbit

Fort La Val - Located in Valdeon, Home of the Otter

Ghent - Located in the Central Mainland Region

Grey Cliff Isles - Located Two Days from Andara's Mainland

Haven Bay - Town located on Marianna

Horner - Island in the Grey Cliff Isles

Larkspur - Island in the Grey Cliff Isles

Lea - Located in the Center of the Commonwealth, Capitol of the UR

Marianna - Smallest Island in the Grey Cliff Isles

Obsidian Citadel - Located in Lea, Headquarters of the Jalora Legion

Palace of Kings - Located in San Leonora, Home of the Lion

Port City - Located on Eastland Isle, Major Airship Port

San Angelica - Located in Valdeon, Home of the Fox

San Leonora - Located in Valdeon, Home of the Lion

San Lucida - Located in Valdeon, Home of the Ferret

San Marimosa - Located in Valdeon, Home of the Jaguar

San Rudalfo - Located in Valdeon, Home of the Wolf

Temple Cave - Located in the Mountains on the Border of Valdeon and Tslavia, Place of Power

Tslavia - Located in the Central Mainland Region, Ancient Enemy of Valdeon

Valdeon - Located in the Southern Mainland Region, Realm of the Lion

Varianne - Located in Valdeon, Home of the Raven

Other Island Nations

Azure Isles - Located South of Andara's Mainland, Ruled by Raiders

Isle of Carlotta - Located Off the Coast of Valdeon

Foreign Nations

Akutar - Located Far to the East of Andara's Mainland, Home of the Jackal

The Pearl Isles - Located Far to the West of Marianna, Home of the Luminawni

Things

Altar of Providence - Stronghold of the Jalora on Andara. Consists of three parts: The Crown of Sorrows, The Lion's Seat and the Orb of Valdeon

Crown of Sorrows - Crown of the King of Valdeon

Lion Ring - Symbol of the Contract Between The D'Antoiné Family and The Jalora

Lion's Seat - Golden Throne of Valdeon

Orb of Valdeon - Conduit of the Jalora's Power to Andara's Rangers

About The Author

C. R. Richards is the award winning author of *The Mutant Casebook Series*. Her literary career began as a part-time columnist for a small entertainment newspaper. She wore several hats: food critic, entertainment reviewer and cranky editor. A lover of horror and dark fantasy stories, she enjoys telling tales of intrigue and adventure. Her most recent literary projects include the horror short story, *Lost Man's Parish* and the newly released novel length dark fantasy thriller, *Pariah*. She is an active member of Rocky Mountain Fiction Writers and Horror Writers Association.

For more information on the author's books and
upcoming events, please visit her website:
www.crrichards.com

Other Books
by
C.R. Richards

THE LORDS OF VALDEON
(Heart of the Warrior Series - Book One)

PARIAH

LOST MAN'S PARISH
(Short Fiction)

PHANTOM HARVEST
(The Mutant Casebook Series)

For more information on the author's books and
upcoming events, please visit her website:
www.crrichards.com

www.ingramcontent.com/pod-product-compliance
Lightning Source LLC
Chambersburg PA
CBHW030646120726
47905CB00001B/81